THE DROWNING LAND

DAVID M. DONACHIE

The Drowning Land
ISBN: 978-1-913781-06-4
Published by CAAB Publishing Ltd (Reg no 12484492)

C . A . A . B
PUBLISHING

Serenity House, Foxbridge drive, Chichester, UK
www.caabpublishing.co.uk

First Published 2021
Printed in the UK

British Library Cataloguing in Publication data
available

To the crew of the trawler Colinda, whose chance find of a fishing point in the North Sea first revealed the existence of a hidden world, and to all the dedicated scientists who have laboured to bring it to light since then.

To Time Team, for telling me about it, to my family of patient readers, to Kay, for suffering my drafts, and to my wife Victoria, as always.

THE SUMMER LANDS

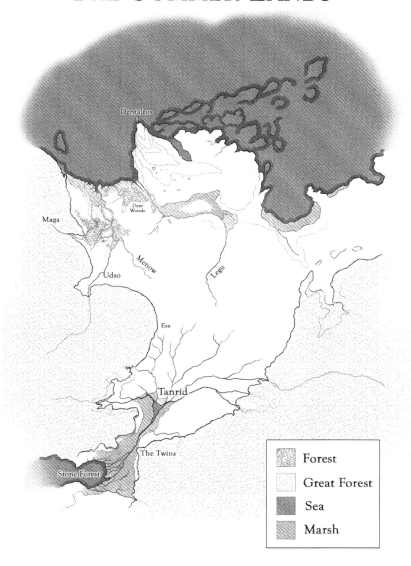

Dentaltos

Deer Woods

Maga

Menow

Legu

Udso

Esa

Tanrid

The Twins

Stone Forest

Forest

Great Forest

Sea

Marsh

1. Edan

From the back of the line, Edan could see the rain clouds coming. Granite-grey and bellicose, they rushed across the flat plains of the Summer Lands from the distant northern sea. Funnelled between mountains and forest, they swept out over the marshes where Edan's tribe was struggling its way north.

Edan pulled the sealskin of his jacket up around his neck as the rain began again.

Bluebottle-fat raindrops drummed over them, soaking the soft leather of their clothes and rattling the reed beds. Falling curtains of rain hid the pale spring sun, turning the world close and grey. When it became clear that this was more than a passing shower, they looked for shelter.

The Elder, whose knowledge of the land was legendary, kept insisting that shelter was just ahead, beyond the next dip, or behind the next rise — but the only things that emerged from the rain were leafless willows and gurgling sedge.

"We're lost, aren't we?" said Uch, who was Second Hunter and often voiced his dissent. "You don't know where we are."

"Of course I know!"

Edan held his tongue. Though he was the tribe's Fisher, he was also the youngest male, and it wasn't his place to speak out. Of course, he trusted the Elder's wisdom, but the once-familiar landscape of the Summer Lands had changed almost beyond recognition, vanishing under creeping waters and floods that never receded. Seven days before, when they had set out from the Winter Home to make for the Summer Hunting Grounds, the route had been familiar enough, worn by the feet of countless generations; but with each passing day they recognised less and less.

The journey had been ill-omened from the start. The winter snows had lingered, wrapping the edge of The Great Wood in ice, well into the spring, and they were short of food when they set out. When the girls — Brina and Morna — had gone to fill the beech nut sacks, they had come back with the sacks half empty. And Cinnia — who was now Second Mother — had given birth to her first child at the tail end of winter. She carried the baby swaddled in elk fur, for extra warmth, but he was still so small and frail. Would a few weeks more in the winter country have been so bad? Tradition demanded that they set out when the first Full Moon of spring rose over the Long Stone, and arrive at the coast by the following dark; but would the moon really have been angered if they had waited until the baby had been named before they left? Edan didn't think so. He grimaced at the raindrops trickling down the back of his neck and thought bad things about Tradition.

Eventually, the rain slackened off, but not before most of them were wet through and tired. Only then did the Elder call a halt, striding off alone and stiff-backed, up a rise to 'survey the land ahead'.

Edan crouched down by the edge of the trail, trying to recognise something, anything familiar in the land around him. Had this curve of water been the meadow where they had camped last spring? Was the flat rock out beneath the water the same boulder from which he had caught that magnificent pike in the autumn? He couldn't tell.

A little way ahead, at the base of the rise, Lavena was organising the others into a makeshift camp. Lavena was First Mother, and all matters of food and fire were hers. She had picked a dry spot by a stand of alder trees, which clustered at the edge of the water — Edan thought that they looked like arrows thrust tail-first into the earth. By the time he had caught them up, the rest of the tribe had settled gratefully on the dry ground, dropping their burdens and hanging their wet clothes on the branches.

Edan remained on the edge, his pack still on his back and his fishing spear in his hand. First Mother produced the gamey haunch that was all that remained of the roe deer buck they had caught three days ago. She set to work slicing thin strips of meat with precise cuts of a flint blade, wolfing down the first before passing out the others. The sight of the meat made Edan's stomach rumble, but he made no move towards them. First Mother always put him last for food, for he was the least important, and cursed besides.

He stared out over the mere instead, trying to spot the landmarks that the Elder would be looking for. All he could see were reed beds and murky water, spreading out in every direction. There were dead birch trees out there, pale against the grey water. The sun drew mist out of the reeds, and it curled around the tree trunks like a living thing.

Over in the camp, the girls produced a few beech nuts from the depths of their bags, while Grandmother, whose teeth were worn almost to stubs, began to chew dry roots, softening them with her spit for the others to eat. It was a poor supplement for the meat. Cinnia's baby began to cry, its plaintive wail echoing out over the mere until she pulled the furs close around them both and curled up against an alder trunk. In moments she was asleep. The journey had been especially hard on her.

Edan waited for Maccus to take up his bow or spear. Maccus was First Hunter, as well as Lavena's mate, and Tradition left it to him to call for a hunt — but he only pulled his buckskins closer and stared northwards in silence. Uch, as Second Hunter, could have raised the matter, but he paced uneasily near to Cinnia and their baby, his eyes on the path that the Elder had taken.

What was Maccus thinking? It was hard to guess — Maccus always kept his own counsel. Maybe he was thinking that if Cinnia's baby thrived, then she might soon be First Mother. Maybe he was thinking she would make Uch First Hunter if she did, and then feeding the tribe would be his problem instead of Maccus'. Maybe he was thinking that the infant might not survive the trip. Edan checked himself; bad thoughts, ill chance. Better to think of something else.

Edan's belly rumbled again. He could see that there were birds on the water, and surely there would be fish as well. He might not be the Hunter, but he was still the Fisher, for what that was worth. He did not have a bow or sling to hunt the birds, but he had his fishing spear, which for the past seven days he had used as a walking stick, with a bag of soft hide over the head to protect the sinew bindings from the rain. Surely the spirit of the spear would be honoured if he hunted with it now, or so he told himself.

Edan's Father had made the spear back when he had been Fisher. He had crafted the two points from deer antler, notching them with teeth before binding them to the shaft with sinew and pine resin. That had been at their old home by the sea; before the sea had washed it away; before everything had changed. Across the space of years, Edan could still smell the pungent wood smoke and the sharp tang of fresh resin. Father's fingers had been stained dark from the pine pitch, but they had been quick and sure, binding the points with

5

practiced ease while Edan had watched with wide eyes from the shelter of the hut door. He'd tried tying his own sinew knots with the scraps that Father had left over, but his fingers didn't have the knack of it. It would honour his Father too, to use the spear ... and fill his belly.

Recklessly Edan unlaced his leggings and slipped away into the reeds — pausing only to check that the water was not deep. Cold water immersed him to the knees, but he hurried away from the rise before anyone could notice or call him back, feeling his way through the water with his toes, kicking at roots, and jumping at the tickle of little fish.

The sounds of his family faded away behind him, replaced by the buzz of insects and the soft splash of frogs, and he felt himself relax for the first time in days. It was not that he disliked the tribe — they were all he knew — but he chafed against the confines of Tradition and those, like the Elder, or First Mother, who placed the most store in them. Even surrounded by family, he felt an outsider.

There were trout lurking amongst the sedge, hovering at the edge of the current. Edan could see the golden glint of their scales in the brown water, constantly sliding away as he approached them, and he felt vindicated. Surely the others would be pleased when he returned with food.

He brushed his fishing charm with the tips of his fingers for luck, feeling the soft indents of carvings worn smooth by countless such touches, then tested the water again, relieved to see that it was still shallow. He approached the fish slowly, his spear raised, and arms spread like a crane's wings, so that they did not see the edge of his shadow crossing them and scare.

Most of the fish made quick exits as he came close, but one fat trout was nibbling at some shoots and lagged behind. With a quick strike, he snared it between the two prongs of his spear, jerking it from the river in a bright spray of water, and grabbed it before it could get away from him. It struggled in his grasp, strong and cold, before he got his fingers in its mouth and snapped its neck. When it stopped thrashing, he put it in the woven satchel at his hip and looked for another, but the shoal had sped away on the current.

He glanced back at the hill and the alder trees, surprised to see how far he had already come. Only one figure was visible, a splash of pale fur and a shock of tangled black hair

6

— Uch, still pacing. Time to go back? No. One little fish would hardly feed all of them, nor would it make Lavena happy. There was no choice but to keep looking.

Away from the reed beds, the water ran faster and more powerfully, pushing insistently at Edan's legs as he waded into it. He stepped back, hesitating on the edge of the open water, his guts clenching in sudden fear. 'What good are you', he berated himself, 'a man afraid of water in a land covered in it.' He didn't want to think about *why* he was afraid. He put it out of his mind. He made himself go on.

Tentatively he prodded ahead with the shaft of his spear — persuading himself that it wasn't so deep after all — then forced himself to stop wasting time and stride forward like a proper Fisher. The water was amber brown, filled with drowned grass and silt, and he went straight into a hidden drop, the water surging up to his waist. At once the old familiar terror returned full force, the tumble of black water in the night, the numbing cold, the grasping hands, and he almost lost his footing. He jerked backwards, colliding with something solid under the water. His questing hands found cold wood, invisible in the water's murk, and he scrambled onto a submerged structure sunk into the river's muddy depths.

Reaching down, Edan felt at the solid wood under his feet, cool and smooth in the current. His fingertips explored beams stripped of bark and posts festooned with weed and algae; all reassuringly solid. It called up a childhood memory of the Marsh People who had once made their homes along the inland rivers. When the tribe had passed by on their journeys the Marsh People would come out to watch, standing in silent groups at the mouths of huts built out into the water. Edan could picture their serious faces, painted white with clay like the faces of coots. The Marsh People had driven stakes into the river bed and laid boles of wood on top of them, edged with woven hurdles, forming paths across the water. Maybe the solid wood beneath Edan's feet was the remains of one of their pathways, swallowed by the water? No other trace of the Marsh People remained above the rushing water.

Edan followed the submerged walkway deeper into the braided channels, and swaying reeds. The sun was hot overhead, and the water was cool. Little fish, too small for him to catch, darted around his ankles as he moved along, while a pair of ducks watched him from a distance, bobbing with the current. Ahead, a ridge cast a long shadow across the water, the dark slope cloaked with leafless trees. Drifts of brushwood clogged the dead trunks where some surge of water had left them. Edan stared at the debris for a long time before he realised that he was seeing the wreckage of wooden platforms and birch back roofing, swollen and darkened by the water. Some trace of the Marsh People remained after all, and this was it. The realisation changed the view before his eyes. The pallid roots in the murky water became fingers, grasping blindly for some trace of life. Driftwood skeletons clung to the ruin of their former homes, festooned with cattail hair and golden flowers for eyes, clutching for what was once theirs despite the rushing water. Within the weed-choked ruin, the silent shapes of the dead watched him with cold, serious faces. This was a taboo place, sacred ground, forbidden to the living. Only the old wood beneath his feet, placed so that the living might cross the water, kept him safe.

The sun passed behind gathering clouds, and the sudden chill broke Edan from his daze. The skeletons became branches, the grasping hands became roots, and the pale faces faded back into the water's depths and were gone. He dragged his eyes away from the ruin of the Marsh People's huts, up to the ridge and its living trees, and received a second shock.

On the ridge-top beyond the empty huts a figure had appeared, just a silhouette against the pale sun. He held a long spear in his hands, and his head was crested with an animal's fur and ears. For a long terrifying moment Edan took him for another spirit, and his hand went instinctively to the charms strung about his neck, the hunting charm, and the mother's charm, and the carved tooth that had been his first. If this was an ancestor of the Marsh People come to punish him for breaking taboo, then there was nothing that he could do but hope that his own spirits might protect him. The figure was silent, unmoving. Then more figures joined the first, spear-armed men without the features of animals. Not spirits then but strangers, people not of the tribe.

His first instinct was to raise his spear in a sign of greeting, but caution stayed his hand. There had been tales of violence in the Summer Lands, of people breaking all Tradition by laying spear and axe on one another. Tradition said he should bid the strangers welcome, but fear said otherwise.

A surge of water and the sudden touch of a hand on his arm made him cry out, but it was not a ghost of the drowned, only Maccus, come to chastise him for hunting out of turn. The Hunter had also seen the distant figures and any punishment was forgotten for now. "Stand still," he whispered, "stay silent." And then, "not all strangers are welcome in these days."

The warning came too late. Edan and Maccus had been seen. On the shadowed ridge the first of the distant figures raised a spear, held horizontal against the sun in the sign of greeting. There would be a meeting after all.

2. Tara

Red-nose, as Tara thought of him, had a braying laugh that made him sound constantly on the verge of choking. When he spoke, he punctuated each sentence with a burst of laughter. Red-nose had been the one chosen to guard her when the rest of her captors went ahead, and he seized the opportunity to taunt her.

"You should be glad it's me that's watching you," he said. "Some of the others, they wouldn't be so gentle. Ha, Ha." Red-nose paced as he talked, one hand on his spear, the other scratching idly at the berry-like stain on his nose. It always looked like it itched terribly. "They call you a monster, girl, say we ought to kill you. Not me. You know you can trust me, heh, heh." Another bray.

They had bound Tara with strips of rawhide, wrists and ankles both lashed to a stout sapling so that her arms were pulled behind her and she could not rise. It forced her to crouch, knees spread and shoulders back, and she could see how Red-nose's gaze was fixed upon her bared breasts. She knew that he wanted her to look away, but she met his gaze defiantly, let him look!

For the most part, her captors held her in contempt. She was not like them, not of their kind. Some of them even feared her or hated her; her kind were probably the stuff of the stories they told to frighten their children. Not Red–nose though, he saw past the monster and desired the woman, which was no better! She'd felt his eyes on her when the others had been around, and he had wheedled his way into the job of guarding her when the others were gone, but now he hesitated. Maybe he was remembering what she had done to Dog–breath when he'd been lazy with her bindings. His arm would heal, but only because he'd had companions close at hand. Red-nose, alone, would get no such rescue.

Red-nose was still talking. Tara didn't understand half of what her captors said, but his tone had been honey-sweet over a violent edge.

Whatever he'd said must have raised his courage, because he moved closer with his hand outstretched to grasp at her, but she was ready for him. Snarling, she bared her teeth, pulling back her lips to reveal a bite as wide as his hand, and snapped at his fingers. He gave a cry of shock and stumbled back, snatching his hand away as if he'd been burnt.

"Animal!" He snarled. "Beast! I'd rather rut with the dogs, at least they know how to listen!" He spat in her face, from a safe distance, and backed off laughing.

It was a poor victory. She was still bound, and he would be plotting his revenge.

She wondered if it would have made a difference if she had been able to talk to them. She knew that her captors thought that she was too stupid to speak or understand them, but it was simply that their language was coarse and hard to fit her tongue around. Amongst The People, speech contained as many gestures as it did sounds, but these men's hands were dumb. They jabbered their words in a tumbling stream, without finesse or meaning. She understood them only with difficulty and was not sure that she could have them understand her even if she had wanted too. As for their names, the mocking nicknames that she had given them suited them far better than their own.

As well as Red-nose and Dog-breath, she had named: Four-finger, who seemed to have lost the smallest finger of his left hand, Forkbeard, Face-licker, who fawned for favour like a young hound, Gaptooth, Rat-tongue, Faint-heart, and Burnt. Then there was the leader, who called himself Phelan. That was the only name she had made herself learn. He was the one who had captured her, and the only one of them that she truly feared. The eyes of the others showed no more than lust or disgust when they looked at her, but the eyes of Phelan showed a glimpse of a beast within. She would happily have fought any of the others, but not him.

Sometimes, in the night, Phelan would talk in front of her, though he clearly didn't care whether she could understand him. The little she could grasp scared her even more than Phelan's gaze. He talked of fate, and blood, and destiny. Whatever he wanted her for, she didn't want to be around to find out.

If only they hadn't captured her, if only she'd had a chance to fight them. Prepared, she could have fought them or evaded them at least, but she had let down her guard and been captured in her sleep. It would be laughable really, if only it was happening to someone else.

Red-nose moved away, and Tara allowed herself to sink into the comfort of memories, where she ran no risk of attracting his attention. If only she had avoided them. If only she could have found a way to avoid them, short of staying in the Stone Forest where she belonged, but she had removed that possibility herself, on the day when the moon took its first bite from the sun. That had been the day that had sent her north, away from the lands of The People and into the hands of these dog-lovers.

The Old Ones had come first, travelling from the river. They followed the old path, even though salt water now covered it up to their ankles and dirty mud covered the flower meadows.

The Seers made their home at the edge of the Stone Forest. Their hut was made from wood polished with age and roofed with sagging turf, so that it looked like a natural mound rather than a built thing. At the door were a pair of tusks as large as a man and heavier. Successive generations of Seers had carved the ivory with symbols of sun and moon, until little of it remained unmarked.

When they saw the Old Ones approaching, the Seers cut fresh withies of willow, stripping them quickly to make white wands. They put furs across their shoulders and marked their faces with ash before joining them. Ama, who was the oldest of them, led the way, then Tara, and finally Esa, who had found her sight only the year before. Ama began the chant, a rumble in her chest in time with their walking, and the others joined her. Tara was pleased to see that long hours of practice had turned Esa's hesitant chant into one worthy of the Seers.

The Old Ones had come because of worrying signs they had divined in bones washed up upon the shore. They came to seek the Seers' guidance. With words and gestures they asked for a vision, to learn if there was anything The People could do before this doom came to pass.

Ama and the others agreed. They piled briar and broom inside the boundaries of the Stone Forest and brought a spark of flame from the carefully tended fire inside their house to light it, knowing that the Spirits would come to the fragrant smoke. The Old Ones had brought hollow logs on which they tapped a relentless beat, echoing the stamping feet of kin who no longer lived. For three days, while the winter moon was full, they stamped and danced around the fire, their heads full of smoke and their bellies empty, until the moon turned upon the sun.

That was when the vision came to Tara. She was exhausted, her feet sore, her head spinning. Ama's chant and the Old Ones' beat had merged into a living thing that she could feel but no longer hear. Instead, she thought that she heard the sea, pounding and surging as it crashed against the land. Then the water rushed over her head and she was tumbling beneath the waves. Below her, she could see the Summer Lands, as if she had risen to the moon's height, but the sea was still about her and the sun was black. She was not alone in the ocean. In the north she saw dark shapes within the sea, shapes that drove the water forwards on its relentless course. The ocean rose at their command, and the Summer Lands fell. She tried to chase them, becoming a fish to forge the waves, and then a seal, silver as the moonlight, but they were faster than her, racing through the mud and the foam towards a single finger of stone that rose at the edge of the sea. She knew, with sudden clarity, that this was where they would gather when the land's final doom came.

That this was a true vision, all agreed. The land would drown, and The People would pass from the world when the moon swallowed the sun entire, at the willing of those Tara had seen within the water's depths. They did not agree on what they should do about it. The oldest of the Old Ones said that she had seen the spirits of the dead. The second believed that it was monsters who led the sea. The last said that they did not know enough, to which the others grudgingly agreed. Ama said that they should return to the Stones until another vision made things clear. It had been Tara that had argued that the answers must lie in the north, in the realm of the ones she had seen, and that someone must go there to learn more. Ama told them that she knew the stone from the vision. Its tale had been passed to her by the elders of her youth, even as she now taught Esa the same tales in the winter months. She named it with a gesture for height and the sea, Dentaltos the tooth of the North.

Once the suggestion was made it was clear that Tara must be the one to travel to the tooth. Ama was too old, and Esa too young. Now she cursed herself for the pride she'd felt. If her Sight had been better, she would have seen the fate that awaited her. Captured and trussed like a hunted doe; prodded and abused by unkind hands. To think that Esa had been jealous of her! Now it seemed that she would never reach the northern sea, let alone learn the secret she sought. She rolled her eyes at her past self.

"What are you looking at, eh!?" Tara realised that she had accidentally caught Red-nose's eye. He was crouched a few paces away from her, working a chunk of flint with the aid of a pebble and a buckskin mat, striking off sharp flakes with every blow. Now he snatched one up and was at her side before she could react, grasping her face with one hand as he pressed the sharp edge against her cheek.

"Looking at me with those eyes!" The laugh had no humour now. "I ought to cut them out! Let's see what witch powers you have then!" The hot stink of his body was overwhelming, the rancid smell of badly cured hides and unwashed flesh. She could hear the growl of one of the dogs, awoken by the sudden commotion, but the mirror-bright edge of the flint filled her vision. She tried to struggle — if she could only break her bonds and get her hands on him — but that just dug the blade into her flesh deep enough to draw blood. Red-nose laughed and pressed closer, his flesh against hers, pushing her down. He spoke low and dangerous now, his breath gusting into her face as if he wanted to fill her up with it. "Phelan wants you alive, I don't know why, but that won't stop me blinding you." She rolled her eyes wildly, as if she could escape the slowly approaching edge of stone, but there was no way out. It was against the soft flesh beneath her eye, now against the lid, now pressing ever so lightly against her eye as he drew out the torture.

"Cahal, stop! Down!" The order echoed through the trees and Red-nose jerked like a chastised hound, pulling back and crouching down, teeth bared and eyes wide. The flint blade dropped from his hand into the rough grass at Tara's feet.

Phelan and two more of his men emerged from the bushes, spears rattling in their hands. Phelan wore his headdress of wolf-skin, ears pricked and teeth framing his face. His cold eyes took in the damage to Tara's face, then flicked back to Red-nose.

"I said she was not to be harmed," Phelan said this in an even tone, almost bored, but even Tara could feel the threat. Red-nose obviously felt it too, mumbling an apology that Tara didn't fully understand. Phelan hefted an axe of green jadeite in his hands. Its head was so polished that it caught the sun like water. No other in Phelan's band carried such a weapon. Red-nose tried to keep his eyes on the ground and on the moving axe at the same time, and Tara heard him gulp in fear. No laughter for Red-nose now.

The confrontation was over almost as quickly as it had begun. Forkbeard, who seemed to be Phelan's most trusted, emerged from the trees, and the wolf-men's leader seemed to forget about Red-nose and his offence. He turned aside and began to direct his companions to gather up the packages of fur and hide that they had left behind. "We go to a meeting," he said to Red-nose, without turning around to look him in the eye. "There are others in the marsh, hunters, fishermen. Since you cannot be trusted with the girl, you can carry the packs."

Forkbeard carried a hollow horn full of seal fat, with which he slicked his hair and twisted his beard into spikes. While he toyed with his hair, and the others laughed at Red-nose's shame, no one spared a glance for Tara at the tree. Slowly, painfully, she stretched her fingers, trying to reach the discarded blade while looking away from it, but it was just beyond her. Daring everything, she waited until the packing of the camp had started, and strained against her bonds, twisting her leg until she felt the cold flint against the sole of her foot. With a stifled grunt of effort, she nudged it close enough to grab.

Forkbeard chose that moment to turn his attention to her. For a horrible instant, she thought that he had seen what she was doing, but Forkbeard had not seen the blade fall, and if he noticed that his prisoner was writhing in her bonds he did not seem to spare a thought for why. With rough hands and simple words, he loosed her bonds and then dragged them tight once more, lashing her wrists to a leather cord so that she could be led, and knotting a second cord from ankle to ankle so that she could stumble but not run. To be trussed and led in this way was shameful, intolerable, but she did not protest, even when she was prodded forward with the butt of Gaptooth's spear, because what Forkbeard had not seen, what no one had seen, was the knife-sharp flake of flint grasped tight inside her fist.

3. Edan

The tribe and the strangers met at the edge of a grey and restless mere which stretched to the north and west of the Marsh People's ruins. The Elder had come down from his hill in response to Maccus' entreaties, and the temporary camp had been hastily cleared. All of the tribe had come to the meeting, partly as a show of strength, and partly for safety.

There were ten of the tribe and only eight of the strangers, but that was little comfort to Edan. Where the tribe had only three men able to defend themselves, Edan included, the stranger's group was all men, each carrying an ash spear in their hand or a bow slung over their shoulder. To Edan's eye, the strangers were dangerous and menacing, covered in old scars. One was missing a finger on the hand that gripped his spear, another had lost his front teeth, while a third showed livid burn scars on the left side of his face. None wore the familiar laced leggings and breechcloths of the tribe, instead, their clothing was trimmed with brindled fur arranged in tails and tufts that he was sure were wolf, and by this, he knew that they were Daesani.

Edan had heard tales of the Daesani, the wolf-men, the taboo breakers. Old Ulat, a wanderer who sometimes came to the tribe's winter hearths to trade meat and stories, had called them the Clan of the Wolf — a great mass of men and women, impossibly numerous. In her story they were taboo-breakers. Men and women who rejected family and kin to make one huge tribe, led by a spirit, or a ghost, or a wolf who had taken human form. Ulat had told this tale as a horror story, gossip of an insane tribe who none of them would ever expect to meet, entertainment for the long cold nights when the snow piled high around their shelters and there was nowhere else to go. Edan had shivered along with the others as required and thought no more about them.

Now he was face to face with them, and they were worryingly real.

"I greet you, strangers. I am First Hunter of the tribe, and these are my family. My name is Maccus. What name shall I call you?"

There had been silence when the two groups had met, broken only by the plaintive cry of a moorhen somewhere out amongst the reeds. The elders took the front, with Edan and Morna behind, her body pressed nervously against his side. Brina, unusually, was not with her sister, but pushed forward, her eyes roving over the strangers.

By rights, the Elder should have spoken for the tribe, but he had kept quiet, so now Maccus addressed himself to the man that looked to be the Daesani leader.

This man wore the scalp of a wolf on his head, the ears raised in tufts, and the upper fangs framing severe features. He had a narrow nose, sharp like an axe blade, and grey eyes. His beard was short and black, trimmed where his companions' hair was wild. Edan could see how the others watched him, careful not to block his steps or stand too close to him.

"I am Phelan, of the Daesani, follower of the Great Wolf. I greet you Hunter Maccus and your family." Phelan's voice was light and friendly, but Edan thought that his eyes were dangerous.

"I am a hunter also, and these few are my companions." He named a number of them. A man with a forked beard was called Duah, while the older man with the missing finger was Kaman. Another, Uchdryd, pale-haired and sullen faced, nursed an injured arm bound up with moss and rawhide. Duah smiled a greeting, turning an eye towards Lavena, and a grin at Brina. Kaman nodded, while Uchdryd merely snorted and said nothing.

"Where are you going?" Phelan asked. "The way is long, and you seem light on food and few in number to be leading old women and children through this marsh. Have you lost your homes to the sea?"

Maccus shook his head. "No. We travel from the Winter Lands to the coast, as we have always done in the spring." The Elder nodded his head and murmured, "Our Traditions work for us."

Edan could have laughed at that, were the situation not so serious. Every year he had to rebuild fish traps lost to the encroaching sea, and every year the catch was less. But he held his tongue.

"Then you are lucky," Phelan said. "Many have no home to return to. These lands are vanishing faster than the memories of old men." Phelan gestured forward another

Daesani, the one with the livid burn scar on his face, who stepped forward to address them.

"My name is Newlyn," the newcomer said. His voice was gruff, accented differently from Phelan's. As he spoke, he twisted the burnt side of his face away from them. It gave him an oddly coy manner. "My people were of the Crow. Our home was in the north, on the shores of the sea. We had the mountains at our backs and the water at our feet. When the snows came, the hills gave us shelter, and we hunted elk amongst them. In the summer we caught birds on the water's edge. It was a good land. I had a family there, as you have.

But the lands of the Crow are no more. The sea ate them. The waters crash against the mountains now. It came so fast, faster than you can believe. Now I have no family in the north." His voice cracked as he spoke but Edan hardly noticed, a vision of rushing waters filled his mind instead. They were drowning him, pouring into his mouth, filling his lungs as he struggled in the darkness and the roar of the sea!

He stumbled back half a step, quailing, and might have fallen if Brina, always protective, had not put a hand on his arm to steady him. It gave him the chance to recover himself. Luckily Maccus and the Elder had their eyes on the Daesani and did not notice his lapse, but Edan could feel Phelan's gaze upon him, evaluating.

"The ocean took your land," said Uch.

"No!" Newlyn shook his head emphatically, "It was the Fomor, the sea devils, the ice riders. They sent the sea to my land, as they will send it to this one."

Fomor? The word meant nothing to Edan or his tribe, and they passed it back and forth between them in confusion. Maccus said, "we do not know this word. Who are these Fomor?"

Phelan answered now. "This is the name for the devils of the sea. The waves are under their command. Do not think that these floods will end. The Fomor will drown us all."

"You have seen these people?"

Phelan nodded, but Edan was not convinced. "Some of us have seen them."

The Elder spoke at last. "Why do you tell us these things?"

Phelan's eyes became hooded, and Uch shifted uncomfortably, taking a firmer grip on his spear, but the wolf-man appeared to let the comment pass. "It does not have to be for you as it was for Newlyn, or for many others. The Daesani are not a Clan of blood-kin. The Great Wolf, who is our chieftain, takes in any who wish to join us. Our numbers are very great, and because of this we can do great things." A strange note of fervour, the first emotion that Edan had seen in the man, came into Phelan's voice as he spoke. "The wolf who hunts alone can be brought down with a spear or a bow like any other animal, but when he hunts in a pack, nothing stands against him. So, it is with the Daesani. Nothing can stand against us."

"You go to fight the Fomor?" Edan blurted out the question before he could think better of it. He heard First Mother snap "Edan!" but ignored the insult implied by the use of his name and not his title.

Again, the stare of grey eyes, but the chief said nothing. Instead, it was Duah, the one with the catfish whiskers, who spoke. "No. The Great Wolf has chosen a different way. We will not stay and drown with these lands as others have. Instead, we will go west, to the high lands, and make for ourselves a new country, a better country than this. Let the Fomor have their waves, they will not have us."

"You will live in the forests? In The Great Wood?" Maccus asked.

"We will cut down the forest! We will fell The Great Wood with our axes!" Duah pounded his fist against his palm as he spoke.

There was a gasp from the tribe. Edan was not sure who had made it, perhaps it had been all of them. "Unthinkable," whispered First Mother, and "Blasphemy!" gasped the Elder. Did they not understand Tradition? How could you explain the obvious if they did not know it? Nevertheless, the Elder tried, his voice adopting the practiced singsong of tales told a hundred times.

"In times long ago," he began, "the forefather of our tribe who we call First Man, wandered alone in the Summer Lands. He was a great hunter, but there were no deer to hunt, and no birds, no rabbits, and no fish because the great winter had come down from the north and swallowed them all." Edan had heard this tale, the Winter-time tale, many times, but never in the Summer Lands or before a stranger. "For two times ten days the First Man had gone without food, and for two times ten days the First Man had seen only snow and ice as he walked, till he was close to death.

On the next day, which was one score and one day, when the sun rose above the snow, the First Man saw that he had come to the edge of a Great Wood, which spread as far as his eyes could see across the hills and down the valleys. Now, the First Man was cold, and he was hungry, and he had drunk only by sucking the snow and ice in his mouth till his insides were as cold as his outsides. When he saw The Great Wood he forgot the warnings of his Ancestors and thought only of the warm fire that he might make from the trees, and of the animals he might hunt beneath their branches, or the tea he might brew from their bark."

The Daesani had fallen silent. Edan thought that Phelan and Duah and Newlyn were listening; but Kaman and Uchdryd with the injured arm bent their heads to one another and exchanged whispered words, while the others shifted restlessly in the damp grass. Or were they spreading out to surround the tribe? Lavena was watching the Daesani men as if Ulat's tales had unnerved her.

The Elder pushed on: "First Man took up his axe, which was of white quartz, and as sharp as any flint, and he struck one of the trees. As he struck his blow there was a terrible cry, and the First Man looked all about to see who had cried out, but he saw nothing but snow. So, he raised his axe and struck a second blow, and again a voice cried out in pain, and red sap ran from the tree. First Man was afraid, but he was also desperate, so he raised his axe again for a third and final blow, but before he could strike, the tree changed and became a woman. Her hair was as black as tree roots and her skin as pale as snow, and she was bloody from where his axe had struck her.

'I beg you, do not strike again', said the woman, who we call First Woman. 'But I am hungry and cold', said First Man, 'and your wood will warm me, and your branches may hide food for me'. 'If you put down your axe', she told him, 'I will bring you wood to burn, and branches for shelter, and food to eat'. First Man agreed to this, and so First Woman brought him branches to burn, and boughs for shelter, and the meat and shoots of the forest to eat. In time she bore him children, and these too she provided for, so long as each kept the law that The Great Wood was taboo ground. In the summertime, their family travelled to the coast, from where First Man had come, but in the winter, they returned to First Woman's home and lived at the edge of The Great Wood. So, it has always been for our tribe, and so it will always be." The Elder lifted his chin defiantly as he finished, daring the Daesani to contradict his tale.

Duah and Phelan shared a glance, and Edan saw in it everything he needed to know about the wolf-men's opinion on Tradition. The Daesani leader fixed the Elder with his grey eyes, and Edan noticed for the first time that he had chains of wolf teeth strung on rawhide laces about his neck.

"Many peoples have such tales," said Phelan. "No sacred law protects the forest. I have seen many trees cut down. When the woods are gone there are hills and rivers, there are beech nuts and acorns to gather, and fish to catch. It is a new land that we are building."

The Elder was obstinate. "We do not need a new land. There is nothing wrong with the old lands and the old ways."

"Are you blind old man? This world is dying." Now Phelan sounded angry. "Did Newlyn's words mean nothing to you? The Fomor will come and take your lands away from you! You cannot fight them. You could not fight anything." His eyes narrowed. "You have but six adults and two are not full-grown. You are not burdened with food; I can see the hunger in your eyes. I think that you have already suffered tragedy, am I wrong?" None of the tribe answered him. He was not wrong, but they did not speak of the missing ones. Still, Edan wondered, was he right?

"It is Tradition."

Edan thought that Phelan would argue further, and he welcomed it. If Tradition forced them to walk these meres and marshes with a babe in arms and no food in their bellies, then Tradition was wrong. Maybe the wolf-men had a place for an orphan fisher that was better than the one First Mother allowed. However, the Daesani leader seemed to make some decision and did not press the matter. "I hope that you are correct, old man, and that your family fares well, but remember if disaster comes the Great Wolf will be waiting. There is a place called Tanrid, the camp at the lake, to the south where the rivers meet. You can still come to the Daesani and find shelter," Edan thought for a moment that he was looking pointedly at Uch, or at him. "Any of you."

The meeting ended as it had begun, with an uncomfortable silence. By unspoken agreement the tribe took to the south-western shore of the mere, while the Daesani, with many glances towards the departing family, went east, fading slowly into the sighing birches.

The Elder led the way through the bull rushes with a stiff and obstinate back, ignoring everything behind him. Grandmother, who alone of them could change the Elder's mind when he was angry, followed, equally silent, while the others came behind full of chatter. Had those really been men or wolves in human form as Ulat had insisted in her winter tale? What had happened to Newlyn to leave the terrible burn on his face? Were their tales of sea-demons true knowledge or simply the fantasy of scared minds? Lavena chided the girls when their excitement boiled over into nervous giggles. Maccus urged speed, while Uch and Cinnia complained that they had been too quick to rebuff the Daesani.

"We should have traded," Uch insisted. "We are short on food. They might have had fish, birds, eels, or at least nuts. Perhaps they had seen deer or boar on their way south?"

Cinnia agreed with her mate, directing her complaints at the Elder's back, but he only bent his head to Grandmother and muttered words that the others could not hear.

Edan lagged along at the back, trailing the butt of his spear through the shallow water. New words were rolling around in his head: Clan, Fomor, Great Wolf. What did these things mean? What would it be like to leave the tribe behind and become part of something greater? The others still had bonds of family to bind them, but Edan did not. Of course, Maccus and Lavena had raised him when his parents were gone. But was his future only to be a mate for Brina or Morna, who were like his sisters now? Was it really to follow the same trail over and over until the Summer Lands were gone?

He hoped not.

Edan pulled out the worn tooth strung around his neck and held it in his palm. The old ivory had been carved into the shape of a diving seal, flippers together and head thrust forward with eyes open. He knew every nick and curve of the little figure, but he could hardly remember his Mother's face. How could that be? Did Newlyn carry a similar relic of his missing family? Had they drowned too?

Lost in thought, Edan fell back even further, dallying at the edge of the water. He saw that there was another of the Marsh People's flooded walkways just beneath the surface. Had they abandoned their homes before the end? or stayed to die with them?

A sudden noise made him turn, and he saw the strangest sight. A woman burst from the tree line across the mere and barrelled straight into the water, ploughing through it, waist deep. Then a man, who plunged into the water no more than two dozen paces behind her. The woman had hair as red as fire and ran awkwardly. The man wielded a spear, and with a jolt, Edan realised that he was chasing her. Even as he watched, the man cocked back his arm and launched the spear straight at the woman! She gave a strangled cry and collapsed into the water, and he thought she had been struck, but she was up and moving again a moment later.

If the man had been using a bow, she would have died!

Edan willed the woman to pick up the spear, but she forged her way past it, struggling against the water. Her hands were bound behind her back! The Hunter's hands were free, and he snatched up the floating spear as he passed it.

Edan wanted to help, but the water was so deep! The trackway! On the trackway, he could catch them. He sprang onto the submerged platform and ran, his fishing spear in his hands. His only thought was to reach the fleeing woman before the hunter brought her down with his spear. If he had a Hunter's bow things would be different. Without one, his only option was to get between them.

His feet skidded on the slick wood and rushes sliced at him as he ran. The spear carrier had seen him coming, sprinting across the water like a goose about to take flight, and slowed down in confusion — he couldn't see the trackway under the water. Edan saw grease black hair plaited in thick bunches, framing a face red with exertion and a fang-like grimace of anger. It was the gap-toothed Daesani!

The fleeing woman took advantage of Edan's arrival to get behind him, and he had his second shock in as many moments as she looked up at him, because she wasn't human. He saw a broad face, large flat nose, wide mouth, and skin pale like snow. Her bare shoulders bulged with straining muscles, and though she waded through the mud, she was nearly as tall as him. He had never seen anything like her, but he knew what she was from old Ulat's tales, a Troll! He almost fled, but Troll or not her hands were still lashed behind her back, she was still bleeding and bruised, and the wide pale eyes beneath the strong brows were full of fear.

Suddenly the hunter was on him. With a cry, he jabbed his spear at Edan, the row of tiny blades at its tip aimed up at his belly. Edan instinctively shoved his own spear in the way, but the impact knocked him back. The man jabbed again before he could regain his footing. Another desperate block, the sharp clack of wood vibrating through his wrists, and he fell back again. There was no hesitation in the wolf-man's attacks. This was not his first fight. Facing him was madness.

Edan could sense the Troll woman crawling onto the platform behind him, but his eyes were fixed on the advancing spear. The Daesani had taken it in a two-handed grip and was grinning as he closed on him.

"Bad choice boy!" he snarled, his accent strange and heavy. "The Troll is ours. Get out of my way and I will let you live!" His words said one thing, but his mad white eyes said another — no mercy.

Desperately Edan swung his fishing spear like a club, aiming for the man's head, but the hunter easily ducked under the clumsy blow and struck into the opening Edan had left. Edan saw it coming at the last moment and threw himself backwards, but the spear's tip still cut a bloody line across his chest, and the hunter pushed in for the kill. Edan should have died then, but the Daesani didn't know what he was standing on. His foot caught in the walkway's old beams and he stumbled; straight into Edan's flailing blow.

The butt of Edan's spear caught the Daesani in the side of the head with a sickening crunch, and he toppled, vanishing off the side of the trackway in a fountain of water and bubbles.

Edan stared dumbfounded at the swirling water, willing the man to reappear, but the bubbles stopped, and the water settled, and there was nothing to be seen. The hunter was dead, and back on the further shore the rest of the Daesani were already gathering, bows and spears in their hands.

Despairing, Edan grabbed the Troll woman by the arm and ran.

4. Phelan

Phelan's thoughts turned dark, seeing his prisoner gone and the tribe fleeing, but he forced himself to focus on the practical.

"Get him out of there." Phelan gestured at the spot where Keir had gone into the water. Kaman and Cuall, the dependable and the eager to please, threw aside their packs to wade out into the mere.

Was Keir dead? It would serve him right for letting the Troll woman escape. Phelan didn't spare more thoughts for him; his attention was on the waving reeds beyond the water into which the Troll and the boy had run. A planned attack? No. An impetuous boy, undisciplined, acting without thought — just like *he* had been before he had met the Great Wolf and learnt discipline. A pity. He had been sure that the little family would have come to the Daesani of their own will before Summer's end. Little chance of that now.

"Duah, go back and break camp. You and Cahal and Uchdryd must catch us up. They will go west, keeping the water between us, we will go after them."

"Why?"

Phelan had been expecting a challenge. He had lost a prisoner and a hunter; a challenge was natural. Just as natural that it was Duah that asked the question. Phelan knew that he had his eyes set on Phelan's place at the Great Wolf's side.

Amongst the small tribes, the families and kin-folk that made up the people of the Summer Lands, there was no chief, no headman. Every man was his own headman, the saying went. If you did not like what others did, then there was enough room to go your own way. The Daesani could not afford such luxuries. Where most tribes sported handfuls of members there were more of the Wolf-Clan than Phelan could count. As with any pack there had to be leaders, and as with any pack, there were always those waiting to take leadership for themselves.

"What's that Troll-blood girl got that makes her worth the effort?" Duah continued, addressing his words to the others as well as Phelan. "A bit of bare flesh? We can get that anywhere. Muscle she will never use willingly for us? We were sent to find people happy to join the Clan, or at least to lend us the strength of their arms, and we've found neither. People like us are worth a dozen marsh hunters or freak women. I say we forget them and head home."

His words were greeted with a murmur of approval by some, but Phelan noted that Cahal and Uchdryd didn't join in. The Troll woman had slighted them both and he was sure that they burned for revenge. If he fanned their anger with words of vengeance, for Keir and for themselves, he'd win them round easily enough and put Duah back in his place. But then what? Get them angry enough and they'd kill the lot of them, he didn't want that. Especially not the Troll.

When Phelan had first found his way to the Great Wolf's side, he had been a boy on the edge of manhood, the last survivor of a dead tribe. He had finished his growing in the old man's shadow and become the foremost of his followers. When the Great Wolf spoke of creating a new world for his people, Phelan trusted him implicitly. When he conceived the idea of creating one tribe from all the scattered people, Phelan had been the first to cast off his old name and take a wolf one instead. When the Daesani needed new hands for its work, Phelan had been the one to gather them, and if there was sometimes force involved, or a certain ruthlessness. Well, they were wolves after all.

And yet, for all that, it was hard to escape the lessons of his childhood. Phelan's own kind had come from a far darker world. A world that cowered in fear of hateful things that could not be fought nor reasoned with, only turned aside with offerings of blood and sacrifice. Fate; Famine; Death. In the darkness of the shaman's tent, the sharp sting of the marking-knife had taught him that the weak paid the price so that others could be strong.

No matter how much Phelan wanted to believe that the Great Wolf's dream could be achieved simply with hard work and kinship, his own scars told him otherwise. In the end, blood must be spilt; lives must be lost; an offering must be made to the very things he so much wished to leave behind — for such a fate as they needed to avoid it would have to be a great offering indeed.

So, when they had come across the Troll woman — a thing out of story — a creature touched by the Spirits, he had known. Her blood, and hers alone, would do. He had to capture her, to take her back, to offer her up in return for the rest of them.

Of course, these were things he could not say to the others.

Duah took Phelan's silence as a sign that he had already won. He relaxed and turned to the others, chuckling at a shared joke, slipping easily into his new role as leader of the moment.

Phelan's first blow took Duah utterly by surprise. He swung the butt of his spear low, catching Duah across the shins and knocking him to the ground. It was a move that Phelan had practiced on deer and men alike. Snarling, Duah tried to rise, but Phelan's second blow, this time with a fist, took him in the side of the face and he went down again.

Cahal took a half-step forward, and the dogs leapt up from the grass, barking and confused at the sudden violence, but all of them fell silent as Phelan threw the spear aside and pulled a razor-keen blade of black stone from his belt, holding it loose and ready to strike. Duah looked up at him, seeing the wolf shadow against the pale sky, and held his tongue.

Phelan looked at Cahal and Trehar, then Nyle and Newlyn. "We will chase down these people because no one, no Troll, no lecturing old man, no milk-tooth boy, steals a kill from the jaws of the Great Wolf and gets away with it!" His voice was cold, certain, betraying nothing.

"I'd rather chase them into the claws of the Fomor than return to the Clan with my tail between my legs." Uchdryd murmured his agreement and Trehar nodded.

Phelan dropped his gaze to Duah. "Agreed?" Duah met his eyes for an instant, one last flicker of defiance, then bared his neck to show his obedience.

"Good." Phelan sheathed the knife and held out a hand, hauling Duah back to his feet. Such fights were quickly forgotten. Duah clenched his hand a little too hard, just for a moment, then turned to gather the others. Cahal threw Uchdryd a glance. They knew that Phelan would take only those he could trust not to kill the Troll as his chasers.

"We split into two. Newlyn, Nyle, Trehar, come with me. The rest of you break camp and deal with the body; if he's dead." Phelan's chosen hunters grabbed their spears while the others shuffled off.

"Swende!" Phelan gave the order to hunt, calling the dogs to his side. He broke into a run, the two hounds bounding after him, while the others raced alongside through the shallow water at the edge of the mere. The dogs were faster than a human in a sprint, and stronger too, but Phelan knew that they needed to see their prey before they could hunt it.

"Cross the water?" Nyle's question was clipped, saving his breath for running.

Phelan shook his head. The boy and his tribe would be on the run, breaking scared into the country beyond the mere; but he wouldn't risk another ambush on a hunch. These hunters might know the land better than them, but they couldn't outrun them, not unless they dumped the old and the young. Phelan had enough time to be careful.

The four Daesani crossed the water where a shallow stream fed the pool, their leather-clad feet slapping off rocks and casting spray behind them. Brown and white geese burst honking from the tangled rushes as they forced their way through, the dogs snapping and snarling at their wings. On the further bank Newlyn, with his longer legs, naturally took the lead. Phelan would have preferred Kamal as his tracker, but Newlyn was the best present and Phelan let him go.

Beyond the open mere, they wove through sighing willows and peat brown streams, following Newlyn's instincts and the hounds' noses. The lake fell behind them to the right, and tree-thick hills appeared to the left. Open mudflats dotted with wading birds ran between braided channels. Here the hunters were forced to slow to a cautious pace, casting around amongst the channels and gravel for some sign of their prey. The tracks they had been following became confused, crossing back and forth over each other. Newlyn hesitated, backtracking. Phelan wondered if more men had joined the ones they were chasing. No sooner had they chosen what they thought was the true route than the tracks vanished entirely.

Tricks and false trails, Phelan almost smiled. The fleeing tribe had set these tricks to confuse them, then melted away into the marsh without a trace, but the Troll woman had no such skill. A half-collapsed mud bank betrayed where she had stumbled, a broken patch of reeds showed where she had grasped for balance. By these signs, they tracked them across the marsh, reaching the edge of a pale birch forest as the daylight began to fade.

A deer trail led between the trees, running up into the mouth of a narrow canyon, barely more than a wrinkle in the red rocks draped with ferns. Phelan hesitated at the gully's mouth, scanning the gloomy rock faces and the sighing birches. There were a dozen places where someone could hide.

"Ambush?" Trehar crouched next to Phelan, the wolf teeth chains around his neck and wrists rattling softly.

"I don't know."

"They are just hunters. If I was running from us, I wouldn't stop to make traps, I'd keep running."

"So would I ... but they are hunters, as you say. They know how to drive game and catch it." Phelan tried to imagine himself in the mind of the old hunter, Maccus, with his stalker's build and cautious eyes. Would he risk capture to plan an ambush? Would the rash boy? Would the others let him?

Phelan slid up behind a tree. With quick hand gestures he motioned Newlyn forward. The big man took a firmer grasp on his spear and moved ahead, glancing from side to side as he went. He had not gone more than ten paces forward when there was a crack and clatter: an arrow, stone tipped, clipped a tree trunk a foot to Newlyn's side and bounced to the ground. Newlyn cried out, threw his spear up into the undergrowth, and jumped into cover without waiting to see where it landed.

"Hunt!" Trehar released the dogs with a cry and they streaked forwards, bounding through the bilberries and up the ravine. For a minute they could hear them crashing around in the undergrowth, barking and howling. Phelan shook his head to himself; it was clear that they had found nothing.

"What sort of throw was that meant to be?" Trehar asked Newlyn.

"I didn't come here to kill men," Newlyn replied. "We came to find people to join the Wolf, to save them before they drown, not to spear them."

"Even men who are taking shots at you?"

Newlyn snorted. "He didn't mean to hit me any more than I meant to hit him."

Trehar watched the hounds come slinking back, dog wet, and empty jawed. "So? Up and after them? Even if he ran, he can't be far ahead."

The warrior in Phelan wanted to agree and press the chase, but not the hunter. Maybe Maccus' tribe had more members than they had seen. They had certainly looked evasive when he had commented on their numbers. It would explain the confusion of tracks that they had found in the mudflats. Moreover, Duah and the others would be waiting for them back by the lake. If they were separated for too long, who knew where they would go.

"No. There might be a dozen of them hidden, for all we know, and the light is failing. We will go back and find the others."

Phelan turned away. "Time enough to catch them tomorrow."

5. Edan

"Run!"

For a brief moment the tribe just stared at Edan as he fled up the grassy bank towards them with the Troll woman in tow. Then they took in the dripping water, the Troll's bound hands, the red blood streaming down Edan's chest, and most of all the distant shouting, like the baying of hounds.

"Run!" Edan shouted again. He flung his arm back in the direction of the Daesani hunters across the lake.

The tribe seemed to understand all at once. They turned and ran. Reeds cut at them. Tangles of nettles caught at their feet. Maccus grabbed Morna in his arms and carried her bodily up the ridge. It was all out flight, bound to exhaust them, but no one was thinking clearly.

They ran until they found cover — a thicket of rowans hidden from the mere by a ridge of heather and stinging nettles. They huddled together in the shelter of the branches; eyes wild for their pursuers. The branches shook, and Uch went for a blade, but it was only a deer bolting away from them.

"Edan, what have you done?!" Lavena berated him like one of her own children, not even dignifying him with his adult title. It rankled, but he held his temper. He wasn't her child anymore, he never really had been, and he was determined to hold his own for once.

"I've saved this woman, First Mother," he said, aiming for an Elder-like formality. "They had her tied like a caught deer!"

"Then we give her back, quickly!" Uch's voice was full of panic. "If they see we didn't mean to steal her, then they might let us go!"

"You can't steal people," Maccus snapped, "and I won't hand her back to anyone who thinks you can. If our Fisher thinks she needed to be rescued, then we should trust him."

Edan tried to keep from smiling at Maccus' endorsement but heard him mutter, "We'll talk about your choice later."

Maccus drew a bone-handled knife from his pouch and stepped towards the Troll woman, clearly intending to release her, but she pulled back in fear, putting Edan between herself and Maccus — as if he could somehow protect her.

Maccus tried to explain, "Your bonds, I'll cut them," but she just cowered further. Either she did not understand him, or she did not trust him. Only when Edan took the knife would she let her hands be freed.

"What is she?" Morna asked, clinging to Grandmother's side. "She's so ugly!"

The Elder replied simply, "A Troll."

"Go now. You're free!" Maccus tried to gesture the Troll away with flapping hands, but she did not move.

"There is no time for that," said First Mother. "The wolf-men will come. We cannot stay here." She laid her hand on Maccus' arm. "You are First Hunter; you know the ways of prey and how to catch it. Now we must be the prey. You will lead us."

Lavena's words brought the discussion to a halt, and only then did Edan start to wonder exactly what he had done. He'd killed a man. Once the others understood that, then what would they do? Maccus probably thought that the wolf-men would give up their pursuit by night. If he knew that a death was involved, then he'd understand that it was quite a different matter!

Maccus interrupted Edan's thoughts with quick instructions, organising the tribe for flight. The burdens of the weakest, Morna and Grandmother, were rapidly divided amongst the rest of them, and they set off down deer trails and boar paths, always keeping undergrowth and trees between themselves and the water, so that the Daesani would not see them. The Elder spoke of a woodland ridge where they could find safety, half a day away, and so Maccus had the tribe adopt the long-striding jog that the hunters used to follow prey in open country, and which they could maintain for hours, even days if they must.

They followed a stream, to throw off the Daesani's dogs, and ducked their way under pine branches, where they might leave no footprints. They saw no sign of the wolf-men, could not even tell if they were following, but no one suggested stopping. All the way the Troll followed, keeping at Edan's heels.

Eventually, they emerged at the edge of a wide mudflat, where a shallow river washed its way through gravel beds and sandbanks. The water thronged with black-headed gulls. On the far side Edan could see a line of hills, cloaked with the rich green of pine forest.

"We will be safe there," the Elder declared, but they could all see that there was a mile or more of open ground between themselves and the hills, with only scattered clumps of marsh grass for cover. If the Daesani caught up with them in the open ground, there would be no escape.

"We split up," Uch insisted. "Three groups. Cross back and forth. Make maximum use of the cover." He pointed towards the far side of the mudflats, where thick banks of sedge spread out below the forest ridge. "When we get to the far side, we meet up again, find some rocks, and get out without a trace."

"No! We should run now, get to the trees before they find us!" Lavena sounded almost as panicked as Uch had, as if she had grown more frightened as they fled. "We don't have time for false trails."

Edan found himself agreeing with her. The wolf-men might be right behind them. He wanted to run and never stop, to increase their lead; but the two Hunters were in agreement. The rest of the tribe scattered. Heart thumping in his chest like a hammerstone, Edan joined them.

He scrambled down the gravel banks and onto the open mudflat, and once again the Troll was right behind him. He risked a glance back. He'd rescued her, wasn't that enough? He wanted to turn and shout her away, but there was no point. She wouldn't understand, and the noise might give him away.

At first, they dashed over open ground, with hard mud under their feet. Then the river channel, and a bank of sand beyond it. After the sandbank, the open flat dissolved into tangled channels that wound between clumps of long grass. The water here was calf-deep, and every frantic step echoed as loudly as Edan's pounding heart until he finally forced himself to slow down.

'Imagine that you are stalking fish,' he told himself, trying to calm his panic, 'you know how to do this.' He forced a deep breath and eased himself forward, stepping carefully. Now the only sound was the slurp of the Troll's feet behind him. To Edan's surprise, she was almost as quiet in the water as he was.

A splash nearby made him jump in terror, the barely controlled panic surging up once more. He dropped to his knees in the water, desperately fumbling at his pouches for a weapon, anything he could use to defend himself other than the spear which had already taken a life.

A heavy hand descended onto Edan's shoulder, gripping him gently but firmly. He looked up into the face of the Troll woman. She shook her head slowly and pointed with her other hand, and he realised that the noise had been nothing more than a pair of gulls coming in to land. The hand pulled him up, and then nudged him forward, setting him back on his way.

In this way, they crossed the remainder of the marsh and came to the hills beyond. Birch and fern crowded the lower slopes, with dark green pines above. Edan met the others at the base of a rocky outcrop that reared above the lower land, where they could scramble up to the bluff.

In the gloom of the trees, Maccus took the lead again, picking out the faintest of trails for them to follow. They formed a rough line behind him, pushing Edan and the Troll to the back. He accepted this with a sigh, then realised that Uch had remained at the top of the rocks. When he hesitated, Uch met his eye, and he took it as an invitation to speak.

"Second Hunter, what is it?"

"I can see them." Uch kept to the shadows of the trees, his eyes fixed on the marshlands. "There. At the edge of the water."

Maccus hurried back, squeezing in beside them. "The light is failing," he declared, "they won't catch us before it's dark." But his tone was uncertain, and his face was grim.

"Someone should make sure of it. Hang back, shoot some arrows at them," Uch said. Edan felt a surge of panic at the thought of violence, seeing once again the churning waters that had swallowed the Daesani. He'd killed a man. How could Uch talk of bloodshed? But of course, they still didn't know.

Maccus appeared to consider the suggestion. "I'll wait, see if they get close. You can lead the others and I'll catch up." Edan wondered what Maccus was thinking. Uch was the best of them with a bow — why would Maccus insist on staying behind? Did he feel responsible? Or did he not trust Uch alone with the Daesani?

They pushed on into the forest. Maccus joined them as the light failed, his face grim. His eyes told them enough to know that they had to keep going. Only when the gloom made the path impossible to follow did they finally collapse, each seeking their own place against a tree or stone. They did not dare to light a fire — for fear that the Daesani would glimpse it through the trees — so they ate Edan's single trout cold. Little remained of First Mother's meat or Brina's beech nuts, but they passed around what they had, even to Edan. Only the Troll was offered nothing, though she looked as hungry as the rest of them.

Edan expected the inquisition to resume. He had tried to formulate some sort of explanation for his actions, something that might make sense to the others, and himself, but no one asked. Lavena spared him one long glance that told him everything about how interested she was in his excuses, then turned away. In the end, he forced himself to approach Maccus and tell him about the Daesani, but even he seemed to have nothing to say. One by one the tribe wrapped itself in furs and silence and went to sleep.

Edan lay down with the others, but rest wouldn't come. As soon as he closed his eyes he was back in the mere, seeing the Daesani vanish into the water over and over again. Again, and again he heard the crack of the spear shaft striking bone and the gurgle of the water as it swallowed the man's face.

Horrified, he tried to focus on something else; on Brina's interest in the Daesani, on Lavena's scorn, on Maccus' unexpected approval, on the Troll woman, but the mere water rolled back over his thoughts, roiling and rising until he felt himself vanish in it, sinking into a confusion of guilt and nightmare. Ice strewn waves crashed in his mind's eye, and he was sinking … sinking. Once again, the spear crack rang out, but this time he was the one tumbling into the water, hands flailing, trying to grasp hold of something that was slipping away from him. When he opened his mouth to call for help, he drowned instead.

Spear shafts of light pierced the water above him. Then a man's hand reached down towards him. Desperately he tried to get to the surface, but the figure planted a fishing spear in the middle of Edan's chest and pushed him back into the mud. First, it was the gap-toothed man, then his father, and finally the wolf clan leader, Phelan, only the wolf skin on his head had transformed him into a real wolf with a man's body. Edan grabbed at the spear, trying to push it away, but something grasped his arms from behind and pulled them away. The clawing hands turned him over, and he looked down into yawning depths as deep as the sky. There was a sun beneath the waves, black and rimmed with fire. Dark shapes poured out of it. Spike-covered and claw handed, they pulled him down into the drowning depths.

Edan started awake in the darkness, cold and clammy, clawing himself free of the nightmare. Mist had crept between the trees, soaking his blankets and robbing them of warmth. He shivered, pulling the dressed pelts closer about him, and tried to ignore the creaking of the trees in the darkness. Had that been a footstep!? No — just the scrape of one branch against another.

Edan closed his eyes, but remained on edge, startling at every noise. 'What have I done?' He asked himself the question directly, but he had no answer. He had seen a woman running, but what business was that of his? The tribe kept to itself. The tribe was all he had, and he had put them at risk for a woman. A Troll woman. A winter tale thing, not something real.

She wasn't even beautiful. She looked nothing like the tribe's women. She was pale where they were dark, large where they were small. Her skin was like thistle-milk or ice, lacking the ruddy colours of human flesh. Where the tribe had dark hair, hers was orange-red, like the embers of a fire. Even her clothing was strange. The garments of the tribe were light and flexible, but she wore plates of hard hide tied with thongs of leather. If he hadn't touched her flesh, he wouldn't think she was real, solid, living.

Edan caught himself. He'd killed a man! What did it matter what the Troll looked like? In the stories they told by firelight when the snow was deep and cold, the Trolls were old things, dead and gone a hundred generations past.

When he and Brina had been young, perhaps seven winters old, they had found a leg bone sticking from a bank of peat. It had been as large as them, mud-dark and heavy as a stone. They had named it a Troll bone, imagining a man as large as a tree and as furry as a bear. Edan's father had played the Troll, lurching through the snow with arms raised, a shaggy fur across his back. Edan and Brina had tackled him, pretending to cut off his arms with an axe. For a moment he'd endured their tickling, arms behind his back, but then he'd roared and grabbed at them, because Troll's limbs grew back as soon as they were gone. They had screamed and run away, but the screams had been full of laughter, you couldn't really be afraid of something that didn't exist.

And yet, here she was, this Troll. Where had the Daesani found her? Why had they bound her? He realised that he had no idea why she had been their prisoner.

Something made him open his eyes again, and he stared frightened into the darkness, searching for whatever had disturbed him. A pale moon had crept into the sky, just bright enough to outline the branches above and little else. But there was something else — a white shape that hung between the trees. With a start, he realised that the Troll was staring at him.

The rest of the tribe had curled themselves into little knots, huddled against the roots of trees, sleeping with their faces hidden from the cold, but the Troll woman had simply squatted down and waited. She crouched only a pace away from him, with her large hands clasped in front of her, and her strange eyes still open.

"What do you want?" he hissed at her, keeping his voice low. "I already rescued you, isn't that enough? Why don't you just go away? Then they won't chase us anymore!"

The Troll woman cocked her head, like a dog listening to a human voice, her wide lips pressed together in an expression he couldn't decipher. He tried again. "Do you understand what I am saying? No? Do your kind speak?" He attempted to mime speech, putting his fingers to his lips and then pulling them away to give the shape of words coming out. To his surprise, the Troll raised a hand to her lips and did the same. Intrigued, Edan pushed himself upright against the tree, his irritation fading.

"Speak. Yes? You understand?" Slowly the Troll woman nodded, but she did not reply. Instead, she made a complex gesture, half visible in the moonlight, her fingers curling into odd shapes.

Edan tried something simpler. "My name is Edan ... Edan." He repeated his name slowly, pointing at himself. "Edan".

He saw the pale eyes drop to his pointing fingers and then back to his face. "Yes, you understand?"

"Ee-dan" the Troll's voice was deep, low and rumbling like distant thunder, and slow. For a moment Edan didn't realise that she had spoken his name at all. Then, with more confidence, "Edan". Copying Edan's gesture she pointed slowly at herself: "Tara".

"Tara? Your name is Tara?"

She shook her head and repeated the word. This time Edan realised that she made a peculiar movement of her hand as she did so, touching her broad thumb to the first two fingers. "Tara?" He did his best to make the same movement, and her face split into a wide grin, revealing teeth as broad as axe-heads.

As if encouraged by this success, she launched into a more urgent speech, half-words, and half-gestures. It felt to Edan like a heartfelt plea, an outpouring of pent-up information, of which he could make out nothing. He tried his best to understand, repeating a word here or there, but it was no use. The Troll — Tara — must have seen the incomprehension on his face, because she fell silent, letting her hands drop, and said no more.

Edan let his eyes close again. Tara. Her name was Tara.

6. Tara

A steady cascade of water streamed off the stones at the entrance to the cave in which the tribe sheltered. Outside, torrential rain drenched the drooping upland pines, turning the deer paths into rivulets and brooks. Tara sat with her back against a rough block of stone, her knees drawn up to her chest as she watched the rain.

It had taken three days of exhausted flight before the human family had finally shaken off the wolf-men. Although they could see nothing certain, nor hear anything definite, the fear of pursuit had been everywhere. Every creak of a branch had sounded like a muffled footstep, each crow's croak a stifled cough, as if Phelan was constantly about to spring out on them. Real or phantom, the Daesani had driven them up out of the marshlands and into a mess of hills, close to the great woods and mountains of the west, home to the broad-antlered elk called the Weru-dan. There at last, under the cover of storms and endless rain, they seemed to have lost the hunters.

Tara knew that these humans had saved her life, but she had learnt little more about them. She thought that she had timed her escape perfectly, using the stolen blade to cut the bonds between her legs and barging Faint-heart to the ground just as the others were returning to the woods, so that they didn't know at first that she had got away from them. But she had no idea where she was running and had underestimated how quickly Gap-tooth would follow. And his spear, how could she have known that he could throw it through the air as he had? The People did not throw spears. If the man — Edan — had not intervened she would have been captured again. But what now? Had she swapped one set of captors for another? No … not captors; but not yet allies.

She turned to look at the shadowy interior of the cave where the humans had gathered. She had watched them light a fire, using a wooden spindle that the oldest woman had turned furiously with her hands until some dry moss they had with them burst into flame. Was this human magic? It was ironic — she, who had spent countless winter nights learning at Ama's knee until she was considered wise, knew almost nothing about these people who had conquered the Summer Lands.

She studied them now. They were small-framed, with ruddy river-clay skin. Shaggy dark hair, tailed and braided, framed small faces with narrow noses and bright eyes. They were dark and quick where she was pale and strong. They wore leather skirts around their waists that covered them to mid-thigh, men and women alike, with leggings underneath tied with criss-cross lacings. Most wore coats of seal-fur. All of them had many trinkets of bone or horn strung around their necks on leather cords. The men had narrow strips of hide bound around their hair, while the women wore tight caps with pale bark stitched in a zig-zag around their edges. She had been more than happy to mock the Daesani by giving them nicknames and had made little attempt to learn their language, but it meant that she had no way to speak to these people either. She wished that she had tried harder.

There were ten of them if she counted the infant. The eldest two, a man and a woman, seemed to be in charge. That at least was the same as it was amongst The People. Then came two pairs with children, and the children themselves.

The adults seemed to have two names each, and Tara could not tell what rules governed their usage. Both of the mothers seemed to be called Matir, and both of the fathers Helyad, but sometimes there were other names. The hunter with the grey streaked hair was sometimes called Hammer. Tara thought that he was father to the two girl children and was sure that the darker haired woman was their mother. Her other name appeared to be Joy, which hardly seemed appropriate, for she was stern and grim.

The younger pair were called Matir Dau and Helyad Dau, as if Dau were their family. But then the man was sometimes called Cross as well, a name that suited him — he seemed constantly angry. Matir Dau, who carried a scrawny baby in her arms, had curly brown hair that escaped her cap in little ringlets. Lacking a better name Tara called her Ring-hair. She had no idea if the baby had a name at all.

And then there was Edan. Long-limbed and beardless, his skin was smooth, free of scars. He wore his hair tied back in a loose braid, secured with a loop of rawhide. He didn't seem to be the child of any of them, even though he was just a boy himself. Or perhaps not, these humans grew at a different rate from The People. Maybe he was a man full-grown, ready to leave this tribe and find a mate in another, assuming that was how it worked amongst them.

Though she had travelled alongside them as they fled from the Daesani, few of them had acknowledged her presence with more than fearful glances. The old man had looked at her and declared her Eshu — a Troll — while the old woman made a warding sign. The new parents kept together, and away from her, while the one called Hammer watched her appraisingly. Only Edan had thought to speak to her, and their few faltering attempts to exchange words had only flustered her. He had learnt her name, but little else.

For hours now Edan had been the centre of attention amongst his kin. The others had scooped up water in a leather bag and used it to wash him down, then painted spirals of mud on his body. Now the mud had dried in the fire-heat, turning pale and white on his dark skin. Joy had braided his hair, and he had cast off most of his clothing to kneel, head bowed, by the fire, while the others made a circle around him. Each of the others took one of the odd carved objects they wore around their necks and placed it in front of them.

She understood that Edan had broken some form of taboo, most likely when he had struck the Daesani warrior. Violence did not seem familiar to them, just as it had not been familiar to The People when their kind had been young. Back then, so the Seers' tales said, The People had been many and the land theirs. There had been great beasts for the hunting, more than enough to meet the needs of all The People. But then the humans had come; fast, numerous, spreading everywhere. The People had tried to ignore them, the tales said, then to avoid them, finally to fight them — none of these things had worked. Those of The People that survived hid in the mountains, in the woods, in the bad lands, in the places where the humans had no desire to go. They had learnt to fight in those places. Now perhaps the humans would learn to fight too; were already learning. It wouldn't help them, not if her vision ran its course. The People and the humans would drown side by side.

She did not mourn the dead wolf-man. She had not intended him to die, it was simply a thing that had happened, and he would not have wept for her if she had been the one to drown. She felt more sympathy for the boy; eyes down, muscles surely cramping in discomfort. He was the one who bore the blood-mark; and for what? Her? What had made him rush out to help her? She had no idea.

The kneeling family began to sing, a low rhythmic chant of syllables, wordless to Tara's ears. Were they calling on the spirits, she wondered, on the ghosts of their ancestors, or the powers of the land? Suddenly she felt that she was intruding, and turned away, resuming her vigil over the forest.

Sometime later, the sound of a soft footstep crunching on the damp grit of the cave floor called her attention back inside. The youngest girl hesitated a few paces away with a handful of beech nuts held in her hand. When Tara turned the girl took half a step back, then held her ground, slowly extending the hand that held the nuts.

"Meru Tu." Tara spoke slowly and carefully, aware that her voice was a rumble, hoping that she had managed to say, 'Thank You'.

The child smiled a gap-toothed smile and replied, "Merasta." So Tara did the same. These people seemed to run their words together in a rush, without gestures to give meaning to the sounds. She extended her hand slowly, and the girl emptied the nuts into it. Tara pointed at her own chest with her other hand. "Tara," she said. "I am Tara."

"Morna," said the girl.

"Morna." Tara thought the word meant beloved. "Thank you, Morna, for the food." The child nodded seriously. Tara knew that they were barely communicating, but she had to try. "Morna. Listen. It is very important. We must go to the Great Stone; do you know it? To stop the sea. We must ..." Tara realised that her hands were fluttering in agitation, supplying the meanings she couldn't speak. The child cocked her head like she was trying to understand, but then she giggled out: "Ni Mi kweillia!" and hurried away, back to her family.

Tara sighed and let her hands drop. Not yet. She would give a lot for the Old One's wisdom now. Language, men's learning, was more their thing. Slowly she shelled the nuts with her fingers, eating them one at a time to make them last longer. Then she curled up against the rock and watched the daylight fade into night, lulled to sleep by the rain and the song of the tribe.

* * *

42

The next morning, the rain finally eased. The solid grey clouds broke apart into rough tatters, letting the spring sun shine through. The ground and the pine trees were still saturated with water, it dripped and tapped, giving off a faint mist as it evaporated. Gnats and other small insects fluttered around the cave mouth, a few settling on Tara's skin and then buzzing off again when they found her too tough to bite. Glossy starlings hopped amongst the wet grass, gorging themselves on the flies, and Tara found herself wishing that she could find food as easily. The gift of nuts had been welcome, but she had not eaten well in weeks now and her belly hurt for it.

It appeared that the tribe felt the same. Sometime in the night they had finished their ritual, and now they prepared to hunt. Cross had lumps of yellow chert to work, and from these he knapped curving crescents of blades, sharp as ice, which he handed to the women. A cave rock, quickly shaped, provided Hammer with an axe blade which he fitted to an antler haft and gave to Edan. Edan took the axe and left the cave, glancing at Tara as he passed, and set to work felling the narrow saplings that crowded amongst the rocks. The poles went to the women, who shaped them into spears with sure strokes of the chert blades, then placed the points in the fire to harden. One spear went to each hunter, and to the elder Matir too.

When the spears were done, and Tara had risen, she cautiously approached Edan. The younger Matir gave her a hostile look, but Edan seemed to welcome her. From his careful words and amusing hand-gestures, she couldn't help but grin when he held his splayed hands to the side of his head to indicate antlers, she gathered that they planned to try and hunt the Weru-dan. Her empty stomach rumbled at the thought of such rich meat and she offered, "I hunt with you!"

One word at least must have made sense to them, for the younger Helyad snorted, shaking his head sharply as if affronted, then glanced at the senior. "You are not a hunter," he said. He spoke slowly, then gestured at those who were not carrying spears, the old, the children, and the mother with the baby. His meaning was clear. "You Gerro," he said. "Chase. Scare."

Tara bristled. She might be a Seer, but she had hunted the deer and the boar before, but the man had already turned away to organise the others. Soon the whole family headed out of the cave, pausing only to bank the fire with ashes, and she trailed after them.

It was damp and close amongst the pine trees. Thick green ferns choked the hillsides, resisting every step and showering them with droplets of the previous day's rain. Tara was quickly soaked despite her heavy clothing. Narrow aspen trunks emerged from the morning mist like ghosts. Where the others slipped between the trees with almost no sound, she trod heavily, more than one branch catching her in the chest. This was not how The People hunted. Where they could, they kept to open land, taking their prey on the run, driving it against brush or cliffs or other places it could not go before they brought it down with club and spear.

The tribe had a different way. The four hunters went first, following animal trails through the ferns, crouching to the ground to look for tracks, or to sniff the droppings that they found, crushing them between their fingertips to see how fresh they were. With gestures and whispered words, Hammer split the hunters into groups. He and the brown-eyed woman went one way, while the remaining men took the next trail. The rest of the family spread out in a loose line, pushing through the ferns, making no attempt to be quiet. Tara realised that it was their job to drive the prey onto the spears of the others. Now she could be as noisy as she liked.

They clambered to the top of a ridge and then down into a valley on the other side. The sun had fully risen, scattering the patchy clouds and burning away the drifting mists. Water glinted from the lowlands below, flashing through the gaps between the trees where landslips and fallen pines revealed it. Columns of dancing flies gathered wherever the sunlight pierced the canopy. Little red-winged birds zipped through the patchy shadows, catching insects on the wing.

The land was beautiful, peaceful after days on the run from Phelan's warriors, but Tara found herself on edge. The hairs were rising all over her body. She dropped behind the others, glancing this way and that, trying to understand the danger. In the buzzing shadows between the twisted pines she thought that she saw figures: pelt-draped, spike-haired, and beast-masked, shaking clubs and hammer stones, and was about to cry out a warning, before she recognised them as vision spirits, come from the forest to warn her of danger.

44

The spirits faded one by one, putting their fingers to their mouths, and she smelt the hot smell of blood. Something was stalking them.

A shout came from up ahead, then a whooping cry — the hunters had seen their prey. The line of chasers was ahead of Tara, and even as she tried to call a warning to them, they broke into a run, crashing away through the undergrowth. Desperately she started running as well, aware that something else was near, somewhere in the trees.

She caught flashes of movement and heard the splintering of branches as the Weru-dan crashed through the woodland. Somewhere down the slope the hunters must be waiting, spears set, but she could not see them. She could not even see the chasers, she just had to hope that she was still running in the right direction.

A scream split the forest, cutting over the noise of crashing feet and running animals. It was a desperate scream of fear and pain, quite unlike the yells and cries of the hunt. Had someone fallen? Had the elk turned on the pursuers? She did not believe it.

Tara burst out of the ferns and into a clearing. A pine tree had fallen in some storm, tearing its roots out of the soil as it crashed to the earth, leaving a space that the smaller trees had yet to cover. Ring-hair was sprawled on the ground, terrified and bloody, with her baby clutched convulsively in her arms. Padding towards her, its eyes fixed on its prey, a huge cat snorted its hungry breath. Tara had only ever seen its likeness painted on the walls of sacred caves or scratched into antlers as old as The People, but she knew it nevertheless; Lero, cave lion, a beast crawled out of legend.

It was old, brindle-furred and starvation thin, as if it had dragged itself from a hibernation as long as generations, somewhere amongst the snow and the old forest. Its body was orange brown, marked by scars that spoke of rivals conquered and spear wounds scorned. Its tufted tail lashed behind it as it sensed Tara's arrival, and it snarled a snag-toothed challenge as it turned towards her.

Tara's hectic bravery vanished as she met its gaze. Its eyes were like the embers of a fire, bright in a mask black fur. Even old and thin it was as large as her. She hesitated, unsure what to do, and as if to warn her off it pounced at Ring-hair, toying with her, its massive paws tearing apart her leather clothing, and lunging at the baby in her arms. The woman lashed out wildly with a rock that she scrabbled from the ground, catching the lion on the side of its muzzle, but her defiance only angered it and sent it in for the kill.

Before it could strike, Tara wrapped her arms around it from behind, straining with all her strength until she could link her hands around its huge chest. She planted her feet wide, trying to hold the lero back. The People were strong, but it was stronger, and it surely weighed more than her. "Get back!" she grunted, hoping that the women understood. The lion scrabbled backward with its claws, slashing at her legs, but the angle was bad and though she felt the blood welling she knew that the cuts were not deep. The lion roared and writhed in her grasp, trying to turn and get its teeth and claws into her, but she held on desperately. If it turned, she would die.

With a yell of effort, she pivoted back, smashing both herself and the lion against the jagged roots of the upturned pine. "Get away! Get away!" she shouted in her head, trying to will the woman out of the way, but she couldn't see if she was gone or not. Tara thought that the mother and baby were still screaming, but her ears were full of the pounding of her heart and the snarling of the lion.

She shoved her knee into the lero's back, trying to force it away from her and into the mass of earth and roots. It dug its fore claws into the wood and pulled away. She felt a claw slice through the salt-tough deer hide on her shoulders. She was bleeding from a dozen blows she hadn't even felt land. She was half aware that the other beaters had entered the clearing, but they were children and old men. All they could do was drag Matir out of the way of the thrashing and deadly combat.

The lion arched back convulsively, snapping at her face, its breath a hot stink of blood and rage. She jerked her head back in terror and smashed it against the hard wood of the tree. The shock blurred her vision and blinded her. Her legs went weak, her muscles ached, but somehow, she held on just a moment longer. Then her fingers pulled apart, one from another, and she felt something tear in her shoulder as the lion broke free. She had lost the fight.

With shouts and leaps and the clash of spears the hunters came. The Weru-dan was long escaped, but now they surrounded the lion with jabbing spears and moving bodies.

In normal times they would have fled before the wrath of such a beast, but Tara had pinned it long enough for them to close with it. At the bite of their spears the lion jerked around, tossing Tara to the ground as if their struggle had been nothing but a play fight.

She watched the rest of the battle from the ground, willing the humans to win. The lero leapt snarling at Cross, but he danced away from it, spear in the way. Hammer yelled, attracting the lion's attention to himself, and gave Edan and Joy the opening to strike again, their broad-headed spears stabbing into its flanks.

Encircled, outnumbered, wounded and surprised, the lero was still magnificent. Snarling and hissing between bared fangs the old beast tried again and again to escape the clearing, clawing at the points of the hunters' spears. Even when the others joined in with branches and stones it fought on, until at last one of the hunters landed a final two-handed blow that pierced its heart.

After the beast was dead the tribe surrounded it, marvelling at it. It was clearly as foreign to them as it was to Tara. The elder Hunter prodded it with his spear, as if not convinced that it was dead, then bent to lift one of its massive paws. He pulled back the muzzle to expose the giant teeth, and the toes to show its claws, shaking his head and making gestures to the others.

Then, practical, they lashed the body to a sled made from spear poles and dragged it back to the cave for butchering.

Back in the cave, the tribe relit their fire and set to work once again. This time, however, they made a space for Tara, patting the flat stone to show that she should join them. Now, at last, they introduced themselves, sharing names she had been forced to guess: Maccus, Uch, Lavena, Cinnia. With halting words and many repetitions, they thanked her for saving Matir-Dau, Second Mother, from the lero. The woman had taken wounds to one of her arms and one of her legs, wounds which her mother, the old woman, had padded with moss and bound with knotted grasses.

Maccus, the hunter that Tara had called Hammer, cut out the lero's heart with quick slices and offered it to her, giving her the honour of the kill even though it had been he who had landed the fatal thrust. Uch and Brina and Lavena cut the Lion's pelt cleanly back, preserving the warm fur, and set strips of meat on the fire. The old woman offered Tara her moss and healing herbs but her wounds, though numerous, had already crusted over with blood and sealed themselves. Morna, when she had recovered her bravery, ventured out into the afternoon sunlight to gather mustard root leaves near the cave mouth, which Matir-Nan, the Grandmother, added to the meat. It was lean and spicy, rich and blackened.

They devoted the rest of the day to extracting everything useful from the lion's corpse. The meat was cut into joints and wrapped in parcels of fern leaf, the sinew stripped from the bones and the guts separated out. The claws were easy to remove, while the teeth required the bashing of a heavy rock to loosen. Maccus took the big fangs for himself and shared the claws between the hunters. Tara lent her strength to cracking the bones for the marrow, splitting them lengthways with an axe-stone after the flesh had been scraped from them. There was an argument, good-natured enough, about the preparation of the meat. Tara gathered that they would normally find oak wood and smoke the meat, drying it to keep it longer, but the Eldest was already unhappy that they had delayed their journey for so long. She thought that there was some sort of taboo at work, that frowned upon spending too long on the road. Maccus seemed to be arguing that wasting meat also went against their traditions, making emphatic gestures that she didn't understand.

Tara remembered her visions. Had the forest spirits merely come to warn her about the lion, or did they have a bigger danger in mind? She decided to try once more to persuade the tribe to go to Dentaltos.

She waited until the bloodiest work was done, and most of the tribe had settled to the time-consuming work of scraping the hide. The sun was dropping over the hills, the light shining up the length of the cave to cast strange shapes on the inner wall.

"You go north?" she asked Edan, pointing.

The youngest hunter looked up from his work, driving holes in a piece of deerskin with a bone point. He looked surprised that she had spoken something he could understand, but he answered with a smile. "Yes," he nodded, "North. To the Summer Hunting Grounds." She cocked her head. "Winter, we go to the forest, to the edge of the forest. Then in Spring we go to the sea."

She felt a sudden hope and asked "The sea? Do you know Dentaltos?" She made the gestures she had seen Ama make, then remembered that his kind did not speak with their hands as The People did and tried again. "The great rock." She pulled images from her vision and tried to explain. "By the sea, a high place." She gestured height, and with her left hand the ocean. "And then a rock like a finger." She held up a finger. Edan shook his head.

"It is important!" Her two hands came together, clenching. "The sea rises, the land drowns, the secret is there." She was sure that Edan understood only half of what she said, but a look of fear came over his face, and in his eyes.

"No." This time it was the Eldest that spoke. "We go home. It is Tradition."

Edan brightened. "You will love it there."

7. Edan

Trolls, Lero, Daesani. It seemed to Edan that everything in old Ulat's Winter stories was coming true at once. More than once he caught himself glancing towards the distant hills in case one of the Giants of the West, Gok or Mag or Bal, should rise up from their death sleep and come crashing down towards them.

In the tribe's winter home, alongside the sculpted figures of First Man and First Woman, there was an ancient root, dark and twisted, carved in the shape of Bal. As a little child Edan had been terrified of the figure, with its bone-chip teeth and glaring shell-white eye. He always hid his face in his Mother's hair when they told the tale of Bal. How he had fought with his brothers Gok and Mag, slaying them and cutting up their bodies to form the mountains of the West and East — the boundaries of the Summer Lands. One night of tragedy had replaced those childhood fears with others, far more real, and he had forgotten his terror of Bal. But now he wondered, if the Eshu and the Lero were real, then why not Bal too? And if Bal, then why not the Fomor demons that the Daesani claimed were driving up the sea?

His rescue of Tara had not gone down well with the tribe and being chased by the Daesani as a consequence even less so. Only when she had rushed in to save Cinnia from the lion had the others begun to relent and accept her presence; but that was not the same as forgiving Edan.

It wasn't the first time Edan had done something impulsive, and he knew it. It was the tribe's rule that Tradition bound everyone equally. When Tradition was broken, Tradition would also dictate what must be done to fix the breach, naming the ritual that must be performed or the Spirit who must be placated. Edan was unfortunately rather familiar with the process. The Elder or Grandmother would search the Winter tales for something that matched whatever he had done and spell out what he was required to do as a result. The punishments were usually laborious and involved a lot of apologising to one thing or another.

Tradition had nothing to say about Edan's current crime. The others could not even agree on what offence was to be punished. Was it striking another man? Possibly killing another man? Was it trespassing at the edge of The Great Wood, or perhaps failing to reach the Summer Hunting grounds by the dark of the moon? Maybe adding a Troll woman to the tribe was what offended the spirits the most? What they did agree on, when they had finally evaded the Daesani, was that the offence was major. Three days of fear and struggle in the tangled forest and the rain; no food, no safety, and no rest.

The question of what to do was a constant refrain all the time they were fleeing, and it became a full-blown argument when they finally reached the shelter of the mountain cave. Everyone knew that the Spirits must be placated, but the wrong ritual would do no good. The Elder cared nothing for the dead Daesani. In his view, the delay of the annual journey was the greatest offence. It was a matter of pride for him that he reached the coast by the dark of the moon every single year, despite the changing landscape. It was the moon upon which they must entreat, he said, or else the spirits of The Great Wood, into whose edge they had almost strayed.

Grandmother had a different view. Since the passing of her own Mother she had carried the charm of the Eagle Hunter, a raptor's talon, yellow and cracked with age, with the feathered face and wings of the hunter carved into its surface. In the darkness of the cave she took the charm from her neck and told the Eagle Hunter's tale.

"There were in those days two brothers, Windos and Tamesis. Windos had golden hair and pale skin, while Tamesis was dark; but in all other things they were much alike. Each was a master of the bow and arrow. They knew well how to strike a broad arrow for the deer, or a thin one for the rabbit. Their greatest skill was in making the forked arrows, with which they hunted the birds of the air and water.

The duck they hunted and the goose, the blackbird and the sparrow, but the greatest prize was the Eagle that lived in the high rocks above the sea. Now, Windos looked upon the Eagle and saw that it was as golden as him, and he desired to catch it for its feathers and make a cloak of them. When Tamesis heard this, he grew jealous, because Windos was thought beautiful and he was not. He tried to talk his brother out of his hunt, but the two fell to arguing and would no longer speak.

Now each brother rose before the dawn, climbing the high rocks to hunt the Eagle. Windos hunted it for its feathers, but Tamesis hunted only to prevent his brother from catching his prize.

All the long days they hunted, and the nights, till at last Tamesis saw the Eagle on the wind above him and brought it down with his arrows. The great bird fell dead at his feet with blood on its golden feathers. Then the spirit of the Eagle spoke to him in anger, because he had not killed it for its feathers or for its meat, but only to spite his brother. 'Who now will soar the winds and keep the high rocks? Who now will your brother hunt?' it asked him. When he heard this Tamesis knew that he had done wrong, for he had killed without need, and he was filled with sorrow. He took the Eagle's wings, and with them its shape. Now it is Tamesis who soars above the high rock, while his brother hunts him."

In this way Grandmother persuaded the others that Edan's highest offence had been to the spirit of the man he had struck without need. Edan held his own counsel on that. As far as he could see there had been plenty of need, even if he had not meant to strike the blow. Tara owed her freedom and perhaps his life to that.

The tribe had no totem to represent the Daesani, so instead they asked their own spirits to carry their apology. Edan was washed with rainwater and marked so that the spirits would see him. One by one each of the tribe took the charm representing their chosen guardian from their necks and placed them in the circle: the Eagle Hunter for Grandmother, the Guide for the Elder and so on, until at last there were eight of them. Brina gave him a strange look and chose the Crying Man, which was not a happy sign, but Morna came last, choosing the delicate charm of the Swan Woman, which Edan hoped meant that she — at least — had forgiven him.

After the ritual came the hunt, and after the hunt another five days in the cave while Second Mother recovered from her wounds. The killing of the lero persuaded the Elder that the Moon was no longer offended by the time they were taking, and so they took the time to hunt, though always with a wary eye out for other beasts. In the following days they caught little deer and squirrel amongst the trees — there was no further sign of the Weru-dan — and gathered sorrel and fern shoots into baskets that First Mother wove from strips of bark. When she was strong enough, Second Mother sewed new clothes from lion pelt to replace those that Tara had lost in the fight. What meat remained after their feasting they hung on poles in the fire smoke to cure. For the first time since the winter, they had enough to eat.

The rest gave Edan five days to make amends with the tribe, and to learn more of the strange creature that he had saved. Now that the others had accepted her, it was his job to show her their ways. Language, however, remained the biggest barrier. The brief burst of words on the evening of the hunt seemed to have exhausted her fluency, and so he set himself the task of teaching her the tribe's language, and of learning hers.

"Rock", Edan would say, pointing, or "Knife. Tree. Sky." then Tara would respond in her own way, a clenched fist for the rock perhaps, a cutting motion and a half-hummed "Ska" for knife. Or perhaps not. The same sound seemed to serve for sky as well, or for all Edan knew, the clouds or the sun. Sometimes Tara would repeat his own words, but it seemed that Edan was a terrible teacher, or Tara a terrible student.

Thankfully, Morna soon overcame her shyness and joined them in their daily sessions. Whatever gift with language Edan or Tara lacked came easily to her. At first haltingly, but then day by day ever faster, the words came. Morna was the first to realise that many of their words were the same, but that Tara's language made do with fewer, using gesture to distinguish between one word and another.

"See," Morna told him, excited at her discovery, "She says Skia for knife, like we do, but it's the same word for the horizon, and for cutting, I think, but the gestures are different." Morna mimed a slicing motion with the edge of her hand, and then another gesture, one hand flat, the other cupped above.

Edan was tempted to hand the whole of the language lessons over to Morna, but Tara had other ideas. Even after the rest of the tribe began to accept her, she still followed Edan wherever he went, night and day, always watching. When his nightmares woke him, she would be there in the darkness, until he began to wonder if she ever slept herself. Disturbed, but also touched by her attention, Edan put extra effort into bridging the gap of language, speaking his dreams aloud in the darkness in the hope that she might understand.

He realised that Tara understood more of his words than he had first thought, especially if he spoke slowly, but that she had great trouble speaking them, as if her tongue could not quite make their shapes — every new word mastered was a struggle.

The tribe left the cave on the sixth day when the moon was a sliver in the pale morning sky. The next day was spent in the forest, as was much of the one after it. At first, they went cautiously — Edan, Maccus, and Uch moving ahead of the rest, eyes wary — but if the Daesani still hunted for them they were far away and they saw no sign of them. By the second day, they relaxed for the first time since the meeting with Phelan and his men, moving in a loose group as they hunted for wood sours and bear's garlic amongst the trees. Following the Elder's directions, they came down out of the hills, emerging from the forest at the head of a rolling valley of windswept grass. The land fell away in front of them, scattered with white and yellow flowers, down to where wetlands and river channels sparkled in the sunlight, and maybe just a glimpse of the sea far away to the north.

None of them had seen this land before, but the Elder was in his element. Setting his old eyes on a coastline the rest of them could not even see, he set off with the wind in his face, guiding them north and east towards the hunting grounds.

Edan and Morna kept to Tara's side as they walked, naming one thing after another while Tara listened. "This one is Cuckooflower," he told her, pointing at the purple flowers, "because it flowers at the same time as the cuckoo comes. You know ... the cuckoo?" Edan tried to make a cuckoo's call, miming flapping wings with his arms until Morna ran about them laughing, flapping her arms and shouting "Cuckoo!" at the top of her voice. Edan saw First Mother smile at the sound, before deftly plucking the flower stems into her basket.

"You are happy," Tara said. "Tribe all happy. Because you go home?"

Morna grabbed Edan's hand, giggling, trying to get him to join her game, but he held his ground. "Home? Yes, one of our homes anyway, our home for when the snow is gone."

Morna shoved him, making him stumble and her laugh, but he saw sadness on Tara's face. "Why are you sad?" He touched a fingertip to his eye and down his cheek to show crying.

"My home is far away." Tara pointed back across the hills towards the south. "This place, I do not know. Do not know if I see The People again. I am afraid."

"Afraid? There's no need for that! This is a good place, a good land. You will love it here. You can stay, stay with us here, don't worry." Edan saw Maccus glance in his direction. He couldn't tell if his words were what Tara needed to hear, but he ploughed on anyway.

"We live right by the coast. There are beaches full of whelks, you can gather them in handfuls, clams too, if you dig for them. There are three rivers that come down through the marshes. We call them Maga, Menow, and Legu: Big, Little and Littlest, after the three sisters in the story. We set traps in the water there, for the fish." He tried to indicate the shape of the traps with his hands. "They swim right in, then they get trapped in these little pools and we can catch them easily. And there is a wood there, by the sea, full of deer, and then in the autumn we can gather so many nuts that they keep us going all year!"

The rest of the tribe were now ahead of them down the slope of the meadow, even Morna had fallen silent a few steps away. Tara looked at him. "But the sea, Edan. I fear the sea."

A stomach clenching flash of raging water leapt into Edan's mind, filled with black claws and scaled bodies. No! He refused to think about it.

"No need for that Tara, no need." Edan spoke with forced lightness. "Of course, the sea rises. Sometimes you can even see it move. You see a rock in the morning on the shore, by evening it's in the water. Sometimes a whole patch of bushes might have vanished over the winter, but the Hunting Grounds are large."

"It will be fine, you'll see."

* * *

At the end of the day, the tribe set its camp in the shelter of a willow tree where the valley met the marshes. Reeds and rushes nodded in a fitful breeze a little way beyond. They had carried bundles of hide all the way from the Winter Lands, ready to build shelters for themselves, but the night was mild and they did not intend to stay, so they simply heaped up rocks and grass and broom to make a fire. The others were already talking of the hunting grounds — Edan could feel their excitement. Brina longed for the taste of whelks fresh from the rocks, Uch began the work of making a harpoon point from antler, talking all the while about catching a seal, while Maccus and First Mother discussed the familiar tasks that would need to be done when they arrived at their first camp near the deer woods.

Edan found himself oddly uncomfortable at the happy talk. Tara's fear played on his mind, mixing with his own doubts about Tradition, and with the memories he was trying to avoid. The cheerful voices grated. He had the nagging feeling that something bad was going to happen.

Edan looked for a distraction. He had broken some lumps of hardened sap from the trunk of a wounded pine tree as he passed, and now he set about turning them into glue. A piece of the lion's shoulder bone made for a shallow dish, and he placed it and the lumps near the fire to let the resin melt. While they did so he took a lump of soft charcoal from his bag and ground it on a nearby rock until it was fine and black. When he mixed it with the soft sap, it formed a translucent pitch that he twirled on the end of a stick. Unbidden, he felt the touch of his father's hands, guiding his own. It had been his habit to teach Edan in this way — taking his little hands in his own weathered ones to guide him — showing how to catch soft glue on a twig, or thread a bone needle, or put weight on a scraper. His touch was strong but gentle. Edan loved to sit near to him in the shelter of a summer hut, or amidst the bustle of a hunting camp, trying to copy his sure movements.

An acrid smell filled the air. With a start Edan realised that he had burnt his glue. Hastily he snatched the bone dish away from the fire, tipping the smoking pitch onto the damp grass. If his father had only been there. For a moment Edan thought that he heard his voice, gently chiding him for his inattention. The sensation was so real that he started half-way to his feet, almost crying out his name — but there was no one there.

He sank back to the ground, the greeting unspoken. Brina looked up at him questioningly, but he turned away, pulling the furs up around his neck and staring out at the blue-grey of the marsh.

The sun had set, but the sky still glowed with a faint wash of light, picking out the feathery tops of the reeds and hiding the rest of the marsh in shadow. An eerie cry echoed out of the darkness, some waterbird mourning the setting of the sun. The constant daytime wind had dropped to a faint breeze, sighing through reed stems and bringing a faint scent of salt and shallow waters. A sudden movement in the gloom caught Edan's eye — just a trick of the wind; but then he was sure he saw the reed-fronds dip as something passed. He stared into the growing darkness, straining his eyes to see what it was, a fox perhaps, or a Daesani hunter! The eerie cry came again, and with it an odd splashing, surreptitious and furtive, like many feet shuffling through the water. The sound came closer and closer, scraping and snapping through the reeds, and the shadows seemed to advance with it, spreading out across the grass towards him.

No. Not shadow, but inky water, black and thick as the pine tar, rising, ever rising. Edan gripped his fishing spear in fear, not even aware of having picked it up, as the water crept about him, lapping at his feet and extinguishing the fire. He tried to scramble away, but the water was like glue. It flowed inexorably up his legs, forming a shimmering coating that dragged him down to the ground and into it. Then he saw the hands: murk black, bear clawed, and fish scaled. They emerged from the water, rising up impossibly long, arms as thin as those of a skeleton, reaching for him ...

Edan jerked awake. The night was dark and cold; the furs had slipped from his shoulders. Behind him the fire had cooled to embers. It had only been a dream; only another dream. He had dozed off, staring at the marsh and dreamt it all.

"Edan?" The voice caught him off-guard, and it took a moment for him to realise that Tara was close by. "Are you ill?"

"I had a dream. A bad dream."

"A dream? Or a vision?"

He hesitated, on the verge of lying down. "What do you mean?"

Tara shifted, her clothing creaking softly in the darkness. "You have ... stain, of death, of spirit on you." She gestured. "I think you have vision. You have seen something."

"A vision? No. I've seen nothing." Edan couldn't bring himself to speak of what he'd seen, so he changed the subject quickly. "You know about visions?"

Tara crouched beside him. "In my people I am ... I do not know your word; I see things. The Spirits show me things. When I am little, I go to Stone Forest, to learn from others who see. I know what is vision and what is simply dream. This is why I am here, in this place, because I see."

"What? What did you see?"

"I see this." She gestured with her arm, indicating the sweep of darkened landscape. "I see all of this land drowning. I see the end of us. I see the creatures who do this, in the sea." Edan felt an irrational hope that she would not find the words to say what she was saying, but she kept on. "There is a place. By the sea, north and east I think, a great rock rising from the water. We must go there. It is why I left The People. It is why the wolf-men capture me. If we go there, we can stop them. Maybe."

"Them?" But Edan knew the answer to his own question. "The Fomor"

Tara nodded, a shadow in the darkness. "Phelan wolf-man's word. Yes. Edan we must not go to your hunting grounds. We must go there."

"No!"

Edan and Tara jumped, surprised by the interruption. A figure stood over them, faintly outlined by the fire embers' glow — the Elder, quivering with anger.

"Enough of this! Eshu! Boy!" The Elder's voice was as taut as his body. "Have you not done enough? Have we not suffered enough? The sea rises, the land still provides. We have defied Tradition long enough. We will go to the hunting grounds as we always have. That is the end of the discussion."

* * *

On the second day beyond the forest the tribe crossed the reed marshes, and on the third they finally re-joined the course they had been following before the Daesani came. Their ancestors had worn the route into the sandy soil with generations of passing feet, marking the final leg of the route to the coast. By noon they were on the edge of the Hunting

Grounds. The deer woods were a day north and two east, the Menow river was ahead down the trail — the first camp site, the place where the tribe always settled when they arrived after winter — was two days ahead, where the land met the sea.

Only, something was wrong. On either side of the trackway there should have been fields of spring flowers, nodding in the sun. Instead the land was lank, strewn with sand as if it had been plunged beneath the ocean and had only just gasped its way back to the surface. Strands of dry seaweed, thin as sinew and brittle as dead leaves, clung blackly to the grass as far as they could see. Pale white shells crunched beneath their feet. The Elder and Grandmother stopped and stared, wordless, while Lavena picked the broken shells from the ground and held them silently in the palm of her hand.

They continued north, under dark clouds and lowering skies. Storm clouds piled up over the distant sea, rising up in churning stacks before spreading out on the back of a rising wind. Walking in silence, clothing pulled tight against the wind, they passed through land where the year before they had gathered broom and bilberries, and dry grass to weave their shelters. Now, brown standing water pooled in every dip and depression, its edges crusted with faint grey bands of salt and sand.

Later, rain began to fall, but they pushed on, trying to reach the banks of the Menow. They had to see. To the left of them there was a hill crowned with pines, its slopes shaped a little like a hand axe on its side, falling away sharply to the north and tailing gently to the south. Edan was sure he recognised it. The river would be in view as soon as they rounded it, surrounded by water meadows and open grass. He wanted to see it; needed to know what had happened, and yet he dreaded what he would find. Without meaning to, he quickened his step, pulling ahead of the others as he crossed the last few dozen yards beneath the slope of the hill.

Water splashed beneath Edan's feet and he jerked back, eyes wide. There were no water meadows before him, no drooping willows and shallow rushing river. Instead, a swollen mass of brown water churned its way through the curtains of rain. Freshly scoured slopes of mud had swallowed the trackway, puddled with water and strewn with detritus. Edan searched in vain for the familiar: the stakes and hurdles of the fish runs, the outcrop where he had often sat to watch the water, the sharp bend in the river course that left a little island that you could almost jump to without getting your feet wet. He could see none of it.

The rest of the tribe joined him one by one, clutching their packs and bundles close as they tried to make sense of it. After a little while, Maccus set off down the slope, slogging his way through the mud to the edge of the water. Edan saw him crouch for a moment and dip a hand into the churning river.

"Salt. The water is salt," Maccus said when he returned. "These plants will not grow again."

The Elder picked up his bundle and set off north without a word. The afternoon was shading into evening, and the air was full of rain. In normal times they would have set camp by the river and have an easy walk to the shore the next day, but these were no longer normal times. When Grandmother set off after the Elder the rest followed.

It should have taken them a day and a half more to reach the coast and the First Camp, but they did not have nearly so far to go before they truly understood the fate of their hunting grounds. By evening they reached the edge of a dark and restless sea. All the coast they knew had vanished beneath it, and the land had been cropped away in chunks, scalloped like the edge of a leaf in one place, sunk beneath the water in another. The trackway ended precariously at a slope of wave-washed gravel. A single tree clung to the lip of the cliff; half of its roots exposed to the empty air. Edan could see other trees, uprooted entirely, appear and vanish under each rushing wave.

The rain stopped, and a ghostly light plunged in rays through the clouds and water, picking out details here and there. Edan saw stands of trees stranded in the midst of waves. He saw the skeletons of gorse bushes tangled in seaweed as red as drying blood. Strangest of all he saw fields of marigolds and grass beneath the water, green and perfect, as if the sea could roll back where it belonged at any moment and restore them untouched. For a moment Edan thought he had lost his mind, but the others saw it too.

They wandered aimlessly through the dusk, coming to rest almost at random amongst an outcrop of jumbled rocks perched at the top of a slope that ran unbroken straight beneath the water. It was no great campsite, without wood, or water, or stone suitable for working, but then no one was setting camp. Lavena and Maccus, Cinnia and Uch, Grandmother and the Elder; each pair crouched apart amongst the stones. Unbidden, Brina and Morna sought comfort at their mother's side, leaving Edan and Tara on the edge.

Edan spoke softly, trying to keep his words for Tara alone, but the sea wind snatched them up and scattered them amongst the tribe just as the sea had scattered the land. "Is this what you meant? Is this the drowning of our land?"

Tara's eyes were sad. "No Edan. This is only the start. When it is done there will be nothing. No Summer Lands, no Winter Lands. No tribe, no People. If we do not find a way, there will be only sea."

In the end, it was First Mother, pulling her blanket of goatskin around her shoulders, who came to them. The wind whipped at her loose hair and snatched at her blanket, but she stood firm, her eyes fixed on Tara.

"Tell me everything. Tell me what you know, and what we must do."

8. Tara

When Tara was still a child she had lived with her parents amongst caves and rocky uplands that no other creature wanted.

Her family was a small group. Her older brother had found a rock of brilliant green shot through with veins of crystal white the year before and had gone in search of a mate to give it to — so now she was her mother's only child. Her mother depended on her to help with the gathering of food. She learnt to tell between edible plants and poisonous ones, to separate grains from grass and to sew the hides that the males scraped clean on the rocks outside the cave. She also learnt the basic rules of families and people, when to speak and when to stay quiet, how to comfort the sad or cheer the glum.

When she had her first vision it was beyond her comprehension. For three days and nights she lay as if in a fever. The inside of the family cave was illuminated by three balls of fire that would not go away, one bright and sharp, one red as blood, and one black yet brilliant. They were like indoor suns and moons that neither rose nor set. When Tara finally recovered, she did not understand what had happened, but her mother did. Even though she was depriving herself of her only child and helper, Tara's mother took her far away to the Stone Forest, to give her over to the Seers.

At the Stone Forest, Tara forgot everything she knew of plants and grains and sewing hides, and learnt instead of history, and omens, and the names of spirits. Old Ama became her family, and her lessons taught nothing of how to speak, or comfort, or cheer. Yet now these human people wanted her to tell them what to do.

Explaining her vision to Lavena had proven to be the easy part of the task. Carefully, with the help of Edan and Morna, she described what she had seen at the need fire, and how The People had interpreted it. If they could only reach Dentaltos, she said, they would learn the true nature of the Fomor and perhaps find a way to stop them. It was the speech she had longed, and tried, to give since the moment they had escaped the Daesani.

What she had not anticipated was the effect her words would have. No sooner had she finished than the whole tribe fell to argument and dismay. Lavena clutched her children to her, terrified by the thought that this disaster could get worse. Maccus sprang to his feet and paced up and down in the evening light, talking faster than she could follow, and though Edan spoke up in her defence, he did so timidly. Was he turning on her, or struggling with his own fears? Tara wasn't sure that she knew how to tell.

"We should turn around now! There is nothing here for us anymore. Staying will only kill us faster!" Uch raised his voice and waved his arms as he spoke, appealing directly to Maccus. "First Hunter — if we go south, we can find food. Then we could go to the Daesani. They have a way out of this."

The Elder was crouched, silent and hunched, just where he had collapsed to the ground, and so it was the old Grandmother who argued with Uch.

"Crazy man!" She spat on the ground noisily. "We live and die by Tradition! The Great Wood is taboo! We cannot go there."

Cinnia leapt to her mate's defence. "Second Hunter is right! We were in the wood already Mother, on the edge of it anyway, and there was food there. More than here." She didn't mention the lero that had nearly killed her.

"Silly girl. We can't go to the wolf-men. We killed one of them." The old woman chided her daughter more gently than she had chastised Uch. "Go to them and they will kill us faster. We can find a new place, build again, we did it before."

"This isn't just some flood!" Cinnia had her face almost in her mother's, her lank hair wild and tangled. "Look around you. Everything is gone, the whole Hunting Grounds."

The old woman merely shrugged her bony shoulders, refusing to be persuaded. "Pointless," Cinnia said to no one in particular, "She won't listen to reason!"

Tara racked her mind, trying to think of a way to stop the fighting. Ironically it was Uch who came to her rescue, pushing himself up from the rock to stand in front of her. "Eshu; tell her. There is way out of this vision of yours isn't there?"

She hesitated, remembering the sun that was not a sun and the malevolent figures beneath the sea. "I do not know. I have to go to the stone, to find out."

Her words had a surprising effect. The argument faltered and went silent. She looked at Edan, but he looked away. Eventually Maccus spoke. "Do you mean that there might be a way to undo this? Pull back the sea? Give us the land back again?" His voice was filled with sudden hope.

Tara wanted to answer with truth, to tell him that visions could be changed, but never thwarted; but she didn't have the words to make it right. Without meaning to she found herself saying, "I don't know. Maybe."

The tribe seized upon her words as if she had promised them a miracle. The thought that the land could be saved, no matter how implausible, was better than the truth. Tara had to ask herself if it could. She thought about the fields of grass and flowers drifting beneath the waves. They looked as if the sea might simply roll back and release them again. But the creatures she had seen in her vision would not give back what they had claimed. Even if they fought with them, spoke with them, traded with them, it would not re-root the trees or rebuild the land. She shivered at the thought of them, bodies of thorns and malice under a black sun. She should try again to tell the tribe that there was no hope. She should tell them to seek a new home. She should ... but she needed them.

"If there's a way ..." Lavena began.

Brina interrupted excitedly, "If there is a way we have to try, don't we?" She looked at Lavena and Maccus.

Maccus seemed to consider, then finally — "It doesn't matter. I don't know this place called Dentaltos. Do any of you?" One by one the others shook their heads or said no. "What about you?" he asked Tara.

"I have seen it," she said, "in the vision. I would know it." She gestured her regret. "But no, I do not know how to get there."

Maccus made to reply, but Grandmother interrupted him. "I do."

The others stared, but she waved them off. "I have heard of it, at least. But it was long ago, many summers and winters. Someone told me of it, not one of the tribe, a stranger." She scowled and tapped the side of her head. "I don't remember so well now. The tales, now those I know! But for other things you must ask him." She jutted her chin towards where the Elder huddled in the twilight gloom. "He always remembers."

Maccus looked at the Elder — who crouched, head down, arms wrapped about himself — and balked. "Eh. Perhaps you should speak with him, Grandmother."

"Not me. I want no part of this foolishness."

"You should ask." Cinnia said to Uch, but Uch stayed where he was. After a few moments she pulled herself from his arms and went to the Elder. Tara couldn't make out what she said to the old man, or what he replied, but she turned away with a snort of disgust and picked her way back to Uch's side, shaking her head to show that she had gotten nowhere.

It was fully dark now. The moon was waxing, half full, but Tara couldn't see it behind the clouds. Even the stars hid themselves, unwilling to look down on the ruined land. The night air was cold, and there was no warmth and little shelter in the rocks, but no one moved to light a fire. The wind was full of the smell of salt and sea, and Tara had to struggle not to imagine the Fomor creeping their way up the shingle towards them. Nervously she rose and walked beyond the edge of the stones, staring into the darkness. She thought that her eyes might be a little keener in the dark than those of the others, and her ears a little sharper, but she could detect nothing but the restless surge and rush of the waves. When she moved uphill, she could hear something creaking, but even though she strained her eyes, she could not tell what it was.

Almost accidentally she found herself at the boulder where the Elder still crouched. She could just pick out the grey of his hair in the dark.

"Elder?" She paused, waiting to see if he would respond, but there was only silence. Was his mind damaged, or was he ignoring her because she was an Eshu?

"Elder. I am not of your tribe, but I need your help. I must find something." Still only silence. Had she mis-spoken the words?

She sank down on the stone beside the Elder.

"I do not know how you are feeling. I cannot know. I am sorry." She trailed off and then there was only silence all the long night through.

* * *

Dawn broke with glacial slowness over the inundated coast. The sun dragged itself up out of grey clouds and greyer waters. Tara woke equally slowly, opening her eyes to a view of the slate-coloured sea. A flock of little birds blew up from the east and passed over them in a rush. When she sat up, she saw that the girls had gone down to the water's edge, searching fruitlessly for shellfish amongst the rocks. The smell of damp wood rose from a small fire, and she realised that she had been awake deep into the night and slept later than the rest. She glanced up at the Elder and was surprised to meet his gaze.

It seemed to Tara that he had grown even older in the night. His hair looked white in the pale morning light, and his cheeks were sunken above his beard; but his eyes were sharp. She was surprised to see that they were blue-grey, like an overcast sky.

"So, it's you, Eshu. Ech! I suppose it had to be someone. Come to tell me I've lost my nerve?"

"No! No, I had a question." She took a chance and asked it before he could close up again. "There is a place, Elder. If we go there, we can learn why this is happening and maybe if there is anything we can do about it. I know the name and look of this place, but I do not know *where* it is. My people call it the Tooth of the north, I am hoping that you know of it."

"Eh? Of course I know. It's my job to know, hill and brook, wood and river, every hand of it. A lot of good that does me now!"

"Then, you can tell us how to get there."

"I could ... but what would be the point? This is our land, and it is gone. I denied it, but I was a fool. The sea will keep coming. Maybe it will be slow, maybe it will quicken, but we are done. My tribe has dwindled, now it will die away. You think you can stop that?"

"I do not know."

"Then let me tell you. You cannot. You and the boy will not rebuild the tribe. I have seen your coy glances, but our kind and yours do not breed. And we will not join the wolf-men and the tree-killers in The Great Wood. We will keep to our ways and die with this land."

For a moment Tara was speechless. What did he mean about her and Edan? No, that was a question for another time. She wracked her mind for further arguments. "But what about the Fomor?"

"There are no Fomor. They are only the imagination of the Daesani, something from dreams."

"Then what is causing this?"

"It is because we have broken Tradition. Tradition is not merely custom; it is the law by which we live. When you break it, you must fix the break and return to the old ways, the strong ways, our ancestor's ways." He fumbled at his neck and produced what to Tara's eyes seemed a piece of antler that had been carved in the rough shape of a human and bound about with grass-stem twine, holding it up so that she could see it.

"You have no charms, but maybe your Eshu-kind have Tradition too, eh? I don't know. Maybe you don't, and you are just paying the price for the sins of the rest of us, bad luck you! But I believe that Tradition has been broken. Maybe not by us, by my tribe, but by others; the Daesani, maybe people we have never met. We all share one land, so we all share one punishment. I don't even know what law has been broken, so I can't fix it. That is why the land sinks beneath us, the Spirits are taking it away from us."

"Then … you will not tell me what I need to know?"

The Elder sighed and looked away at last. "Pfft, what would be the point in that? You will go anyway, I think. The boy will go with you, the girls too maybe. Perhaps, even, you are right, and I am wrong, I don't know. So yes, I'll tell you."

* * *

The Elder's route led them east along the coastline, and then inland to where they might cross the river that the tribe called the Legu, the least of the three rivers. After that it turned north, making for a headland that jutted out somewhere far into the sea. The Elder had scratched an image of the land into the dirt with a stick, a trick that both fascinated and confused Tara. Maccus had studied the image and decreed that they must pass through the Deer Woods and then into the hills beyond.

They came to the edge of the woods on the second day after leaving the rocks — a pale wall of trees half lost in shimmering water. It seemed to Tara that most of the land they passed through was now as foreign to the tribe as it was to her, but now and again they would see something that was familiar to them: a cliff, a tree, a stream or the shape of a hill. Places where in previous years they had lived and hunted.

"Look," Morna pointed for Tara. "The woods are there, across that valley. Usually we go that way," she pointed west, "but we come here to hunt deer, and you can find lots of plants to eat in the valley here." Tara stared at the valley before them, shimmering under a blanket of shallow water. "Or at least you could," Morna finished sadly.

Tara glanced over at Edan, trying to guess what he was feeling, but he was the same as he had been since reaching the coast, eyes fixed on the ground at his feet, hardly paying attention to anything around him. She knew that she should try to speak to him, to help somehow if she could. But ... what had the Elder meant about glances? Of course, she stayed close to him. He had saved her life, had been her one friend when she had joined the tribe. That didn't mean that she wanted him for a mate. And he couldn't want her, could he?

If only she knew what he was thinking. Even the Elder seemed to have recovered from his shock enough to function, but Edan was a mystery. What did he fear? Why did he cry out at night and keep as far from the sea as their path would allow? Had the shock simply affected him more or was there something else? She felt frustrated. She had the feeling that he had already given her the answers, back in the cave, when he talked to her in the night, but she hadn't understood his words then, and couldn't remember them now.

"We will go around to the south," Maccus was saying. "There are trails that Second Hunter and I know well that lead east through the woods. But the river must be flooded too. We will need to reach higher ground before we cross it." He pointed towards a distant hillside where thicker woodland could just be seen amongst the patchy sun and cloud-shadow.

As they started on their way again, Tara dropped back to walk closer to Edan, hoping to get his attention, but he seemed lost in his own thoughts. Even though she was watching him, and he was looking at his feet, he was the one who tripped over something in the grass that the others had bypassed without noticing.

"What's that?" Tara saw that the stone Edan had dislodged was black on its inner face.

Edan looked at the stone without interest, and then said, "Stones ... burnt stones." Tara pushed back the grass and revealed a ring of stones — the remains of a fire. Someone had made an attempt to hide it, brushing away the charcoal and flattening the grass over it, but it had been casually done.

"There is still a little warmth, deep down," she said, looking up to see that Maccus had crouched down beside her. The hunter put his own hand in the fireplace, pulling up a handful of ashes and letting it fall through his fingers. "Yes. Not enough for it to have been lit today, nor in the night. Yesterday, perhaps."

"There is someone else here?"

Maccus considered. "We have never seen strangers in this place before, except once four summers past, but they were on the far side of the Legu and did not cross it. But nothing is normal now. We cannot be the only ones driven from our homes. It is not a surprise that someone else has come this way, is it?"

Tara was not so sure. She glanced up at the open moorland, sun-dappled under patchy cloud, thinking how easily a watcher could be hidden up there. She hurried back to join the others.

Another hour took them into the Deer Wood. The silver birches were gaunt and silent. Some of the trees had struggled out a few leaves, but most were as dead as winter. The bare branches creaked and rubbed eerily in the wind.

The woodlands were awash up to their ankles. The tribe moved with bare feet, removing their shoes so that the rawhide bindings would not soften in the water. Tara felt the fine hairs on her arms and neck prickle. There was something about the woods that set her on edge, and she looked everywhere for a reason, but there were no spirits in this forest to offer her warnings, only her own heightened nerves.

Lines of sight opened briefly as the spindly trees aligned then vanished again, hemming them in. The sun was stifling, and the dead trees provided little shade. Shoals of sand flies swarmed about their feet, drawn to the vegetation rotting in the water, but they had no interest in people. The hidden fire pit nagged at her thoughts. The night had been cold, any traveller alone might light a fire, but why go to the pain of hiding it? Maybe the fire lighter was as far from home as she was, and with just as many reasons to distrust the unknown. Or maybe he was the one out to cause harm.

Despite Maccus' earlier confidence, the tribe struggled to find a path through the woods that led away from the water. The sea had made the woods into a maze. Once, trying to find a better route, Maccus accidentally led them into deeper water. For the first time since they reached the Hunting Grounds Tara saw Edan react with something other than blind plodding progress, but it was only to balk at the water, stopping dead in the midst of the woods as if he has lost the power to move. She went to his side, but he shook off her attention; Brina had to take his arm and lead him away.

Frustrated, she asked Morna why Edan was afraid. "He doesn't like the water. Not deep water," she said.

"Doesn't like the water? Why?" For a moment she thought that Morna was about to tell her something important, but the girl just shook her head and said, "He just doesn't."

Maccus chose a different route, and all that long day and into the next they dragged themselves through the still water and dead trees, making what camp they could where a patch of dry ground emerged amongst the trees. Though Tara tried to be constantly alert, nothing happened to justify her fear. But the fear remained.

Finally, after yet another day, they found a route that led away from the water, up a low line of bluffs swathed in a tangled mess of alder and rowan. Thickets of nettle and blackthorn clogged the gaps between the trees, and they struggled with brittle deadwood and clinging thorns as they pushed uphill.

At first the hunters took the lead, but Tara saw how the thorns plucked at their flesh, and how they strained with the knotted branches. How had The People lost so much of their land to such weaklings? Gently she pushed them aside and took their place, heaving the fallen branches aside. The barbs of the blackthorn stabbed at her, but her tough clothing turned most of them and her skin the rest. The work was exhausting, and the air still and hot, buzzing with little flies attracted to the sweat trickling down the back of her neck, but she had the strength for it.

By the time they reached the top of the ridge above the Deer Woods, Tara was covered in scratches as fine as hairs, but at last the woodland opened out into an overshadowed glade where tiny flowers littered the ground like stars. Narrow fern-edged trails wound away between black alders. Tara thought she heard an animal move in the brush, but the sound was gone as soon as it came.

She rested against a tree trunk to catch her breath as the others trailed into the clearing. Cinnia complained loudly that she needed to rest, as if she had been doing the work instead of Tara, while Uch grumbled something about going the wrong way.

Maccus pointed through the trees. "I think we came here years ago, and there was a better place to rest over that way, a hillside free of trees, dry ground to sit on?" He directed the question at Uch who grunted noncommittally. "Come on." He chose a little trail between the trees and started down it.

Tara hesitated, tilting her head. There it was again, that noise — a crashing or a cracking — like something charging through the undergrowth at speed. It was to the left of them, no, behind them, growing closer.

"What's that?" Cinnia had heard the noise now, and her voice rose in fear. "A boar? Another lero!"

Not a lero. A bear? Tara tried to picture a bear crashing towards them, but it sounded wrong. She strained her eyes as well as her ears. Where was it?

Then, suddenly, a flash of movement in the brush, a pale streak like a thrown spear. Before she could react, it burst from the undergrowth, jaws wide and ears back. A hunting dog! Barrel chested and brindle-furred it came straight at Uch, snatching away a mouthful of furs and leathers with its first bite. This was no wild animal; it was a Daesani hound!

"Run!" Maccus shouted. He plucked Morna from her feet and bolted down the trail. Cinnia went after him. The others broke apart, scattering chaotically before the dogs could surround them. The first hound went after Uch, but Tara could hear more coming.

She was halfway out of the glade herself before she saw that Edan had not moved. Shock? She didn't have time to think. She grabbed his arm and fled.

They ran helter-skelter through the woods. The dogs were baying behind them. Whip-snags of thorn and brush lashed them, and unseen branches tried to bring them down. Tara had no idea where she was going. She had to get them somewhere safe. She thrust one arm in front of her face to keep the branches off, dragging Edan with the other until she was sure that he was running on his own. There was already blood on her arm. Stupid, stupid, stupid! She cursed herself. Who else but the Daesani would be sneaking around hiding campfires? It was obvious, and yet she had gone on blindly, smashing her way through the woods so loudly that a stone could have heard her coming. How long had they been following them? Were they being driven into a trap?

Dense thickets appeared to one side of them and she veered away, smashing through a screen of fallen branches instead. Should they be hiding? Was stealth better than speed? No. They had to run! Run from the dogs and the cries of the huntsmen echoing through the trees.

She saw sunlight shining through the trees ahead and ran towards it, thinking that they might have reached the open hillside Maccus had mentioned, instead she scrambled to a stop at the top of a cliff that fell away to the flooded land below.

Tara grabbed a tree trunk, teetering on the edge. Too steep to go down safely, but where else? Before she could begin to think of an answer, one of the dogs burst out of the bushes behind them and leapt at Edan. He cried out in pain and fell back with the shaft of his spear wedged between them. The dog worried at the spear, trying to yank it out of Edan's hands, giving Tara the time to leap forward and kick it in the side. The dog thudded against a tree but sprang back to its feet in an instant, snarling, hackles raised. Tara grabbed a fallen branch for a weapon, hoping that if she fought side by side with Edan they might be able to hold it off. But Edan froze again, eyes wide, and she cursed. Not now!

Tara and the hound leapt together. The dog was faster, but she was closer. Before the beast could strike, she did the only thing she could think of. She grabbed Edan in her arms and threw them both off the edge.

9. Edan

The breath was knocked from Edan's body, and then he was flying through air and sunlight. Leaves and bushes broke his fall, but he was still tumbling and rolling, crashing through bushes as he skidded down a steep slope. He tried to hold on to Tara with one hand, his father's spear with the other, but both were jolted from his grasp and went flying away.

He felt water on his face and thrashed in panic. He had gone into the river; he was drowning! For a moment he flopped about, until he realised that there was solid ground beneath his back and under his hands. He had rolled into mud rather than water.

A strange redness swam into view in front of his eyes — a mat of crimson weed, slick and shiny, little fronds waving in an inch of water. He blinked, focussing on the tiny curls closest to him, and then closed his eyes to make them disappear. They were still there when he dared to look again.

Edan heaved himself onto one elbow. His whole body protested. He was cut and bruised all over. He felt like he had been in a dream, and then had woken up into another dream. The ground he lay on was awash with seawater and as wrinkled as a fingertip soaked in water. It was horrible; it was beautiful; it was confirmation, if any were needed, that the land belonged to the Fomor now. But ... where was Tara?

He forced himself to sit up properly and look around. "Tara!" he yelled, "Where are you? Are you all right? Are you hurt?" There. She lay a handful of yards away, unmoving. "Tara!"

Edan dragged himself to her side; his legs weren't up to standing yet. Somewhere far away he could hear a dog barking furiously, but it didn't seem to matter. "Tara?" Tentatively, he laid a hand on her side. Relief flooded through him — she was still breathing. He shook her gently. "Wake up."

She blinked, slowly opening her eyes, and then rolled onto her back to look up at him. "Did we get away? Are we safe?"

Edan looked around again, scanning the flatlands more carefully for hunting dogs or running people, but he could see nothing but the strange crimson saltmarsh, and beyond it the restless gleam of water. Was this some new thing, or a feature of the land by the Legu that he had never seen before? He couldn't tell. Behind them, the land rose up sharply to the woods above. The gash of crushed and broken plants where they had tumbled made it clear that he hadn't imagined the fall.

"I think so."

They helped each other to their feet, leaning together until the pain faded and strength returned to them. Somehow neither of them had broken a bone, or sprained a limb, or had a branch thrust through them. Edan offered thanks to the spirits for watching over them both.

Edan did not let Tara go until he was sure that she could stand unaided. Pieces of his belongings were scattered all about them, a stone flake here, a bone point there. Tara stopped and hauled his bedroll from the ground, shaking the water from the tightly packed furs while Edan went in search of his fishing spear. He found the haft undamaged, floating on shallow water a dozen feet away, but both of the antler points were missing. With increasing desperation, he cast about for them. The spear was the last physical link he had to his father, to the past — it was all washing away. At last he spied something pale against the red and plucked one of the points from the shallow water, of the other there was no sign.

"Edan, we have to move."

He looked up from the spear point in his hand. "What do you mean?"

"The Daesani. They won't stop. They will see us here." In the distance the dog was still barking. "We need to get some cover or get further away."

Edan wanted to protest at the futility of it all. The land was gone, the water was coming. He'd listened to everything Tara had told the others, but he knew that he was beyond saving. He belonged to the water. He had belonged to the water for years, ever since that night ... He'd tried not to think about it, but that hadn't changed a thing. He might as well walk into the water now, for all the difference it would make. Only, perhaps, if he offered himself as a sacrifice, the others might get away. He couldn't have long, not in a place as touched by the Fomor as this, but there might be a chance for the others, there might be a chance for Tara.

Edan looked at the slope they had fallen down, spreading to east and west — not that way. He turned around, looking for a way that didn't mean going closer to the water, but there wasn't one. "That way." he said reluctantly, pointing at the open water to the north. "We go to the edge of the sea and then follow it till we get to the Legu, then we will find the others."

They crossed the salt marsh as quickly as they dared. The sun shimmered amongst strange pillars of cloud, which hovered above the northern horizon like clay-red islands. The ground was deceptively soft beneath Edan's feet. The little mounds of red slime collapsed at the slightest pressure, dissolving into puffs of silt and crimson particles that sank quickly into the water. He leant heavily on the spear haft, using it as a walking stick. Soon it was caked in mud from being thrust into the ground.

A sudden noise made Edan jerk his gaze seaward. A huge mass of birds hurtled inland, skimming over the marsh in a jumble. He barely had time to throw his hands up in front of his face before they rushed over him in a confusion of battering wings and raucous cries. One collided with his arm, then the whole flock was past them, racing in a swirling panic towards the woods.

"What was that? What scared them?" Tara shook her head; she had no answer.

The sun was dipping towards the horizon by the time they reached the edge of the water. Edan had glanced back toward the woodlands and the hills many times, hoping to see others of the tribe, expecting to see the Daesani in full hunt; but he saw neither. Now he gazed across the water with equal confusion. No more than three or four hundred yards away more land was visible, steep and green-grey in the evening light. Had a new island risen from the sea? Was this some work of the Fomor? It took him a long time to understand that he was not looking at an island, and that he was not standing at the shores of the sea.

"I thought you said Legu was the smallest of the rivers." Tara said, looking at the water.

"It was." Edan gazed in fear at what the little river had become. Hesitantly, he dipped the spear-shaft into the water to test its depth, but it immediately sank in over half its length, and the rushing current nearly plucked it from his hand.

Edan leapt away with a cry, sloshing backwards through the water until he was back on what passed for dry land. For a moment he thought that the water was coming after him. Not yet! He had to get Tara away first. Only then could he let it take him. Only then.

With an effort, he made himself sound calm. "Not here. No, not here. Maybe further upstream?" He forced a smile. "Crossing here wouldn't be any use anyway. We need to find the others, and Maccus was going to cross further inland, wasn't he?"

Tara nodded, but her pale eyes were narrowed. She must suspect something. Not that he planned to drown, not that, but something else. Did she think that he meant to let the Daesani have him, in the hope that they would ignore her? He would, he realised, if it came to that, but he was sure that she would never let him.

Quickly Edan swung around and hurried south along the river shore, back towards the woods. "The sun will set soon. If we can't find the others before dark, we may never do."

"Edan!" Tara called out behind him, and he was sure that she would challenge him, but she did not. "Those birds. Something is wrong. I have felt it for days. I thought it must be the dog-men I sensed, but now I think it is something else."

"I ... I have no answer for that. Nothing here makes sense to me anymore. If the land is drowning, if the soil is turned to blood," he directed an angry stamp at the red-tinged ground beneath them, "then perhaps the birds have gone mad. I don't know." Edan spotted the heads of reeds poking their tops above the water a little way ahead, marking the edge of the red plain. They swayed this way and that amongst the stems of headless knotweed and leafless meadowsweet killed by the inundating water.

To their right, a hill had been cut away by the rushing waters, exposing brown earth and the tangled roots of the trees that perched on top. To their left, small islands of gravel and stranded trees dotted the water, perhaps the other half of the fallen hill. They were hard against the edge of the forest now, but forty feet below it, hidden by shrubs and saplings that ran right to the edge of the swollen river. Past the slumped hill the land rose sharply, and Edan was sure that the river must narrow back to its original course somewhere up ahead. That was where Maccus would lead the tribe ... if they had escaped the hunters. If the hunters weren't looking down on them right now.

Edan was sure that once they got into the cover of the slope, they would be safe. The sun was low to the horizon now, and the forest cast long shadows across the water. If they reached those shadows, between the water and the cliff, no one would find them.

A sudden shaking of the undergrowth ahead told Edan that someone else had had the same idea. He had just enough time to hope that it was one of the tribe before he saw that it wasn't. The man that emerged from the bushes was as old as Maccus, and broader at the shoulders, but something about him seemed hunched and evasive. His hair was long, lank-braided and streaked with chalk. Strings of wolf teeth rattled at his neck and wrists, and his forearms were wrapped in grey fur bound with strips of dark leather. He carried a stone-tipped spear which he immediately grasped in both hands, aiming it first at one of them and then the other.

"Stop! Both of you!" Edan was surprised to hear fear in the man's voice. "Don't come any closer."

"That's Rat-tongue" Tara whispered in his ear. "He's the one that looks after the dogs."

"I know you" Rat-tongue said. "You're the boy who killed Keir. Phelan's going to reward me well for finding you two."

Tara stepped up to Edan's side, spreading her hands wide, ready to grab at the man. "We kill you too if you don't drop that spear," she snarled, but Edan felt his legs waver at the Daesani's words. Killed? Surely, he hadn't killed him. No matter what Grandmother had said about spirits and purification he'd been sure, deep down, that the gap-toothed man had simply been stunned when he went into the water, that he was fine. He wasn't a murderer.

"Edan, what are you doing." Tara hissed at him, and he realised that he'd let the broken fishing spear fall to the ground at his feet. "We have to fight!"

"No fighting here." The Daesani said, and to Edan's surprise he began to edge away, carefully retreating across the rough ground until he was well out of their reach.

"I didn't mean to!" The words burst out of Edan. "I didn't mean to kill anyone!"

Rat-tongue seemed to regard him over the wavering point of his spear, his eyes narrowing into slits. "Didn't mean to, never brought anyone back from the dead." Then, "You're just a boy, aren't you? Just some beardless boy who got lucky. Keir must be having a fit, knowing he got killed by you. To think that Phelan's been worrying your tribe had a whole bunch of warriors we'd never seen." He snorted out a laugh. "Well, no more running now!" He put two fingers in his mouth and blew a shrill whistle.

A few moments later, the whistle was answered, first from one part of the shadowy slope and then another. Rat-tongue let out another cruel chuckle. "See boy, here they come." A crashing noise told Edan that the dogs were on their way, and then he saw figures break from the tree line above, arms windmilling as they ran down the slope. "Uchdryd! I got him for you, got them both!" Rat-tongue was shouting now, his spear levelled towards Edan's throat.

Edan saw instead the face of the man he had killed, his eyes wide with confusion as he sank beneath the water. Edan had cheated death that day, let someone else die, but the water always got what it wanted in the end, and here was his punishment, catching up with him at last.

The ground seemed to lurch beneath Edan's feet, and he began to topple. For a moment he thought that he was fainting, and almost welcomed the thought of closing his eyes on all that was coming — then he saw that the Daesani was swaying too, grabbing randomly at the bushes as he tried to keep his balance. Birds burst in panicked clouds from the woodland trees as clumps of rock and earth toppled from the exposed cliff, plunging into the water amidst spouts of spray. The ground really was moving!

A roar filled the air, like the challenge of an enormous beast, pouring from every direction. Edan clapped his hands to his ears to try and drown it out. Rat-tongue covered his own ears and fell to his knees, his mouth open in a yell that Edan couldn't hear.

He felt Tara grab him, holding him up while the earth heaved. Water surged past their feet, washing through the undergrowth and foaming against the hillside. Behind the surge the river seemed to empty for a moment, as all the water was flung against the shore, exposing a wet gravel bed before the water rushed back. Tara tried to sign something to him with one hand, but he couldn't understand it.

"Into the water! Our chance! Now!" She put her lips to his ear and yelled, pointing across the water to the nearest island. "Escape!"

"No!" Edan shouted into a sudden silence. The roar had ended as abruptly as it had started, but if anything the shaking had grown worse, threatening to throw them both to the ground. His determination to sacrifice himself vanished instantly at the threat of going into the river. Not the water, anything but that. Without meaning to, he gasped the words out loud.

Tara's eyes widened with emotion, then narrowed, hardened. "I'm sorry Edan."

"Sorry for wha—" Edan never finished the question. In one quick move Tara wrapped her arms around him and plucked him up. He barely had time to take a terrified breath before she waded into the water, carrying him over one shoulder. Terror overcame him. Without reason he struggled, panicked, kicked, scratched, screamed, all to no avail. He caught a brief glimpse of one of the Daesani running into the edge of the water and losing his footing, swept off his feet in an instant and tumbling away downstream. He'd failed, they were both going to drown. She couldn't fight the sea, no matter how strong she was. Even dying, he'd saved no one.

With a final wail, he screwed up his eyes, unable to face the cold embrace that he knew was coming.

10. Phelan

If the Daesani were anything, they were a people without traditions. They were creating themselves new, patching together the scraps of a score of tribes and families into something that was none of them. Nevertheless, it had already become custom that when one of them died, they would take the body back to the Great Wolf's camp at the edge of the forest and place them as high in the hills as they could. Too many of them had already lost brothers, sisters, children, parents to the sea. They were determined to give it no more.

When Phelan returned to the mere and discovered that Keir had been dragged dead from the water his first thought — after the anger had cooled — was that they must take him back, if not to the Great Wolf, at least to the camp at Tanrid where the rest of the Daesani gathered. But to take his body south would be to let the Troll and her rescuer go free, and even Newlyn, when he learnt that Keir had died in the mere, did not suggest that. He left it instead to Uchdryd, who had been of the same tribe as Keir before they joined the wolf, to decide what to do with his body.

At Uchdryd's instruction they cut saplings into poles and fashioned a platform from them, notching the green wood with their axes so that they rested one across the other atop the rock they had chosen. They washed the mud and muck from Keir's body, trimmed his beard and folded his hands together. Then they raised his body to the top of the tower of branches and placed it there. Uchdryd shot a greylag with his bow and put the severed wings beside the body, one by either shoulder.

"At home we would have placed him on the highest ground, to get away from the rats and foxes," Uchdryd said, when their work was done. "He belongs to the birds now. Let him fly away with them and forget this pain."

Afterwards they remembered Keir in Daesani fashion, telling tales of him across the fire. They roasted the carcass of the goose in the flames and passed it around, each man taking a bite and thanking Keir for it. Then the practical — dividing out his blades, his furs, his talismans and tools between them.

The next day they made another attempt to track the killer's tribe, searching beyond the mudflats and along the edge of the woods. To Phelan's frustration they found nothing certain. It was possible that the trail they were following wasn't even the right one, after a day of rain had washed through it. Alternatively, Phelan wondered if he had underestimated the Hunter, whatever his name had been. Shoot a few arrows to scare them off and buy the time to hide their trail? He kept his men searching, but as the day wore on it was obvious that they were finding nothing. It was frustrating. Every hour wasted here gave the tribe more of a lead. Duah took his anger out on the others, cursing their incompetence, but Phelan was better at keeping his anger hidden — when he wanted to.

Instead, he called off the search while the others were still eager to hunt and sought a new plan. They gathered at the edge of a bluff looking over the river, the dogs milling and yipping excitedly about their feet. Phelan gazed out over the grey marshlands and then asked for ideas.

"The dogs can't get a scent after the rain," Trehar said. "But deeper into the woods we might be able to get something."

"We could search the woods for days and find nothing," Duah mocked. "Better we pull some of that Troll bitch's stuff out of wherever Uchdryd stashed them and try and get a scent off that." Some of the others agreed, but Trehar said that scent would be too old now, and that was that.

"The old man said they were going to the coast," Newlyn suggested. "We could just go there and wait, if ... you are determined to catch them?" His eyes flicked up to look at Phelan as he said it.

"I am." Phelan was thinking about fate. "We need them, all of them. We need them because they hurt us, because they killed one of us, and we can't let that go. And we need our prisoner, but we need the rest too. Every stupid idiot who goes and gets themselves killed out here is another tally for the Fomor, another mark on their death count." In his mind he could see the idols his people had carved, the squat wooden bodies, the fangs and claws, their desperate idea of a Fomor, stained black with blood. It hadn't been the right blood.

"You want to bring them back?" Duah was incredulous.

"I'll kill them myself before I let the Fomor have them, but it doesn't have to be that way." He glanced at Newlyn. "Not for all of them." His other reasons were his own.

"So ..." Kaman idly scratched at his maimed hand, "I'm a good tracker if I say it myself, but there's a lot of coast up there."

Phelan looked down at the broad wash of water below them, following it north with his eyes. "Lots of coast, but we know the way they were headed before they ran." He gestured over the landscape with one hand. "River to the west of them, river to the east. And the Troll, Uchdryd, what did it say it wanted?"

"Cliffs? Cliffs by the sea? I think."

"Only cliffs up there are east of us," said Kaman, "East of the river too if I remember. Been a few years."

Phelan nodded. "And everything keeps changing. I understand. But we know where they are going, and we have no need to skulk in a wood like frightened prey." He let his voice rise. "We are Wolves, we hunt!" He saw the excitement rising in their faces and he smiled. They were the future, his new tribe. Let these lands drown so long as they survived. Let them.

They were five days on the river banks, skirting between the rippling reeds and the thicker brush. They kept an easy pace, loping northwards with their spears in their hands. They kept their camps small, taking water from peat stained pools, and hunting birds on the move. There seemed to be no sign of the elk and auroch, boars and red deer that they had hunted in Phelan's youth. The land was already dying. Phelan remembered a fight against the Boar tribe when they had been tracked by their camp remains and told the others to cover the fires when they moved on.

After five days, the river curved to the west, winding its way around a tree-crowned upland. When they scaled the ridge, they saw that all the land beyond was now under water. Newlyn, looking out along the coast, was silent and grim, but Kaman just joked that the Fomor had made their jobs easy. "A lot fewer places to look," he snorted.

Phelan didn't appreciate the joke. They were looking at land under the heel of the Fomor. They were pushing it down until it vanished under the waves like a drowning man, never to rise again. The very sight of their creeping ocean made him want to get under cover.

"Then find them."

They ranged far and wide over the following days, searching along the edge of the sea. Here and there they found a sign of habitation: the remains of a fish trap in the water, the stone footings of a fireplace, the skeleton poles of a hut awash with sand. Enough to tell that these lands were some tribe's home. Kaman was nearly as good a tracker as he thought he was, and all of Phelan's pack had experience on their side, but even so then they nearly missed the killer's tribe when they arrived. The land was vast and empty, a handful of men couldn't cover all of it.

In the end, they found them almost by chance. Newlyn had split off into the hills, searching the brush-choked valleys, while the others followed a wooded ridge that wound its way towards a river valley beyond, hugging the tree shadows to stay out of the sun. They planned to meet up later in the day by a distant outcrop of stone.

Cuall, ever keen, kept his eyes scanning the woods below as the rest forged ahead. "Phelan! There!" Phelan turned in time to see a flash of movement on the hillside below, the shape of figures vanishing into the trees. "I saw the Troll," Cuall hissed with excitement.

Phelan put his fingers to his lips and gave a short whistle, calling the others back. He gestured quickly, mindful that any loud noise could warn their prey. He split them into two groups, sending Trehar, Uchdryd, Cahal, and the dogs straight down the slope while he took the rest to the right, curving down through the trees to catch them in the flank: wolf wisdom.

Phelan and the others spread out through the trees, slipping through the dim green like fish through water. They kept low to the ground, in case one of the tribe happened to glance up and see them against the sky. Then they heard the distant clamour of the dogs and broke into a run. There was no need for silence then. Phelan plunged full tilt, leaping a fallen tree when it blocked his way, ducking beneath twisting branches.

After a few moments Phelan realised that he had lost sight of the others. He slowed, placing his feet more carefully. Somewhere to his left the dogs were barking. A sharp rustle came from a bush to his right and he whirled around, but it was only a squirrel scampering for a tree.

A shout echoed from along the slope and he switched direction. Figures were running full tilt between the trunks. He saw Duah on one side, Nyle on the other, chasing ragged figures in brown. Duah threw his spear, but it smacked against a tree and fell to the ground. A bow twanged, and an arrow hissed through the foliage. Phelan came up at Cuall's side just as he snatched at the back of a fleeing woman, but his feet caught on a fallen branch and he went tumbling into the undergrowth instead. The woman and two smaller figures went left, two more scattered right, and another skidded downslope.

The pack broke up again, driving the tribe towards the river. Phelan left Cuall to pick himself up and went after the lone figure, aware that Nyle and Kaman had gone right, vanishing through a screen of rowan branches. Phelan grinned wide at the sound of his pack in full chase.

Scattered sunlight shone through the trees ahead, giving Phelan a glimpse of open ground. His muscles ached from the pace he was keeping, sweat plastering his hair to his head, but he thrilled at the chase, doggedly following the lone hunter as he twisted and turned through the woodland. He snatched off his wolf-skin crown to wipe the sweat away with one arm. Better, but there were shadows ahead, and the hunter had vanished amongst them.

Had the pack caught the rest of them? He could hear the rush of water nearby, then a whoop or cry, but he couldn't tell who had made it or where it came from. One of the dogs barked again, and he was sure it was below him now, somewhere off the wooded bluff.

He edged forward again, tucking the wolf-crown at his waist. The knowledge that there was a man bow-armed made him cautious, and he crept along for a while, keeping low to the ground and parting the ferns ahead of him with the tip of his spear as he moved. Where was the man?

The trees came to an end, and he found himself at the top of a steep slope swathed in green that dropped down to a wide rushing river hemmed in by canyon walls and banks. A plain as red as split blood spooled away to the left, a steep bare slope to the right. His eyes darted from side to side, taking in the scene. There were figures down there in both directions. Five or six had found their way to the river upstream of him. It looked like they were struggling in the shallows, spears flashing in the water spray, trying to link up with a second group closer to his vantage point. To the other side there were men running down the slope, Uchdryd's pale hair was hard to miss, and there, at the edge of the water, large and small, the Troll and the boy!

With a cry, the hunter burst from cover mere yards away and slammed into him, striking the spear from his hand and knocking them both down the slope. A fist came for his face, but he blocked the Hunter's arm and kicked him back. The man was strong, lean, desperate, but he had no experience fighting other men. Before he could get a grip, Phelan arched his back, throwing him off, and leapt to his feet, flint-blade in hand.

The ground beneath them seemed to tremble, and then the hillside shrugged, throwing them off as easily as a man brushes off a fly. They both tumbled uncontrollably down the slope. The Hunter went backwards, heels over head, crashing through bushes and down into the water.

Phelan managed to get his feet under him, but the loose soil of the slope turned to sand and cascaded into the river. Phelan cascaded with it, ploughing thigh deep into water that hadn't been there a moment before. What madness was this? The world had been turned upside down. The land was covered with water and the river was bare stone and soaking gravel. The air trembled with the echo of some enormous noise that he didn't even remember hearing, or maybe it was just his ears ringing.

He hauled himself upright, bracing against the water, which was rushing past him from behind, thick with leaves and broken branches, and something pale and floating. There was no sign of Uchdryd or the others to his left. Had the water carried them away? Had the earth devoured them? Were the Fomor here, now? He had felt the ground shake once before, months earlier, but it had been nothing like this. There were people in the river to the right, just shadows against the water. His men? The tribe's? He had no way to tell.

And there, a dozen yards across the streaming water, on the edge of a shingle bank, the Troll and the boy.

11. Edan

Edan felt hard stones pressing against his back, and the chill of air on wet skin. He smelt sea-stink and salt, as if something had been dredged up from the bottom of the ocean — maybe it was him. He knew that Tara had hauled him somewhere out into the river. He'd run from the water for years, hid inside himself when he'd seen what it had done to the Hunting Grounds — and yet as soon as he resigned himself to letting it have him, here he was. The inevitability of it all almost made him laugh.

He listened to the hiss of the river with his eyes closed. It didn't matter that he was out of the water now, he'd be back in it soon enough. He could feel lapping hungrily at his feet. Don't worry, he told it, you'll have me soon enough.

He knew that he should have died long ago. His life was owed to the sea. Others had drowned in his place; his Father, his Mother, the wolf-man Keir, but their deaths wouldn't save him. The Fomor were of the sea, and so they would come to take him now. They had to, they must, or they would take everyone else. It was all clear to him now. The thought made him oddly calm. He had run out of terror or passed beyond it; too tired to be frightened.

Edan half expected to see the Fomor already waiting in the river when he opened his eyes. Instead he saw a shingle bank, a green-grey narrow of surging water, and Phelan, staring at him from the further shore.

The sight of Phelan shattered the strange feeling of serenity. He had no place in Edan's vision. Edan reached back for his spear, sending a shower of pebbles skittering into the water, before he remembered that it was still somewhere on the other shore. Beside him, Tara heaved a wet black stone out of the water, ready to use it as a weapon.

"Better not." Phelan's voice was clear and even over the chaos of the river. He leant down to grasp at something in the water and hauled up a soaking shape, holding it knee-high against his leg by its hair. With a start Edan realised that the shape was an unconscious man; Maccus.

"Your friend's not dead. Not yet anyway. So why don't you drop that rock before I drop him back into the river?"

Tara glanced down at him and he shook his head. They couldn't risk it. She held on to the rock a few moments longer and then slowly lowered it to the ground.

"You seem to have gotten yourself into quite a mess. Killing Keir was a big mistake."

"I didn't mean to kill him." Edan spoke up despite himself.

"I know, I know. But I don't think the others will see it that way. But maybe ... maybe I can put in a word to change their minds."

"Change their minds?"

"How old are you?" Phelan asked. "Seventeen, Eighteen winters?" Edan didn't reply. "I was about your age when I joined the Great Wolf, struck my first man. Didn't kill him, not that one. Now here we are," Phelan spread his hands wide, letting Maccus slump down towards the water, "both lost our spears, both look like we fell down a hill backwards."

"What I did once, you could do. The Great Wolf needs people willing to do decisive things, and you seem to have a knack for that."

Edan looked at the water lapping at his feet. Each ebbing ripple seemed to expose more of the gravel bank to the evening sun, as if the water were pouring away through an unseen gap in the river bed. That wasn't right. The water should be coming for him, not slipping away. He flicked his eyes back to the figure across the channel.

"You must see that this world is doomed," Phelan continued, apparently not having noticed where Edan had been looking. "There is no future here. The Great Wolf leads us to a new world, so what does it matter if we have to burn down the old one to make it. No one will care when all this is under the waves."

Edan knew that it was true, but: "I would care."

"You think that you would, but everything old can be replaced. All you'd have to do is join us." Phelan flashed a wolf's grin.

Join them? Edan allowed himself a sudden, desperate hope. The Daesani planned to quit this world for the mountains and the forest. There were no seas there, no Fomor. In their world he might not have to die. He tried to imagine what that would mean for the rest of the tribe, for Tara. Maybe if he ran away, they could still be saved? But he couldn't be certain, couldn't know for sure. He tried to judge the odds, to fathom the minds of the Fomor, but his thoughts were knots and circles.

"You don't want to die here, do you boy? You want to live. I can see it in you. I like that. You could be a wolf."

A nasty little part of Edan crowed at the thought, welling up out of the recesses where he'd hidden his past. He didn't have to be the scared boy waiting for the sea to drown him. He had killed a man. He had stolen a Troll. He had led the Daesani running all over the Summer Lands. He was a man now and could cross his own rivers. He didn't even have to feel bad about it, because it would save the others just as well as his death would.

Tara shifted uneasily at his side. Was she worried by how long he was taking to answer? Let her, said the nasty part, but the rest of him remembered how she came to be at his side, and why Phelan was hunting him in the first place.

"What about Keir?"

"Oh Keir." Phelan made a dismissive gesture with his hands, casting off something irrelevant. "That won't go down well with some of the others I admit." He lowered his hands. "But there is a way …"

"Give me the Troll."

"What!" Edan felt the gravel shift as Tara stepped back in shock. "Give you Tara?" He stared wide eyed at Phelan. His eyes darted over the wolf-fur ruffs on his clothing, on the water ebbing around his calves, on the knife of black stone that he had slid from behind his back and came to rest on Phelan's face. Even from across the water he could see the grey of his eyes.

"Oh, I could take her. I will, if you don't give her to me. But if you give her to me, then you are one of us."

"Edan, no!"

Edan ignored Tara. His eyes were still on Phelan's face, and because they were, he had seen the little sidelong glance he'd given when he spoke. He was stalling for time, Edan realised. Right now, he was alone against the two of them, with only a knife as a weapon, but if he just had a few moments more, then his men would join him, and it would be over.

But if he let Phelan take Tara now, he could join them too. Just because Phelan was stalling didn't mean that the offer was a lie. Do it, the horrible part said. You want a way out? Then don't throw away your life to save the others. Phelan and the Daesani will catch them anyway, no matter what you do. This way you can come out of it on top, instead of ending up like Keir.

'And be what?', the rest of Edan asked. 'One of a band of wild men? Kinless blood-soaked wild men, running from the real fight?' Perhaps he could be one of them, but he didn't want to be. The wheedling little voice in his head was terror and nothing more. The bit of him that was scared of the sacrifice he had to make. Was dying so terribly bad? Not as bad as living like them.

"I've got all the family I need!" he shouted, scrambling to his feet. He grabbed a stone from the bank and tossed it in his hand to test the weight, scanning the river at the same time. Now that he looked for them, he could see that there were others in the water, closing from left and right. The sound of cries and struggling were suddenly sharp and clear, ringing out over the swirling waves. Uch was wrestling with one of the Daesani while the girls were grasped in the arms of another, kicking and screaming. All around him the tribe was fighting for its life.

And he saw too that the river was changing. The water around their little island had fallen back a yard or more, exposing slimy weed and flopping fish. The channel that Tara had dragged him through was now only ankle deep.

Phelan took his chance while Edan was distracted, dropping Maccus back into the water and launching himself forward, his black blade glinting in the light. But before he could close the distance someone else came hurtling at him from the other direction. Phelan lurched aside with First Mother clawing at his face. Edan barely had time to see it happen, before yet another figure came running at him from the other side, bow in hand. Tara hurled her rock two-handed at the bow-carrier, and he tumbled limply on the slick stones.

A rushing hiss filled the air. The last of the water drained into the gravel bed of the river; vanished. Someone shouted, "The land is coming back!"

"Edan, come on!" Tara grabbed another rock and hurled it at the man on the ground, but he rolled out of the way. "We have to go and help them."

Edan didn't move, even when Tara grabbed him by the arm. Couldn't she see? The Fomor controlled the waves, the sea, no one else. The river emptied at their command. Time was up.

They were coming.

A dull roar gathered at the horizon, echoing between the steep banks and across the weed-choked river bed. At the edge of vision, where the distant ocean met the sky, something was growing. A grey wind swept up the river channel, swallowing the sun and plucking at the trees until the air above them filled with swirling leaves. A wall of water came behind it, rushing over the land as if a giant hand was pushing it, swallowing marsh and river and hills alike.

The Fomor came with the wave. Edan saw them suspended within the water, chiefs or hunters or shamans of the sea, he couldn't tell which. They rode within the crest of the wave like eagles soaring on the wind, claws ready to stoop. They flickered in his vision, now spear-armed and bone-crowned, now many limbed and seal fast, now tangles of black and red and claws. They split as they came, birthing seaweed tangles and shattered trees, turning inside out through themselves until they were no more than flotsam in the flood.

Some of them swept west, out across the saltmarshes and into the Summer Lands, others east, vanishing behind the wave-swallowed cliffs. The last one came tearing up the river bed atop the cresting wave. For a moment Edan lost sight of it amongst the debris, then he saw it again, spike covered and spindle-limbed, one-eyed and crested with the black of crow feathers. It levelled a spear of spume and driftwood, aimed straight at his heart.

Freezing water plucked Edan up and carried him upriver like a twig on a stream. The water was dark, full of silt and seaweed and stones. Edan instantly lost all sense of up and down, left and right, forward and back. He was spinning through darkness. Something slammed across his back. In his mind it was the Fomor's spear, but he could see nothing in the water except a faint blue glow, growing brighter as he sank towards it.

He could struggle. He still knew how to swim, even after all these years avoiding the deep water. The surface was somewhere above him; he should be trying to reach it; but his limbs stayed still. He had gone down into this darkness before. The last time he had been saved, dragged out of the water and back into the light, to live on alone. Not this time. This time the whole world was going to drown. But maybe, maybe he had done enough. With that thought he closed his eyes. It was nice to hope that he had given the others enough time to get away — that Tara had gotten away.

Something took hold of him, grabbing a handful of hair and clothing in its grasp. Edan jerked like a fish on a spear, thinking that the Fomor had come for him, but the hand was dragging him upwards against the current, hauling him out of the water.

No! If he lived, everyone else would die!

He caught hold of the arm above the hand — trying to wrench himself free — but it dragged him, choking and spluttering, out of the sea.

He gasped a breath; coughed water; lived and went limp, letting Tara drag him from the hungry sea.

12. Tara

Darkness and surging waters surrounded Tara as she dragged Edan from the flood. Waves crashed into her and over her, threatening to carry her away, but she ploughed on, using Edan's weight as ballast. For a moment he had seemed about to let himself drown, only to struggle when she grabbed him. Now he was limp again.

She could barely see the slope she finally crawled out on. Night had fallen along with the monstrous wave. Wherever it was, it felt like wet earth and smelt like the sea. Slick masses moved under her fingertips as she pulled Edan fully out of the water. She couldn't tell if they were seaweed or something else. She bent her head to Edan's chest and was relieved to hear the murmur of his heart: not dead.

When she felt he was breathing steadily, and was in no danger of being washed away, she forced herself to climb back down the slope to the edge of the water in the hope of finding other survivors. She ought to be looking at the river, but now it was the sea, restlessly feeling out its new bounds. Tara strained into the gloom, calling out, but no one answered. When the moonlight broke through the ragged clouds it picked out debris on the water, branches and leaves and sea foam, but no men, alive or dead. She and Edan were the only life on that lonely shore.

Something spun by in the flood that she was sure was moving on its own. With a last burst of energy, she scrambled into the water to grab it. For a moment the weight of it resisted her, and she hoped that it might be one of the others, but when it popped free, showering water, she saw that it was only a branch, green and roughly broken.

The soft soil shifted under her feet, slumping down into the sea as the rushing water undermined it. The land was still receding. She inched away up the slope, struggling to keep her footing in the dark, back to where Edan lay. He was still unconscious. She got a hand under each of his armpits and dragged him further up the hill. When she thought that they were high enough to be out of danger, she let him go and flopped down by his side.

Edan stirred when she put him down for the second time, coughing water. She bent over him, and he grasped wildly at her arms. "Tara? No! You are alive. What have you done?"

"Saved you, when you wouldn't save yourself."

He slumped in her grip. "What about the others? My family?"

She shook her head, knowing that she would be only half visible in the moonlight. "I am sorry Edan, I cannot find them." She felt his body shiver with one brief gust of emotion, but then he was still again. When he spoke, it was in a murmur, half to himself, so that she had to strain to hear him. "It isn't your fault. I should be dead."

Tara started back in surprise. "Dead? What do you mean? Why would you want to die?"

Edan looked up at her from under mouse-tails of damp hair. She thought that his face was as pale and overcast as the moon above. "They were coming for me, don't you see? They wanted me. You should have let them have me."

"Who?"

"The Fomor. Didn't you see them? In the wave? You must have."

Tara pulled him close again, to keep him warm, and gestured an apology. "I am sorry Edan, I saw nothing. The people of course, the wave, maybe broken plants and seaweed in the water. Nothing more." Edan looked away in confusion. "Maybe you just need to rest, Edan, think more clearly."

"No. I'm clear. This is the first time I've been clear. It's just like before. I should have known."

"Then tell me!" Exhaustion made her snap in irritation, and it took an effort to make herself calm again.

"Please Edan, I think I need to know. You've been so strange. Why did you want to drown? I don't understand. You are terrified of the water, and then you throw yourself into it."

She thought she saw Edan nod.

"Yes. I'll tell you."

Edan relaxed a little in her grip. When he spoke again his voice had the sing-song tone of one of the tribe's tales.

"Long ago — many summers and winters — when I was still small, the tribe was a bigger thing. You could not count its members on two hands or four. There was more than one family then, though each were kin.

In those days we had two places, the Winter Place and the Summer. We built homes in the Places, from which we could range to gather what we needed. In the Summer Place we had houses made of earth and grass and wood. We dug them into the banks of sand and soil, by the river. They had walls made of wooden poles held up by the earth, and above them more poles to hold a sea grass roof. They were dark inside, and smelled of smoke, and they were cool when the sun shone and warm when the rain came, and had so many precious things in them ..."

A pause, long enough to make her think he had fallen asleep, before he started again.

"The Summer Place was where the river met the sea. In those days the ocean did not steal land with every winter, and so we were not worried by it. Each summer we might have to set our traps a little closer to the house, or gather whelks a little higher on the shore, but the sea was full of fish and the shore was full of whelks, and sometimes there was a deer or an auroch or a boar to share.

My Father was the Fisher. My Mother had only me to raise and so we were all always in the water. We thought we knew the ways of it. I could swim near as soon as I could walk. The sea was like The Great Wood, sacred in its own way, something to be respected, but we lived always by its edge and were thankful for it. Until ..."

A second pause, and this time when he started speaking, he stopped again. Tara heard him swallowing tears in the darkness. All her annoyance was gone. She wanted to tell him that she did not need to hear his tale — but something told her that he needed to tell it, and so she held her tongue.

"It was late in summer," he said at last. "I remember that we had started to dry our fish on racks over the fire, ready for the journey to the winter lands. Mother would put alder wood into the flames to flavour the meat, you could smell it everywhere. There had been storms the night before, but strange, all lightning and thunder but no rain. Just heat and clouds that were red at dusk. I couldn't sleep, so I crawled in beside Mother and Father.

The sea came with the dawn, in the half-light, just like now. I remember that I heard it coming, like something was sneaking into the hut. Water was seeping through the door, black water, putting out the embers. I was up and out before my parents even knew what was happening. I remember standing in the middle of the Place. The path that led down to the river was already awash, and I could see this surge of water. It wasn't fast, not like today, but slow, like something heaving itself out of the sea with water pouring off it, only it wasn't anything but water.

I started to go towards it. The water was my friend. I was curious. I heard someone calling for me to come back, but I didn't listen. The water was cold, it was up to my ankles, my knees, I wasn't afraid." He let out a long breath, shaking.

"And then suddenly I couldn't feel the bottom. Suddenly there was water everywhere, all around me, and it was throwing me back and sucking me down, pulling me away in the undertow. There was no hope for me, do you see? But there was for the others. They could have run. Like you should have run. You should have left me."

"What happened Edan?"

"They came after me. Mother, Father, others. I was already halfway down the river, but they dived in anyway. I didn't see it; I was told afterwards. My Father pulled me from the water, somehow managed to pass me to my Mother who passed me on to someone else and so on. They got me out, but they didn't get out. They drowned for me."

Tara tried to find comforting words. "This was not your fault Edan. You did not do this."

The silence before he responded was heart-breaking. "No, of course not. I know that. I do know that. But don't you see, it doesn't matter. I should have died, and I didn't. I am blood-price, owed to the Fomor. I used to think it was just the sea that I was bound to, but when we met the Daesani and I heard about the Fomor, I knew the truth of it. They came for me today, I saw them. If you'd only let me drown, the others would not have been taken."

To Tara's mind this was poisoned thinking. Edan's family had saved him, so now he assumed that anyone who saved him would die in the same way, and that by dying unsaved he could save others in turn. The twisted thoughts required to believe this were beyond her. She wanted to tell him that he was being stupid. She wanted to tell him that she would save him again, and she didn't care what he thought. But she imagined how she would feel if she were the last of The People. How would she feel if she was alive when they were dead? She shivered, feeling the wet clothes cold against her skin.

"I understand," she said. "You have a death mark on you. That is why you could see the Fomor in the wave and I could not."

"You believe me?"

"Of course. I know what it is to see what others cannot."

"Thank you." Unexpectedly, Edan reached up a hand and touched her cheek. "Thank you for believing me." He made a noise, somewhere between a chuckle and a groan. "I hardly believe it myself." He let his hand fall.

In spite of herself, Tara had to stifle a yawn. She could barely see Edan now, and the chill wind from the sea cut through to her skin.

"Don't worry," Edan said, "My eyes are closed already."

"We should set a camp," she said; then, "but I don't think we have anything to set one with. Your pack is somewhere in the river, mine too."

"We will just have to make the best of it."

They were too tired to do more than find a sheltered corner, where broom branches kept off the worst of the night wind and a bank hid the heaving sea from view. Tara still had the two tightly rolled furs that she had taken from Morna on the way through the Deer Woods. The packed hide had turned away the worst of the water. She gave one to Edan, and he wrapped himself tightly in it. In moments he was asleep, his breathing soft against the distant swell of the sea.

Tara put a hand to her cheek, feeling the faint warmth where Edan had touched her. For some reason she felt herself smile. Then she hurriedly threw the one remaining fur around her shoulders and lay down to sleep.

* * *

The flood had left Edan and Tara with little in the way of supplies or belongings. When morning came, they pooled what they had: two deer skins stained with salt, clothing torn and damaged, a flint blade, a hammer stone, fishbones and thorn hooks, scraps of fur, one shoe of buckskin, a glue stick, a few pieces of sinew and the single spear point Edan had recovered from the marsh.

Edan weighed the antler point in his hand. "That was just about the only thing I had of them, after the flood," he said. Tara knew that he meant the fishing spear. "They found it floating when the waters receded, amongst the debris. They gave it to me when I was old enough. That and this charm." His hand went to his neck, holding out an ivory-yellow carving in the shape of a seal for Tara to see. "My Mother made that for me, when I was small."

By the washed-out light of day, they could see that a new sea had wrapped itself around the headland they sheltered on. The woods through which they had run had become islands in a grey expanse — the river Legu was now the mouth of a bay that curled to the south of them. A solid raft of cloud hid the sky, though a fitful wind blew constantly from the north. Cold spits and spats of rain came when the wind was strongest, speckling their faces with water.

Edan spent a long time pacing the ridge above the uneasy sea, calling out through cupped hands for First Hunter, First Mother, Brina and the rest. Tara watched him until he finally turned away.

"They can't all have drowned ... can they?"

Tara had her doubts. They did not have her strength, and she had barely managed to get out of the water. That truth would hurt Edan however.

"I am sure they were just washed away inshore."

"We should go down. Look for them. We might find something useful, tools, furs. Shouldn't we?" Edan didn't sound enthusiastic.

In her mind she saw a sudden image of Morna or Brina cast up dead on the shore, pale and lifeless, eyes as blank as a fish on a hook. She would not let him see that.

"We have no food, no shelter." Tara gestured to indicate loss, pinching her fingers as if she held something and then letting it fall. "I am not keen to spend another night on this hillside."

With unspoken agreement they turned away from the lashing waves and headed uphill, seeking a better spot to make a camp.

A wind-swept cape thrust north into the sea beyond the Summer Lands, sloping up ahead of them as it went northwards. They saw few rocks and fewer trees. Everything seemed to be peat and gravel, soft under their feet and waterlogged, collapsing under every step. Only in one place, away to the north, did there seem to be bare rock, jutting up above the undulating landscape. It was a poor place to hunt, and a poor place to make a home. It reminded Tara of the place where she had been born, a bad land that no one else would want.

In the afternoon they reached level ground, a moorland of brown pools and grey banks. Scrubby bilberry and crowberry plants hugged the ground wherever the banks gave shelter from the wind, and they stuffed their mouths greedily with berries until they finally felt full. Then they filled Edan's knife pouch with as many more as would fit in it.

Eventually they came across a thicket of scrubby birch trees cowering in the shelter of a shallow gully. Grey rocks stained with lichen poked through an underbrush of nettles and bear's garlic, and they approached it cautiously in case a real bear might have made its home amongst the trees, but there was no sign of anything larger than a bird, save them.

They worked to set a fire. Tara gathered loose brush into a pile at the edge of the trees while Edan used his blade to scrape dry bark for kindling. She watched as he quickly cut some of the dry wood into a rod and a disk, rubbing the spindle furiously between his hands, the bottom pressed into the disk, until it began to blacken and smoke. This was the fire making magic she had watched before. Now Edan had her come close and help, blowing air gently onto the wood to coax embers into life, and then quickly transferring them to the nest of bark shavings. The first flickers of flame were a comfort in the darkness.

Tara woke early to find that it had rained in the night, quenching the fire and threading rivulets of yellow-brown water through the woods. Overhead, the strange clouds had not moved, and faint rumbles of thunder echoed from the north. She knew that their journey to Dentaltos had not ended. They should move on, but not today. The previous day she had been driven by powerful emotions, determined to put the ruined coast behind her. Today she was simply tired.

They did their best to make a proper shelter. Tara picked through the scattered stones until she found one she thought might serve as an axe. She hefted it in her hand until it felt comfortable, then struck the other end over and over again with a second stone until she'd shaped a rough point. It was not good rock, but it would have to do. With it, she set about felling the two smallest saplings she could locate. The rhythmic pounding of the stone against the green wood woke Edan, and he headed back to the bog in search of food.

By the time he returned with a few small fish in his hands, Tara had cut down the birches and set them at an angle against an overhanging branch. Between them she placed smaller branches, the straightest she could find, thrusting them into the soft earth to make upright stakes. They wove smaller branches between them, bending them under and over the stakes and then tapping them down with the round end of the axe to make them tight.

They relit the fire and roasted the little fish in the flames. They were as silent now as when Tara had first joined the tribe, but she felt no desperation to speak. They were both drained of words, but the silence was comfortable, comforting.

After their meal, they wandered slowly amongst the birches looking for food. Amongst The People gathering plants was women's work, just as hunting the great animals was for the men, but Tara knew only the lands around the Stone Forest. Edan proved more knowledgeable in this terrain, plucking shoots she'd passed by to add to their little stock of berries. The nettles and jakkios which had provided meals back at the edge of The Great Wood were flowering now and had grown bitter, but Edan picked the heart-shaped leaves of wood sours and the broader ones of ramsons, and even the shoots of snakeweed, which Tara knew only as a root The People used to tan leather.

"I'd feel safer if I had a bow," Edan told her when they had returned to their sheltered fire. "Too many Daesani taking shots at me."

The Seers did not use bows, though Tara knew that some of The People had adopted them, so she did not know much about them. "Could you make one?"

Edan yawned but summoned up an answer. "If I had enough time perhaps, and something to make a bowstring from, fresh deer hide would be perfect. But you don't really want to use green wood, better to cut it in the winter and let it rest. That's what First Hunter always says … said." He stopped for a moment. "But we don't have time, do we? We need to go on."

Tara didn't reply to that. She wasn't ready to break this bubble of rest they seemed to have wandered into.

Edan seemed to take her silence for agreement. "Well, maybe I can think of something else tomorrow." He wrapped himself in his deerskin and closed his eyes.

Sleep came quickly for Tara that night, but not pleasantly. Exhaustion dragged her down through what seemed like an ocean of blackness, until suddenly she was falling from a raft of cloud towards a bleak and wind-blasted landscape. Overhead, a blazing ball of ruddy fire, wreathed about with ropes of smoke, cast blood-shadows on the rolling moors. She spread her arms into eagle's wings and snatched herself out of the fall, speeding northward, following the red light.

She wheeled upwards into vision sky until she reached the red ball of fire. The sky was dark and cold despite the flame. There seemed to be water to the west of her and water to the east, and water to the north and south as well. All the world had vanished beneath the sea except for this one final desolate scrap of land.

She came at last to a great cliff, beyond which a needle of stone rose from an ocean of blood: black water reflecting the red sun. The chief of the Fomor waited on top of the pillar. She knew without a doubt that it was the creature from Edan's nightmares. It wrapped around the stone like a weed, moving and shifting in an unseen tide, cloaked in shadow. She thought it wore a crown of antlers, but then she saw that they were the toothed jaws of whales, angled like the limbs of a crescent moon. It was a lord of endless ocean, of boundless hunger. When it raised its hand, the sea convulsed and rushed forward, crashing against the rocks and surging up through the air to pummel her with spray and drown her in spume.

She opened her eyes and thought for a moment that the sea spray had followed her from her vision, dancing in front of her eyes. Then she realised that it was only the stars, which shone keen and silent through the narrow gap of the shelter door. It was the middle of the night, still and cold.

The vision told her what she already knew; that she could not linger on the edge of the Fomor's realm, playing at houses. She remembered the three balls of fire from her childhood vision, the white, the red, and the black, and realised that the white light had already come that day at the Stone Forest when the moon had turned the bright sun grey. Now the second light, the red, would soon be upon them.

Tara felt a sudden desperate need to talk and put out a hand to shake Edan by the shoulder, but she didn't touch him. For once he seemed to be sleeping easily, it would be a shame to wake him. Instead, she watched the rise and fall of his breathing, the way that the moonlight picked out his chest.

Better to let him sleep.

Quietly she wrapped the sleeping fur around her shoulders and stepped out of the shelter, into the grey and black of the moorland's edge. The dew was cold on her bare feet, but the silent darkness was good for thinking. She had left The People full of purpose, certain of the need to come here and see the Fomor with her own eyes, not just with the eyes of vision. That sense of purpose had sent her weeks inland across the southern marshes alone in a little skin boat. Even when the wolf-men had plucked her from the water and made her prisoner she stayed focused on that one goal: reach Dentaltos, confront the creatures, save the land.

It seemed so foolish now, after the reality of the flood. These Fomor would not reason, they would not negotiate. If she went to the Tooth of the North, what then? Would they finally claim Edan for their own? He might think that his sacrifice could save the land, but that was just another sort of madness. His death would accomplish nothing, except to break her heart.

She stopped dead in the moonlight. Where had that thought come from? Edan wasn't her mate. He had not offered her a partner-gift. It was just a silly thought put in her head by that poor old man. Edan would never think of her that way. Or would he? She remembered the touch of his fingers on her face. Was it fear for herself that made her hesitate now, or fear for him. He'd suffered as much as any of them, more than her. He'd lost his family, not once but twice, and his land too. What more would he suffer if they kept on going?

The dream of hiding out on the headland came back full force. Far away from the Daesani, far away from The People — and the need to go back and tell them that she had failed. Just her and Edan. They could make a life here.

The dream fled as quickly as it had risen. The Fomor's new sea was right there, a day's walk away. How long until even this upland moor vanished beneath the waves? Her visions told her the answer: not long if she lost the courage to act. Even if they somehow did not, it would be more than cruel to ask Edan to make a home overlooking the devastation of the Summer Hunting Grounds, the graves of all his family. The dead that lay beneath the Stone Forest had gone peacefully into the ground, and they were still unnerving enough. The dead of the tribe were not likely to stay so peaceful. She chided herself for her cowardice. She had not hesitated to face Uchdryd, or the Iero, or Rat-tongue's hounds, she could not hesitate in this either.

Tara realised that the dawn had come while she had been lost in thought. The moon had vanished again behind the scudding clouds, but pale light was creeping in from the east. She looked back the way she had come, seeing the pale birches in the dell below. She'd wandered further than she had meant, as well as for longer.

By the time she made it back to the shelter, Edan was already awake, yawning in the early morning light as he coaxed the cinders of the fire back to life. He'd found a flat stone and crushed the snakeweed roots into a gritty powder. Now he mixed it with ramson and sorrel and a dribble of water to make some patties, wrapped them in large leaves, and placed them in the ashes to cook. "It's not much," he shrugged, "but better than nothing."

Tara had so many things to say, but not the words for most of them. Instead she said, "We need to leave. We still have to go to the stone."

Edan nodded. "I know. I dreamt of the Fomor again. They won't stop if we don't find a way to stop them."

Tara found herself smiling. "I am glad you see it the same way!"

"Still," Edan held up his single shoe, "I think a little more preparation won't hurt us."

Grudgingly, Tara gave them another day. They gathered cattails from the marsh, digging into the peat with sticks to get the roots out of the ground while talking of meaningless, inconsequential things: stories of years well past.

It was hard work, muddy and damp, but they came back with armfuls of the plants. They roasted the roots and the green flower spikes beside the fire until the roots were blackened, and the flowers were hot and soft. They snatched the flowers from the ash and ate them whole. The roots were harder work — after the burnt shell was split off, they had to

102

drag the fibres between their teeth to scrape off the edible part. Once she'd had enough to eat, Tara spat each mouthful of pulp out into a leaf, building up a store of white tacky balls that could be cooked and eaten later.

Edan, meanwhile, took the sharpest of the stone flakes that she had struck from her makeshift axe and used them to cut a scrap of deer hide into something roughly like the shape of his foot but larger. He used a bone point scrounged from the bottom of his one remaining pouch to pierce the edge with holes. With a little noise of regret he teased the stiff leather headband out of his hair and chewed it until it was soft enough to slice into thin strips which he used to lace up his new shoe, crossing them back and forth as he tied it to his foot.

One last preparation was in order. Tara went to the lonely ash tree and cut the straightest branch that she could see, stripping the bark with long draws of a stone flake until it was smooth and white. She handed it to Edan, watching as he took his Father's spearpoint and bound it to the haft, weaving strands of sinew back and across, wetting each piece in his mouth to make it stick. When the binding was dry, he warmed his pine-tar glue over the fire until it was sticky and black, coating the join until it was thoroughly waterproofed. When it was dry, he lifted the spear, turning it in his hand, round and around.

"You look like a warrior," she said.

13. Edan

The land above the little wood where they had sheltered was open and bleak. Rough heather hid a multitude of boggy holes and scattered rocks, so that every step threatened to twist an ankle or bruise a toe. Like every other day since the flood the weather was oppressive, hot but grey, pressed flat by the endless deck of clouds above. Faint hints of thunder rumbled, but no rain fell. It seemed as if the whole world was waiting for them to reach Dentaltos.

Edan felt the same: pressed down, paralysed, suspended waiting for something to happen. What? He did not know. For a miracle to bring his family back? For the world to start making sense again? For the anger inside him to find a target?

At first, when Tara hauled him from the water, he had been too drained, too numb, to really understand what had happened. He had let himself be led out of the flooded valley like it was a dream and curled up in the scant shelter of the wood in a daze; but slowly sensation had returned, and the reality had hit him full force.

His tribe was dead. Even if the people in it had somehow survived the flood, they could never return to the Traditions that had made the tribe what it was. The Summer Hunting Grounds were gone, the Winter Lands might soon belong to the Daesani, even as The Great Wood might. Even if the tribe could somehow continue, he would never be just Edan the Fisher again.

After the numbness came anger; a formless, targetless rage. It rose from some part of his mind he didn't know existed, bubbling up through the grief like seeping water. It trickled into his dreams, tainting every action. Every little annoyance became an unbearable slight. His unbound hair kept falling in his eyes; the charms tangled at his neck; his new shoe leaked; his new spear was rough in his hand; his tribe was dead. By the time he was consciously aware of the rage, it was lodged inside him like a snake coiled up in his belly.

The anger demanded action, violence, revenge. Revenge on whom he was not sure. He could not fight the sea, and the Fomor were spirits or fever dreams, beyond his reach in either case. Not himself, and not Tara — she had saved him out of kindness, not malice. Instead, his thoughts focussed on

Phelan. Phelan had driven the tribe into the river. Phelan had chased them across the Summer Lands. He could hurt Phelan, if he found him, if he wasn't dead.

But Phelan wasn't there. Crossing the moorlands, struggling north, he found that a distance had grown between himself and Tara. He couldn't articulate what he was feeling to her. He tried to concentrate on the land ahead; on what little Tara had told him about their destination; on anything, in fact, that might distract him, but the anger wouldn't go away. It raged under every thought. He quivered with the need to do *something*.

Edan stabbed the haft of his spear into the soft peat, wrenching a slab of it away with a fierce twist of the wood. The rough wood grazed his palms, and the pain brought a little bit of calm. Looking at the broken ground and the quivering spear, he felt a sudden sense of shame. His Father had been a peaceful man, just as his Mother had been a loving woman — neither would have been happy to see what Edan was doing with the fishing spear, or himself.

Hurriedly he snatched the spear back out of the soil, wondering if Tara had noticed. Thinking about her, about what she might be feeling, was the one thing that distracted him from the anger. Amongst all the pain and confusion of the night at the river, he clung to one half-coherent memory of Tara holding him in her arms. She had seemed so strong, and yet so soft.

Edan coughed down a blush. Why would his mind not behave? Instead he called across the heather, "Tell me about Dentaltos again."

"I only know what I've seen in visions, and what I was told."

Tara made an attempt to get closer, ploughing through the grey-green and the brown, but the craggy peat divided them, and she had to raise her voice and gesture wildly to reply.

"The oldest of the Seers, Ama, told me that the Tooth of the North marked an ancient home of The People, somewhere that we lived before the invaders … before your people came. I do not think that The People live here any longer, but I can't be sure. There are not many of us left. We do not always know who lives and who does not. In my visions the tooth is a spear of rock at the edge of the sea, or in it, it changes." She gave a little shrug of frustration. "I am sorry, I do not answer clearly. Knowing so little … this is why I came to see for myself."

Edan felt a pang of guilt that pushed the anger away for a moment. "I've poured out all my problems at your feet and expected you to listen, but I've never even asked exactly how the Daesani came to capture you."

"Oh!" She made a little squeak of surprise, and he realised that she was embarrassed.

"Well, it was a stupid thing. I told you that I had volunteered to learn more about my vision. Our place, the Seer's place, is by the mouth of a river that runs far into the Summer Lands. The Old Ones had a boat of skins, and I made my way up the river in it.

I remember there was a lake, all covered in rain, so big it took days to edge my way around it. Somewhere along the way it turned into a marsh, and there were more days, and I got lost. There were so many channels, and in all that rain I couldn't tell where to go." She gave a rueful little smile that Edan found oddly pretty on her broad lips.

"So, I pulled my boat up on a bank somewhere and went to sleep under it. When the rain stopped, I was still asleep, and that's when they found me. There wasn't even a fight, I woke up already caught."

Edan gave her a smile that he hoped looked sympathetic.

"But what did they want with you?"

Tara shrugged. "I do not really know. They dragged me across the middle lands, kept me prisoner, and never said." She paused to take a jump from one springy clump to the next, flinging her arms forward for balance.

"Information?"

"No, they did not ask me questions. They did not think I could speak. I thought it was to make sure I did not fight the Fomor, but now I am less sure. I do not think that most of them knew why I was their prisoner. It was always Phelan." Edan saw her visibly shiver. "He had some desire for me." She made a sign that Edan did not recognise.

"Desire? He wanted you for … to …"

"Oh!" He saw her blush. "No, not in that way; in fact, he kept the others away from me. I have used the wrong word perhaps. I think that he wanted me dead, but I do not know why. Do you know that he has scars, all over?" She brushed her arms with her hands to show him where. "Like a knife's cuts." A slicing motion of the hands. "I saw them once, but he hid them from the others."

"But he showed you?"

"Sometimes he talked to me, at night. I don't think he knew I could understand some of it. If he had, he'd have said nothing. It was more like a confession."

Edan felt a surge of jealousy. How dare Phelan talk to her like that! In the night, the same way he had.

"What did he say?"

She shook her head. "I did not understand that much. Fate. He talked about Fate, and blood. Sacrifice too. Something about his past."

What had Phelan wanted? Edan tried to puzzle it out. To kill Tara as an enemy? No. He'd had plenty of chances to do that. Maybe to take her to the Fomor? But again no, the Daesani had been fleeing the Fomor and the coast. To use her as a sacrifice? Even the Daesani would not think to do that. He had no answers.

Thinking of Phelan brought the anger back. 'Stupid questions.' He told himself he would never see Phelan again. Time for another change of subject.

"So, what do you think we will find at Dentaltos now?"

"Something bad."

Startled, Edan tripped, almost fell, and she clarified. "My visions say one of the Fomor waits for us there, a chieftain of their kind, I am sure of it. His eyes, I can't describe them, pale in the darkness, like stars, or shells."

"Bal," Edan said. The thought came to him unexpectedly, along with the image of the horrible statue in the Winter Place. "It is Bal."

"I have heard the name," Tara admitted, "but not the tale."

"I don't have the charm to tell it right," Edan replied, "but the Elder said that it was the oldest tale. I heard it often enough, so I can try." He called up a memory of the Elder's voice from the shadows of the Winter Place.

"In the days before First Man and before First Woman, before even the Summer Lands, there lived three giant brothers. In those days there was no Great Wood, no mountains, no rivers and no plains. The land was covered in ice, as the eye could see.

The three brothers lived on the ice. Their names were Gok, and Mag, and Bal, and they were the only things that lived. They hunted the seals and the whales that lived under the ice. Now, Gok and Mag were fair to see. Their hair was long and dark, their skin as smooth as slate and ruddy as clay, their arms strong and their eyes bright. Bal was none of these things. His skin was rough as roots, his limbs were twisted, his one eye was white as milk and blind and his other red as blood.

The heart of Bal was as ugly as his body, and he hated his brothers' fairness from the depths of it. He longed to destroy them but knew that he could not overcome their strength. The only talent in which he excelled was in holding his breath.

Now one day Gok and Mag set out to hunt upon the ice, where the sea was under it. Bal knew of this plan of theirs and saw his chance. Taking a deep breath, he swam far beneath the water, and with his knife of bone cut deep into the ice above. When his brothers stepped on the weakened ice it cracked in two, dropping them into the freezing sea and his waiting arms.

Great was the slaughter that day. Bal cut his brothers into pieces and flung their remains to the horizon. Gok he threw to the west, where his bones became mountains, and his flesh became forests, and his hair became the storms over The Great Wood. Mag he threw the other way, so that his flesh became the brown mountains of the east. The hot blood of the brothers ran freely, melting the ice and pooling between them, so that land came where there had been ocean, and these were the Summer Lands."

"What happened to Bal?"

"I don't know. The tales don't say. There is a statue of him, in our winter home. It always scared me."

"A strange thing to keep a statue of."

"Yes. I always wished it wasn't there. It looks appropriate now, doesn't it, if what you say about Dentaltos is true. Bal created the Summer Lands and now he will destroy them." There wasn't much more to say after that.

Edan found that his tale had carried them out of the peat bog and onto a windswept upland of scattered boulders and breeze-cropped grass. The grey stones were spattered with lichen. Pale flowers huddled amongst the roots of the grass, their petals curling in to hide their hearts. He presumed that this was the edge of the Summer Lands. He expected to see the sea, just over the next hill, but the rise and fall of the land was deceptive. The top of each ridge revealed only further land ahead, bare and treeless.

The heather slopes had taken them most of the morning to climb, and now the lands above consumed the afternoon. When the grey day began to darken into an equally grey evening, there was still no sign of the coast. Had they had lost their way? They had nothing but the Elder's half-remembered drawing and Tara's visions to guide them. Edan wondered if they were somehow travelling parallel to the coast, if they had already left Dentaltos far behind. He was on the verge of suggesting that they turn back when they saw a sign that they were on the right track after all.

At first Edan did not realise that he was looking at something made by man. Yet another rise had revealed a grassy slope strewn with hummocks, stretching up towards a higher bank topped with waving grass. Small birds sped away in a flap of black and red as they approached.

When he looked closer, he saw that the mounds were heaps of mussel shells, overgrown with grass and earth. When he ran his fingers through them, he found them as dry as ancient driftwood and as white as chalk. The mounds were taller than either of them, compacted under their own weight. Even the grass they stood on hid more shells.

"Whoever lived here is long gone," Edan said quietly.

Beyond the mounds, the steep bank was punctuated with the mouths of caves, shallow spaces with their backs to the sea. The stone within was dusted with wind-curls of white sand. Edan bent down to look through one opening, seeing a cave floor strewn with bones. He scanned the gloom, nervous that this was some creature's den, but there was no sign of movement. He sniffed, smelt nothing living.

Inside, the stone was cold through the thin leather of his shoes and the air smelt of damp and dust. The bones inside the cave were heaped as deep as the shells outside. They were as dense and heavy as stone, from some beast more massive than any the tribe had ever hunted.

Tara made a circuit of the space, running her hands across the walls. "See here." She called him over, showing him marks cut into the hard stone of the wall. When he ran his own hand over the stone, he felt a criss-cross of lines carved as deep as the first joint on his little finger. There were other shapes too, curves and what might have been circles, stained with the faintest hint of old ochre.

"You recognise these?"

"Yes. Ancestors of The People lived here."

Edan looked at the ancient bones and the dry shells outside. "It must have been very long ago."

"Very long." Tara kept her eyes on the carvings. "My people have been dying for a long time Edan." She signed the passing of ages. "They are only tales now."

Edan ducked back out into the evening light and climbed the bank above the caves. From the top he saw the distant sea, no more than a faint grey line above yet another hill. Not something they would reach that day.

When he returned to the valley, Tara was crouching by the cave entrance, staring over the quiet mounds. His footsteps were soft on the grass and she did not hear him coming. For a moment he stood and stared, watching as the wind ruffled her hair, red like restless flames. At the touch of his gaze she looked up and saw him, so he hurried the rest of the way down.

"It's too far to the sea to go on, and there is nowhere else to shelter. We should stay here."

Tara looked uneasy. "Here? I don't think I like this place."

Edan wondered, "is that the Seer talking?"

She chuckled, a pleasant throaty sound. "No. No visions. Just a feeling that we don't belong here. This is someone else's place."

Edan joined her, looking at the last slivers of sunlight as they faded over the hillside. He imagined that he could see the shadows of Tara's People moving amongst the mounds, just vague shapes of light and shade, so distant that even their memories had been washed away, but it was only a trick of the light.

"I think that they are too long gone for that," he looked at her, "and if not, they won't mind you being here."

"Is that the death mark speaking?"

Now it was his turn to laugh. "No, just a feeling."

14. Tara

The Summer Lands ended in a cliff, dizzyingly high and as sharp as an axe cut. Tara and Edan stood at the edge, looking straight down into a sea as green and pellucid as ice, and as unnaturally still. Gale mown grass formed a thin layer over slanted slabs of loose stone, forming a treacherous edge. Kittiwakes and Herring gulls wheeled below them, their cries full of anguish and loss.

This was the place of the Tooth of the North. In all Tara's dreams and visions the rock spire had risen just beyond the cliff, sometimes sheer, sometimes twisted, sometimes wave lashed. That very morning, before the dawn, she thought that she had seen Bal of the Fomor beckoning her onwards from the great stone. It had been as clear as if she had already stood before it.

Only now that she was actually there, Tara saw no such thing, for Dentaltos had fallen.

Huge wedges of rock, impossibly large when she forced herself to think of them in motion, lay where they had toppled into the sea, half submerged. She imagined stacking the shattered pieces back together into a finger of rock. What sort of force could make it fall? Had the Fomor broken their own perch? Why would they?

The night before, in the darkness of the cave, she had confessed to Edan that she had no idea what she would do when they reached Dentaltos. She had come north with the intention of learning the nature of the creatures that controlled the sea, and she had certainly done that! But her goal had transformed over the weeks she had spent with Edan. Now she was determined to stop the Fomor, but how? With the confrontation almost upon her, she had had no idea.

Edan had said that if the Fomor were like Spirits, then they could be placated, while if they were like Men, then they would have desires and reasons for acting as they did. Either way, all she had to do was learn what they wanted. Privately, she doubted it would be so easy. After all, the Daesani were men, and she had no idea what motivated them. Nevertheless, the idea had comforted her. She had gone to sleep planning what she might say and awoken with tentative words on her lips. She had practised the conversation in her mind as they had crossed the final stretch of headland, going over each part a dozen times. The one thing she had not considered was that there might be no Fomor to confront.

The base of the sea stack had been two or three hundred feet from the cliff's edge. Tara reckoned that if it still stood, its top would have been on a level with the clifftop, or even higher. When she craned forward, nervous of getting too close to the edge, she could see patches of green amongst the jumbled stones that might have come from a grass covered top. Everything matched her vision of the Fomor waiting on the sea-stack's top, except that it was no longer there. Could the rock have shattered in the great wave? The exposed faces of rock were raw enough. But if so, why? Could she have been wrong all along? Did the Fomor even exist?

Feeling suddenly dizzy she backed away from the edge, raising her eyes to the horizon. Great white shapes, as pale as the sky, lurked in the ocean. For a moment she took them for clouds, then realised that they were huge masses of ice, grey-white bergs drifting down from the north. There were dozens of them, more than she could count.

Sometimes in the winter the river by the Stone Forest froze. Transparent ice would creep in from the edges, spreading out from the snow-covered banks until the rushing waters vanished under it. In her first year at the Stones, when the winter had been very cold, the ice had met in the middle of the stream and hid the water entirely. Tara had marvelled at that ice, but what lay in the ocean before her was no winter creeping, gone with the summer sun, but the great ice of the earliest songs, creaking and booming as it jostled in the tide. She remembered Edan's story of Bal and his brothers, a tale drawn from a world of ice and snow. Were the Fomor bringing the ice as well as the sea? She imagined every corner of the Summer Lands drowned and buried, frozen beneath black water and featureless ice. Everything The People had ever done would be forgotten. The thought filled her with horror. Wasn't it enough that they would die? Must nothing remain of them? The thought was so terrible that she turned to run.

"There's something down there, at the edge of the water." Edan's voice brought her back to her senses. While she had been distracted, he had lain down at the edge of the cliff, full length on the grass and rocks, and was peering over the brink.

He looked back over his shoulder and beckoned her to join him.

Tara got down on her knees, shuffled closer, hesitated, and then lay down beside him, clutching at the rock as if it might come to life and pitch her over. Far below, past the backs of the wheeling gulls, she could make out a strip of shingle beach. Something lay at its edge, pale coloured, longer than wide, moving fitfully like a sleeping animal. After a moment she realised that it was the sea that was moving, nudging the object back and forth with each sluggish wave. She tried to estimate its size but could see nothing to measure it by.

"I can't tell what it is."

"We have to go down there," Edan said, "we need to see."

"Edan, I don't think we should." In her mind the sea was filled with a thousand Fomor; writhing, clawing, waiting for them to come too close. The world seemed to spin, and she grabbed at the ground to stop herself falling. She closed her eyes for a moment to fight the vertigo, but it just made the terror worse. It was all she could do to edge back, inch by inch, until the sea was safely out of view.

She took deep breaths, trying to force the fear away. "They could be down there, waiting."

"Let them." There was an unfamiliar edge of anger in Edan's voice. Edan sprung up from the edge and strode over to where he had placed his new-made spear, snatching it up from the ground. "I'm not afraid of them." For a moment she was almost afraid of him, but then his face softened into something more anguished. "It might be, it could be, a survivor."

A survivor? Impossible. No one could have survived that flood. But then they had both survived, why couldn't someone else? Another pulse of fear: what if it was one of the wolf-men? But what if it was one of Edan's family?

She made herself look back towards the edge, the sheer drop. "How exactly do we get down?"

* * *

There were no easy ways down to the edge of the sea, so they chose a hard one, a narrow gully at the head of an equally narrow chasm where the sea had split the solid rock in two. A cascade of wave fractured rocks tumbled to a narrow ribbon of pale white sand a hundred feet below.

113

Tara tested the first boulder carefully, making sure that it wasn't going to give way when she put her weight on it. Using the dry stone as a handhold, she let herself down gradually towards the next one, feeling the crunch of salt and sand under her feet. She grasped the rock beneath her with her toes, getting a solid hold, shifting the bundle strapped to her back so that it did not unbalance her, and put her full weight on the next stone down. When she felt secure, she helped Edan down to join her.

They descended the fissure in this fashion, squeezing together for space on each ledge in turn. Some of the rocks seemed freshly fallen, others were bedded in with earth as fine as sand and streaked with guano. Nesting seabirds thronged the cliffs to either side, squawking and flapping. The air was a confusion of them, circling up and down between nest and sea. When they got too close, the birds cascaded from their perches, diving at their heads and bombarding them with droppings.

Tara threw up her arm to ward off the assault of a diving gull, and instantly lost her balance, teetering on the edge of the ledge. She windmilled her arms, trying to grasp something solid or tip herself back against the rock, but she felt her feet slide towards the sea. In the same instant, Edan grabbed the rolled-up furs on her back and pulled her away from the edge, holding her close. She flung her arms around him, pressing them both against the rock until her heart stopped pounding in her ears. After that they went slowly, always with a hand on one another.

It was afternoon by the time they reached the bottom. Blue-grey shadows painted the depths of the fissure. Tara saw that the beach was not made of sand at all, but countless shells, each as white as the ice on the sea. They crunched underfoot. The gulls sped past, no longer interested in them now that they were away from their nests, and Tara saw that they were feasting on things cast up from the sea. She stooped to look at one, shooing the gulls away with a wave of her arms, but it was an unrecognisable shape, soft and silt covered.

Tide pools and narrow strips of wet stone formed a path at the base of the cliffs, on which they worked their way back around the coast towards the fallen tooth. The noise of the seagulls fell behind them, leaving only the soft slurp of the sea as it slid around their feet. The water, not as calm as it had seemed from above, lapped hungrily around the rocks they clambered over. Suddenly it swelled, surged up, spumed past them and slunk back, frosted with rings of foam.

Part of Tara hoped that when they finally rounded the last outcrop and came to the beach beside Dentaltos that the thing in the sea would be gone, carried away back wherever it had come from. Then there would be no chance of a Fomor trap, no chance of Edan being hurt again, because she felt a cold certainty that he was going to be hurt, whatever they found. But when they stepped onto the rubble strewn shingle the body was still there, abandoned by the receding water.

And it was most certainly a body. She could see one arm outstretched on the pebbles, a hint of sea-pale flesh, a wet sprawl of hair. Please let it be Forkbeard, she thought, his hair was dark. Or the hound-master, no one would be sad to see him dead. Or someone they had never seen before. 'The whole north must have felt that wave', she thought, surely someone might have died elsewhere and been carried here, it wasn't impossible. She begged for all these things but knew it would be otherwise.

Edan dropped his spear on the ground and ran forward, first eagerly, and then slow and hesitant. Tara watched him approach the body and then sink down by its side, gently moving the tangled hair away from its face. She could see from the slump of his shoulders that it was not a Daesani, not a stranger. Let it not be one of the girls at least, she thought, not Morna.

When she came closer, she could see that the dead man was Maccus. The hunter's body had been bashed and smashed amongst the rocks, but the sea had washed away the blood and left him looking almost peaceful. The water had robbed him of his headband and the bow he had always carried, leaving him oddly anonymous. Streaks of grey showed in his hair, as if he had aged in the days since his death, but they were only sand and dirt. Tara wondered if he had ever recovered consciousness after his fall into the river. Had he even been alive then? She preferred to think that he hadn't.

Edan lifted the body from the gravel, cradling its head in his arms. With one shaking hand he smoothed the hair around Maccus' face, making it neat. He had his back to her, hunched over, and she felt an urge to stroke his hair too, to wrap her own arms around him. She wanted to say something, to ease his pain. Instead, she was struck with a realisation, chilling in its clarity.

"This is their answer," she said. She was speaking to Edan's back, but she was sure that he heard her. "We came here to challenge them, to learn what they want, to find out if there was a way to make them stop. This is their answer."

"I won't leave him here."

Tara tried to imagine carrying a body back the way they had come. It couldn't be done, but it had to be. Edan was right, they couldn't leave Maccus to the Fomor.

Tara bent and took the body from Edan. The corpse was waterlogged, limp and heavy, but she lifted it without complaint, settling it over one shoulder like she would the carcass of a deer. The body ought to have stunk of rot, but instead it smelt of brine and ice, as if it had been carried to the distant bergs and back again.

Knowing that they could not scale the fissure with the body, they headed in the opposite direction, west towards the distant river. Edan strode ahead, back stiff, and Tara came behind. She wanted Edan to turn and speak to her, but she knew he was trying not to look at Maccus and she couldn't blame him for that.

The tide was at its ebb now. The cold green sea had drawn back, exposing an endless expanse of gravel that sapped the strength from every step, reducing them to a slow slog. Branches, broken and stripped white, were scattered along the tideline amongst heaps of uprooted kelp and hard black wrack that showed how high the sea would come if they could not outrun it. Even though they had seen the fallen pillar and found the washed-up body, Tara had the feeling that there was still more to come. The air was too still, the strange clouds too unmoving. She could feel the gaze of the Fomor on her like an oppressive weight. The sea was always in the corner of her vision, ready to disgorge Bal or his creatures. The longer that nothing further happened, the more terrified she felt. She had seen the Fomor in her visions, had they seen her too? What were they planning?

The trek seemed endless, unbearable. She wanted to turn back and scream at the sea, 'come out and face me!' She wanted to drop the body and run back for the fissure. When they were forced to abandon a possible route up and go back to the beach she wanted to lie down and hide, but instead she took a new grip on her burden and started forward again.

The corpse slung across her shoulder writhed, swelled, and split, coming apart like an overripe fruit. Stinking ichor flooded down her body, and then came tentacles, black, sucker-mouthed and claw tipped, spilling out of the hollow body and wrapping her in a death grip.

Tara staggered, gasped, stumbled out of the hallucination, losing her footing for a moment on the skittering pebbles and nearly dropping Maccus' body. Her first instinct was to hurl it aside and run, but there were no tentacles, no ooze. Not a true vision, she told herself, just exhaustion and fear.

With a start she realised that most of the day had slipped by. The sea had slunk back across the open flats, slyly extending feelers of water. Now it was snapping at their heels, encircling them like a wolf pack, swallowing whole sections of gravel with every surge. She was convinced that the Fomor were just going to watch them drown.

But escape came, in the form of an irregular slope that switch-backed its way up through sloping beds of rock and gale scoured pitches of grass. They scrambled their way up it in the evening light, now shouldering the body alone, now carrying it between them, finally reaching the top as dusk fell.

They laid Maccus on the flat stones at the back of the headland and flopped down exhausted a little distance away. To the south, the valley of the cave had already vanished into darkness. The setting sun was a lidded bead of fire in the west. Tara knew that she couldn't carry the body any further that day, but it didn't matter. They were safe now. The night softened the fear of the Fomor's realm into something more bearable, and they talked instead of the burial of the dead.

Amongst The People it was the custom to place the dead in pits, knees bent to the chest, arms wrapped around them and heads bowed, as a baby was cradled inside its mother before birth. Sometimes the scattered families brought their dead to the Stone Forest, making the long trek, so that their loved ones could lie amongst their ancestors. Old Ama would spread marigold blossoms over the bodies if it was summer. More often the dead came in the winter and they would place holly leaves or pine cones into the grave.

Edan told her that the tribe had also buried its dead, though he was less clear on the details. When his parents had died there had been no bodies to bury, and so he tried to recall for her the death of an old woman whose name he could hardly remember. He thought that she had been laid on her side, and he remembered the Elder placing handfuls of boar teeth into the grave, scattering them like snow. Since they could not return Maccus to his own land, it seemed appropriate to them both that they might bury him amongst the remains in front of the cave, where the dead already lay.

As Edan spoke, Tara began to relax, her heart no longer thumping quite so hard, the fear fading. The day had passed, they had gone to the very edge of the world and come away again without any sign of the Fomor. Maybe her visions had misled her. Maybe the Fomor had simply never been there. Her earlier fears began to seem foolish. She had worked herself up over the course of months, ever since she had left the stones, tying together a half-remembered childhood dream with the black sun of her latest vision and then spinning a story out of it. Perhaps the Elder had been right, and the Fomor were just a nightmare of the wolf-men and nothing more.

Then the clouds parted, and the red moon rose.

Tatters of cloud spun away like leaves on water, fleeing from the moon. The disk was huge, close to the horizon, moving fast enough that they could see it rise. The moon was red, shading to orange, like it had been dipped in blood or set on fire. It was the second light of Tara's vision, the harbinger of the Black Sun.

Now she knew real terror. She had no doubt that the blood moon was the Fomor's sign, a brand placed on the sky, the war banner of the coming flood. She thought of Bal's eyes, one red and one white. It was him! Staring down at them!

She ran, wailing in terror, but the eye of Bal followed. Edan grabbed her hand, and together they bolted, seeking some sort of cover, some shelter, to escape the awful sight. She skidded on slick grass and loose stone, then careened down the steep slope that had taken them half the morning to climb, dragging Edan behind her. Above them, the moon blazed, soared, slipped into cloud, lost its sheen of blood. Tara ran on regardless, not stopping until they were huddled in the cave — where the sky was hidden, and the moonlight could not reach them.

Wracking sobs shook her. She couldn't breathe, couldn't think. All the horrors of the day came crashing down at once, overwhelming her. From a great distance, she heard Edan's voice trying to comfort her, but the words meant nothing. He put his arms around her, telling her that everything was all right, that the crying could stop, but she couldn't stop. She grabbed him back, holding on as tight as she had in the river, to keep herself above the flood tide.

Tara felt his hands on her arms, and then suddenly she was reaching under his seal-fur coat, feeling blood warm skin, the curve of muscle, the quiver of breath, while he in turn was reaching for her. Their bodies met in the darkness, then their lips, hot and salt-wet and banishing all other thoughts, so that for a little while they found the comfort they were seeking.

15. Edan

Edan dozed, feeling warmth on his back and warmth on his front. His mind painted a familiar picture behind his closed eyes, the big room of the Winter Home, with the heat of the banked fire at his back and the crowded bodies of his kin on the other side.

The walls of the Winter Home were made from stout wattles, woven between upright pillars of wood, and daubed with clay. Countless generations' worth of wood smoke had stained them black and dried them out, so that the hair mixed with the clay poked out in tufts. Edan's place was near the fire at the centre of the hut. The elders had the luxury of little bays by the walls, separated from each other by the large pillars that supported the roof, while the children huddled together on the floor.

Edan felt someone standing over him, and knew that it was First Hunter, awake earlier than all the rest as always. He knew that he should get up, dress, go hunting, but for some reason he didn't want to open his eyes.

"Edan." First Hunter's voice was as soft as the pre-dawn light, and strangely hollow. Of course, that was it, First Hunter was dead — drowned by Phelan and the Fomor. It was only the ghost of Maccus that was speaking to him.

Edan tried to block out the voice, scrunching his eyes closed, but it went on, rising and falling like the tide, whispering of the ocean and the ice. 'Maccus', he thought, 'what happened to you?'

Although he had not spoken the words out loud, the voice responded. "I have been to the lands of the Fomor, where all is ice beneath the sea, and come back with a message."

What message?

"Edan, be careful," the voice came again, "beware the stranger. The Fomor will walk the land before the drowning."

Edan thought of monsters dragged from the bottom of the sea, stalking the Summer Lands, but again the dead man answered his thought. "They have taken human form. They are us now, we are them."

As men!

"Oh Edan," a human note of anguish came into the ghost's hollow voice for the first time, "I have seen the Black Sun! You must run, deer-fast, lynx-silent. Run for the hills, for the forest, they are coming ..."

The voice faded, and with it the sense of presence; the familiar smell of wood smoke; the creak of the wooden walls and softness of the earth floor. Edan realised that he was not in the Winter Home at all, but in the cave on the headland. The warmth behind him was the sun, angling in through the cave mouth, and the warmth in front was Tara, nestled close.

Edan blinked his eyes open, and the dream of Maccus faded into the sunlight and shade of mid-morning. He focussed instead on the bare shoulder a few inches from his nose. The pale skin was dappled with freckles, and it rose and fell by the slightest of margins as Tara breathed. A curl of red hair trailed across the exposed part of her back, ending in a little spiral. Tentatively, he reached up one hand and stroked her shoulder with his fingertips and was surprised to feel the roughness of tiny scratches. Her skin was criss-crossed with them. He wondered how many of them had come from the past weeks, how many from saving him? She healed fast. The gross wounds were gone, but the scars remained. Curious, he ran his finger along the length of Tara's arm, brushing the invisible marks. She shifted slightly, pressing more firmly against him, but did not wake.

Edan remembered the night before and blushed. Of course, he was familiar with the ways of Mothers and Fathers. More than once he had caught a glimpse of what went on under the furs but doing was quite different from seeing! And it was more different than that, he was a man, and she was a Troll; they would not become Mothers or Fathers from this union!

Tara stirred beside him and rolled over, looking up at him. She yawned and then smiled. "So soon? Ready for more?" Edan felt the blood rush somewhere other than his face. Boldly he lent down and kissed her, feeling her hands on his shoulders. He started to move forward, but to his consternation she pushed him back. "Something is wrong, I see it. What is it?"

A sudden echo of Maccus' dry voice cooled his ardour, but he tried to put it aside. "It was just a dream."

She brushed the hair back from his face, but she also sat up and away from him. "A dream of what?"

He put his hand on her leg again, but she was focussed on the dream now and he knew he would have to talk about it.

"Maccus. He spoke to me." Mentioning the dream brought back a frisson of fear, but he pushed on, doing his best to describe it, unconsciously shaping the troll signs as he spoke.

"A strange warning. Worrying. As for Maccus ..." she looked out of the cave towards the sunlit hillside, "we have to bury him."

* * *

They laid Maccus to rest at the bottom of the slope, in the shadow of one of the grass-covered mounds. They dug a shallow pit in the sandy soil and lined it with white shells, before placing Maccus on his site, in the tribe's fashion.

He looked small, to Edan's eyes, diminished by death. It was hard to imagine the First Hunter squeezed into a simple hole in the ground. The sight roused the anger that the previous night had dampened. Maccus was no longer the Hunter, but he deserved better.

They had no boar's teeth to scatter over him, or marigold blossoms, or any of the other things that they had talked of; so they placed a little of their food in the grave instead, along with a scrap of woven grass as a blanket, and a stone blade, in case the Fomor should disturb the sleeping spirit. Edan had gone through the few things that the sea had left to Maccus, the sharp flint knife, the water soaked tinder, but all Edan took from him were the charms from his neck: the Hunter, the Owl Maiden, and the Father's charm.

"What are they?" Tara asked. "They are not the same as the ones you wear."

The question surprised him. The charms were so much a part of the tribe — had been so much a part of the tribe — that he had never considered that they might be a mystery. Of course, he knew that Tara had no charms, but at some point, he had just assumed that the Daesani had taken them from her.

"The charms ... They are our stories, I suppose." They were sitting near one another at the entrance to the cave in the evening sun. He held up the Owl Maiden's charm, a piece of wood so burnished by age that it was as smooth as a sea pebble. He showed her how it had been carved to show an Owl's eyes above a human mouth, with both hands and wings suggested below. "Each one represents a story, or a person in a story, a piece of the tribe's wisdom. The charm carries the tales. When we take a charm, we learn its tales, to guide us in Tradition.

Sometimes there are many charms for the same story, like the Mother's charm, that a Mother gives to her child, or the Maiden, that a girl has before she becomes a Mother. Others are, were, given to a person because of the things they did, like the Hunter's charm, or the Fishing charm. Do you not have such things?"

"We have tales, but we do not have charms. The People do not make images of things as you do, only simple signs, the sun, the moon, the animals we hunt." Tara picked up the Owl Maiden and held it. It looked so small in her hand. "What is this one?"

"The Owl Maiden. That is a lover's tale."

"Tell it to me."

"It's not my tale," he protested. The telling of the tale came with the gift of the charm. You practiced until you got it right. But still ... He took the charm back from Tara and turned it in his hand. The fragile wood seemed to hold the weight of all the generations of tale tellers who had come before. If he did not tell the tales now, who would?

"So ... well, once there was an Owl Maiden." Edan stopped in frustration, that wasn't how it started.

He began again, growing in confidence as the tale came back to him. "As everyone knows, when a woman is too long without a man, an Owl may help them find one. So, it was with a woman of the tribe. She had seen all the other girls grow up alongside her and become Mothers, but still she had no man of her own, and there were none left in the place to choose.

So, the woman went into the woods when the moon was full and called for an Owl, too-too, too-hoo. Now, as it happens, the only Owl to hear was the Owl Maiden, who had no experience in finding love. Still, she flew down into a tree and looked down on the woman in the moonlight and asked her what she wanted.

'I am growing old, and have no man for my bed, nor a child in my arms', said the woman. 'Please help me to find a mate for my elder days'.

Now, the woman told the Owl Maiden that there were no men left in the tribe for her to court, so the Owl Maiden went seeking through the night, two days, and three days, and two days more. Then by a river bank she found a fisherman who was not of the tribe. She watched the man from the treetops, seeing that he had no woman to share his furs, nor any other family of his own. She watched him cut the trees with an axe of polished stone and pluck the trout from the water with his hands.

The Owl Maiden knew that she should fly back to the woman and tell her that she had found a man for her, but when she looked at the man, she loved him for herself. Each day she told herself that she would fly away when evening came, but each night she perched in the tree above his camp and watched him sleep. Eventually the man noticed that the owl was watching him. 'What do you want, owl?' he said. 'Is there some woman looking for a man? If so, send her to me.'

This was too much for the Owl Maiden. That very night she came down out of the tree and took a woman's form and went to the man's camp. 'I am a woman looking for a man,' she said, 'and the owl sent me' which was not quite a lie. Now, the man liked the look of the beautiful woman with her great bright eyes and downy hair very much, and he took her in to his camp and lay with her.

When the morning came, the man woke next to the Owl Maiden, who was still sleeping. As he looked at her, he saw that her hair really was downy feathers, and that her ears stuck up from amongst them. He realised at once that she was the owl, and not a woman at all, but he did not care. And so, the man and the Owl Maiden lived together, while the unhappy woman went without." Edan laughed self-consciously. "It is a silly story."

Tara grinned. "I liked it. I suppose the lesson is, get your own mate."

Edan laughed. "I suppose it is."

"Well, you did that." She said, and he blushed again. She pointed at the next charm, the Father's charm, and asked, "What about this one?"

"The Father's charm," Edan said, but the charm made him think of Brina, and Morna, and Second Mother's unnamed baby, and he did not want to think of those things.

After the burial, the traces of the ancient People no longer seemed unwelcoming, as if by placing Maccus there they had made it into a kind of home, and the following days were warm and pleasant. By unspoken agreement they stayed away from the sea, but the sound of it followed them, booming and crashing, whispering and hissing, rasping at the cliffs behind them.

Edan could not help but sneak a glance or two at it. He found that the land beyond the river was utterly changed. What had once been the Summer Hunting Grounds were gone. The red sands had become sea, and what was left of the land was now the edge of the Fomor's realm. It was no longer a place for living people, and they concentrated instead on the land on their side of the river, gathering reeds from the marsh and wood from the forest.

The weather was fine and clear, caressed by a warm wind that breezed steadily from the south. There was a life to be made here, and Edan allowed himself to dream of living it — just the two of them. Would it be so bad to turn their backs on the violence and madness? Let someone else fight the Fomor, if they had to be fought. So, what if there was only a little wood? Or if they didn't dare to visit the shore? The Eshu-kind had made a home here once and left them a cave for shelter. They could do the same. There was water in the mere and reeds to eat, fish to catch. He could make traps to catch the little trout that lurked beneath the brown waters and smoke them by the fire.

Thinking this way, Edan trekked back to the spinney and pulled down the remains of their makeshift shelter, heaving and hauling the branches back up the slope to the cave in a trail of shed leaves and snapped twigs. Now that they were no longer wandering blind, he found that the wood and the cave were closer than it had seemed on the first day. It was possible to go back and forth twice in a day, and so he moved all the bundles of hurdles and withies, heaping them up outside the cave to rebuild them. In the afternoon he hammered the poles into the ground with a rock and re-wove the wattles, creating a windbreak across half the cave mouth.

Inside, he piled loose armfuls of heather together to make a soft mattress for their bed-skins.

When Tara returned from gathering reeds, she looked at his efforts and raised an eyebrow, but said nothing. Edan hoped that meant that she was happy to stay here as well, but he was reluctant to ask her. She seemed happy enough to sleep in the shelter that night, and happy enough for him to sleep beside her, which was all that really mattered.

The next day, he returned to the spinney and cut a length of straight ash wood as high as his waist. He stripped it of its bark, peeling back the long strips and setting them aside, before placing it in the back of the cave to cure. From this wood, he planned to craft a bow. With a bow he could perhaps kill a deer in the forests at the bottom of the headland or take down one of the great white gulls that hung almost motionless in the winds above the sea cliffs. While Tara was busy gathering reeds from the mere and herbs from the wood he hunted through the heap of bones in the cave until he found a length of deer bone. He smashed it with a rock and picked through the fragments until he had a handful that were suitable for arrowheads.

Outside, where the constant breeze could carry away the dust, he sharpened the fragments on a large flat stone, grinding the rough surfaces smooth and the points keen. Using a sharp edge of rock, he cut indents for binding, and serrations at the tip, as Maccus had taught him. In a month, perhaps, the wood would be ready, and he could shave it down into a bow stave. All he had for a bowstring was rabbit sinew, which would mean a lot of splicing, but he had time to collect it.

Edan knew, in a detached sort of way, that there were important things he was ignoring. The anger that lurked in his hind-brain, the fear that should have come from Maccus' warning, but he had cocooned himself like caddis fly, ignoring everything beyond his little world of cave and mere and spinney. If the Fomor were truly walking the lands of men, then sure there would be a peaceful time, a no-flood time. Danger and fear could come later. 'Who is to say that there won't be seasons,' he told himself, 'or years even, before the Black Sun?' It might not even happen in his lifetime.

That evening, excited, he told Tara what he had been thinking. "After all," he said, "the sea has been rising for a long time, hasn't it. The Elder told us that the Hunting Grounds were larger when he was young, larger still in his father's day. Perhaps there are generations more to come before the end." To his confusion he realised that he sounded plaintive, small, afraid.

"Oh Edan, we can't stay in this place," Tara said.

"We can! Your People managed it once. I can dig a pit here, line it with stone and clay, and we can use it to store water. Once I have a bow, we can hunt down in the valley."

Tara came and sat beside him. She picked up a handful of bark shavings, coiled them in her hand, and then let them fall again. "You know that's not what I mean Edan. The Fomor haven't gone away. You saw what happened as well as I did. The fallen pillar, the body, the blood moon. They might as well have shouted a challenge in our faces."

He didn't want to see it. "But what are we supposed to do about it?"

Tara hung her head. "I wish I knew. Before, on the way here, everything was so clear. The visions guided me every step. Those last few days they were so strong they wouldn't let me sleep. But since then, nothing."

Edan stammered, "Your gift. It isn't ... We didn't ..."

Tara laughed and reached out to touch his cheek with a finger. "Silly. The gift doesn't care about things like that. Girl or Woman; Daughter, Sister, Lover, Mother, it is all the same.

But sometimes the visions come easily, and sometimes it is hard. At the Stone Forest, where the Seers live, we can sometimes call them up, if we do the right things."

"Well," Edan knew she wouldn't be happy just to hide, "can't we do those things here?"

Tara looked up in surprise. "I ... maybe." She toyed with a strip of bark, curling it around her fingers as she mused out loud. "We make a fire, from certain woods, flowers, then breathe the smoke. The smoke helps bring the visions, but there are songs too, chanting. It takes days and many People. We can't do it that way. But old Ama told me of riskier ways, other smokes." She tugged on one end of the bark, pulling it taut. "It is dangerous though. Breathe too much and it can hurt you."

Edan was afraid that a vision would drag him away from the little place, back into the fear and the anger and all the other things he didn't want to face — but he could see that Tara needed this as badly as he feared it.

"Let's do it."

* * *

They started the next day. They had no hut or shelter to keep the smoke in, so they planned to light the fire in the cave mouth instead. Edan wove a little basket from the bark strips — a skill that First Mother had taught him long ago — and they set about filling it with pinecones from the wood. They grubbed about in every corner, teasing the empty cones out of the peaty soil until the basket was full. Pine cones would make a hot fire, but a brief one, a blaze to release the secret smoke from the herbs Tara was seeking.

"In the Stone Forest the oldest of the Seers, Ama, makes the Spirit Smoke for us." Tara had her hands full of pine cones and had to speak without gestures, enunciating every word with exaggerated care. It made it sound like she was delivering a lecture. "I learnt the recipe years ago. There are plants touched by the Spirits, that bring visions. It has hemp in it, and sweetflower, and belios leaves."

Edan didn't recognise the name belios but recognised what the tribe had called sun's flower, when she described it. "I was always taught that sun's flower was a poison," he told her, "we were told to stay clear of it."

"It is. Quite dangerous."

"But we are looking for it?"

"No. There is no belios here, or sweetflower, or hemp."

"Then what?"

"Another plant, and more dangerous — Ah!" she dropped the pine cones and pointed. "This! The Spirits are smiling on me!"

Edan looked at the plant she had spotted, a spike of purple flowers, hood-shaped and stacked like flattened cakes, bright in the shadows of the wood. He answered in a half-whisper. "That? I know it too. Troll's cap, we call it. One touch, the Elder said, could kill a man."

"Troll's cap?" Tara quirked an eyebrow, and Edan felt himself redden. "Well, the Elder was right. It is touched by bad spirits; very dangerous. But they are powerful spirits too. I hope Ama taught me the right way of it." Tara took some large fresh leaves and used them to protect her hand as she carefully plucked a few of the flowers, holding them well out

128

in front of her as she dropped them into an empty leather pouch.

On the way back to the cave, carrying the basket of pine cones and an armful of deadwood, Edan kept eyeing the pouch, irrationally afraid that it might come alive and attack him. It was a little thing of deer-leather and feather-shaft beads that Brina had made, but it was hard to see it as beautiful when it contained poison. He wondered if he could persuade Tara to forget the whole thing. Probably not.

They gave the pine cones and the deadwood a day to dry, spreading them out on the rocks in front of the cave while the sun still shone. Edan gathered more heather for tinder, and spent an afternoon arranging rocks into a circle to hold the fire. He knew that he was wasting time. He should be stockpiling food, making tools, preparing to leave. But then, maybe the vision would tell them to stay.

That evening the stars were bright in a black sky, flocking in the shelter of a sliver moon. Edan watched the moon as he set the fire, daring it to turn red again, but it remained as white as ever. Tara had prepared for the ritual with great care, insisting that neither of them ate after their morning meal. As the dusk crept in, she began to chant, a low and hypnotic refrain without words that rose and fell like the sluggish motion of the sea.

Edan worked the fire-drill until his tinder caught light, cupping it in his hands and blowing on it until flame bloomed. When he transferred it to the pine cones, they blazed up fiercely, filling the air with their sharp scent. Quickly he piled wood onto the fire, and then more cones. Flames shot up, flickering in the darkness of the cave, and he felt a blast of heat on his face. Smoke swirled out into the night, shot through with sparks.

Tara knelt by the fire, still singing. She passed a hand through the smoke, back and forth, and then took up the little piece of bark in which she had placed the purple flowers. She held it for a moment in front of her, and then cast them into the flames with a quick movement.

Edan half expected purple flames, or brightly coloured smoke, but nothing seemed to change. Had the ritual failed? Tara's chant continued to rise and fall just the same as before, as she leant forwards towards the fire, breathing in the smoke. Curls of smoke wound around her hair, like tiny snakes. Her hair was curling too, rippling in the firelight and then blazing up with its own fire. Fire-head woman, he thought.

The sparks of light separated from Tara's hair, swirling up into the sky, from which the stars were gently falling. They wove together and fell on him like rain. Edan felt a strange tingling in his hands and feet — the stars were getting under his skin. He felt invigorated and numb at the same time, his heart drumming in his chest.

Shouting came from outside, and shadows danced across the wall, angular, jerking, crashing into one another and juddering free. Edan crawled to the cave mouth and saw that the hillside was covered in struggling figures, frenzied, grappling, stabbing with their spears. Blood flew in arcs, red as fire, from bodies pierced by the sharp points of bone, slashed by claws, crushed in fists, grasped between teeth of ice and bone. Endless ranks of people, more people than he could imagine, surrounded the battle, waiting for their turn to fight. They filled the hillside beneath the whirling stars and beyond. Surely it was every man and woman that lived.

Something hurtled from the darkness. A sharp spear impaled him through the chest. He grasped the wooden shaft dumbly as if he could pluck it out, but the spear would not move. The blood flowed out from him in an ever-growing stream, filling the cave. For some reason the blood was ice cold and ocean black. His bloodless body grew numb and heavy, until even breathing was beyond him. The shadows crept forward, crook-backed and jagged, with mirror eyes as round and blank as the moon above mouths filled with transparent fangs.

He tried to pull away, to cry out for help, but the spear pinned him to the ground. His breath was stopped up. He could not move. Only the rage moved, beating at the inside of his skull. He wanted to strike out his killers, to punish them. But all he could do was struggle like a fish caught in the jaws of a spear, filled with impotent anger.

Then the fire blazed up, flooding the cave with blood-red light, and he saw that the creature that held the spear was not a Fomor at all, fish-faced and scale covered, but Phelan, grinning under his wolf's head crown as he struck the death blow.

130

16. Tara

Tara took deep breaths from the fire, filling her lungs with smoke and chanting it out again, shaping the words that unlocked the visions. The smoke was thick, bitter and choking, but the discipline of years kept her breathing steady. A sense of dislocation came over her, familiar, yet different from that produced by the secret smoke of the Stone Forest. It came quickly, light headedly; dropping the solid world of the cave away as her attention focussed on the star-filled sky instead.

The stars began to move, swirling around a central point like a flock of starlings around a tree. Next, they began to fall, first one, two, and then more and more, until they cascaded down like rain. She stepped into the air, leaving her solid body behind, and soared free, swooping through the points of light until they began to warp and merge behind her.

Coming together the stars formed figures, ranked in shadow on the edge of a precipitous drop. A field of shimmering light spread out behind them, a hillside of cobwebs and dewdrops, while in front of them there was only darkness. Within the darkness the sea heaved up sick green phosphorescence, forming a second array of figures opposing the first. Not orderly, this second mass, but chaotic, jostling, jumbled and twisting, surging and receding. She tried to focus on them, make sense of them, but they shattered into geometry under her gaze; squares and triangles that danced and would not stay still.

She saw that there were two races here. One that would surge in like the tide, and one who stood to oppose them. Weathered, ancient, these second ones, like a line of stone set to hold back the wind. The dark figures had no features, no faces, but she knew them for The People, come together one last time at the edge of the world.

Tara's heart ached for them. This was The People's final stand. They would make war as only they could. Her sorrow and pride became birds, one white, and one dark, that soared away into the night. Below her the two sides crashed together like waves. Churned. Intermingled. Who won and who lost? She could not tell.

The sounds of battle filled the air. Men and women dying, screaming, choking, coughing and gasping in the smoke that swirled from sweating bodies and hot blood. Something stirred at the edge of her awareness. There should be no smoke here. Even as the thought crossed her mind the smoke swirled thicker, became chains, dragged her down. The sound of choking was louder now, close by, real. Edan!

Tara became aware that she was lying on her back in the cave. She tried to lift her arm, but it was heavy; sluggish as if rocks had been piled on it. Her heart was drumming like thunder in her chest. The coughing came again, weaker this time, off to one side. She could just make out Edan, lying half in and half out of the cave, his body shaking as he struggled to breathe.

She forced herself to her knees, then her feet, blundering against the stone. Somehow, she got her arms around Edan and hauled him out. She slipped and dragged them both down the dew-damp slope until they were free of the smoke. When she let him drop, he coughed, gasped, and rolled over weakly, vomiting on the grass. Her own limbs were tingling and numb, but she forced him to sit up and rest his back against one of the mounds of shells.

"Edan. Take deep breaths, the smoke is still in you. Let the vision go."

He couldn't speak, but he nodded weakly, and the coughing seemed to fade in intensity, so she let herself rest beside him. She leant back, feeling the shells shift under her weight, and looked up at the stars, which had returned to their proper places. The night was cold and clear, and she felt the chill slowly return the feeling to her limbs.

"I saw ..." Edan's voice was cut off by another ragged cough, "I saw people fighting, dying." He rubbed at his chest as if it pained him. "Phelan was there."

Tara frowned. There had been no place for Phelan in her vision. "Are you sure it was him? I saw The People and the Fomor fighting, not the wolf-men."

"Maybe we saw what we wanted to see? Or what we didn't."

"No." Tara was sure that the vision had been a true one. Edan was not, could not be, a Seer. The gift of vision only came to girl children. She shouldn't put any trust in what he thought he'd seen. But what did she know of humans? Maybe amongst them it was the men that had the Sight. He had been touched by the Spirits just as she had. He had seen the Fomor in the waves, and the ghosts in the mounds. But then, why had his vision differed from hers? She tried to think of answers, but her mind was as sluggish as her body.

Edan supplied his own explanation. "Perhaps we saw the same thing."

Tara looked up, surprised, as Edan continued. "Maccus. In the dream he told me that the Fomor had a human shape. You say your People will go to fight the Fomor. I saw the Daesani fighting. Maybe they are the Fomor, in human shape." There was a note of relish in Edan's voice as he accused the Daesani that sent a chill up her spine.

"Or maybe the wolf-men will fight with us?" Tara was too tired to argue clearly, said the first thing that came to her, then wondered why she had said it.

There was a long silence before Edan said, "So, your People will come here? If we wait?"

Despite the cold wind blustering down across the headland, Tara found that she had drifted into sleep, and that Edan's question had woken her. She understood why Ama had warned against using Troll's Cap. If they stayed out here through the night, they might die of it.

"No. No, I don't think so."

"Then what must we do?" Tara was already pushing herself to her feet as Edan asked the question. "We need to get up and light a fire."

By will alone, it seemed, they forced themselves back to the cave, and the embers of the poisoned fire. Tara went first, holding her breath, and kicked the ashes out into the darkness. Only when she was sure that all the smoke was gone did she allow Edan to light a new fire, to drive the chill of the night from them.

She lay down gratefully on the bed of heather, letting tiredness overtake her; snuggling against Edan when he stretched out beside her.

"You didn't answer my question."

She yawned, sleepy. "What question?"

"If your People will not come here, what do we do?"

"We must go there. We must go to the Stone Forest and make them."

* * *

133

They headed south into high summer, following the trickling waters of the Legu until they vanished into a vast inland mere. They had stayed at the cave as long as Tara could bear, which was too long for her comfort, and probably not enough to prepare for the trip they would have to make. She would happily have set out the very next morning, leaving the unbearable sense of the Fomor's presence behind her. She was practically out of the camp and on her way before Edan could talk her back, pointing out that they had weeks of travel to get ready for.

By unspoken agreement they kept to the south side of the headland, away from the ocean. They knew that if they returned to the base of the cliffs they might find all that they needed: sea grass for weaving, beach pebbles for hammer stones, flint nodules for working, whelks and mussels, fish and seaweed, but going back was out of the question. Neither wanted to risk that realm of sly waves and tainted deaths a second time. Instead, they filled their bark baskets with gull's eggs and rabbit meat, garlic leaves and reed hearts. It was a meagre harvest that would not keep.

In the late afternoons, when their gathering was done, they had tried to argue out a route that would avoid the lands of the Daesani; difficult because neither of them were sure exactly where they lay. Edan told her that Phelan had once mentioned a place called Tanrid, some camp of the Daesani that might lie in their way. In the hope of avoiding it they decided to go east, into lands that neither of them had ever seen.

Edan had crafted himself a bow, complaining that the wood was still too green, but sure that he could catch them a deer as soon as they came down off the headland. They found little to hunt however, and barely more to forage. Spring was done, and the summer was barren. They crossed plains of tufted grass, knee-high and dry brown, where deer or aurochs should have roamed, but the landscape was as empty of big game as it was of people, human or troll. Once they came across the remains of a hunting camp, but the place was long abandoned. Only a few bent hurdles showed where the shelters had stood, and the fire stones had been deliberately scattered, marking the place as dead. Cautiously they picked through the remains, in the hope that something useful might have been left behind, but all they could find were a few flakes of flint and a blackened scallop shell. They offered an apology to whatever ghosts might remain and took them anyway.

Even the skies over the plains were empty, save for persistent swarms of flies that dogged them across the grasslands as keenly as Phelan's hounds. When their course led through silent woods of birch and alder, they scoured the ground for traces of deer and the trees for squirrels, but all they found was a pack of boars that they did not dare to face alone.

Instead, they had to depend on the fish that Edan managed to pluck from the little west-flowing streams and the sun-drained marshes that they flowed from, along with whatever wilted greens they could find along the way. It was not enough, and day by day Tara felt the hunger growing in her belly. The Seers had kept to the ancient ways of The People, preferring meat to plants, but they often went without, depending on the generosity of the few of their kin that visited the stones to keep them going. Tara had thought that she was used to lean times, but the constant hunger gnawed at both of them and left them thin.

Now and again a faint tremble passed through the ground beneath them, sending them scrambling away from water in fear, but no waves came crashing down on them, and no Fomor rose from the meres to catch them. Tara knew it would not last. She had seen the crescent sun and the blood moon; the black sun was still to come.

The thought was almost intolerable, but it was not her burden alone. Edan had seen everything that she had seen. When night came, she lay beside him talking, and learnt that he too had glimpsed the Black Sun, burning in the waters' depths, in his dreams. They tried to guess what it might mean, other than a sign of the Fomor's coming. Was it a symbol of Bal's plucked out eye? Was it something that they could fight? Edan tried to paint a picture of brave warriors casting their spears at the sun, at the moon, drawing on tales that he had been told by some old woman, but they were children's fantasies. Tara could see that Edan knew nothing of war.

"But can't your people survive any injury?" Edan asked her. "In the tales a Troll can grow back an arm, or a leg, or even a head." He trailed off, apparently aware how foolish he sounded.

135

They had taken shelter from a rain burst, huddling together under an uprooted pine which had fallen against its neighbours to form a sort of natural arch. They shared the space with a single bedraggled crow, sheltering itself from the drumming raindrops while watching them suspiciously.

"What else do your tales say about us?" Tara asked, brushing damp hair away from her face.

"Well, all sorts. They say that Trolls grow as big as bears, or mountains. That they are strong enough to catch a boar with their bare hands. That their skin can turn aside a spear thrust." He laughed. "Like I said, lots of things. They aren't true then? Any of them?"

She smiled at the hopeful tone in his voice. "No, I am afraid not."

He sighed "I was hoping that maybe your warriors were a little more like that. But I guess they were just things old Ulat told us children to keep us amused."

A big drop of water snuck round one of the branches above and splashed down on Tara's face, and she pressed herself more firmly against him, trying to avoid the next drop. "We do have our own tales, not so different. Tales of the past."

"The People, we are not what we were. If the tales are true. Once maybe we were like your stories said, and we changed."

It felt strange — to talk aloud about The People's long decline. It was a known thing, but not a spoken one. As each year turned, fewer of The People came to call back the sun on the longest night. Fewer still than Ama recalled from her distant youth. The empty ruins at Dentaltos had only confirmed what she already knew — The People were dying out. She talked of fighting to protect their land, their way of life, but what was there, truly, to save? The People had no taboos to prevent them going west or east to escape the floods, and they had lost the Summer Lands to the humans long ago. What would make them go to Dentaltos? She only had bad answers — they would not go hoping to save themselves, but because they would already believe themselves to be past saving.

"Changed, how?"

Tara shook herself free of her black thoughts. "It is hard to say. The tales talk of a time when we were the only ones in this land. But that was long ago. In the ice time, the cold time, the great beast time. It was so long ago that there are hardly any tales left, only the one really, the story of how we lost our land and became less.

Maybe we were mightier then? I do not know. I do know that there were beasts, larger than the biggest auroch or elk, and that my ancestors killed them and made their homes from their bones, so perhaps they were larger too. Perhaps they grew as big as bears and wrestled boars with their bare hands." She sighed, suddenly sad. "If they were, it was not enough. The People are all but gone now."

They travelled on in this fashion while the moon grew from dark to full, then waned to dark again. A little before dawn a few days later, when a sliver of moon lit a clear sky shading to morning, Edan finally found deer tracks. They had set camp by a muddy pool, and the tracks were still fresh in the soft ground, leading from the bank into the scattered fringe of a birch wood. Tara watched as Edan strung his bow and went after it, arrows in hand. She followed behind him, but not too close, she was well aware that she had no gift for stealth.

Edan vanished like a ghost amongst the silver trunks, leaving her alone in the gloom. Somewhere in the woods a few birds began to greet the dawn. Wan light spilled through the screen of trees in tenuous bands. The woods proved little more than a few trees deep, thick with bushes. From somewhere nearby Tara heard the soft tock of an arrow, then a whoop of excitement, followed by a crashing in the undergrowth. A moment later Edan emerged, lithe and quick, but empty-handed.

"What happened?"

Edan held the bow up ruefully. "The wood split. But I wounded it with the first arrow." He pointed towards a scrub covered rise. "That way, help me find it."

They headed up the slope, keeping parallel courses as they searched. Edan vanished again amongst the broom, his eyes on the ground. Tara scanned the horizon instead and saw that the rise ended in a drop, a cliff side edged in thick bushes against which the deer might be trapped.

Doing her best to be stealthy, she moved to the edge, keeping low and moving slowly. The wind was blowing in her face, carrying the smell of peat and water, and the sound of voices! For an impossible moment she thought they were tribe voices, but the language was guttural, unfamiliar, neither tribe nor Daesani.

She made herself even lower, creeping forward through the broom, keeping a slight screen of branches in front of her as she peered over the edge. Way down below, an arc of open water lapped at the base of the cliff, spreading along the edge of a vast lake-like bog of standing water and trailing weed.

A group of men stood at the channel's edge. Tara counted five. One was younger than the rest, and naked, daubed in white clay and red mud. The other four had capes of black feathers slung around their shoulders and draped over their heads so that she could not see their faces. The young man stood facing the water, his head bowed, while the others stood behind him. One had his hand on the boy's shoulder, his arm straight, as if supporting him. Whatever it was that they had been saying, they seemed to be finished now: there was no sound but the gulping of the water.

She was about to call down to them, or to stand and wave, but she felt Edan come up suddenly behind her, a hand raised in warning. "Stay still," he whispered, his eyes wide, "stay silent." He crouched beside her, veiled by the yellow flowers.

"Edan? What is wrong?" Tara used The People's signs to ask the question, barely speaking aloud. It limited her to simple words that she hoped Edan would understand. "We are hungry. We need help. They are not the wolf-men."

"No. Look. Don't you see? That one there," Edan uncurled a trembling finger, pointing down at the man who rested his hand on the boy's shoulder, "He's not a man. He's a Fomor."

She jerked her eyes back to the scene below, scanning the hooded figure in the hope of detecting some abnormality that could prove Edan right. Were his shoulders hunched unnaturally? Was he oddly tall, or were the other men merely short? Was the paleness of his arm that of a drowned thing? She could not tell. Did Edan have some gift that could uncover the Fomor's hidden shape? She could not tell that either.

As if it could hear her thoughts, the figure unwrapped its feather hood and threw it back. She was sure it was a man, but a rustling curtain of shell-white strands hid his face. She struggled to see what lay behind the veil, but the figure was turned half away from her.

The voice came again: "The water is tainted!" She could not tell which of the figures had spoken, but at once the three hooded ones raised their arms in the air. Tara saw that one held an axe in its hand, another a sharp stone that glinted in the half light.

"The animals vanish. The earth shakes, the Moon bleeds." Tara was sure that it was the man in front who was speaking. "Great spirits, accept this sacrifice, thrice dead, and have mercy on us."

A sudden movement: a sharp and ugly thud, the figure with the axe had struck the boy across the back of the head. At once the boy sagged, but the veiled man held him up so that the next man could sink his blade into his belly. Now the boy cried out, a single agonised moan of pain, stifled in an instant as the last figure put a cord around his neck and throttled him into silence. The boy twisted and spasmed, flopping about, soiling himself with blood and water.

Tara stifled her own moan of horror. She had a crazy idea of rushing down to save the boy, but it was already over. The spasms slowed, then stopped, and the last man lowered the boy to the ground, leaving the cord he had used to strangle him wrapped around his neck. The veiled man, the one who had rested a comforting hand on the boy's shoulder, knelt down and forced a handful of dirt into the dead boy's open mouth. Then with an almost casual heave he tipped the body into the open channel, watching it sink into the murky depths until the surface of the water grew calm. Then, one by one, they turned and vanished away into the trees.

Tara sank down again, turning her back on the water. She felt sick to her stomach. Had that really been a Fomor in human form? If they had washed up onto the land with the flood, would they have had time to drive a tribe mad? How long had they been walking? How far had they spread their poison?

This, she realised with dread, was the answer to her question. This was why The People would come north and fight. Not to save themselves, and not to save anyone's way of life. They would fight because the Fomor's taint could not be endured. They would fight because someone had to.

She turned to say this to Edan; but he was nowhere to be seen.

17. Edan

A shock of cold hit Edan like a slap across the face. He was waist deep in open water, and a dark current was plucking at him, eager to drag him down to join the dead. With a strangled cry he back-pedalled, hauling himself out onto the muddy shore at the bottom of the cliff.

Why was he here? For a moment he couldn't think. It came back to him slowly; the anger had taken control. He had wanted to kill the Fomor men, so badly that he had forgotten everything in his desperation to get to them, even his safety, even the water, and had rushed down here after them.

Now the anger had vanished as abruptly as it had appeared. No. It was it still there, coiled up somewhere inside him, waiting. The thought scared him even more than the water still lapping around his ankles.

He realised suddenly that he was still standing in the open and might be seen. At the edge of the water three figures were staring out of the curling mist. Hollow-eyed and stick limbed, crowned with broken branches, they looked at him with sorrow on their faces. Then the mist drew back, and he saw that they were only the leafless skeletons of stunted trees.

"Edan!"

He looked round to see Tara skidding down the hill behind him.

"Edan, what are you doing?"

He looked at the empty shore again, still confused. He managed to stumble out the words: "Go after them. Kill them."

"With what?"

He looked down at the bow in his hand. The wood had cracked from one tip to the middle, following some weakness. Even if it had been intact, he only had two arrows — he'd left one in the wounded deer and one in the bushes somewhere. He didn't even have his spear, that was still back at their camp.

"With nothing."

He brushed past her before she could ask him questions that he wouldn't be able to answer. The Fomor men were hard enough to explain, even if you accepted that the dream warning had been true, but the anger inside him had been something else entirely. The desire for revenge, the need to hurt, it shamed him, and he wouldn't talk to her about it.

Back on the bluff they could find no sign of the wounded deer or Edan's missing arrows, and they returned to their camp by the pond with hours wasted and no more than a handful of gooseberries to show for it. They packed their camp in silence, neither mentioning what they had seen at the river bank.

Edan had made himself a pack from bent canes and rabbit skins, sewn together with rawhide lacings and with two fur straps to fit his shoulders. It was a small thing, but large enough for the few possessions that did not fit the pouch at his waist. He coiled the bow string into a circle and placed it in the pack along with the two remaining arrows and tossed the cracked bow stave aside.

Still they did not turn west. What they had seen at the mere's edge only increased their terror of meeting the Daesani again. If the Fomor could drive the people of the marsh into such an insane sacrifice, what might they do to a whole tribe of men who were already mad? In Edan's mind Phelan had become synonymous with Bal, and he imagined each of his hunters replaced with one of the terrible creatures he had seen in the murderous wave.

He could remember a hundred details of those creatures and yet could not grasp the whole of them. Only impressions remained, constantly changing and protean. He knew that the creature that had ridden the wave at the left of Bal had been fang-toothed like a lero, and that its wrack-black hands had borne too many fingers, but he couldn't picture the whole thing together. Instead he imagined Duah inhabited by the creature, and Uchdryd, Tara's tormentor, transformed into the Fomor that had come at Bal's right hand, a formless evil with a lamprey's rings of teeth.

These images and others tormented Edan as they journeyed onwards. He tossed and turned through confused nightmares populated with drowned boys who bore his own face, and pale things on beaches that he knew were Brina and Morna and Second Mother's baby all cast up from the ocean depths. More than once he dreamt that something black and wet, like a tendril of seaweed, was creeping inside him, thrusting its way through his chest to wrap around his heart. With each dream he grew more haunted, and more certain it was the curse, the old curse that the Fomor had placed on him as a boy, come back again to mark the man. Only now it was worse, now no self-sacrifice would be enough. Whatever the Fomor planned for him was still to come, and he both dreaded it and welcomed it. Let it come, he told himself, let Phelan come and see if he was still the helpless boy from the river.

Beyond the sluggish river and the mist-shrouded marsh they travelled another three days east across a desolate plain, thick with sun-bleached grass and little else. Now and again a small hill would break through the surface of the grass, like an island emerging from the sea, its sides invariably strewn with countless flowers: purple, red and yellow. They ate the few blossoms that they recognised as edible for want of anything else.

There were plants enough on the plain, and the ever-present insects, but the game on which the tribe had always relied was almost absent. Edan wondered if some power of the Fomor had driven the life from the land, or perhaps the eastern lands had always been this empty and they had blundered into starvation? Perhaps the distant mountains he could see ahead of them, purple and indistinct in the grassland haze, rose higher because all the weight of beasts was in the west? 'You're thinking crazy thoughts now,' he told himself with delirious clarity.

It was hard to think about anything other than food. The hunger pains twisted up his gut, he began to wonder if Phelan really had stabbed him with his spear. Once he saw a group of wild horses, off into the distance, and ran after them, spear in hand, but he didn't even get close to them. His strength gave out before they even bothered to run away.

He was close to giving up, but he could see that Tara was suffering even worse than him. She lagged behind, stumbled sometimes, complained of being dizzy, and even when they found food, she sometimes did not seem able to eat it. Edan had seen the signs of the hunger sickness before and knew it would only grow worse if they did not find real food.

He had just come to the conclusion that they must turn back west, when Tara spotted the smoke.

They had come upon another hill, this one crowned by two large stones, grey and splotched with lichen, that lay slumbering amongst the waving grass. White and purple flowers were scattered down the side of the hill like stars in the night sky. Tara climbed to the crest, leaving Edan at the bottom amongst the shadowed clover. He nipped a few of the blossoms off between his fingers and popped them in his mouth, savouring the sweetness, then sank to the grass, exhausted. The sky danced with tiny flies. When they landed on his face, he didn't have the strength to brush them off.

"Edan!" He looked up at Tara's call and saw her silhouetted against the afternoon sky, pointing at something beyond the hill. He dug down for some last reserve of energy and rose to join her.

From the top of the hill he saw the smoke, a lazy curl drifting into the sky in the mid-distance, just visible against the backdrop of the mountains: a campfire.

"There are people. Come on." Tara started eagerly down the further slope, but he caught her arm and pulled her back.

"Have you forgotten the river? The boy?" he asked. "What if these are the same people?"

"They aren't, they can't be. We left their marshes behind days ago."

"Then what if they have their own Fomor, or they are like the Daesani, or …"

"Your tribe could have been any of those things, and I trusted you." Tara shook off his grasp. "You know that we will never reach the Stone Forest if we don't get help from someone. Just a bit of food, some meat, some directions." She lowered her voice. "We have to trust someone, sometime."

Hunger wrestled with fear in Edan's head.

"We'll take a closer look."

By the time they had come close enough to the smoke to see its source, they had seen many other signs of human presence: grass crushed into trails, leaves plucked from their stems and roots uprooted. From another small rise they looked down into the camp where the fire burned.

Four tall shelters were arrayed loosely around a central fire pit. Each was a tall cone of dry grass, with multiple layers of neatly aligned straw reaching up to a tufted point from which the tops of long wooden poles protruded. Arch shaped entrances faced the fire, each with its own projecting shelter of straw. A yellow dog lay panting in the long grass.

Through one opening they could see flashes of people moving around. From somewhere there came the sound of a child's giggles, and a smell of cooking meat that made Edan's mouth water.

A figure emerged from the rightmost shelter, ducking through the entranceway, a woman with long hair and a dress almost the same shape as the house. She carried an empty water skin in her hand, and Edan saw that she was heading towards a small pond on the far side of the camp.

There was nothing of the Fomor about her. Her face was not hidden; Edan's hackles did not rise; nevertheless, he hesitated. He had no second sight; how could he be sure? Before he could decide, something made the woman look up and see him, and she dropped her water skin in shock. Hastily Edan held his spear out flat in the sign of friendship, and after a moment she raised her own hand, beckoning them down.

Close up he could see that she was middle-aged, perhaps she was Grandmother to these people? The thick rattails of her hair were streaked with grey, and her weathered face was nut brown and wrinkled except in a dark band across her eyes where charcoal had been applied to her skin. Her dress was hung with countless leather tassels, descending from sleeve and hem, so that she looked like a piece of the grasslands turned upside down. Around her neck was a necklace made from flowers, crude but cheerful, like a child's work.

Edan tried to imagine how he looked to her in his salt-stained shreds of clothing. Hungry and tired, he thought, thin as anyone who had not eaten well in a month or more. Not too much like a monster or a killer, he hoped.

"Aren't you going to introduce yourself?" the woman said, in an accent both long and mellow.

Edan realised that he had stupidly been waiting for someone else to begin, as the Elder or Maccus would once have done, but there was no one else. "My name is Edan. I was wondering if you might have any food to spare." He tried hard to give the sort of greeting that Tradition demanded and failed. "Only we haven't eaten for days …"

"We?" the woman raised a quizzical eyebrow. She raised her voice. "Why don't the rest of you come down!"

There was a rustle of grass as Tara stood, and in a moment, she stood behind him. "This is Tara," he began, "she's—"

"An Eshu-kind, eh?" the woman said, and to Edan's surprise she made a rough approximation of the gesture of

145

greeting. "I know your People. One of them passed through here not so long ago, and we saw him on the plain." She nodded as she spoke. "Just the two of you then? Welcome. I am Satha, and we are the Grass People. We are of this land, or we were."

"Were?"

"Soon this land will have no people, I think," she said, "but that is a story for later. You look hungry, and we do not turn away strangers in need. Come in, come in."

They were not the Grass People's only guest. The Grass families had already made room in their lodges for a man from the east, a heavily moustached traveller who called himself Morikatus, who emerged amidst a rush of curious children and adults come to see the new visitors. For precious minutes Edan regarded the stranger with distrust — was this a Fomor after all, hiding his true face behind that concealing hair? He wanted to be sure, but the smell of food and water was too much to resist.

Edan let himself be led to a place by the communal fire. Heaps of grass and brush burned lazily, sending wisps of smoke up into the darkening sky. The Grass People took hot rocks from the embers and used them to boil water in which they had steeped herbs and flowers gathered from the plains. Edan had seen many of the same plants on their journey but had not known that they were edible.

It seemed part of the Grass People's pride to give sustenance to those crossing the plain, where water was scarce and food scarcer to those who did not know its secrets. More than one of Satha's relations told Edan some version of this fact before he'd even managed to eat anything.

One of the children, there were four or five and he'd lost track of which was which almost as soon as they'd been introduced, brought him a wooden bowl filled with steaming water taken from the pit of herbs. Cautiously he sniffed, breathing in the fragrant steam, then sipped. "It's good!" Hungrily he drained the bowl, nearly burning his tongue in the process. When his bowl was filled a second time, the broth contained meat and leaves stewed together and came with a flat, cooked cake of something warm and gritty. This time he didn't even bother trying to offer thanks, he was too busy stuffing the food into his mouth.

"How did you come to be travelling alone and hungry?" Satha asked at last, when Edan was finally done eating. "A Man and an Eshu together."

Telling the tale of a journey was another skill for an Elder, but it came easily enough to Edan now. He told the Grass People about the flooded north, about the great wave, about the death of his tribe, and about the Fomor. He left out only the Daesani and their part. He had no desire to brand himself a killer or terrorise their hosts with the threat of Phelan. Instead he spoke about what he and Tara had seen at Dentaltos, and their plan to travel to the Stone Forest. By the time he had finished it was properly evening. The fire blazed brighter in the gloom, and the younger children had taken shelter behind their parents. The adults looked grave.

"This is a worrying tale you tell, Edan," said Satha, who appeared to be a leader or wise-one amongst the Grass People. "Sadly, it is not entirely new to us. We have also seen the way the land is changing, though we are as far from the sea as you may go in the Summer Lands. The animals have gone, and we must follow them or perish.

It is for this reason that the Grass People have decided to leave our ancient home." There was a murmur of subdued agreement from the others. "You find us mid-journey. We are travelling east out of the Summer Lands and do not expect to return, though your story of defying the Fomor gives me some hope."

'But you don't expect us to succeed,' Edan thought to himself. Out loud he asked, "Where will you go?"

Satha point into the darkness, in the direction of the distant hills. "The lands to the east are high, higher than the rising tide. We hope that when the sea has taken this land, they will still remain. Morikatus has told us of these places."

The traveller looked up at the mention of his name and came closer to the fire, entering the conversation. His face, Edan saw, was marked with faded patterns on each cheek, the washed-out blue spirals of old tattoos. His black hair had been tightly braided into many rows and slicked back across his head, while his drooping moustache covered his mouth entirely. It made him seem fierce, but also oddly mournful. When he spoke, his accent was so thick that Edan had to concentrate on each word.

"I am Morikatus of the Tungri. I have journeyed many moons from my land, for trade." He thumped a fist against his chest as he said this. "In my land too, the sea rises. But the land is steep, we go inland, is a good place. There is much hunting, fine green stone. There is space, inland, where people may settle."

"And my people?" Edan was startled by Tara's voice, he had not heard her speak since they sat down. "Are there any of my people in your land?"

The traveller shook his head. "I do not know your people."

Edan tried to imagine leaving the Summer Lands for good. The world was bigger than the lands between Gok and Mag's mountains, bigger than the tribe's tales and Traditions, but everything he knew was here. What was the difference between what the Grass People planned and what the Daesani were doing, save that one went east and one west? If the tribe had lived in these plains would Tradition have made the mountains as forbidden as The Great Wood? He had no good answers to these questions. Only a few months ago he had been the one chafing at Tradition, questioning every rule, yearning to break free and strike out for some half-understood future. Now he ached to have that simple life back, along with the family he had lost.

He turned back to Satha. "This is where you are going? To Morikatus' land?"

One of the other Grass People, a strong-looking man who appeared to be Father to some of the children, answered. "To this or to a place like it. We are not the only Grass People. There are other families on the plain, some of whom have already left for the east, and others who may go this year, or the next. We have heard that there is plenty of space for the taking."

"But ... if you could stay, if you could drive out the Fomor? Defeat them?"

The man shook his head sadly. "It is a good thing that you are doing, but we will not stay and fight. We have all seen the marshes growing and felt the earth shake. When the moon rose red, we trembled and feared. Even if you drive back the Fomor to the sea, what will you gain? Will the sea return to its place and give us back everything that has been lost, or will the waters continue to creep inwards, the rivers grow salty, the trees die, and the beasts vanish? This is what I think will happen."

Edan felt the coiling anger, rising up to contradict this doubter, and said nothing.

"I will not insult your bravery," the Father continued, "but the offer is open, if you wish to join us. There are many of us. Two more mouths will not see us hungry, but two more sets of hands and eyes might serve us well. If you come with us to the eastern lands, you may settle where we settle."

"Is that what you will do?" Again, Tara addressed a question to the traveller, and again he shook his head. "No, I will go south and west, for trade." He paused a moment and then "I will leave tomorrow I think." There was a jumble of protests from his hosts. "You have been good hosts, very good, but I will not burden you more when you have new guests." He looked back at Tara, and then at Edan. "We could travel together, if you wish. I have supplies, and you know the land."

Edan felt only confusion. West? East? Stay? Fight? He needed time to think.

As if sensing his confusion, Satha clapped her hands. "No more of this tonight. It is late now, and our guests are tired. Time enough to think on these things in the morning."

* * *

They were given space in the lodge closest to the pond, in which Morikatus also slept. Inside, the Grass People's dwellings were surprisingly spacious, with room for a central fire and heaps of bedding around the edges. As well as Morikatus, Edan and Tara found themselves sharing with two of the younger children, a brother and a sister named Cal and Aine who cowered in their blankets when Tara entered. Exhausted as she was, she took no affront at their behaviour, instead she crouched down and offered them a hand, telling them that there was nothing to fear. At first, they continued to hide, just two pairs of eyes peeping out from beneath their woven covers, but Tara had a way with children, and soon they were comparing her huge pale hand to their own small dark ones. Once they had overcome their fear of her, their curiosity was insatiable, and it was all she could do to disentangle herself and lie down. When she did, the little girl crept to her side and lay down next to her, apparently entranced by Tara's hair.

In the morning the sun sent tiny needles of light through gaps in the grass thatching, slipping in through pin prick holes and spaces. To Edan's sleep-filled eyes they looked like spears. He realised that some noise had awoken him, and turned over to see Morikatus in the doorway, a bag held in his hands. Edan started to say good morning but the big man hushed him, putting a finger to his lips and looking significantly at the corner where Tara and the children still slept. When he saw that Edan understood he slipped quietly outside.

Carefully, Edan untangled himself from his blanket and tied his breechcloth in place around his waist, then drew on his jacket. Even in the dim light of the lodge he could see how worn and ragged it had become, the seal-fur trim matted with dirt and salt. It was a wonder that Satha had offered them hospitality when they looked like this.

Outside he found Morikatus by the ashes of the fire, surrounded by half packed buckskin bags and pouches. He had drawn a flat warm stone from the embers and was busy making some sort of patty of meat wrapped in paste, dusting it with a dry plant powder. Edan could see no other sign of life.

Edan crossed to his side, the dew wet on his bare feet, and sat down on one of the patches of bare earth near the fire pit.

"Are you leaving so soon?" he asked softly, nodding at the traveller's bags and baggage.

"I want to be on my way today, but Grass People will say many goodbyes, so I get up early to get ready, make food, get water."

Edan looked at the half-filled bags. "No bow, no spear?"

"Is no deer, no boar, no big things to hunt," said Morikatus, "no need for big weapons." He tugged one of the bags forward and showed Edan a loosely coiled sling and a pouch of pale, water-rounded stones. "Is nothing here but birds, like we eat last night. Is enough."

Edan almost asked him if he wasn't afraid of other men, but then he remembered that he had left the Daesani out of his story. Instead he said, "Aren't you afraid of the Fomor? They could be anywhere now."

Morikatus nodded gravely, one hand unconsciously tugging at his moustache, then equally unconsciously patting it back into shape. "Yes. I listen to story, is a bad omen. I wonder if these creatures make sea rise in my land also. It would be better if you are to come with me, help me avoid them. Will you do this? Come with me today?"

Edan had totally forgotten about the man's offer from the night before. By the time they had curled up to sleep he'd been far too exhausted, and too belly-full, to think about it. There was no denying the usefulness of a fellow traveller; but the cold light of morning did not leave him trusting. 'What if he is a Fomor-friend after all?' whispered the coiling thing. Here amongst the Grass People they might be safe, but neither he nor Tara were in any state to defend themselves. 'No trust,' the anger whispered.

"We haven't talked about it yet."

"She is your mate, yes, your pale woman?"

Edan flushed, it was one thing to know it, another to say it out loud. "Yes."

"Maybe you like my trinkets then, as a gift." Morikatus delved amongst the half-stowed goods, unwrapping soft rabbit fur bundles to show Edan the treasures within. He saw strings of beads, delicate and as red as his face had gone, blue shells that had been pierced with holes and disks of horn as thin as stretched hide. In another bundle there were axe heads of polished stone, translucent grey-green and as smooth as ice. Edan had never seen their like.

"These are wonderful," Edan breathed, his distrust momentarily forgotten. Carefully he lifted one of the strings of beads. The morning sunlight glowed through the carnelian stones, making them seem like miniature suns. He held it a moment and then regretfully put it back down. "I'm sorry, we have nothing to trade," he said. He plucked at his ragged jacket. "We barely have clothes to cover ourselves."

"Ach, this I can see." The trader picked up the necklace himself, running the stone beads through his fingers. Then he thrust out a hand, offering it to Edan.

"Here, take it. I have more and is the colour of your woman's hair. A new lover needs a proper gift."

"Are you sure?"

"Yes, yes. But you promise, you talk with her about my offer."

"Of course!" Edan took the necklace, letting it coil in the palm of his hand.

"Talk to me about what?" Tara's voice came from behind him, accompanied by cheerful giggles and squeals. Edan looked back to see her emerge onto the dew-covered grass, with the two children at her heels, one tugging at her hand, the other peeping out from behind her. Someone had pulled a comb through her fiery hair, so that it coiled down loosely over her shoulders. 'She's beautiful!' he thought.

Seeing her so happy, so relaxed, Edan knew at once that they could not leave with Morikatus that day, or the next, nor still the day after, even if he stayed so long to wait for them. She had not looked so well, so alive, in weeks. Rest must win out over revenge. But still, he'd promised to ask.

Quickly he rose to his feet and crossed the camp to her. She smiled, almost shyly, as he came, and then embraced him. "What's that in your hand, Edan?"

He opened his fist to show her the necklace. There was a squeal of delight from the little girl, Aine, and a breath of one from Tara. "Is that for me?"

Smiling, he helped her put the necklace on, knotting the dark leather cord at the nape of her neck. Morikatus had been right, it matched her hair perfectly.

"It was a gift from Morikatus." he said softly.

"Oh! I should thank him!" She made to move, but he put a hand on her arm to stop her.

"He wanted me to ask you, if we would go with him?"

"Today?" She shooed the kids away with a flap of her arm, telling them that she would just be a moment.

"Yes, today. He is getting ready to go already. He wants us to be his guides, help him avoid the Fomor, or any other danger." He felt her tense again.

"And what do you think?"

"I think ... that it would be great to have a companion. That we have important things that cannot wait." He saw her face fall, gave in. "And that none of that matters. We need to rest. We should stay here."

Tara's face broke into a smile, and she brushed his cheek with her fingers. "Oh Edan, for a moment I thought you were going to try and make us go again, and then I would have had to pick you up and dump you in that pond, and tell you no."

He laughed out loud, and the children joined in, excited. At the sound of his laughter, the snake of anger pulled its head back in and he forgot about it. He put his arm round

Tara and turned back to Morikatus, who was busily putting the last of his belongings into his pack. "I'm sorry, Morikatus, but I don't think we are ready to leave so soon."

The traveller shrugged good naturally. "I am not surprised. Maybe I am sad you do not come with me; I think you would have been good companions. But I am enjoying the company of the Grass People many days, now it is your turn."

"So, you'll stay, eh?" The new voice was Satha's, addressing the question to the air as she stooped her way out of her hut and stood, hands pressed against the small of her back. "Oh, my aching bones!" she intoned. "Every year I am less like the grass and more like a stone."

"Well, of course we will be glad to have you." She looked at the children, who flanked Tara and Edan, one on either side. "It seems you have settled in well already." The boy, Cal, tugged at the arm of Edan's jacket. "Come and make breakfast with us!"

"I think it is time for me to leave," said Morikatus, hoisting his pack onto his back and slinging the water-skin over one shoulder, "before you feed me so full, I cannot move again." With his pack settled, he walked over to Satha and bowed his head in respect, clasping her hands in his own. "Grandmother, you have kept me very well and I am in your debt for it." He drew something from his belt pouch and held it out to her. "I cannot make as fine a necklace as young Aine, but this gift is for you." Then, leaning forward, he kissed Satha once on each cheek, before heading away through the wind-ruffled grass.

'South and East towards the Daesani,' the coiling voice whispered, and Edan narrowed his eyes.

18. Tara

One day with the Grass People rapidly became two, became three, four, five and more. Tara had foolishly assumed, on that first day, that they had somehow arrived at the exact moment when the Grass People planned to uproot their houses, gather their belongings, and head east never to return. Instead, she quickly learnt that they had no intention of moving before the end of the summer, or perhaps not even until the following year, joining the slow exodus of their kind towards the mountains.

Tara and Edan's story, the description of the great wave and the sea full of ice, the warning about the Black Sun, had thrown them into confusion. Although they remained calm in front of their guests, Tara knew that heated debates raged inside the shelters.

Tara learnt most of this from Neala, a woman who seemed to be about her age, though she found gauging the age of humans difficult. There were three families in the Grass People camp, not including Satha, meaning a dozen adults and nearly as many children. Neala was Aine's older sister, the eldest of six children in the largest of the families. Tara had tried her best to learn their names, but there were more names and more faces than she had seen anywhere but at The People's largest gatherings, and she could not keep track of them all. She had the uncomfortable feeling that there might be more children in this one camp than she had ever seen amongst The People, even at the naming day that followed the longest night.

She learnt from Neala that the families voted amongst themselves on decisions of importance. Satha was not their leader but rather a healer and a wise-woman, respected and heeded, but not in charge. If a family did not agree with a course of action, then they might pack their shelters and set out on their own instead. To avoid this outcome they argued, day after day, how best to respond to Tara and Edan's warnings.

"But why would you want to stay in the plains?" Tara asked Neala one afternoon, as the two of them sat near the hearth. They were making the dough paste that the Grass

People called bread, which was to say that Neala was maki
it, while Tara was trying.

Making bread involved stripping the seeds from the
fronded grass, grinding them between stones, mixing th
with water, and spreading the paste on to the hot rocks to
cook. Neala's nimble fingers made the process look easy,
plucking the seeds from each stem in a single quick
movement, but Tara couldn't seem to get the knack of it,
though she kept trying. Edan, naturally, had picked up the art
at once, and then abandoned it.

Neala looked confused by the question. "Why would we
not want to stay on the plains, Tara? There is everything we
need here."

"Everything?" Tara put down her handful of mangled
grass stems, glad of an excuse to abandon her attempts. A fat-
bodied fly, disturbed, droned back and forth through the
wisps of fire smoke. "There is nothing here." With a sweep of
one hand she indicated the wind-swept grasslands around
them. "Nothing but grass, and flowers," the fly buzzed into
her face and she swatted it away, "and insects!"

"But Tara, we eat the grass, and the flowers, and yes," she
laughed, "we eat the insects too, if that is all there is.

"Let me ask; what is it like where you come from?"

"Well," Tara considered, "now I live at the edge of a
marsh, but when I was small, I lived with my family in the
hills. I suppose it would have been," she craned her neck, as if
it would actually let her see into the distance, "that way." She
pointed south and east, towards the far-off mountains.

"What were they like, these hills?"

"Not like here." Tara delved into her memories for the
right words. "Steep, rocky. There were many caves, places
that you could take shelter from the rain or the snow. There
were trees all over, the wind and the rocks twisted them into
strange shapes." A memory came to her with startling clarity,
gathering beech nuts one autumn day in the valley bottom
amongst plants as tall as herself. "There were boulders
everywhere, big ones and little ones, all bound up in the tree
roots, like flies in spider webs. In some places the trees almost
grew sideways." It occurred to Tara, all of a sudden, that the
place she was remembering might have been beyond the
Summer Lands, in Morikatus' world. "But there was plenty of

game. There were deer all up and down the slopes, and boar in the valley bottoms."

"So, you could not carry the lodge-poles of our shelters there?"

The question startled Tara from the spell of memories. "No, you would hit the trees."

"And there would be no grass to cover them with? No seeds to make our bread? No clear skies for bird hunting?"

Tara nodded, understanding. "These lands are what you know. The lands Morikatus spoke of will be as strange to you as the plains are to me."

"Just so. Is it a wonder that we drag our feet in going? If what you say is true, we may never be able to come back. It scares us." Neala looked up, gazing at something behind Tara. "As it scares him, I think."

Tara turned around, following Neala's gaze up towards the hill behind the camp, where Edan stood, back towards them, looking out over the grasslands beyond. One of the Grass People was with him, a cousin of Neala's whose name Tara could not remember. As she watched, the man pointed at something, away across the horizon, and then turned away, descending towards the camp and leaving Edan alone to his vigil.

"He broods, doesn't he." Neala dropped her voice to a conspiratorial whisper, glancing sidelong to indicate Edan.

Tara struggled to answer. For reasons that escaped her, half the women in the camp seemed to be fascinated by her relationship with Edan. The older ones shared what she assumed was wise advice, sometimes directly, more often obliquely, as if advising the thin air rather than her. The younger girls, Neala especially, acted as if they were privy to some special knowledge of Edan's mind that Tara knew nothing of. Only Satha, the wise-woman, kept her own counsel, for which Tara was glad.

"He worries that we are staying too long, that's all."

"Something Adair has said has upset him."

Adair, that was his name. "I had better see what it was." Tara rose from the fireside, intending to climb the hill to Edan's side, but no sooner had she stood than there came the pelting of feet and she was surrounded: Cal on one side and Aine on the other, with Bove, the youngest, toddling solemnly behind.

156

"Oh Tara, Tara, come play with us!" The older children grabbed one of her hands, straining with mock effort to pull her towards the pond, while Bove looked on uncertain. "Come down to the pond and we'll show you the flowers!"

She looked back up towards the hill, but Edan had vanished from view somewhere over the far side: the moment had passed. "Come on!" Aine wheedled, and she relented, allowing the children to pull her away from the camp and towards the pond at the further end of the dip.

The pond was the source of the Grass People's water, a reed covered pool that seemed to bubble up from the earth itself, with no stream in and no stream out. Wild flowers surrounded the water in a chaotic profusion, tumbling twenty or thirty feet in every direction. Bee buzzed and wind-blown, some were familiar to Tara. Golden globe and marsh yellows, hardhead and thistle, she had seen before, but there were a dozen others, each with some secret use that the Grass People knew. Learning the name and powers of each plant was a vital skill for the Grass People's children, and Cal and Aine, who seemed to regard her as especially theirs, delighted in showing off their knowledge to her.

"This one is avens," Aine told her seriously, "remember?" Tara had a sudden memory of Morna doing just the same, in the valley below the woodland's edge, but that was too sad a thought for such a day and she pushed it away.

"I do," she said, and it was true — the flower was called avens and was used to drive moths away from furs and clothing.

Aine wanted to gather avens roots for Satha, but little Bove ran off chasing butterflies and Cal went after him, screaming and laughing. Tara followed, making sure that Bove didn't end up in the water. Soon she was stomping around, with Bove hanging from one arm and Cal from the other, lifting them into the air with each swing. The children were in awe of her strength, and she easily carried them on her shoulders, or swung them over the water. It filled her with a carefree joy that she had not felt in months.

At that very moment a spear of pain seemed to lance into her belly, as if some Fomor claw had struck her in the moment of her happiness. She pressed her hand to her side, dropping Cal into the water. The boy just giggled, but Aine noticed that something was wrong. "Tara, are you ill?"

"No, no," Tara lied, "only tired."

Aine smiled, her concern forgotten as quickly as it had come. "Tell us a story then!" The others quickly joined in: "Story! Story!"

Tara carried Bove away from the water and put him down amongst the clover blossoms, grateful for the excuse to sit down herself. Bees buzzed away as she settled, circling lazily towards new blooms until Aine and Cal's arrival startled them off. Once she sat down, the pain quickly faded, and she turned her attention to the children instead.

Tara had learnt many tales at the Stone Forest, repeating them time and time again in the winter months, until they were ingrained in her memory as surely as marks carved in stone. But they were the long tales, the great tales, told at midwinter and midsummer and the naming day. She had learned to sing those tales with voice and hand, so that the knowledge of the sun and the moon, the great spirits and the ancestors, would be preserved. They were not tales for telling children, and if her own mother had told her stories back in the mountain caves, she did not remember them.

What she did remember were the tales that she, much younger, and Esa, newly arrived at the Stone Forest, had whispered to one another in the darkness of the Seer's hut, when the sea winds lashed the coast and the ancient tusks that bore the roof creaked and shifted. They had been stupid tales, of grandfathers as large as hills, or grandmothers as strong as bears, who wrestled with elk or plucked up trees to use as toothpicks. They were stories that had reminded Esa of home; she remembered now, because they had told such tales back where she had come from.

She passed the stories on to the Grass People's children as they sat around her in the warm grass of the water meadow. Cal and Aine were rapt as she described how Grandmother had come to remove a sleeping bear from her den, carrying it on top of her head through the winter snow, while Bove laughed and clapped his hands in glee when she did the bear's roar, and flapped her arms around to show how it had struggled in Grandmother's grasp.

It was easy for Tara to imagine a life surrounded by the Grass People. Edan had wanted to hide from the catastrophe to come by living alone on the headland, but it made far more sense to leave with the Grass People instead and go to the mountains of the east where she had been born. It was not impossible that The People might do the same thing, not impossible that she could meet her own kin again, when the Summer Lands were drowned and the Fomor were done.

But Tara knew that the Fomor would never be done. The sea would continue to rise, the land would continue to vanish, onwards and onwards into a future she could not even grasp. Who would ever stop them if they did not do it now? The People must go north to oppose them, and that meant that she must leave the Grass People behind.

The world, it seemed, had different ideas, throwing up obstacles to delay them. That evening Edan showed her another one.

For days he had obsessed over a scrap of scraped hide, marking it with charcoal from the fire. He called it a map, a way to represent the land they had crossed — and that which still lay ahead. Tara struggled to understand it. Edan told her that this mark meant a river, this wavy line a coast, this blotch a hill, but she could not grasp the trick of putting these things together into a landscape. When she had crossed the Summer Lands, both alone and in the hands of the wolf-men, she had measured the route in terms of landmarks, sunrises and moonsets. She could walk it, but she could not draw it.

Edan's map resembled the bole of a tree, with a strong trunk and spreading branches. He had filled the centre with a dark spiral of angry lines from which other lines spread like roots or fingers. Edan stabbed the black circle with a finger and said, "Tanrid!"

Tara recognised the name. "The Daesani camp?"

"Yes. This is Tanrid, and this," he indicated a mark off to the right, "is us."

Tara looked again, trying to understand. If this line was the river, and this the plain ... "I see it now." She placed her own finger on the broad mark that resembled the trunk of the tree, running down towards the coast. "This is the river that runs to the Stone Forest, isn't it?"

"I think so."

She saw now that the river, running north from the coast, ran straight to the black mark of Tanrid. "No wonder the wolf-men captured me, Edan. I must have paddled straight by them in the marshes."

Edan nodded grimly. "The Grass People say there is a great lake there, surrounded by marshlands. We cannot avoid it; we must pass by it." His eyes narrowed. "We will see Phelan again."

She looked up in alarm. In the background the flames of the campfire were licking the air, and the Grass People were rippling shadows before the light, but the two of them were away to one side where the night was falling. "You place too much store in your nightmares Edan." She was sure that he had seen something terrible concerning Phelan, that night at the cave.

"My nightmares are less to be heeded than your visions then?"

"No. Only, what we see in visions is seldom clear. They seem to mean one thing, but in the end, they mean another. Your gift is new born, untried. You think you know the way things will happen, but there are other possibilities." She took a breath. "Perhaps if you told me what you saw?"

Edan did not reply but stared at his map instead. It was not the first time she had asked, nor the first time he had refused to answer. Part of her wanted to press the issue, or give him silence in return, but her heart relented. "You'll tell me when you are ready, and not before, I know it." A smile of relief crept onto his face and the shadows faded. "Just remember, nothing is fixed. Visions, fate, the future, these things can all be changed."

He glanced back at the map. "Only if we can get past the Daesani."

The threat of the Daesani hung over them that night, making it hard to enjoy the Grass People's food and the songs they sung around the fire. Rather than try to join in the music, Tara asked Neala what she knew about the wolf-men and Tanrid. The answer appeared to be very little: some of the Daesani had come to the plains once, a year before, looking for people to join their tribe, but the Grass People had turned them down. The families knew that the wolf-men planned to go west, towards The Great Wood, and had already decided to go east instead. Of Tanrid they knew even less, only that it was built on the shore of a huge lake, larger than any river, and that it was equally immense, bigger than any camp the Grass People had heard of. None of this knowledge was first hand, however, it was only hearsay and breeze-tales, carried by travellers and distant cousins. Even these few questions seemed to make the Grass People uncomfortable, so she held back from asking more.

The thought of being captured by Phelan again was a good reason to stay longer with the Grass People, but Tara had another reason, one that she kept to herself.

Tara had fallen ill on their long trek from the north. Her stomach was sick, and her strength had faltered; even her monthly bleeding had run dry. They had both starved, but where rest and food had helped Edan recover, in body at least, she felt no better, and in some ways worse. She ate, but still felt hungry. She was hungry but could not stomach food. She slept but was tired, and rested but felt heavy and sluggish. In some ways she felt bloated and swollen, in others dried up and empty.

She worried that she had carried a curse from the Fomor's lands. Had the water been tainted by Fomor blood? Or human corpses? Had the Blood-Moon touched her when she was under its rays and left a lingering poison behind? Night after night she dreamt uneasy dreams, not quite nightmares and not quite visions, in which she gathered the dead things on the Fomor's beaches and ate them as if they were food, wolfing down mouthfuls of corruption that spread within her unseen.

She did not want to tell Edan. There was nothing he could do except worry and insist that they stay with the Grass People even longer; but, waking once again soaked with sweat, she had to speak to someone.

Satha's hut, uniquely, was hers alone. Where the other shelters held nooks for many people to sleep and store their possessions, Satha's was given over to herbs and medicines. Tara had glimpsed them through the shelter's low lintelled entranceway, never quite daring to go too close. Sometimes, when the night fell and the others gathered around the common fire, Satha's hut would glow with its own light, flickering and dim.

Tara slipped out of the shared hut in the pale brightness just after dawn, when all the rest of the camp was sleeping. The debris of the past night's revels were scattered around the ashes of the fire, stark in the washed-out morning light. A white mist hung over the grasslands, without a breath of wind to stir it, so that by the time she reached Satha's shelter the rest of the camp had vanished behind her. When she hesitated by the entranceway, the harsh croak of a crow startled her, and she looked up to see the bird perched at the hut's crooked top. The bird cocked its head and regarded her for a moment with one glinting eye, and then launched itself off into the mist.

"Come in."

The sudden voice from inside the shelter was almost enough to make Tara back away, but she gathered her courage and stepped inside. It took a moment for her eyes to adjust to the gloom — the hut was lit only by the light that filtered down through the smoke hole. Bundles of herbs hung from the slanting lodge posts on strings of grass twine. Faded strings of flowers ran from post to post, looping through the half-light. Woven grass curtains, darkly marked with moon and sun, concealed further mysteries.

Tara took a step forward, bending down to look at the fireplace, where cut herbs lay in bunches on flat grey rocks. The scent of smoke, heavy and fragrant, clung to the inside of the shelter, though the fire was cold.

"Child, what ails you?" Satha emerged from behind one of the curtains. Her eyes were puffy from interrupted sleep, the charcoal marks around them smudged and pale.

"What ... what makes you think I am ill?"

The old woman chuckled, creaking her way into the middle of the hut. "There are only a few other reasons for someone to come to me alone when everyone else is sleeping. I don't think you have an enemy in the tribe, so it must be a matter of health. Unless it is a matter of the heart you wish me to solve?"

Tara shook her head.

"Well then, come in, sit if you want." She gestured at a clear spot by the fire. "I have some flower tea if you want it, though I am afraid it is cold." She lifted a little woven container, dark with the stain of beeswax, and looked inside, frowning. "Ahh, it seems to have leaked away. So now, tell me what is wrong."

Tara relaxed a little, calmed by Satha's cheerful manner. It was hard to find the words to describe her symptoms, more than once she had to fall back upon gestures, but the wise-woman knew the ills of her body better than she understood them herself, or so it seemed, and prompted her where words failed.

"Up, up, then!" Satha gestured, bidding Tara to stand again. "Let's have a look at you."

Tara rose obediently, standing still with arms half-raised as the old woman poked and prodded, humming to herself as she pressed first a hand and then an ear against her body. "Here, you said the pain was, eh?" Tara gasped as Satha jabbed a finger into her side. "Yes!"

Satha nodded as if her pain confirmed some thought. "And you've felt this sickness a month or more?" She pressed a hand against Tara's belly, raising a wave of nausea. Again, "Yes."

The wise woman stepped back, and a wide smile split her weathered face, wrinkling her cheeks. "Then be happy, for this illness will run its course by winter's middle and bear its fruit by spring."

Tara blinked, confused. "I don't understand, what sickness is it, why should I be happy?"

Satha shook her head disbelievingly. "Silly girl, you are with child!"

19. Phelan

Phelan's private chamber — a curtained off space at the back of his pack's hut — was a privilege that he had awarded himself as the Great Wolf's chosen. Many times, it had offered a refuge, a valuable isolation from the demands of running Tanrid; a quiet place in which to contemplate the Daesani's destiny. Now it seemed like a cage, a prison in which he had trapped himself.

Phelan's mind was filled with thoughts that churned and whirled and snapped at their own tails. Should he have killed the Troll when he had had the chance? Should he have turned back before they ever reached that cursed river?

The river haunted him. Phelan usually scorned those who were mastered by fear, but time and again, when he lay down to sleep, he saw that monstrous wave come rushing in, crushing and drowning and carrying him away like flotsam. That water had been full of hands, grasping, clutching at him then ripped away. He did not know if they had been the hands of living men, or the claws of Fomor. Both possibilities were unthinkable.

Phelan struggled to think of these events as anything other than a punishment from Fate. Had he suffered because he had failed to kill the Troll, or because he had planned to kill her in the first place? He wondered if his obsession with sacrifice came from the bad blood of his people still running through his veins. His people had believed that some were born with bad blood. It could be bled out of you, but never fully removed. Phelan's wolf skins concealed the livid scars from a hundred such bleedings, cut with sharpened edges of shell and bone. He had been so sure that the Troll woman's blood was the way to buy Fate's blessing for the Great Wolf's plan, but maybe that was his people's curse, still tainting his mind.

Phelan shivered despite the heat. He could feel them behind him — his people — crowding the dark corners of his chamber with their ghosts. There was the scent of blood in the air, burnt, dark, thick, and the sound of drumming, the constant tapping of fingers on a hollow log. Death by drowning, death by throttling, death to turn away death. He could almost hear the shaman's whispers: kill the Troll, turn back the sea.

Phelan found himself standing, trembling with his blade of obsidian in his hand, not sure when he had risen. He looked around wildly, but of course there was no one in the chamber with him. His people were dead and gone, and he was the better for it.

But he wondered. He had been told that the Trolls were gathering in the south, filtering their way through the marshes in ones and twos and families together. What were they doing? His scouts told him that warriors were gathering near the mouth of the great river, more Trolls than any man could remember having seen before. Did they mean to make war on the Daesani? Phelan feared that they might. What if the Troll woman had somehow survived the flood as well? Could she already be there, mustering her kind to march on Tanrid? If she had, if she somehow had, then it would be Fate's ultimate revenge on him.

Or could the Trolls intend to make war on the Fomor? The boy — Edan — had asked him why they could not face the Fomor together. It had cost the boy his life to learn the answer to that question. But what if the Trolls did fight alongside them? Could they defeat the Fomor together? Phelan's Daesani, for all their might, were only men, they could not fight the monsters of the sea. But the Trolls were monsters too, perhaps they could.

For a few moments Phelan allowed himself to savour the dream of an army of Trolls and men forging north at his command, casting the Fomor back into their ocean. What glory that would be, glory enough to erase any stain in his blood. In his head he saw himself leading a hundred warriors against the sea devils, striking left and right with his spear, bowling them down and back into the sea.

And suddenly the Shaman was there, old one eye, old cruelty, with shells strung in his hair and bones in his beard. From under the hood of sealskin, in a face black with pitch, the single bloodshot eye pinned him in place. "You've got bad blood boy," he said, "and you know what that means." One clawed finger reached out to touch his heart.

Phelan staggered back, choking with fear. It couldn't be! He was dead! They were all dead, Phelan had made sure of it; but the Shaman grinned a Fomor grin, with needle-sharp fishbone teeth in a mouth as wide as a snake. And then the knife was in the black-clawed hand. "Bad blood should bleed!"

"No!" Phelan screamed, trying to strike the knife away — but there was no one in the chamber but him.

Phelan sank back on his furs, every muscle trembling. Just a nightmare ... a waking nightmare. He cursed the memory, and the fantasy of fighting the Fomor too. The Trolls had no place in his future. The only thing they could do was lend their blood to fuel his destiny.

There was a rustle beyond the hide curtain that separated Phelan's chamber from the rest of the hut, and then Duah's oily tones: "Phelan? Chief? Is something the matter?"

Phelan stood, scanning the room with restless eyes to be sure that there was nothing there. No Fomor, no ghosts, only him. Just the fears and nightmares of the past, as dead to him as the people who featured in them. Deliberately he turned his back on the shadows and lifted the curtain.

"What do you want?"

Duah, standing half way between the curtain and the doorway of the hut, bowed his head a little as if in apology for disturbing him. The long chain of wolf claws wrapped around his neck, an affection he had adopted since they had returned from the north, rattled as he moved. "A stranger has come, not a refugee but a trader. I thought you might like to speak with him." Phelan saw how his quick eyes darted around his room, taking in everything. "Was I wrong?"

Phelan scowled. He wanted some reason to put Duah in his place, but he had to get out of the shadows. "No, you were not wrong. Show me this stranger."

Duah smiled and stroked the forks of his beard. "Of course, of course, he is this way."

Outside, the sun was shining from a cloudless sky, beating down over the rooftops of Tanrid. Dogs lounged in the shadows, and people were everywhere. In one direction Phelan saw a party of hunters returning with a deer slung from a pole, in the other a group of women pounded hemp leaves with stones, singing some unfamiliar song in time with the work. At the door of the next hut along, a thin woman with long braided hair peeped out fearfully from the shadows — another new arrival. The sight of the Daesani's industry, their numbers, their might, lifted Phelan's heart, as it always did. In the dark, alone, he could fear the Fomor and his past, but out here he knew that the Wolf-clan was his future.

Duah hurried along behind him, battering him with questions. Shouldn't we return to Eburakos while the weather is still clear? Why are we still gathering food when the storehouses contain more than we can carry? Why should we worry about a few Trolls, they aren't that strong? Duah thought of himself as second only to Phelan, someone who might rise to even greater power when Phelan took the Great Wolf's place, but he knew nothing. Fate. It all came down to Fate. To leave before this curse was lifted, that would be madness.

They found the stranger close to the shore of the lake, watching the fishermen casting their nets out in the water. He was a big man, broad shouldered and strong looking, with long black hair and fierce tattoos. He seemed to recognise Phelan's authority at once and clapped a fist to his chest in greeting when he saw him.

"Please, you are the Great Wolf?" The man's voice was deep, heavily accented, but respectful.

"No. But I am his representative here." Phelan had the disturbing feeling that Duah was smirking behind his back but did not turn. "I am Phelan. You are welcome in Tanrid."

The trader clapped his chest again. "Forgive my mistake. My name is Morikatus. I have come from the east to find the Daesani. Your name is known far and wide, great Phelan, as are your people." He turned to look at the many huts of Tanrid, spreading up the shore. "I confess I am in awe. I had heard much of Tanrid, but what I see before me is greater still."

Phelan knew the words for mere flattery but felt their effect even so. He liked this man at once. Strong, friendly, respectful — he needed more of his sort.

The trader continued. "So many people. I do not think I have seen so many together at once. How many are there here?"

"Who can count? More every day. Ten score at least, more. But this is not our greatest camp, that lies at Eburakos, where the Great Wolf forges our new land." Phelan knew the number of people at Tanrid nearly to the last man and child, but he kept the figure to himself. "But tell me, Morikatus, you say you came from the east. I have travelled that way myself, beyond the marshes and the two rivers there is nothing but hills and grass. Had I seen a tribe of men as striking as you, I think I would have remembered them."

"Oh no, not there." The trader spread his hands in a gesture of honesty. "I cross these lands on my way here, yes, but I am from much further away, in the hills, beyond these low lands."

"From beyond the Summer Lands?"

"Yes. My people, we are driven from the lands we once lived in by the sea, and so we take to the hills and make new lands. This was generations ago now, before my Grandfather's time. Now we prosper, and so we trade. This is what your great tribe plans, is it not?"

Phelan felt a thrill at the man's words. This was a vindication of the Great Wolf's dream, a tribe who had already done in the east what they planned to do in the west. His mind filled with questions he wanted to ask: how had they felled the great trees? How did they manage the winters without access to limpets from the shore? How did they thatch their houses without reeds? But he kept quiet. Acting impressed now would only weaken his position later when it came to trade.

Instead he took Morikatus by the arm and led him into the heart of Tanrid, showing him the fifteen big houses, each with their walls of woven hazel and rooves of bundled reeds, and the smaller shelters of peat and wood that served as workshops, processing the wood and stone, hide and horn, that they gathered to send to Eburakos. Duah followed behind, but Phelan ignored him, let him plot and scheme — Phelan led here.

They talked as they walked. Phelan was happy to answer the trader's questions, especially when they gave him the chance to learn more about the trader in turn. He felt his dark mood slip fully away. Let his ghosts haunt the shadows if they wanted. He was walking in the light, and would leave them all behind.

"Did you not find it hard to come here? The way is very long, and this land can be ... difficult."

Morikatus nodded in agreement, stroking his moustaches with his hand. "Yes. Is very hard. Many times I come to a place where I expect to find people, and all is abandoned. Or

I am expecting forest or plains, and instead I find a river, or a bog."

"Many people have already joined us … or vanished."

"Yes. I am expecting to make much trade on the plains, but instead I find only one group of the Grass People, so I stay with them many days."

"I know the Grass People. They are very welcoming."

"They are!" The trader grinned and rubbed his belly in appreciation. "They make good food, sing songs. I am not the only one they help. Just as I leave a Troll comes to stay with them also."

They were just reaching the entrance to the long hut where Phelan had his chambers, but at Morikatus' words he stopped dead, so that Duah nearly ran into him from behind. Phelan felt a shiver of anticipation, like the tension before the thunder-crack: the touch of Fate. Something was about to happen.

"A Troll?" He knew that he was as taut as a bowstring. "Where was that?"

"With the Grass People." Morikatus spoke slowly, obviously wondering what he had said to cause such a reaction. "It was a strange thing. A Troll woman and a young man travelling together. Lovers, I thought. They made a strange pair. He was like any man, and she so striking, with her red hair and her pale skin."

Now Fate showed its hand... Edan and the Troll. Somehow, they both lived. That one-eyed old ghost had almost had him, almost dragged him down into the darkness with the strangling cord around his throat, just another sacrifice to despair. But now he had another chance. Let the Troll woman raise her monster armies, he would face them. He would give her blood to Fate before the sea drowned them all.

"Duah!" Phelan spun around and his second took a step back in surprise, the wolf teeth strung around his neck rattling like old bones in the wind. "Call my hunters, we have prey to catch." He heard the trader gasp; ignored him. Duah lifted a hand to his beard, opened his mouth to speak, but Phelan cut him off. "And gather the others. The Trolls muster in the south and we will be ready to meet them when they come."

Phelan dared Duah to defy him on this, already bristling for the confrontation. He had questioned him at the mere, all those months ago when Keir was killed, and again, after the great flood, when Phelan had wanted to search the coastline for the Troll's body. That second time he had allowed Duah to prevail. They had been in no condition to do anything but rest, then limp their way back to Tanrid. This time, he would not be dissuaded; but Duah only bowed his head and hurried off.

Phelan looked around, and saw that a small crowd had gathered, drawn by the sight of the stranger, or the sound of Phelan's voice, or the growl of confrontation. As Duah hurried off, he raised his voice to address them. "Daesani! Wolf Clan! Brothers and sisters. A storm is coming. A storm that will drown this world!"

He saw anxious faces. Many were unfamiliar to him, others he knew well. There was Cuall, still limping, there was Newlyn, grimmer than ever, almost all that remained of his pack. He let them surround him, raising his hands as if to bless them.

"There are monsters to the north of us," he felt as if he were speaking, not just to them, but to the ghosts of his past and to his unseen quarry, "and monsters to the south! Any day they may fall upon us, with waves, and spears, and blood." A murmur of fear bounced back and forth between the people surrounding him, but he spoke over it.

"But I am not afraid!" He shouted this, exulting, hurling his defiance at his dead kin. "I am not afraid because I am not alone, I am here, with you, my pack, my clan. I am not afraid because we are the wolves, and no monster will defeat us!"

He lowered his voice into the silence that came after his ringing shout, persuasive. "When the Trolls come, we will not die, we will throw them back because we are Daesani!" There came a buzz of agreement, a whoop of excitement. "When the Fomor come, when the sea comes, we will not drown because we are Daesani!" Now the whole crowd was shouting, roaring.

"The time is coming, brothers and sisters of the wolf! You have watched your lands, your people, be washed away. You have laboured long for the hope of something better. Now it comes! This is fate! This is destiny!" He had them now.

"But this fate is not yet certain." He rotated on his heel, meeting the gaze of one Daesani after another as he turned, so that they knew he spoke to them. "You know of the Trolls

— the crude beasts that haunt the marshes. I have learnt that these creatures serve the Fomor. Even now they are gathering, ready to hunt us."

"Even now!" he punctuated his words with one fist raised, grasping the air, "they take their spears and prepare for killing."

He modulated his tone, allowing a pleading note to enter his voice. "What should we do, brothers and sisters? Should we run?" There was a clamour of objection. "No? Should we stand aside and let these Trolls have their way?" This time he had to raise his hands and voice to be heard over the chorus of anger. "I say no!" The howls of anger became cries of assent.

"We are the wolf! We do not run — we are not hunted. We are the ones who hunt! We are the ones who chase, we are the ones who kill." He pitched his voice for Duah now, somewhere invisible in the press of bodies. "We do not turn our backs out of fear. These Trolls will not stop us. When they come, they will find us waiting. We may not be able to face the Fomor in battle, but we can do this!" The roar this time was deafening.

"So, gather your spears and feather your arrows. When the Trolls come, they will see our numbers and turn back, and if they do not, we will drive them back!" He threw a fist in the air. "Daesani! Daesani!" The crowd chanted back, throwing their own fists in the air.

He turned back from the crowd. The trader looked shocked, Duah was nowhere to be seen, but the ghost, the old ghost, was still there, behind them all.

20. Tara

"A child?" Tara struggled to comprehend the words. "But how can that be?"

Satha chuckled, "I don't think I need to tell you how it works."

Tara was too confused for more than a twinge of embarrassment. "No, but … he is human, and I am of The People. We are not the same."

Satha made a circuit of the unlit fire and lowered herself creakily to the ground; the beaded tassels of her skirt spilled out around her like ruffled hair. She gestured for Tara to sit on the other side of the fire. "Do sit down, girl, can't have you looming over me."

Tara sank down to the earthen floor, her hands creeping to her belly. Could there really be a child within? Of course, there could. She wanted to cry and laugh. All these weeks spent thinking that the pain and the missed bleeding were the symptoms of hunger, and she had missed the obvious.

The wise-woman was silent for a while, then spat phlegm into the cold embers. "I have heard some of the stories that you have told the children," she said. "Is it true that once your People were different from what they are now? Less like us?"

Tara tugged her mind over to the question. Edan had asked her much the same, before ever they had met the Grass People. "I suppose it is," she answered, "if the tales are true."

Satha nodded. "Then it may be that your kind and ours have mixed before. You have become less than you were, more like us. Your blood is no longer pure." She picked up a stick and began to stir the ashes idly. "We have been in this place a long time, our kind. So long that we no longer have stories telling of how we came here, only that your kind was here before." She gave a short laugh. "If we had tales of travelling, then the thought of leaving would be easier."

Not pure blood? The Seers strove to keep the memories of The People pure, to remember the old tales and the great tales. It hurt to think that The People had changed around them without their notice. And yet; Tara thought about the stories Esa had whispered in the dark, and about Edan's tales of Trolls as huge as mountains. If those tales were even half true, then there could be no doubt that The People had changed since they were first spoken. Her skin was white, and her hair was red, and still she was more like Edan than the Trolls in those stories.

She ran a hand over her belly. There was no arguing with the life inside her.

Tara knew instinctively that she would not tell Edan, not yet. Her determination to leave the Grass People had not changed, but now she knew the need was greater. If she told Edan then he would worry, fret, demand that they stay for her own good. If they lingered here too long then the child would make her fat, slow, unable to travel. They had to leave now, at once, and complete the task she had set herself before it was too late — for all of them.

She jumped impulsively to her feet, setting the dry herbs swinging and twirling on their strands of grass cord. The hut suddenly seemed tiny, claustrophobic. "I have to go! I have to get to my People!" She stumbled for the doorway, brushing hard against the wooden frame as she burst out into the swirling mist.

"Girl!" Satha's voice seemed to come from a mile away behind her, but a moment later she felt the old woman's hand on her arm. She stopped but found that she was trembling in the cold morning mist.

"I've given you a shock." Satha said. "Come back inside and have something hot to drink, it will calm your belly."

The surge of panic drained away as quickly as it had risen, and she allowed herself to be led back inside. Satha kindled the fire, and then warmed water in a leather bag until it was hot enough to steep herbs. She bustled back and forth, squeezing past Tara in the gloom of the hut, without speaking, until she could scoop some of her potion into a pale horn cup and hand it over.

Tara took the drink gratefully, clutching it close to her chest so that the heat seeped into her. She drank it cautiously, expecting a wave of sickness, but it was delicate and sweet, like flower blossoms, and it calmed her.

"I can make you a bundle of these herbs, to take with you, if you like." Satha's voice broke the silence, making Tara look up from the fragrant steam. "They should help with the sickness you feel." Tara nodded a grateful thank you.

Satha returned to her side of the fire, holding her palms out to the flames to warm them. Curls of grass glimmered amongst the ashes, twisting as they burnt. Tara wondered if the strange mist was another sign of the Fomor and shivered despite the warming tea. Once you started to look, everything became an omen.

"Perhaps you would be best amongst your own people." Satha said. "But there are things that I would do, to see to the health of your baby, if you will."

"What things?"

"There are herbs I would like to gather, and a ceremony, for the blessing of the Spirits." As Tara listened quietly, Satha explained that amongst the Grass People each new mother was presented to the Spirits in a women's ceremony in the hope that their blessing would see the unborn baby safely birthed. "These are strange times, and we cannot give you much to aid you against the end of the world. Let us at least give you this."

* * *

They came for her at dawn, on the day of the ceremony.

For the past few days, the women had been preparing for their ceremony in a little dip hidden from the main camp over a small rise. The menfolk knew better than to ask what their women were about, and they guided Edan away and encouraged him to concentrate on his maps and plans.

Tara yearned to tell him about the baby. He had lost his whole family, but he would have a new one. Not telling him was far harder than hiding her sickness had been. If only she could be sure that they had the time to wait for the birth, if only she could be certain of his reaction.

Instead, she busied herself amassing supplies for their journey. She gathered every edible plant that Cal and Aine could point out to her, ranging well across the low hills with the hot dry wind from the south gusting around her. Dawn until dusk, returning only when the ember-glow of the campfire guided her back.

And still the Black Sun, shimmering beneath the dark waters of her dreams: Bal's eye fully opened. How long? Days? Months? Years? She felt sure that it could not be years. The visions came again, every day now and every night, swirling insistently from wherever it was that visions came. If there was a message now, she couldn't see it, only the unrelenting knowledge that the end was coming. Alone, amongst the nodding flowers and the dry wind of waning summer, she touched her belly, flat still, but so different. Were the visions for her, or for her child?

They came for her at dawn, but she had been up long before the sun rose. She had gone through her possessions a dozen times already in the previous days, laying out their belongings and packing them away again. The clothes gifted by the Grass People, Edan's rabbit-fur tunic, repaired almost as good as new, strips of meat smoked over the fire and wrapped in grass parcels. She could hardly be more ready to go, but at the same time she did not want to leave.

Neala had woven them packs from stiff grass, and she had dumped them outside the shelter where there was room to lay everything out. She sat down in the short grass as the sun rose and had just loosened the rawhide bindings and hauled out the first bundle of food to start her packing all over again when a shadow fell over her.

They came for her at dawn, startling Tara with their shadows. She squinted up into the early morning sun, then started back in alarm. The figure that loomed over her seemed more than human, shaggy fringed and stoop-shouldered, its domed bird's head bristling with tufts of spines. Others came in quick succession, shadowy and shapeless against the sunrise, rustling as they moved.

Two of the figures reached for her, and for a moment she took them for Fomor, set to drag her to the water, but she felt the touch of warm hands, smelt the musty scent of hay, heard the stifled giggles, and realised that it was the Grass women come to take her to the ceremony. There were half a dozen of them, all the grown women of the tribe. They had dressed in costumes woven from grass and reed, gathered in sprays at wrist and knee so that they looked more like birds than women. Over their heads went hoods that hung down their chests and backs, the tightly plaited fibre dyed red and black with ochre and charcoal.

Dawn was the birth time, when the sun rose new-born, and so they took her east into its rising light, dancing their way over the hills out of the camp and down into a hidden dell. There Tara saw that they had made another shelter, weaving a low tunnel from newly gathered grass that ran to a single peak and then out again. There is only darkness before birth, and so they covered her eyes with their grass feathered hands and led her blind to the low entrance.

175

She crawled through the low arched passage, and then out into the warm gloom of the central space, while the others came after. In this way they hoped to ensure that the real birth, when it came, was as easy as their rehearsal.

Satha waited under the peak, which sheltered a round chamber as large as any of the communal huts, though less sturdy, with curving ribs borrowed from the stock of spare lodge poles bearing up the roof. Bundles of flowers, for fertility, hung blossom down over the browning floor of tamped down grass, with the Grass women ranked up along the edges. At first only Satha wore her human face, but soon some of the others were throwing off the heavy hoods of woven fibre, revealing faces flushed with heat and excitement.

Tara let herself be led to the centre, where sunlight filtered down from the meeting point of the lodge poles, quite overcome. Garlands of flowers were placed around her neck and in her hair, which streamed down behind her. Satha took a fire-blackened shoulder bone from another woman and scraped black ash from it to paint around Tara's eyes and across her face. For this day at least she was one of them.

All around her, the older women began to sing, shaking their clasped hands and bent knees so that the grass ruffs rustled and swished in time with the stamping of their feet. Some of the costumes had seashells and dry seed husks sewn on strings that rattled as they moved. Their words soared and swirled about her, calling on their spirits to watch over her: Ibanna who they called mother, and Damara who was a guide in dark places.

One of the masked women stepped forward to dance Ibanna's part. Her costume was big bellied and laughably buxom, a half dozen straw breasts protruding as she twitched her hips and clapped her hands, always turning. Her bare arms were striped black and yellow with coloured earths, and she wore a bracelet of empty nut shells around each wrist that rattled rhythmically. She danced three times around Tara, and then with a final whoop stepped back to make room for the next dancer.

Tara felt herself sway, light-headed, and thought that the song might carry her away, into a vision under the sun and open air, but then the music faltered. Puzzled, Tara looked around, seeing that the same confusion on other faces. Some of the women lost their rhythm, stumbling in their steps and clutching each other for support. A moment later it was the shelter that moved — it lurched sideways under a mighty blow that uprooted one of the lodge poles and sent damp grass pouring down on them.

The women cried out in terror, and Tara yelled too. The Fomor had come. The ground heaved under their footfalls, and the building heaved. The lashings that bound the poles in place snapped with sharp cracks and puffs of dust. Light lanced in, illuminating air filled with chaff. For a moment Tara thought that she could see the creatures outside, a blur of black limbs and claws, looming as tall as the lodge peak, before everything shook again.

This time the structure of the lodge gave way under the blow, dropping on their heads and plunging them into darkness. Thatch and beams tumbled around them. Tara heard a scream from one of the women and threw up her arm just in time for a falling beam to rebound off it. The blow jarred her, and she stumbled blindly into someone else, yelling against the noise.

After the chaos came silence, save for the settling creak of the shelter's debris and the moans of the women. Tara found herself on the ground, a pole across her back with a weight of wreckage piled on top of it. With an effort she managed to get her hands underneath her and pushed up, heaving her way into the light. Grass showered down around her, and the pole rolled away with a clatter.

Under the open sky, turning, looking for the Fomor, Tara tried to heave up a fallen pole for a weapon, but it wouldn't come free. She twisted, expecting the creature to rear up behind her, but there was nothing to see except for the ruined hut and a few of the women crawling their way out. She spun on the spot, sure that the creature must be hiding, somewhere, impossibly, amongst the nodding grass; but if there had ever been a Fomor it was gone now — leaving the ruin of the blessing ceremony behind it.

Over the low hill, figures came running, the rest of the Grass People, with Edan at their head. He had his new bow in his left hand and two arrows clutched in his right, but he tossed them aside when he saw her, sprinting to reach her — seeing him come, anticipating his questions — Tara resolved then and there to tell him the truth, but then he flung his arms around her, holding her tight and stopping up her words with kisses of concern. By the time she could take a breath, the moment had passed, and she said nothing.

"The whole camp shook," he said, "the shelters nearly fell." As he spoke, the other men arrived, a few steps behind, and broke off to help haul the women from the ruins. Some of them were nerveless with shock, and a few had bruises from where the posts had hit them, but the shelter had been light.

Standing aside, while loved one went to loved one, Tara tried again: "Edan ..."

"I know," he interrupted her, "The Fomor. We have to go."

* * *

They left the next morning, bright and early when the sun still had the whole sky to clamber up. There were embraces and tearful farewells on both sides, but the Grass People were on the move too, gathering their belongings even as Tara and Edan packed theirs.

When they had returned to the camp, they had found the place ruined. The flower meadows were cracked, and the pond was polluted with dirt and mud. The families had consulted and come to agreement. The Grass People would leave as soon as the lodges could be taken down, and the food gathered.

Edan and Tara turned south into the teeth of a blustery wind, down through the grasslands until they reached the valley of a mighty river that cut deep through the peat layers and rushed noisily over the gravel below. It took them three days to reach the valley, and for three days more they followed it westwards, picking their way through fords and rapids to the far bank. It was late summer now, but the days were still long and the moon not yet dark, so they pushed onwards towards the marshlands they knew were ahead while they still had the luxury of prepared food in their packs.

On the fourth day incessant waves of rain drove them to take shelter amongst the osiers that crowded against the riverbank. Behind them aspens creaked in the wind, their sighing leaves as loud as the rain, and they followed the noise up towards dryer ground, where the taller branches of an alder gave proper shelter on the top of a spur of canyon wall.

When the rain showers passed, they clambered to the highest point of the spur, and looked out. Spread out below them was a vast marshland dotted with light and shadow, where a dozen rivers seemed to meet in one vast tangle of channels and pools. Two great rivers flowing from the east and west formed a broad beam, like the lower branches of a tree, while a skein of smaller channels spilled away to the northern horizon. 'Somewhere along those,' Tara thought, 'Phelan and his hunters captured me.'

Where the rivers met, in the middle of the fens, open water glinted. This was their first sight of the lake of Tanrid. It was a vast thing, a day's travel long, surrounded by the spreading stain of flood water. From the vantage point of the high ground Tara was amazed that she hadn't even known it was there — when she had been down amongst the reeds and water. She called herself a Seer, but had known nothing about the land just beyond her own.

They both agreed that they could not cross the lowland without being found — it would take them days to pass through the marshlands close to the lake. Their only hope was to skirt the great depression, staying close to the cliffs of grey and white chalk that jutted up at either side of the marsh. These were the lands of Gok and Mag, pressing close on the Summer Lands like a pair of jaws caught in the act of closing. At the north end of the lake the cliffs were many days apart, but at the south end of the marsh they came together, looming over the single river that drained towards the sea. The People called these gates of rock The Twins, and they would have to pass through them to reach home.

For Tara this was the first glimpse of a land she recognised. Somewhere through that gap the cliffs opened again to each side of the southern coast — the wedge of land where the Stone Forest clove to the sea, and the Seers of The People made their last home. She did not see the steep rock faces and crowding trees that forced them down into the marsh as things of terror, but a sign that her long journey was almost done.

Edan, at her side, did not feel the same. She could sense his fear in his rapid breath, in the way his body tensed for flight. "The Great Wood," he whispered, "it is so close. I could almost reach out and touch it." Tara saw the way his eyes darted from side to side. "You could walk from one edge of the Summer Lands to the other in a day!" Edan was whispering, as if the looming lands might hear him. "I never imagined that the Summer Lands could look so small!" Tara saw that his knuckles were white where he gripped his spear.

She looked down at the lake again. There was a smudge of smoke there, a grey smear against the yellows of the fen-land. She followed it upwind with her gaze, and suddenly, there, she saw Tanrid. By the edge of the lake there were buildings, large enough to be seen even at their distance. On first glance her mind had taken them for a grove of trees, clustering together by the water, but now she saw that they were circular structures, spreading along the northern lakeshore.

"Don't look at the cliffs," she said to Edan, pointing down towards the lake. "That is what we have to fear, the Daesani place. Phelan's place."

Together they tried to count the buildings, but they were beyond the counting of either of them. Even if they had been able to make them out clearly, they had not the fingers to tally them.

When the rain cleared the lake and the sun came out again, Tara saw how close the marsh came to the eastern cliffs, and therefore how close they would be forced to come to the Daesani. They had no choice. If they tried to climb into the uplands, they would take even longer to reach the south. They had to stick to the slopes between the marsh and mountains and hope that they could slip by the Daesani without being noticed.

'Could we pass by at night?' Tara wondered, 'Sneak through when darkness hid them?' Edan must have been thinking the same way, because he said, "The moon is dark tonight. Even if they heard us, they would not be able to see us."

"And we would not be able to see our way." Tara gestured blindness, putting her hand in front of her eyes. "We would stumble and drown."

"Then we must go in the day. Now."

"Today?"

Edan looked round, and she was surprised to see that the signs of fear had vanished. Instead his face was closed to her. "Yes, before our courage fails." He turned his gaze to the clouds drifting above. "And before the light does too. We need to be well past them by nightfall."

Courage, Tara wondered, or something else?

They kept to the cover of the trees for as long as they could. Ahead and downhill the countless ponds and channels sparkled in the afternoon sun, appearing and vanishing as they descended. Tara saw that there were paths there, places where wood had been laid on the soft ground, or tracks worn through the broom and sedge. They were like the strands of a spider's web, stretching out to surround them and pull them in.

They covered as much as a fifth of the distance to Tanrid before Edan suddenly stopped again, bringing her up short. "Look! There are people there!"

Tara followed his pointing finger and saw — a hunting party of men and dogs were moving at speed along the trackway a little to the north of them. She jerked herself back into cover, making sure that they could not glance up and see her, but suddenly there were people everywhere she looked, as if Edan's gesture had conjured them into being. She saw dots moving in the water and realised that they were fishermen. She scanned the slopes nearby and saw tiny figures, bending and stooping as they gathered berries amongst the gorse. There was even one man already above and behind them, who would already have seen them if his back had not been turned.

Tara let out a moan in spite of herself. "Oh Edan! They are everywhere!" She no longer saw a spider's web, but an ants' nest, swarming and crawling over every part of the landscape, blind hands and eyes for Phelan and the Fomor. They were sure to stumble upon them. They had to turn back. They couldn't turn back.

"We just have to make sure that we aren't seen," Edan whispered.

With no other choice, they crept onwards. They slunk through the cover of flowerless broom, slipped across gaps, and dashed where open slopes blocked their way. They kept to dry ground where they could, lest the splash of water gave them away, holding their breath, quiet as mice, when the Daesani gatherers came close.

They came upon a patch of hillside free of bushes, with rocks above and brush below. The open ground was carpeted with a tufted mess of bilberry bushes, knee and ankle high. Only a few yards away a Daesani woman bent nearly double as she deposited handfuls of berries into a leather bag. She was moving slowly up the slope, a baby swaddled on her back, coming ever closer. Tara was sure to be seen by them at any moment.

Tara looked around wildly for a hiding place. The broom was barely waist high, and barely hid her. 'Don't see us. Don't see us,' she chanted to herself. There was cover beyond. If they could just stay hidden a little longer, they might be away and clear.

She felt movement beside her and glanced over at Edan. To her surprise he had risen to his feet, his eyes on something out on the hillside. "What are you doing?!" she hissed, but he ignored her and started forward. Desperately she grabbed for him, got her fingers on the hem of his jacket for a moment, and then he was beyond her reach, out in the open.

21. Edan

The Daesani woman looked up at Edan, shading her face with one hand to ward off the sun. He felt like his heart was lodged in his throat. It was hard to breathe. Had he made a terrible mistake? Now that he was out in the open, he wanted to bolt for cover again, but it was too late.

Finally, the woman spoke, still squinting against the sun, "Edan? What are you doing here?" and he knew that he had been right.

"Second Mother, is that you?" She looked different in Daesani clothes. Her dark hair was no longer bound under the familiar cap but instead worn loose, a single knotted tooth hanging loose on a beaded strand.

She made a sharp gesture, almost irritable. "Not Second Mother. Just Cinnia again now, we don't use those words here."

Edan felt his heart leap, jumping from throat to chest. "We ... the others survived?"

Cinnia shook her head, nodded. "Yes, no, both. Uch is here, with me, and little Matus of course, and Brina, and Lavena. But the rest, I don't know. I like to think that Grandmother and the Elder are living up there, on the coast somewhere, like they wanted, but I don't know."

Edan's mind leapt onto the omissions, Maccus of course, and Morna, little Morna. The sudden stab of joy became grief, became anger, but he kept it out of his voice. "Matus," he said, "lucky — a good name."

Cinnia glanced away from him, half turning to look back along the hillside, so that he saw the baby swaddled on her back for a moment. There were other Daesani further down the hill, just diminutive figures from this distance, but close enough that they might glance up from their work and see them talking. Her hand went nervously to the braid in her hair, twisting and untwisting it around her fingers.

"Edan, what are you doing here?" Cinnia wrapped her arms around herself unhappily.

"I thought you'd be glad to see me?"

"I am, but ..." she trailed off for a moment and then started again, lowering her voice. "Phelan. He is obsessed with you, and with the Troll — Tara. He is convinced that the

Trolls are in league with the Fomor, that you plan to attack us here. Edan, he sets the others against you, sends men to search for you. He will kill you if he finds you, I'm sure of it." She clutched herself tighter. "Oh Edan, I should turn you in."

With a rush and rustle, Tara stepped out of the bushes beside him, a looming presence in the harsh glare of the afternoon sun. He could sense her anger, and he felt it too, the sharp-toothed adder in his gut that had hidden away while they stayed with the Grass People but never gone. Always Phelan, doing the Fomor's work for them.

"I saved your life," Tara said softly, "your baby's life, does that count for nothing?"

As if on cue the baby began to cry, a quiet grizzling sort of noise that could turn into a wail at any moment, and Cinnia took the leather straps that held him in her hands, tugging and knotting them but not undoing them.

"Of course, it does. But you have to understand, it's different now. Uch ..."

"What about Uch?"

"He's one of them now, Phelan's pack, his hunters. It was a long journey back, from the north, and Phelan had lost men. Uch, he's a good hunter, a fine hunter. Phelan was impressed, he came to accept him." She looked up at Edan with defiance in her eyes. "What were we supposed to do? We needed his favour."

Edan's voice was cold. "So, you are Daesani now?"

"Of course, we are." Her voice rose, but she held it back. "I have eyes, I saw what happened in the hunting grounds. It's all true, what you tried to tell the Elder." She looked at Tara as she said this. "The Fomor are coming, the Summer Lands will die. There is no future for us here. Or did you find something? At that place you wanted to go, in the north. Something that changes all of that?"

Edan glanced away. "No."

"Then we have to be Daesani. We have to find a new land, for our future, for our son. And that means that we need to fit in here, to have a place, a position. Uch has worked hard for that, don't hate him for it."

Edan's anger answered for him. "You'd turn in your kin for a position, is that it?"

"No!" Cinnia's hand flew to her mouth, as if shocked by her own voice, then more softly: "No. I won't turn you in at

184

all, either of you, but you have to go, quickly now, before they find you."

"Don't worry, we will." Tara said, brushing past her. "Come, Edan, we need to go."

Edan nodded, stepping forward to follow her, but a hand on his arm stopped him, and he looked back to find Cinnia's face close to his own. "Edan." she said, her voice low now. "Be safe, be well. And please, don't come back to this place, or he will kill you. Phelan, he will kill you both." For a moment he thought of putting his hand on hers, but the anger inside held him back.

"Edan! The others!"

Edan sprang for the bushes, but he could see that it was already too late. Some of the other Daesani had stopped their work, looking up to see what was happening. There was no way that they could mistake Tara for one of their own: they had been seen.

Irrationally, he felt the anger flare higher. These were the people who had killed Maccus, who had killed little Morna — she who had never harmed anyone. He took a pace downhill, shaking his spear at the distant Daesani gatherers. He had no idea of what he would do if they came for him, one man against five, but Tara caught him by the arm and pulled him away before any of them could do more than put down their leather bags.

They plunged through the undergrowth, racing along the ridge above the bilberry slope and down into the thick rushes beyond. Edan tried to remember the lay of the land. How close had those hunters been? How close were the dogs? They'd escaped the hounds and the hunters before, but that had been a handful of men, a couple of dogs. How many were there here? If they came now what should he do? Fight them? Surrender? He wouldn't go down easily.

He heard cries behind him, falling away as they wove and dodged, but not falling silent. The pursuit was coming, and there were Daesani all around. Stupid to have broken cover. Stupid to have started so early, when the cover of darkness was still half a day away.

The ragged rushes gave way to a gravel slope, scooped out by a landslide. There were more steep slopes up to their left, littered with rocks and stunted trees that cowered in the shelter of the cliffs. To the right the land tumbled down through stretches of open ground and brush, stripes of each alternating around the distant lake shore.

Which way? Edan tried to think. If they went uphill, they would have the cover of the rocks and the trees, but they could easily get stuck, trapped against the cliffs waiting for Phelan to come. And the rage didn't want to wait, it wanted to fight. He was filled with the burning desire to confront Phelan. Right here. Right now. He had his spear, his anger, he could kill the Fomor here and now.

Down then. Down was closer to the lake. Closer to the Daesani place, but better footing — the best place to outrun the hunters behind them; the best place to be hunted too. Without a word he started down the hill, leaving Tara to follow behind.

They ran and hid, ran and hid, bolting across the open ground and taking cover amongst the willowherb and gorse, slinking amongst the dead water channels and flood-bound trees. In this manner they crossed a broad arc of the marshland, while the sun crossed an equal part of the sky, sliding into mid-afternoon. A chill wind blew up then, sweeping down from the north and across the grey water of the lake, buffeting them from behind. Edan expected, yearned, to see Phelan before him at any moment, but they saw no one.

The wind carried the sound of the hunt. They heard snatches of raised voices, or the baying of dogs on the wind. Edan's hackles rose, but somehow he knew that Phelan was not behind them. This was the wolf hunt, the Fomor hunt, that had pursued them since the day he had met Tara; but Phelan would be ahead of him if he was anywhere.

The cliffs closed around them, looming over the bloated river course and the wind blasted scree. To the east the rocks were thundercloud grey, while to the west they shone white like snow, each side crowned by the tangled trees of The Great Wood. If they passed the gap by nightfall, they might be able to escape in the open land beyond. If they were caught on Tanrid's side when the sun set, there would be no escape.

Then, suddenly, one of the Daesani was before them.

They had come to the edge of a gulch that cut down through sandy loam, leaving steep dark banks thick with exposed roots. Water had washed through it and drained

away, scouring the soil down to a bare chalk path that
arrowed towards the lake shore through bars of inky shadow.
Edan had jumped down out of the broom just as the Daesani
man had rounded a corner on the trail: each as surprised as
the other.

The Daesani grabbed for something at his belt, eyes wide.
There was murder in those eyes and something else,
something that was not human. He knew this man: Uchdryd,
Tara's tormentor, one of Phelan's own, but he didn't see a
man, he saw a monster, a black smeared creature in a parody
of human form. Fomor!

"You!"

Edan turned his jump into a lunge, thrusting his spear in
front of him. He wanted to drive the antler point through the
monster, just as he had been stabbed, over and over again, in
his nightmares. Just as he had slain Keir at the lake, just as he
would slay Phelan. He put all his weight behind the stroke,
but the Fomor-man twisted his body and knocked the spear
aside with one arm. Edan lost his hold on the spear and went
after him with fists instead.

There was no artistry to it, just a mad assault of clumsy
blows and desperate blocks. The two of them crashed
together and went down in a tangle of limbs and claws,
landing heavily on the hard chalk. Edan smelt the stench of
the sea, felt the shivering cold of the ice and saw black jaws
and needle teeth snap for his face. Someone cried out in pain.

They rolled, clawing at each other, landing glancing blows
but no telling ones. Somehow Edan found himself on top.
The creature immediately struck for his throat, but he blocked
the blow with his forearm and forced the monstrous arm
down, binding Uchdryd for a moment with his weight. Faces
flashed in front of his eyes: Phelan with his spear, Maccus
dead in the water, Morna drowned. So much pain; so much
evil. He would kill it here and now.

Edan saw his spear and snatched for it, intending to run
the creature through, but the two of them had rolled on top
of the haft and it was pinned fast. He fumbled for the sharp
flint at his belt instead, still holding the Fomor down, but that
left him open to a fierce blow across the shoulder spilling him
off his perch. He felt hands, or claws, slice into his back. Now
his face was pressed hard against into the dirt. Still he
scrambled for a weapon. He had to hurt this creature, he had

to kill it! His hand closed around something cold and he struck backwards with it, smashing the Uchdryd-creature off his back.

They both tried to rise, so Edan struck it again, knocking it down. Edan staggered to his feet. There was a rock in his hand, a fist-sized lump of white stone stained red with blood. There was blood in his eyes as well, the all-consuming rage that he had nursed all the way from Maccus' grave.

Edan raised the rock, ready to deliver the death blow, but something caught his arms from behind. Tara. Why? Edan couldn't understand it. The creature was vulnerable, squirming and squealing, lashing the ground with its claws. It tried to speak but he wouldn't listen.

"Edan. Edan don't do this!"

What was she doing? He struggled with her almost as fiercely as he had with Uchdryd. He had to kill him!

He heard his voice shouting, "He's Fomor!".

"No Fomor, just a man."

What did she mean? Couldn't she see the monster? He looked again at the beast, seeing how it twisted and heaved, like a fish caught on a spear, left arm limp and right arm crooked across his face. Edan saw desperate eyes, wide and white in a mask of blood. Frightened. Human.

Wait! It was a man, a man! What was he doing? He tried to lower the rock, but now his arms would not answer him. His hands were not his own. They were still trying to slam the rock down in spite of him. Only Tara's hands still held him back.

Now he struggled with himself, with the black serpent of hatred and murder that coiled around his muscles. This was not him. Not the man he wanted to be. Not the man he would let himself become. Edan felt something break inside him. Spots danced before his eyes and for an instant he thought he saw something black and barbed, sloughing out of him and slithering away. His arms finally answered him. He felt the weight of the stone, opened his fingers, and let it fall to the ground.

"I'm not a killer!" He'd said the same thing to Phelan, at the Legu, the last time he'd seen this very man. He let out a shuddering breath, said it again. "I'm not a killer!" Then more quietly, "But I would have killed him."

The anger. Edan realised that the anger was gone. He'd stored it up inside himself since the river, since Maccus' grave, and it had built into a flood, a storm, a tidal wave, a poison thing. Now it was finally gone. He was not a killer. He had never wanted to be a killer.

"I know." Tara relaxed her grip on his arms, let him lower them. "You were angry."

"No, not just that." He felt cold realisation seeping into the empty places the anger had left behind. Maccus' ghost had warned him to beware of the Fomor in human form, creeping into the Summer Lands to watch their horror close up, and in his arrogance he'd decided that it would be the Daesani and their kind that they would take, when all along it had been him. The anger, the rage, that had taken root in him at Dentaltos, that was the Fomor. They wanted to see fear. They wanted to see anger. They wanted to see men tearing at each other even as the waves came crashing down, and he'd almost done it. Worse: he'd wanted it.

He gulped down a breath, tried again. "I was blind. I saw what the Fomor wanted me to see." Tara had wrapped her arms around him, holding him up. Now he peered over her shoulder at the Daesani. He wasn't moving. "Is he dead? Please don't let him be dead."

Tara carefully let go of him, then bent down to check the still figure at his feet. She touched his chest, then bent to listen. "He's alive."

Edan felt relief wash over him. He wanted to sink to the ground and close his eyes, but if he went down now, he wouldn't get up. "We need to go. Before others come."

At some point his spear had rolled free, and Tara picked it up. He would have been happy to let her carry it, but she held it out to him, and he made himself take it. It was still his father's work, no matter what stupid use he'd tried to put it to, and when he started forward again, he realised he needed it to lean on if nothing else.

They limped southwards, picking their way through the gorse and the furze at the edge of the river. It felt to Edan like the fight had taken forever, and changed everything, but in reality it had only lasted minutes. Nevertheless, the bulk of the day was already behind them, along with the bulk of the lake. Now they were in the throat of The Twins, between the cliff and the peat dark river, masked by the roar of the current and the rush of the water.

To Edan's intense relief, the noise of hunting dogs had fallen far behind. It seemed that the Daesani were still searching the slopes above the lake, unaware that their quarry had slipped away from them. They had a brief moment of opportunity before the others found Uchdryd.

They made it almost as far as the narrowest point before the hunt came in earnest. Cries broke out behind them, ululating and wild, the cry of a hunter to his hounds. Other voices joined the cry. They had found Uchdryd, or their trail, or both. Edan looked back across the ground that had just taken them the balance of the afternoon to cross and realised how small it looked. Could they get to the safety of the Troll lands before the hunters crossed it? He wasn't sure.

Now they had to run again. Edan imagined Phelan leading the pursuit, chasing them to the very southern tip of the Summer Lands, just as he had chased them to the north. His desperation to confront him had vanished along with the Fomor's anger. Now he was happy to run! One endless chase across the face of the world, if that's what it took.

The sun balanced on the edge of the white cliffs with the black branches of The Great Wood reaching up for it like hands. For one brief moment, looking back, Edan thought he could see the hunters at the edge of the water behind them, but then the trees swallowed the sun, and the Summer Lands vanished into darkness.

22. Tara

Morning came slowly, creeping through the branches of the oak tree. Somewhere nearby a crow let out a harsh croak, reminding Tara of the bird that had perched on Satha's house.

In the darkness of the night before, when the valley of the Summer Lands was pitch black, but the sky above still glowed with the last colours of evening, they had clambered as high as they dared into the cliffs above the river. Here they came across a spot where rocks and an overhanging tree created a sort of niche in which they had gone to sleep.

From where she lay, Tara could see a wedge of grey-green marshland and a fragment of wide, slow river. This was her homeland, but she saw it with new eyes now. Somewhere at the mouth of that river, two or three days south, lay the Stone Forest, where she had spent most of her life, and then beyond it a low sweep of land surrounding a long finger of the sea. Were there Fomor in that sea too, she wondered, or were they only in the north? Was that sea also filled with ice?

Suddenly filled with a yearning to see her home, she crawled out under the low branches, careful not to wake Edan. He could use the rest.

Outside the sky was a clear and cloudless eggshell blue, but the air had a chill that said autumn was not so far away. Would there even be an autumn? How close was the Fomor's flood? She thought of the child growing inside her. What sort of world would it be born into? Would it be born at all? Too many questions and no answers.

She clambered up onto a tilted rock to get a better view of the landscape spread out below. The river's edge was almost at the foot of the slope, with a vast expanse of marsh on the other side. The further cliffs, ghostly white in the morning sun, receded almost due west into the haze. She stared the other way, hoping to catch a glimpse of the inlet where the Stone Forest lay, but she could see nothing. It must be further than she had thought.

Down in the valley a thin drift of mist still clung to the osiers and the reed beds, curling gently around the edges of the water and out across the mere. She thought she saw figures — ponderous, stooped, and giant — plodding their way through the water as they had done for years beyond counting. She smiled at the sight of these spirits, feeling sure that they had come to bless her and her unborn child.

She studied herself. Was that a change in the shape of her belly that she could see, or was it her imagination? The sickness she had felt so keenly was already fading, just as Satha had assured her it would, but there was a weight now, pressing down inside her. She had to tell Edan. Today? No. Not after the trauma of the day before. Had he really seen a Fomor in Uchdryd? She had only seen a man, and yet ... she was sure that the Fomor were real. Their touch was on everything around her. The shaking earth, the rising water, the way Second Mother had almost betrayed them.

'So, when do I tell him?' Tara's thoughts wound back on themselves. 'Why haven't I told him already?' She had no answer for that one. She'd almost mentioned it a dozen times after they had left the Grass People and never quite found the moment. She wanted to be sure; she wanted it to be certain Satha had been right. When she could see the change in her belly, yes that would be the time.

A noise intruded on her reverie, the crunch of feet on gravel from down below. For a moment she thought that it was the spirits come back again, but the mist had faded like a dream while she had been lost in thought. It must be one of The People!

Tara scrambled down the slope, excited at the thought of seeing one of her own kind after so long. Crooked rowan trees littered the hillside, and she skittered from one handhold to another until she came to a place where the small cliff dropped down to the river bank below.

There were people moving along the broad gravel shore at the edge of the river, but they were not her kind. Four Daesani hunters, two men and two women, crept along the edge of the marsh. They held makeshift weapons at the ready, an antler pick, a hunting spear, a heavy stone lashed to a wooden haft. They went cautiously, not speaking, their eyes scanning the reed beds and the sand flats.

Tara sank back into the rowan leaves. What if they looked up? Bunches of green berries, not yet ripe, brushed against her hair, but she dared not push them away. She cursed herself for rushing headlong into danger. Of course, it was the Daesani. Phelan had convinced them that they were enemies, they wouldn't give up. Phelan. It always came back to Phelan. If anyone was Fomor-possessed, it was Phelan.

She remembered that once, months ago, she'd dismissed the idea that humans could fight like The People could. Phelan and his band were surely just exceptions. Looking at these four she knew how wrong she had been. Their weapons might be not be made for war, but there was no doubt that the ones who wielded them had become warriors. Phelan again. She still had no idea why he had taken her captive or what he had wanted from her.

Something startled the hunters below. Had they seen her? But no, they were pointing out into the marsh instead, clumping together with their weapons outwards. For a long tense moment they held their place, ready for a fight. Then just as suddenly they turned about and went jogging back along the hard sand and out of sight. Even so, she waited, not daring to move, until she was sure that they were gone. 'Gone for now,' she thought, 'but not for good. They will be back.'

Edan was awake when she returned, though he looked as if he would have welcomed a whole day of sleep. He pushed himself up when he saw her coming, and limped forward with his arms open, but something in her look stopped him.

"What's wrong?"

"Hunters. By the river. Looking for us."

"Of course there are." She saw concern in his face, but no fear. That was new. "Did they see you?"

"No. They took off back towards Tanrid. I think the river must have washed away our tracks, I don't think they knew we were here." She closed the distance and wrapped an arm around him in a quick embrace but pulled away before he could drag her into something more. "They will come back. With dogs. They won't give up."

Edan nodded and grabbed his belongings. His woven pack had been broken in his fight with Uchdryd and they'd had to discard it, so he stowed what he could at his belt. His spear lay in the long grass by the tree, and Tara saw him hesitate before stooping to pick up what she realised must now be a distasteful weapon.

"No. They won't give up. Not as long as Phelan is in charge."

"What then?" She asked. "Do we fight him?"

"I don't want to fight Phelan. I don't want to fight anyone."

"Not even the Fomor?" Edan made no reply, but the answer was clear enough. The sharp anger that had driven Edan all the endless leagues from Dentaltos and right into the enemy's den, had vanished. The warrior was gone right when she needed him. No. She scolded herself at that thought, she'd never wanted a warrior in the first place — never wanted someone like Phelan. Edan the fisherman was back, and she was glad.

"Leave that to The People." She said. "It is their fight now."

"But will they fight?"

She shouldered her own pack. "Only one way to find out."

* * *

Beyond The Twins the two lines of cliffs diverged once more, one turning south and the other west, so that a wedge of land opened up between them. The great river, after churning its way through the gap, split into a hundred channels, spreading out like hair towards the sea. There was dry land there, enough to support stands of osier and willow, but dry land meant trails that the Daesani and their dogs could follow.

Tara knew that Edan would want to stay well away from the water, as much as anyone could these days, especially deep flowing water like the river, and she agonised over the choice even though he stayed silent. If it was only a matter of confusing the trail she might have risked the dry land, but the truth was that following the river was the only way she knew how to find the Stone Forest, which lay at its mouth.

She went with her gut and set off into the heart of the marsh, where running water would wash away their scent and the fog might hide them from view. It didn't take her long to realise that she had made a grave mistake. Down amongst the water and the reeds every direction looked the same, and the mist hid the few landmarks she might have recognised. What she had been sure was the main channel of the river vanished amongst salt-ponds and reed beds, leaving them wading waist deep in water that the washed-out sun did nothing to warm.

Tara had hunted in these marshes before, journeying from the shore with the other Seers to gather bullrushes and little fish, but the water had been lower then, and fresh. Now the sea had crept inland, swallowing all but the tips of the rushes beneath grey waters. When she was certain that she had done the wrong thing, she tried to turn around and find a way back to the higher ground, but the water was everywhere, twisting and turning.

In the end she had to admit the truth to Edan: "I don't understand it, I know this place, but I'm lost."

Edan embraced her as well as he could while still thigh deep in the water. "Everything has changed, just like it was in the north. You'll find the way, just keep to it."

She smiled, and tried her best, but the marsh appeared to have become a maze. Every time they got their feet on dryer ground it turned out to be no more than an isolated blip in a wasteland of water.

They spent a wretched night camped on a sodden hummock of earth, listening to the lap and slurp of the water amongst the reeds. It was too wet to lie down or to light a fire, so they huddled together and waited for dawn.

The next day was no better. They made a valiant attempt to find the river proper, but the land defeated them. Tara jumped from clump to clump, avoiding runnels of black water as viscous as mud. She thought she was making good progress, but Edan fell behind, picking his way ever more slowly around the sudden pools and abrupt channels. It was a strange reversal of roles. For so many of the past weeks, she had been the one trailing behind.

Was it the old fear of water slowing him down, or something more? Had the fight with Dog-breath done more damage than she had suspected? She watched him as he caught her up and realised that he was trying to hide his injuries. In the gloom of the previous night she had caught a glimpse of angry scratches, puffy and red, covering his back and arm. She suspected that they might be infected. By the way he walked, they were growing worse.

Frustrated, she clambered up the nearest mound, telling herself that this time she would catch a glimpse of something, but there was only a sprawl of waterways dissolving into the fog. It was surely impossible. Could the Fomor somehow be responsible? She shivered at the thought. Could they have shifted the river to strand them? Were they waiting just beyond the mist?

As if responding to her thoughts the mist suddenly receded. In moments it had rolled back so that she could see half a mile across the marsh. For the first time in days she felt the sun on her skin and closed her eyes to savour the warmth.

When she opened them again, she saw that there was something a little way off, rising just above the level of the reeds, a platform of branches atop a small mound of earth. Tara wasn't sure if it had been there when her eyes had closed.

Edan appeared to her left, cautiously skirting the edge of the water.

"Edan look!"

"I don't like it. It isn't safe."

Tara felt the same prickle of alarm, but after two days with nothing but mist and her own thoughts, she had to see. She started to clamber down into the channel, but to her surprise found dry ground where she expected water. A bank of sandy earth snaked through the reeds and up towards the platform. The prickle of fear intensified, it was all a little too convenient; but stubbornness made her go forward anyway, with Edan a few steps behind.

The top of the rise was dry and free of reeds, a rough circle having been cleared around the platform. Eight forked branches, each reaching as high as Tara's shoulder, had been driven into the soft ground, and more laid across their tops to form a scaffold. On the scaffold's surface a multitude of bones had been scattered, not animal but human.

"Did your People do this?" Edan had come up the slope behind her, but he hesitated at the edge of the cleared space.

"No."

She picked up one of the bones. It was the lower part of a leg. The upper part had been splintered off, and the marrow was gone. Deep gouges on the broken end made it look like a large animal had gnawed it through, but Tara knew that there were no animals in the marsh capable of doing so.

"Tara."

Edan had gone around to the far side of the platform and picked up something off the ground, which he now held up for her to see. It was a human skull, jawless and white. Tara saw that something violent had happened to it, leaving a hole as round as a spear shaft in the top.

Tara felt a growing sense of terror as she looked at the bones, the claw marks, the looming banks of mist under the unnatural sun. The reeds began to tremble on every side of them — something was coming! All at once the mist began to draw in around the knoll, as if someone was taking a breath and sucking the mist in with it. Tara thought she saw hulking figures advancing just behind the wall of mist where a moment before there had only been stunted trees and rushes. Nightmare black, misshapen; they stained the mist with their bodies like blood pooling in water.

She cried out for Edan, but he was already moving. He grabbed her by the hand and drove down into the reeds. For a moment she had solid ground beneath her feet, and then there was water up to her knees. The reeds closed around her and over her head. It felt like drowning.

Something closed around her ankle, cutting into the flesh. 'A hand!' she thought irrationally. She tried to pull free, but the unseen grip held her. A bitter cold spread up her leg, her groin, her chest. Then, in her womb, something shifted, and she felt a pulse of life that threw back the cold. She lurched free, plunging back into the unwelcome safety of the mists.

They saw no more sign of the Fomor after that, indeed they saw almost nothing at all. The fog was so thick that they gave up any hope of sensible navigation. The days were without sun, the nights without moon or stars. Often, they came across stands of leafless trees, half sunk in the water, but none of them led out of the marsh. They tried to keep to dry land, skirting the mud flats and the wide channels that sometimes emerged in front of them, but for all they knew they were simply going around in circles. Once they came across a line of tracks in the mud, slowly filling with murky water, but they couldn't tell if they were their own or someone else's, and they led nowhere.

More than once she tried to tell Edan; about the baby, about the claw on her ankle, but the endless grey robbed her of the right words. She wanted to tell him that she was glad that he was no longer a warrior. She wanted to tell him that she loved him, and that their love would get them out of this trap, but instead she offered a prayer to the Spirits in the hope that they would show them the way out. There was no answer.

The sound of animals teased them, invisible in the gloom — the splash of otters, the clamouring of birds at dawn and dusk, the slap of fish in the water — but the only creatures they saw were the countless tiny flies that swarmed at the water's surface. The air was bitter, and the water too, so that they had to suck at the moss that coated the dead tree trunks just to get something fresh to drink.

They caught a crab once, a flat red thing with a weed covered shell, and on another day strained a handful of shrimp from the water, but it was far from enough. Edan made one attempt at grabbing the fish that brushed past their feet in the shallows, but it was covered in barbs that stung his hand and he let it go with a cry and a splash. They plucked rushes instead, stripping out the pulp with their teeth and leaving the rest to drift on the tide. It seemed that the marsh had become endless. Tara began to believe, with a despairing certainty, that they would never leave this place; that they were already dead.

"What's that?"

Edan's voice was so unexpected, after days of near silence, that for a moment Tara thought that she had imagined it, but he had stopped and was pointing off into the mist.

She squinted in the same direction. Something wavered in the dimness — dark, half solid, as tall as a man. For a moment she thought that they had managed to stumble straight into one of the hunters after all, but no, it was not a living thing.

"A tree!"

"No?" Edan's voice was questioning as he splashed forward, laying a hand on the black trunk. He coughed, running his hand tentatively down the bark. "Not wood. It is as cold as stone."

Stone? Tara let out a whoop of joy. It seemed like one of the spirits had listened after all. "It is one of the Stone Trees, Edan." She signed the ritual sign for the Stone Forest, clenching her right fist in the open palm of her left hand.

He looked around at the drifting mist. There was nothing to see but water lapping on mud. "This is the Stone Forest?"

"No. Not yet. There are single trees like this around the delta, but it means we are close!"

Edan stood back from the tree, then reached out to touch it again, first brushing it with his fingertips, then knocking with his knuckles. "I can feel bark, but it is as hard as rock. What is it? How did it get here?" His voice was growing with excitement.

"No one knows what they are, beyond what they seem. There are more than we can count, scattered all across the lowlands here. Near the river mouth there are dozens all together, that's what we call the Stone Forest. Some stand, some are fallen in the mud, you would take them for rocks if you didn't look closely." She laid her own hand on the tree, feeling the slickness of algae under her fingers. The sense of hope she had felt when she first saw the delta from The Twins was suddenly there again. She felt herself smile. It was stupid, but despite it all she grinned.

"The stories say that Grandmother put them here because she was trying to make a fish hurdle." Edan laughed, a genuine out loud laugh, and she laughed too. She felt like the sun had come out and driven the mist away, although the real mist was still all around them.

They set off again, using the trees as markers. They worked their way from one to the next, always heading where they seemed thickest. If they went too long without seeing another they turned back, following the ridges of dryer land where the trees stood highest. In this way, after two days more, they reached the Stone Forest.

Tara heard the Stone Forest before she saw it and smelt it before that. The scent of smoke cut through the mist, heavy with the distinctive tang of saltgrass and marram, the smell of the river mouth and the sea. The noise came next, a hum of voices and activity all mixed in with the rush of the river over its bed of stones.

Then at last the mists parted, and they saw the stones. Two rings of the largest trunks, ten within and then fifteen more around them, were set apart on a rounded hill overlooking the river. To the left of them Tara saw the familiar curving bank where the Seer's hut lay, the turf covered top just visible over the hill.

When Tara had set out on her journey there had been nothing more to the Stone Forest than this; the stones, the hut, the path down to the river and the white rocks that marked where Seers of the past had been laid to rest. Now the receding mists revealed more, a whole jumble and scatter of shelters on the high ground beyond the Seer's hut.

Wooden poles had been sunk into the soft ground to support awnings of stitched deerskin and auroch hide, each with a fire pit set outside. Shapes were moving amongst them: men, women, children. The People had come to the Stone Forest.

Tara found herself both amazed and dismayed at the sight. The camp looked crowded enough to eyes expecting empty hillside but compared to the teeming masses of Tanrid it was a sobering sight. Was this all of The People? Was it just that many had stayed away, or had the Eshu race been reduced to a mere few dozen families? A thought crossed her mind. Had her mother come? Did she have family here, other than the Seers?

The fog had retreated fully now, rolling back across the marshland, and Tara could see that there were more figures moving amongst the pillars of the Stone Forest, keeping between the outer ring and the inner where only the Seers were permitted. They must have become visible to The People inside the circle at the same time, because some of them stopped and turned in their direction. A moment later one of them left the stones, striding towards them with a spear in his hand.

Tara watched the warrior approach, wondering from which wandering tribe he had come. He was a hulking brute of a man, his broad chest and thick face dense with ritual scars. His hair had been lathered and spiked with chalk so that it bristled like a hedgehog's spines. When he reached them he thrust his spear butt into the soft ground and then stood silent, glaring at them both.

For a moment Tara wondered why he did not speak, before realising that he was already talking, but in the hunter's manner, using his hands alone, as some of The People did. She had been too long amongst humans and it took her a moment to catch up.

"You are expected, Seer," he signed to her, "but I do not know the human."

"He is … with me."

The warrior responded with a grunt, snatching his spear out of the mud and favouring Edan with a glare. When he spoke again, he used his voice, turning his back on them. "You will come to the Old Ones, and we will see if it is time for war."

23. Edan

The confrontation with Uchdryd had brought about a strange change in Edan. After so long spent in fear, and then anger, the revelation he'd experienced on the shores of Tanrid had left him euphoric, and yet strangely numb. He'd spent the following days detached from everything around him, like an insect, encased in amber. He could see what was happening around him, the endless bog, the mist, the cold rain, the hunger, but he didn't feel it. He was only a spectator. It was as if he'd already made the crossing to the afterlife, and that's what it was, after all of the life he'd known. Even the Fomor's macabre show of bones on the island hadn't broken through this barrier.

When they arrived at the Stone Forest, however, all that changed. Everywhere he looked there was something so strange or so inexplicable, that he could not help but take notice. Tara, once outlandish herself, was now his only constant.

He no longer saw Tara as strange. He had fallen in love with her milk white skin, the flaming hair that wouldn't stay still, even the freckles that had bloomed across her broad cheeks. The things that had once seemed bizarre in her were now beautiful.

The Troll warrior who confronted them was something else. It was not just his height, though he stood a head taller than Edan, but his massive girth. He had the build of an auroch, broad, stocky and muscular. His ruddy skin was covered with old scars and blemishes, as if he wrestled boar as a pastime. Edan remembered how Tara had fought the Iero and thought that it might even be true. He also remembered her tales of The People's decline. If this warrior was an example of a declined Troll, he didn't want to meet the real thing!

The warrior appeared to be called Anagar. He rattled as he walked, each heavy footstep shaking the necklace of antler discs that he wore looped around his broad neck. He communicated as much by gesture as speech, and Edan struggled to understand any of it. He had congratulated himself on his mastery of Troll speech and considered himself fluent in it. Now he realised that Tara had adjusted her language to suit his, and that he had actually been speaking a mishmash of both tongues. And Anagar spoke with his back to Edan, when he deigned to speak to him at all.

It was clear that the Troll warrior didn't think much of him, which was understandable given that he had the Daesani as neighbours. Edan thought that it was only respect for Tara that kept them from throwing him back into the marsh.

Anagar led the two of them towards the double ring of stone trees on the hill, and then around them, following a well-worn path. A third ring stood outside the main two, this one made of thick wooden stakes driven into the ground, and the path led between the wooden ring and the stone. A heap of white pebbles lay at the foot of each stake, and Edan could see pale stains where the rain had washed chalk dust into the soil.

There were many Trolls on the path, a looming welcoming party that glared at him, but touched their hands to their chests when they saw Tara. Faces leapt out of the crowd, dark with red ochre; white with chalk; black with soot; fierce eyes with the pelvis of an auroch for a mask. Few had Tara's complexion of white and red. Edan faltered at the sight of them, but Tara laid a reassuring hand on his arm and they hurried on after Anagar.

Beyond the nested circles of wood and stone, a path led down a steep slope and then up again towards the camp on the opposite hill. A stream in spate cascaded over the path. Edan tested it with one foot, feeling the pressure of the water as it rushed over its rocky bed. It earned him another scathing glance from Anagar, who strode into the flood without a glance.

"I don't think he likes me," Edan whispered to Tara.

"The People have suffered at the hands of your kind."

"Not at my hands!"

"I don't think he sees it like that."

On the other side of the stream was a sandy hilltop where the grass was cropped short by the wind. Each Troll family had pitched their camp a little way from all the others, so that clumps of leather tents were scattered around the hilltop with spaces in between. Somewhere in each clump — sometimes in the centre, sometimes casually to one side — a stripped branch had been thrust into the ground. Edan saw that each one was topped with an animal emblem, roughly shaped from the wood. In front of one camp he saw a boar, in the middle of a second an eagle, and so on. These were not the precise carvings of his own charms, but, like everything else here, both crude and bold.

Trolls — no, The People — Edan silently corrected himself, watched them pass from the mouths of their shelters. Edan saw a jumble of faces and markings, old and young, but no children or infants, and only a very few that he thought were as young as himself. He wanted to ask Tara what that meant, but Anagar strode relentlessly on and he had to hurry to keep up.

At the approximate centre of the camp an enormous fire-pit had been built, well clear of the shelters. Around this sat several Trolls, some crouched on the bare earth in Tara's familiar pose, others seated cross-legged on spread deerskins. Edan counted three old men and one old woman, and then a younger girl, all in a group, with two more men, grave faced, off to one side. From Tara's descriptions he guessed that the older men were the Old Ones, chosen to speak for the Troll-kins and that the women were the Seers.

The girl leapt to her feet as soon as she saw Tara, then ran forward to embrace her. Words and gestures followed, too fast for Edan to follow, before the girl stepped back, an embarrassed grin on her face.

"Edan, this is Esa." Edan made what he hoped was the gesture of greeting, but the girl was shy, and said nothing.

"At last the Seer has returned," one of the old men said. He appeared to be the eldest of the three, with a bristle of beard and tufts of white hair on a head stained with dark spots. He held a cane of pale ash wood in one hand, tapping the bottom of it against one foot as he spoke. Strings of bone beads, and what appeared to be gull beaks, were draped around him like loops of intestine spilling from a carcass. His tone seemed less than welcoming.

"Now our council is complete, and we may plan our way forward."

Tara stepped forward. "I have much news, Cuinn. I have been to the north and returned. Dentaltos has fallen. Creatures that the humans call Fomor are guiding the sea." Behind them Anagar snorted at the mention of humans, but Tara continued. "The wolf-men of Tanrid, beyond The

Twins, are against us too. I believe they have been driven mad by these Fomor …"

Cuinn, the Old One, raised a hand, cutting Tara off with a sharp gesture. "There will be time enough to discuss these matters later." Edan struggled to follow the rapid movements of the Old One's hands. If he suspected that Edan could speak their language he made no allowance for it. "Tonight, we will sing The Great Tale."

Edan read the surprise in Tara's reply. "The Great Tale? But it is not midwinter."

"These are not normal times. We have watched the stones and counted the days. Your Black Sun will rise in one moon's time."

Edan felt a chill go through him. 'So soon!'

"Even more reason for us to speak of these things now," Tara insisted. "We must fight the Fomor, and I fear we must fight the wolf-men too."

"Fighting is a matter for the Warrior to decide."

"The Warrior?"

The Old One made a complacent gesture, as if Tara were an unruly child. "We have chosen a Warrior to lead us in matters of fighting. We will let him decide what we do."

How dare they treat Tara's warning like it didn't matter! "Who is this Warrior?" Edan demanded, looking around. "Where is he?"

Anagar snorted, slapping his broad chest with one hand. "I am here." Edan thought he heard a suppressed snigger from somewhere behind him. "But who are you, human? What are you doing here amongst The People?"

Tara spoke before Edan could. "He is my mate."

Now the murmur of scorn was clearly audible. One of the men by the fire said, "You take a human as a mate? This is not done!"

Tara rounded on them. "These are not normal times; did you not say so yourself?" It was Edan's turn to suppress a laugh of satisfaction. "You should listen to him. He knows his own kind better than we do."

"And what is it that you know, human?" Anagar made the last word an insult.

"I know that the Fomor are real, and that if we do not stop them, they will drown this land. I know that just north of here there is a man called Phelan who has told the wolf-men that you are his enemy, and who will come here to stop us. I know that we must fight them. That is what I know." Edan made a point of using his hands to speak as well as his voice, and when he was done he thrust out his chin, daring the Troll warrior to doubt him, but instead he saw what he thought was a flicker of interest cross Anagar's face.

"Tell me more of this Phe-lan."

"No!" Cuinn slammed the heel of his cane against the stone edge of the fire. "I have said. These matters will wait." With a grunt the old man pushed himself to his feet, the strings of finger bones and wader beaks rattling as he moved. "Tomorrow, or the next day," he pronounced, turning away. "Now we go." Hurriedly, the remaining Old Ones rose to their feet and joined him.

"He will not listen," Edan murmured to Tara.

"He is Cuinn, the oldest of the Old Ones. He is held to be the wisest ... but not the most patient. The other two are Druce and Irin." Her voice brightened, "and this is Ama." Edan saw that the old woman was approaching, leaning on Esa's arm. She seemed older even than Grandmother, and more intimidating than Satha. Faded spirals of blue marked her face, and her long, matted hair was woven through with hundreds of tiny bones stuck crosswise through the braids. Even hunched by age she was taller than Edan and broader. In her youth, she might have challenged Anagar for the Warrior's mantle.

Tara bowed her head in respect as Ama arrived and made a sign that Edan had not seen before, balling both hands into fists and pressing them knuckles together over her breast. "Mother."

"You have been gone many moons," the old woman said. Her voice was like the rumble of distant thunder over the hills, and her gnarled fingers made her signs hard to read. "But I have seen what you have seen." With two gnarled fingers, she tapped the centre of her forehead.

"The sea ... the Blood Moon ... the great battle still to come."

"Yes. Even that."

"I have seen it, dreamt it, but I do not know the outcome. Will The People go? Will they turn back this tide?"

The old woman made a rumble in her throat, not laughter, more like the warning growl of a stag at bay. "I am the crone;

I see only death. And this one," she gripped Esa's shoulder, "is too young. It is time for the woman," a pause, "and the mother. You must finish this vision."

Tara raised her face, and Edan saw that she was clearly unsettled. "I have seen enough to know that everything comes too soon. Cuinn says that the Black Sun comes in one moon's time. It will take every day of that to reach the north. But he wishes to wait. There is no time, I must warn The People now."

"Warn them then." Ama responded to Tara's look of surprise with a bark of laughter. "Are we not the Seers? The Old Ones do not command us."

"But The Great Tale ..."

The old woman made her fingers into a circle. "It is the story of our beginnings. It is fitting that it also be the story of our end. When it is our turn, we will say what needs to be said."

Tara bowed her head again. "Thank you."

"I need no thanks. Did I not say it was not my time? You will be the one to do the talking." Tara made as if to speak but Ama went on. "I am too old either to head north or to run, so it is your time."

"As for you ..." without warning she prodded Edan in the middle of his chest, rocking him backwards, "you will listen and learn. Your turn to speak will come. Be ready." With the same hand she grasped his jaw, turning his head from side to side as she looked at him. Another rumble. "Not the face of a warrior. I see the shadow of fear in your eyes. But something else too; strange times." She released him and he rubbed his jaw ruefully.

"Both of you now, it is time to make ready." Planting her hand back on Esa's shoulder she shuffled away, heading in the opposite direction from the Old Ones.

Tara let her shoulders sag. "It is easy for her to say. Hard for me to do."

Edan had his mind on something Ama had said, and he asked, "Mother?" To his surprise a look of alarm crossed Tara's face.

"What?"

"You called her Mother, but she is not. Is she?"

"Oh! No. But I told you, I was only a little child when I came here. Ama raised me, taught me how to be a Seer. In many ways she was like a Mother to me. She always seemed eternal, but now that I have been away, I can see how old she is. She looks so frail." She trailed off.

"And ... you called me your mate."

A blink of surprise this time. "Why should I not? That is what you are."

Edan felt a sheepish smile creep across his face. "Well ... I. It has been a little while after all, since we ..." Tara reddened and he hurried on, "and when we got here you told Anagar I was just a companion."

Tara's gave a bark of laughter that made her sound just like Ama. "Words! You are worried about words? What does it matter what words I say to Anagar? You care about his opinion?"

He shuffled his feet on the short grass. "No."

She stroked his face with one hand, running her finger gently over the spot where Ama had grabbed him. He thought she was going to say something more, but she kissed him instead, her lips hot on his cold skin. He leaned into her embrace, raising himself on his toes and closing his eyes.

A shy clearing of a throat disturbed them, and Edan pulled reluctantly away to see that the girl, Esa, was standing a few feet away, her hands behind her back. "Tara ... Ama says ..."

"What does she say?"

The girl coughed, signing with her hands close to her chest: "That you have had enough time to play lover and must come and get ready."

Tara blushed again. "Of course. I'll come now." She turned back to Edan. "I must get ready, but I will come back before the tale. My part will not be till the end, so I will try and explain what I can."

Edan found himself alone amongst the bustle of The People's camp, drawing glances from everyone who passed him by. There were a few curious looks, but most of the gazes were hostile or fearful. After being jostled for what felt like the tenth time, he retreated to an empty corner where a stone provided a makeshift seat. A staff topped with the carving of a crow jutted from the soil a yard away, regarding him with one crude wooden eye. Edan had a sudden flash of a Fomor looming above him in a cresting wave, with a crown of severed crow wings framing the blackness where a face should have been and had to look away.

Had he really seen that, or was it an image the Fomor shadow had left in his mind? Could he trust anything he thought he had seen? In the river? In the vision at the cave? But he knew that he had to trust himself and not obsess over shadow-thoughts or he would become a Fomor-man as certainly as Phelan had. He forced himself to look at the totem again, but it was nothing more than a rough carving.

* * *

They had arrived in late afternoon, and now the late summer day was winding its way into evening. Edan watched as The People set about clearing a space in the midst of their camp. Drying racks for fish and birds were pulled aside, and some of the shelters were quickly taken down. The worn hide coverings from the dismantled tents were spread on the ground around the central fire for extra seating. All through the afternoon the Eshu came and went, heaping armfuls of reeds and sea grass onto the fire until it roared up a great mass of flame.

The People had no costumes or dances for their celebration. Instead they sang, pounding hollow logs and rocks on the ground to create a rhythm that quivered inside Edan's chest. It had no words, but instead layers of tone upon tone, growing in complexity as more and more of The People joined the throng, their towering shadows circling the fire. The singing circled too, dragging Edan's thoughts along its loops and swirls until he felt dizzy.

Slabs of meat were thrown onto the edge of the fire, sending sizzling showers of sparks up into the air. The rich smell made Edan realise how desperately hungry he was, and he slunk to the edge of the gathering, taking a place behind the others.

Someone handed him a chunk of meat out of the darkness, and he shoved it greedily into his mouth, letting the hot fat melt on his tongue and run down into the patchy stubble on his chin. The meat was rich and hot and tasted like the best thing he had ever eaten. Only when he had gobbled every last drop did he realise that it had been Tara who had given him the food.

In the flicker of the firelight he could see that she had marked her face with ash or ochre, and that she wore a shaggy pelt wrapped around her shoulders. Absently she started to wipe her greasy fingers on the fur, then thought better of it and cleaned them on the grass instead.

"Shouldn't you be getting ready?" Edan kept his voice low.

"I am as ready as I will get," Tara whispered back, "my part isn't till the end." She rubbed her hands together distractedly. "I don't know if I can do this."

He leant closer. "You faced down Phelan in the middle of a flood. You fought the lero with your bare hands. I think this will be easy."

He could just pick out her smile in the darkness. "So, when does this start?"

"It has already started." He started to ask her what she meant, but she cut him off with a gesture, hissing, "Listen, the first speaker."

Close to the fire, off to his right, someone rose. He could just make out a face framed with wild locks of hair. A woman's voice spoke. Hands gestured.

"I am Lirg, of the Bear's Kin, first and oldest." The woman's words were strange and guttural, and her gestures unfamiliar — not pitched for outside ears.

"I sing of the first time, the ice time, the cold time, the great beast time. Kin then were great as mountains, old as hills." Edan recognised some of her words from a story Tara had once told him of her people's origins, a story it seemed every one of The People knew but could not understand the rest. A ripple of laughter went through the circles of Trolls, but he had missed the joke they were responding too.

Tara leaned in close to translate. "She is speaking of the first age," she whispered, "when snow covered the Summer Lands and there were no humans here."

"Were there really such times?"

"Do not your own tales say the same?" She did not wait for an answer. "Now she tells of the great beasts that were in the land then, do you hear?"

Edan concentrated. Some words he understood, others seemed to make the leap into his mind without the comprehension of his ears, conjuring images he couldn't quite explain. He thought he saw huge lumbering creatures, four footed like an auroch but with their horns below their chins instead of on their brows, plunging through the smoke that billowed from the fire. Or perhaps they were made of smoke. After them came a bewildering procession: shaggy beasts with horns on their noses, slow-moving mounts of fur with ember eyes, rearing deer with antlers that spanned the campground. A hunting beast like a lero, but with fangs as long as a man's arm, pursued them through the smoke and then was gone.

By the time that Edan had realised that Lirg had stopped speaking, she had already stepped down, giving her place to a dour faced man with a drooping nose whose name he did not catch. In a voice as sombre as his expression this man began to speak of a time when the snow was gone, and the humans came in its place. "Many Kins made welcome of the new ones, with open arms and open hearts, but Eagle Kin had keen eyes and did not trust them."

Again, Tara whispered to fill the blanks. "He tells that the first humans were few in number. They came to lands where there were many of The People. Then, we did not know murder or conflict. He says that we were the greatest of hunters and did not fear anything. So, we gave our lands freely to the newcomers."

The second speaker gave way to a third. "I am Kaman, of the Crow's Kin. The Eagle Kin say they were wary, but it was the Crow who saw human treachery before it came.

I sing now of the blood time, the killing time. I sing of the fight for prey, for water. Others will sing of how we fought, I will sing of how we lost."

Edan turned away. He did not need Tara to translate the story of how the humans — how his own kind, had driven The People from the land they once called their own. Out beyond the circle a restless wind boomed and blustered over the sea, sweeping the fire's smoke off into the darkness. Edan watched it go with a feeling of dread. Phelan was out there somewhere. If the Fomor helped him as much as they had hindered Edan, he might be only days away. No matter what The People decided, Phelan might finish the slaughter that other humans had started.

More speakers came and went, telling the tale of Kins long gone, or conflicts lost. Some Tara translated for him, but before long she had to return to her place amongst the Seers and leave him alone. After that he gauged the content of the tales as much by the reaction of the crowd as by the few words he could make out. Unlike the tribe, where each story

210

was bound to the charm it belonged to, it appeared that all of The People knew The Great Tale. Sometimes they spoke the words along with the speaker, and at others they anticipated the words they knew were coming.

The food was heavy in his belly now. He could have done with more, but the meat was all gone. Instead, he was passed an antler beaker filled with cooling blood. He was last in line, probably passed the cup because there was nowhere else for it to go, and the contents were sticky and cloying, but he drank it anyway.

A pause in the tale marked the arrival of a new speaker, as it had done many times before, but this time new fuel was cast on the fire, and the chanting gained new vigour. The Great Tale was ending — it was the Seer's time to speak. Edan craned his neck to see Ama step into the firelight, Esa and Tara in the shadows at her back. The old woman held herself straight now, without a stick or a helper to lean on, and he saw that her costume of simple skin and hides had been replaced with a cape of the purest white that reached almost to her feet. At his distance he could not tell what it was made from, it might as well have been clouds or snow, or the white smoke of dry grass burning.

The Seer raised her hands for silence. When she spoke, it was with a clear enunciation and broad gestures that Edan imagined might have been for him.

"Kinsfolk. Strangers. The Great Tale is nearly told. I am old now, and have in my heart the final words, but I will not speak them." A puzzled murmur passed through the crowd.

"I give my place instead to another, known to you, the Seer Tara. She has been gone long, and travelled far, and has much to tell. Her words will make a more fitting end to our tale than the ones I would speak. Listen to her."

Even from the edge of the throng Edan could hear the objecting voice of Cuinn, but his protests achieved nothing. This was the time of the Seers; it was already done.

Worming embers lit Tara's face from below as she took her place at the fire, hooding her eyes in shadow and making her crimson hair burn brighter than the falling firelight. Edan thought she looked a match for any Fomor.

For a moment he worried that she would not speak, but she was brave. She raised her hands for silence and began.

24. Tara

"The tale I am telling you is not known to you. It is not history — it is now."

Looking out over the sea of fire lit faces, Tara wondered what Ama expected her to say. She'd wrestled all evening with the immensity of the task. So much had happened since she had last stood by the need fire that she hardly felt like the same woman. How was she supposed to condense all of that into one speech?

"When I am finished you will have a choice to make that will decide how our Great Tale ends."

'Start at the beginning' was what Ama had whispered in her ear as she had taken her place, and she clung to that simple instruction.

"My tale begins in the spring, on the day when the moon took its first bite from the sun. Following my vision, I left the Stone Forest and went north, into the land of men, where I was made a prisoner."

As she spoke the words seemed to bubble up from inside her, as if she had tapped into a hidden well of speech. Unconsciously, she shifted into the rhythm of The Great Tale.

"Fearing the black spirits of ocean called the Fomor, these Daesani planned my death. Till strangers, danger risking, broke me free.

Thus, saved from these wolf-men, to the north shore we journeyed. Where the Fomor, from sea fastness, grasp the land in flood fingers.

Chased by Phelan, as a hunter seeks his quarry, never resting in drowning land I saw the Fomor, salt crowned and clawed in darkness."

The crowd was silent. Even the Old Ones were no longer protesting. With quick gestures and flowing words, she described the confrontation at the river: Phelan's challenge, the human's defeat, the coming of the Fomor. Her mind threw up details drawn from Edan's description that she didn't know she knew. Cold-hearted and cunning she called them; monstrous and cruel. Then the words were rushing on again until …

"… to Dentaltos, where in old time kindred People made their dwelling. There the Fomor, with fell might into the sea, threw the great stone and as a sign of their anger froze the ocean, with red blood challenge they stained the moon."

She could feel the tension. Everyone had seen the Blood Moon and must have wondered what the portent meant.

"In forebears' cave, in vision, I saw the Fomor, and The People locked in battle, at the edge of night's darkness, at Dentaltos.

Against the rising of the Black Sun the kins united, spear thronging, our split blood is crow's cost, without this comes the drowning."

If she persuaded them of nothing else, she had to persuade them of this. The People must fight. But even as she spoke Tara felt a pang of fear — if they went, would they die? Abruptly she wanted to unsay what she had said, but the words flowed on regardless. In broad strokes she described the signs of the Fomor: the drowned boy, the earthquake on the plains, and most of all the fanaticism of the Daesani. "In Tanrid, at water's crossing, Wolf Phelan now gathers, scores of wolf-men. False speaking with Fomor's lie to persuade them that The People are their foes. Having failed there to waylay us, or with hound, chase to catch us, to stop my vision; cunning Fomor the great marsh turned against us, mist blinding, till relenting the Stone Trees led us home."

She gestured the word home with arms curving wide, the sign for the embrace of family. The rush of words left her as abruptly as it had come, so she brought her speech to a close without poetry.

"So, called to battle one last time, we must decide. There is still time to flee as the Grass People do — to leave the Summer Lands to the Fomor — or instead to fight them, to go to the place of my vision, to Dentaltos."

Her heart was pounding in her chest. She took deep breaths, trying to slow it down. Four beats; five, then everything was silent, the tale was over. There was nothing now save the sigh of embers; a shower of sparks leaping into the sky; the murmur of water in the darkness. She looked around a tableau of faces, silver with moonlight, red with fire glow. Had she said enough? Had she spoken the right words?

Suddenly the whole gathering of The People seemed to be on its feet, shouting questions, demanding answers. Some clamoured to know more of the Fomor, others asked fearful questions about Phelan, while others still, waving their fists in the air, urged battle. In moments the voices wanting war began to outnumber the rest. "Fight!" Tara heard them shouting, "Fight! Fight!" Fists, axes, even spears, were thrust into the air along with the chanting, and one of the Kin of the Bear, bedecked with trophy claws, leapt over the edge of the fire with a whoop, his tattered bearskin flaring.

She felt a presence to her side and looked up into the glowering face of Anagar. "It is the Warrior's choice!" She had to raise her voice and yell it twice more before the kins settled into a restless jostle. "It is the Warrior's choice" she repeated, then to him, "What do you choose?"

"Will these Fomor truly drown us all?" he asked her, hand-gesturing so that only she could see.

She gave him the only answer she could. "Yes. Truly."

Anagar raised his voice into a bellow. "I choose to fight!"

This time the chaos could not be quelled. The People surged forward, all custom forgotten, and Tara felt herself plucked from her feet and borne aloft, passed from hand to hand amid whoops and hollers. Faces came and went. Hands slapped her on the back or made the sign of respect. Voices overlapped each other, crying, "Fight! Tara! Seer! Fomor!" She looked for Edan in the tumult, but seeing beyond the press of bodies was impossible and the throng was already carrying her away.

They went down off the hilltop and up towards the stones, splashing through the ford by the pointless light of bundles of grass snatched from the fire, which dripped flame and ash into the wind but did nothing to the darkness. Somewhere behind them the drum logs began again, swelling into the victory chant of The People. 'How can they be happy?' she thought, and, 'What have I done?', but for good or ill she had no answer.

Eventually she was put back on her feet, but she was no more in control of where she went. A press of bodies and a blur of faces guided her this way and that through the darkness. Somewhere nearby gruff voices were already discussing the tactics of war against the Fomor and the Daesani, but she paid them no attention.

Somehow, she ended up in the Seer's hut, laid down upon the piled-up furs and dry rushes of her old bed. She nestled into the familiar worn spots of the deerskin base and inhaled the hare-pelt mustiness of her favourite blanket. She had a half-thought of dragging herself up to find Edan, but her exhausted body wouldn't co-operate. She closed her eyes, listening to the muffled sounds of the celebrations outside, but sleep didn't come easily either. Instead, she tossed and turned, tumbling in and out of dreams.

For a moment she thought she heard the rush of waves, and jerked awake, her hand going instinctively to the cold gap beside her where Edan should have been, but the hut was dry and empty. Before she was even fully aware that she'd woken, she dozed again, this time thinking that she heard the hiss of the wind over the grass plains. For a moment she thought that the bed was a cliff of grey stone from which a Fomor was dragging her and she thought that she was falling, but there was no cliff and no stone.

After that, she dreamt that the three Old Ones entered the hut. They stood over her, whispering something that she could not hear. Cuinn leant down and his white hair swelled until it became a circle of light, painfully bright. Druce's red hair became a second ball of fire, and Irin's dark countenance became a third. The shapes of the Old Ones faded away, leaving the three suns burning in the blackness.

All at once she was racing through the black ocean, with the white sun falling behind and the blood moon rising. Once again the vision carried her north, to the edge of the Summer Lands, and once again she saw the battle between The People and the Fomor, raging at the border between land and water. Above it all, the Black Sun rose.

This time, for the first time, the vision did not end with the battle. With a tremendous roar, a wall of water smashed into the shore. It was larger than she could comprehend, higher than the broken sea stack, higher even than the towering cliff. The sea surged and kept on surging, rolling up and over the land like a spill of blood. Fountains of spray hurled themselves over the cliffs; mounds of water poured themselves down the heather slopes; a black wave rolled out across the Summer Lands. Somewhere in that chaos the embattled People vanished.

Tara turned and fled.

She became a fish, became a bird, but something grabbed hold of her leg and dragged her back into the raging water.

She looked back in terror and saw a Fomor bursting from the waves. Its one eye was ice white, and its clawed hand closed around her.

She became a seal, became an eel, and tried to snatch herself from Bal's grasp, but the crab-claw fingers dug into her flesh, snapping her back and forth in the thrashing tide. One of the claws, needle-sharp, sank into her guts, sending sharp pain coursing through her. She saw the shark's jaws open; screamed in terror; awoke.

A figure loomed over her in the dim light within the hut, one of Anagar's warriors. When she opened her eyes, he let go of her arm.

"Get up. Wake your mate. You are needed."

Her hands went to her belly, remembering the sharp stabbing of the Fomor's claw, but there was no pain now. She started up out of the furs, wanting to warn the warrior of what she had seen, but he was already gone.

Tara emerged from the hut to find that the night had slipped by without her noticing. A tenuous dawn was breaking. The sun was a vague bar under a blanket of grey. Ribbons of cloud hung overhead, dissolving into rain that spattered fitfully on the breeze at her back.

A group of warriors were gathered near the stream. Tara could see them gesticulating, pointing at something on the ground before them, and then north towards the stones. More of The People were making their way down the slope towards them, and she hurried across the cold grass after them. One of them was asking, "What is happening?"

"They say a stranger came into the camp ... a human!"

When she reached the group, she saw that Edan had already been found. A loose semi-circle of people stood at the edge of the stream, two or three deep, surrounding a section of the bank. Edan was crouching on the wet grass in front of them, using one arm to support a man who was sprawled on the ground. The man's fur clothing was stained with mud, and his left leg was splayed out painfully in front of him. The flesh of his calf was swollen, blood red and angry with injury. Who was he? Why was his face familiar? She realised that the man was Morikatus. What was he doing here?

"Make way!" Tara heard Anagar's voice as he pushed the others aside. The warrior looked as if he hadn't slept but had still taken the time to apply more chalk to his hair. He gazed down at the two humans. "You. Seer's mate. What does this stranger say?"

Edan looked up at him, and then at Tara. "He says that Phelan of the Daesani is coming to attack you."

Anagar snorted. "For this I was roused? Nothing new here." Tara saw Edan whisper a translation into Morikatus' ear as Anagar spoke.

"You don't understand!" Morikatus' voice was cracked with pain and exhaustion, but he pressed on. "Phelan has gone mad. He has convinced his people that you Trolls are going to attack them and that they need to strike first. He has gathered all his men and is coming here. He wants you, Tara, Edan. They might be here at any moment!"

Consternation swept through the assembled People as Edan translated. "We must wake the others!" one of the kin of the bear insisted, while one of the kin of the auroch countered, "We must fight these humans!"

"No!" Edan's raised his voice into the confusion. "The Fomor are more important, we can't let Phelan stop us. If we waste time, he will block The Twins."

Anagar inclined his chalk-bristle head. "I agree with the human. The Seer has told us we must go north, not waste time on wolf-men. There is barely time enough to make the journey as it is."

Tara could hold it in no longer. "I was wrong!" There was silence. "I was wrong. If we go to the north to fight the Fomor we will die." She looked around at the circle of questioning faces. "I had a vision, another vision. I saw a wave drown the whole Summer Lands." The warriors' eyes were dark in their circles of charcoal and umber. "I am sorry. I was so sure."

Anagar broke the silence. "Our deaths are no surprise, Seer." Now it was Tara's turn to stare in confusion. "Do you think we agreed to fight expecting to return unharmed? No. We understood the danger of what you asked." He gestured at the encampment on the hill. "The old and young have already left for the east, the rest of us will fight."

"Your Vision. Did you see us die?"

Tara shook her head, wordless.

"Did you see these Fomor triumph?"

She shook her head again.

"Then your vision told us nothing that we did not know. Still ..." for a moment he looked at Edan and Morikatus as if it pained him to acknowledge their advice. "The humans are right. We cannot waste days fighting this Phelan and reach the north in time."

To her amazement, the warriors began to argue about strategy again, as if they had not heard her warning at all. Some suggested taking a coast route to avoid the Daesani, others advised a dash through the eastern mountains.

"If we travel the coast, we will be too late to Dentaltos."

"So, we go up into the hills, pass round The Twins, we know the way."

"And then they will come at us from the side, as we attack the auroch when they are on the run. It would be worse than facing them head on." A chorus of agreement.

Edan's voice rose over the throng. "Then we must send some to stop them, and some to face the Fomor." Edan spoke directly to Anagar, and the Warrior responded.

"How would those who go north pass through The Twins when the wolf-men still hold it?"

"They wouldn't have to. Look." Edan tugged a roll of deerskin from his pack and unrolled it on the grass, revealing the smudged map he had drawn in the Grass People's camp. "Here, this shows the route we took. This is the marsh, and here is the river. The Twins are here, below the Daesani's lake." His hand flicked from feature to feature as he spoke. "We can go up the cliffs here, east of The Twins and across the plain, then follow the river. This way we will reach Dentaltos and avoid the Daesani. I can lead you, as long as Phelan is distracted; here." Edan stabbed his finger on the narrow mark that indicated The Twins.

Anagar's brow furrowed as he stared at the markings on the deerskin. Tara took the opportunity to step up to his side, pulling away from the other warriors. "They call it a map. The signs show the landmarks we use to navigate, as a bird might see it."

Anagar blew hot breath into the chill air, but he took another look at the map, crouching down across from Edan. Slowly he picked out Edan's route, touching each mark in turn with a fingertip.

"It could be done." Anagar's tone was grudging, but Tara thought she saw a suppressed excitement in his gestures.

"Yes. If some were willing to stay behind, the rest could escape." To Tara's surprise many of the warriors voiced their agreement — more willing to face the humans than the Fomor perhaps?

She thought: 'Why are they still fighting? Weren't they listening to me?' She could imagine herself facing the Fomor, because she had seen with her own eyes what they could do. Did the rest of these eager hunters understand what they were volunteering for? She had a sudden mental image of Phelan, punching the air as he shouted, whipping the Daesani into a fury with words just like hers. It was an uncomfortable thought.

Anagar called for those who wished to delay the Daesani to come forward and stand to one side. Soon two score or more warriors, mainly of the kin of the auroch, had formed a group close by the tumbling stream. Tara watched, bewildered, as the plan for fighting on two fronts was agreed.

Edan helped Morikatus to sit up, then sprang to his feet and came to her, hands open. His movements spoke of nervous energy, and his eyes searched her face. "Tara, this is it. You did it. You actually persuaded them all. Everyone wants to stand against the Fomor, and Phelan too. Isn't it amazing?" His hands danced through the words with quick, choppy gestures.

"No ... Edan, didn't you hear what I said? The flood will still come."

He took her hands, curling his small fingers around hers. "It doesn't matter. We always knew the flood was coming." She felt a little shiver pass through him at this admission, but he pressed on. "I can't think of a better way to face it than side by side with The People — with you. We can go back to Dentaltos and face them, and who knows what will happen."

"No!" She jerked her hands free. "We can't go to Dentaltos!"

"I don't understand. Don't you want to be together, at the end?"

"You idiot! It is not just about us." Now she took his hands. "Don't you understand yet Edan? You are going to be a father."

To Tara it seemed that the whole crowd fell silent, though in truth only the closest few warriors had even heard her. Edan, though, was genuinely speechless. "That is why we cannot go to Dentaltos, Edan. We must think not only of ourselves, but of our child!"

Edan's mouth opened and closed soundlessly, like a fish gasping.

"I'm so sorry I didn't tell you before! I meant to, but it was never the right time."

Finally, he stammered, "What? How? You are having a baby? But it isn't possible! You said ..."

She cut him off, "I guess we aren't as different as I thought."

A foolish grin crept onto Edan's face. "I'm going to have a daughter, or a son!"

"A daughter," Tara said quickly, surprising herself.

"How can you know?"

She had been suddenly certain. "It is just a feeling. You aren't angry?"

The grin got wider. "Of course not." She felt their fingers entwine. "So ... not to Dentaltos." She shook her head, not trusting herself to speak in case she laughed or cried.

Edan looked round at Morikatus and Anagar. "I am sorry, I won't be able to lead you to Dentaltos after all."

The warrior snorted. "Better this way. Some human needs to go speak to the wolf-men. Can't be this broken one. Better you."

Tara wanted to protest this too, but the words died on her lips. She looked at the volunteers, stamping and laughing and preparing to go. She wouldn't shirk from the danger they were so eagerly embracing. The vision had run its course and her part was done. If they were willing to take the risks she had talked them into, then so was she. Anagar was correct. Someone had to try and talk the wolf-men out of their killing frenzy, and she couldn't imagine the Old Ones going to face the humans. It had to be them. But ... she remembered the last time they had stood face to face with Phelan, in the raging river, with the tribe falling one by one to the hands of the hunters.

"You want me to talk to Phelan?" Edan's voice squeaked a little.

"Yes."

25. Edan

The marshlands spread out before The Twins, brown and grey, framing the wide rushing river. It was late summer, but an unnatural chill had descended on the Summer Lands, and the air tasted of frost.

Edan and Tara had come north with a dozen each of boar-kin and elk-kin, and nearly all of the aurochs. They had made no attempt to be stealthy; instead, they had done their best to be noticed, lighting smoky fires and keeping to the open riverbanks. They were the beaters, catching the attention of the prey while the rest went around out of sight. Only in this hunt there were no waiting spears to drive their enemy onto. The rest of The People were hopefully far away, making for Dentaltos.

The journey had been easy, four days on the riverbank under pale skies. There had been no sign of the mists that had confused and trapped them on their way south, save a vestige of fog-breath, clinging to the shallows and the salt grass. Edan couldn't help but wonder; was it because The People's spirits were with them, or because the Fomor wanted them to encounter Phelan?

When Edan had last been at The Twins it had been on the edge of night. He had had an impression of towering cliffs and jagged rocks that echoed back the gravel-bed hiss of the river and had thought the two sides mere paces apart. Now he saw that the river was at least an hour's walk from the eastern cliff and many hours from the western ones.

A multitude of Daesani were strung out along the east bank of the river, blocking the route that any force from the south would take if it wanted to pass The Twins and Tanrid. A smudge of smoke on the pale morning air betrayed camp fires behind the line of hunters and scouts. Flocks of marsh birds whirled and wheeled in agitation above them, taking wing for the white cliffs beyond the river. There might have been movement in the camp as well, but it was hard to tell.

Edan allowed himself a brief moment of satisfaction. They had done their job. There was no way that the Daesani horde in front of them could hope to catch the rest of the Trolls. The satisfaction faded — now he had to stop Phelan.

On the journey from the Stone Forest he had spoken at length with Morikatus. The trader was weak, and his leg injury grew worse each day despite the Troll's attempts to heal it, but he had insisted on coming with them.

By the campfire, Morikatus had told him a tale that filled them with horror. By his account, Phelan had whipped the Daesani into a frenzy of bloodlust, convincing them with speeches and threats that the Trolls were as much their enemies as the Fomor, or more. To hear him tell it, Phelan had told them that if they didn't stop the Trolls, then they would never escape the doom to come.

Edan wasn't blind to the similarities between Morikatus' story and what had happened at the Troll-moot. In another time he might have found the irony funny; perhaps when he wasn't the one offering to walk into the madness and try to talk them out of it.

Morikatus had said that he had tried to reason with the Daesani. "There was a man. He was called Duah, I think. Forked beard, sly, but I could see that he did not like Phelan." He had stirred the embers of their fire with a stick, looking into the flames. "I spoke to him, tried to make him see reason. It did not work. He might hate Phelan, but the fear runs strong in those people. He listened, but he did nothing, and after that I was watched. They did not call me a prisoner, but I knew that I could not leave."

"I watched them preparing to fight. I knew that Phelan did not care about the Trolls — he cared about you and Tara. It came to me that I had to warn you, so I determined to escape. That's how I get this," he had patted his injured leg, wincing. "I wait until night, take some food from them, make a run for safety. They set the dogs on me. Luckily the one that got a bite at me could not follow up the cliff I was climbing and so I got away."

Morikatus had leant close, the firelight making it look as if his face had been dipped in blood. "He is mad Edan, and he has infected them all with his madness. I know you must try to stop him, but how do you reason with insanity?"

In the chill morning light, Edan remembered his words and wondered, how would he reason with him? Speaking with Phelan seemed like an exercise in futility, he might not even remember him. But who then? Duah? Duah would only turn against Phelan if there was a guaranteed reward in it, and Edan didn't have anything to offer.

He shifted uncomfortably, feeling the hardness of the pebbles through the worn soles of his shoes; all his senses were on edge. The ground was as cold as the air and he thought again of the ice that had crowded the northern sea. His skin felt tight, stretched across his face like frost on a stone, an echo of the old fears, but he would not give in to them.

There was movement for sure now, along the Daesani lines. Tiny man-shaped specks were raising their spears, one by one. At this distance they looked like the stick figures scratched into the edge of the Stalker's charm, hardly real. Some of them gathered at the river banks, pointing their spears south, and he knew that they had been seen.

Edan turned round to look at the line of bulky warriors strung out along the shore behind him and raised his hand to them in the agreed signal. One of the boar-kin came forward and handed him a spear which he held out above his head, parallel to the ground, in the sign of greeting. Hopefully, the Daesani would talk before they fought.

Two groups met in the open land between the lines, approaching each other cautiously until they were sure that the rules of meeting were in force. Edan and Tara were in one, accompanied by Morikatus and two representatives from each of the three kins. In the other Edan saw the familiar forked beard of Duah, and the uncomfortable sight of Uch in Daesani garb, but his focus was on Phelan, striding wolf-eared and grey-eyed, at their head.

They settled into two rough lines, with eight feet of empty space between them. Only Phelan stepped into the gap, claiming it for himself, though Duah stepped up to his side. There were more Daesani than Trolls, but Edan knew how intimidating the kin-warriors must look to Phelan's hunters, and had chosen the largest and fiercest of The People to come forward. One of the auroch-kin, bull's horns jutting from his forehead, took a mock step, lowering his head as if he was going to charge the Daesani line, and half of the wolf-men jerked back; but the auroch only laughed, tossing his head.

The two sides sized each other up. Edan felt Phelan's hard eyes ranging over Tara and himself, predator quick under wolf-tooth brows. No, he'd not been forgotten. The wolf leader looked taller, gaunt, sharp as a knife blade. He'd shaved his face clean; wore a few day's stubble like a shadow, and his eyes, once flat and hooded, seemed to burn with an almost feverish intensity. Edan felt himself squirm in his gimlet gaze. He had prepared words, husbanded them in his head for just this moment, but Phelan struck first.

"It has been a long time since the river."

Blink flashes of the tribe taken prisoner, of the wave mountains tumbling down shivered up Edan's spine. The rush of the river, blood pounded in his ears, foaming its way out of The Twins. Why did they always meet beside water? Edan pushed away the memories of the Legu, he'd faced those fears already.

He opened his mouth to respond, but Phelan struck again. "You cannot face us. Put your tail between your legs, boy, and run. Go back to your Fomor masters and tell them that they cannot stop us."

Edan was almost tempted to take the offer and retreat, job done. But even at that moment a Daesani scout might be running south with news of the other Trolls, who could not be much more than hours ahead and a few miles east. Besides, Morikatus had told him that he and Tara were Phelan's real target. If Phelan was still obsessed with them than that was an opening to play on.

"I didn't come here to fight you."

The grey eyes hardly blinked. "If you came to join us, you are too late. You had your chance for that boy, but you chose the enemy instead." Edan glanced at Duah, trying to get his attention, but the Daesani was looking past him. Was he counting the Troll line? How long before they realised how few in number they were?

"I came here to warn you. There is very little time left. Soon the Fomor will raise a great flood — in twenty days. You were there at the river Legu, you saw what happened. You need to get your people to safety."

Phelan barked a laugh, but there was no humour in it. "Of course you would say this. You are a servant of the Fomor, flood-bringer, kin-drowner. No doubt your masters told you this."

Edan bristled, raised his hackles, and gritted his teeth. Kin-drowner! Phelan knew just the words to get to him. He tried to regain his calm, but Phelan grinned his wolf grin, and Edan felt his heart jump in alarm. It was the grimace of a beast. Was he looking into the face of a man, or of a Fomor? In confusion, he lost his train of words, but Tara spoke for him.

"Do you really believe that Phelan?" Edan saw that she kept her fists balled at her sides, avoiding the gestures of Eshu speech. "You took me prisoner on my way to fight the Fomor! They killed Edan's family, you must know that by now. We would never serve them! It is only your sick imagination that says otherwise."

If Phelan was surprised to learn that Tara could speak as they did, he did not show it, but nor did he reply, and she took advantage of that.

She took a step forward. "You want me for yourself, that's what this is about. Your hunters pawed at me, but you ... you fixed me with your gaze like ..." She faltered, and Edan saw, for the first time, something that looked like genuine emotion in Phelan's eyes. What was it? Anger? Lust? Fear? Yes, it was fear, but not of them. A desperate fear. A fear that drove him to madness.

Edan knew that he had to find a lever to make Duah act before the situation spiralled out of control and violence erupted. Desperately he remembered the things Tara had told him about Phelan. His obsession; his night-time confessions; the scars on his flesh. He remembered the sacrifice at the lake's edge. Phelan had spoken of sacrifice when he held Tara prisoner. Sacrifice! That was it. Suddenly he understood what Phelan had wanted.

Edan took a wild chance. "You know you'll never have her for your sacrifice! Her blood won't save you. Even if you kill us all it won't make you safe!"

At last the mask slipped, and the beast snarled back, "I'll prove you wrong!"

Edan pushed harder. "Because it's fated? Because it is destiny? No! You think you are in control, but you've done nothing! Tara escaped you at the lake; we escaped you in the forest; I beat you at the river. You couldn't get her, and you couldn't get me. Now even the Trolls have escaped you. You've failed, Phelan. You always fail." He was yelling now, not caring if the distant Daesani should hear. He had to make him crack!

An incoherent yell broke from Phelan's lips and he surged forward, shoving Duah aside. "No! I must have her!" His words were wild, panted and foam flecked. "Her blood! Don't you see? The Fomor are coming — the water! All this will be for nothing without Fate's blessing. Her blood for Fate's blessing!"

There it was! A ripple of consternation went through the Eshu behind him, and Edan could see the same shock reflected in Duah's face.

Tara must have seen it too, and she shouted. "You will never have me!"

"I must!" Suddenly the blade of black glass was in Phelan's hand and he lunged for Tara. Duah tried to block him, but the blade flashed, and he crumpled. The wolf leader came at Tara again, but Duah's intervention gave the two Elk-kin enough time to pull Tara back and get in the way, shoving Phelan away.

"Don't just stand there!" Phelan snarled at the other Daesani, "get her!"

Edan saw Uch take a half step forward with the meeting spear in his hand, while the others produced weapons they had hidden in their clothes. Half the people seemed to have weapons too.

"Stop!"

Duah's shout froze the Daesani in their tracks. With a grunt he sprang back to his feet. There was blood running freely from a livid slash across one cheek, but there was iron in his voice.

Phelan rounded on him, his blade flicking back and forth, now pointing at Tara, now Duah. He bared his teeth at Duah, but Duah snarled back.

"Don't defy me!" Phelan barked out the words, but Duah snatched the spear out of Uch's hands and stepped forward to engage him. They circled crabwise, testing the footing of the river bank with cautious steps.

Phelan was taller, leaner, faster, but his movements were almost frenzied. His knife wove eccentric patterns in the air, while Duah held the spear low and steady. To Edan's eyes the two Daesani looked evenly matched.

Both sides pulled back, instinctively forming a loose circle around the two men. It was clearly a fight that had been a long time coming. Edan scanned the distant Daesani lines.

226

Could they see what was happening? Would they join the fight? If they did, then The People would not survive.

"Do you think you can stand against me? Now?" Phelan's voice broke on the last word.

"Do you think you can break peace and not suffer consequences?" Duah's voice was as focussed as Phelan's was wild, pitched for the ears of the listening Daesani. "You've gone mad. You've kept us here all this time out of bloodlust! You've preached war and murder because you are obsessed with one stupid Troll! We've slaved and laboured and lost good men because you are afraid!" Edan could see agreement in the faces of the encircling warriors.

With a yell of rage, Phelan sprang forward, jabbing at Duah, but the attack was wild and Duah turned it aside with his shoulder. Phelan thrust again and again, so that Duah fell back before him, but even Edan could see that the smaller man was the one in control. Once or twice Phelan lashed out with his knife as well as the spear, and then Duah looked harder pressed, taking cuts to his fine fur coat, but always he pulled back, leading Phelan on.

And then suddenly it was over. Phelan lunged and Duah did not retreat — instead he caught the spear and yanked it hard, forcing Phelan off-balance, though he took another slash with the knife for it. Phelan skidded on the loose gravel, trying to turn the lunge into a dash, but Duah cracked him hard across the ankles with the spear and sent him sprawling. He roared up off the shingle, but Duah struck him hard on the side of the face and knocked him back down, sending the wolf headdress flying off into the water. Phelan tried to push himself up a second time, struggling onto hands and knees, but it was obvious that the fight was already over.

Duah made a gesture and the remaining Daesani ran forward to take hold of Phelan and drag him aside; all except Uch, who hung back with a look of utter confusion on his face. Phelan cursed and bucked, but the hunters held him fast.

Duah stepped fastidiously across the disturbed gravel and plucked Phelan's headdress out of the water. He held it up for a moment as if he was planning to try it on for size, but he tucked it through his belt instead. He gave Phelan one brief glance of disgust and then turned to Edan and Tara.

"Phelan is … ill. I will speak for the Daesani."

Tara signed the rest of The People back behind them and waited. For an uncomfortable time Duah appeared to contemplate the rushing water of the river, the migrating birds overhead, even the pebbles at his feet. He spoke, but only to himself, and Edan couldn't make out the words. Finally, he turned his attention back to them.

"You are not our friends … but you do not need to be our enemies. This land is done. We will go to Eburakos, but there is no place for the Eshu there, you must choose another way."

"We have."

Duah stroked his beard absently, then jutted his chin in the direction of The People's line. "This isn't all of you, is it? I counted no more than three score. The rest of them aren't about to attack us from the rear, are they?"

Tara shook her head emphatically, but Edan wondered if they should answer. Would he attack them if he knew that there were no more Trolls in hiding? Apparently, Tara thought otherwise. "They are going where your hunters should have been going — to fight the Fomor."

Duah laughed. "Good luck with that!" Then more seriously, "Do you think you can do it? Save the Summer Lands?" Without waiting for a reply, he answered his own question. "I saw what happened at the river as well as the rest of you. You can't fight that. All we can do is find somewhere else." He turned to go, heading past Uch, then stopped and came back to Edan. "You know, the rest of your tribe are with us now. You could leave these Trolls and join us. No? Suit yourself."

Later, when the Daesani and The People had withdrawn to their respective camps, Second Mother came to repeat Duah's offer. She crossed the open ground alone in the half-light, picking her way around the smoke that drifted from The People's cooking fires. Cinnia, Edan reminded himself, not Second Mother. She looked happier than the last time he had seen her, and she wore a simple buckskin cap, reminiscent of the one she had worn with the tribe.

Edan made a space for her by the fire, patting the earth to invite her to sit down, but she hovered uncomfortably at the edge of the circle, eyeing the kin-warriors cautiously.

"Cinnia!" Edan tried to put as much warmth into his voice as he could. "Will you join us? We have a little hare on the fire. Are the others here?" He wasn't surprised when she shook her head uncomfortably.

"No, I should get back to the Daesani camp. Uch, he … he hasn't taken it well, what happened to Phelan."

"Phelan is a madman." Edan didn't try to make his voice warm this time.

"I know. I know. They are saying he is moon-touched, that they will put him out of the Clan. I think Duah will lead now. But Uch — Phelan was the reason he was accepted. It will be harder now that he is gone."

"I'm sorry." To his surprise Edan found that he meant it. If he had found himself amongst the Daesani, he might have looked for a patron as well.

"You could come and join us, you know — the rest of the tribe. It was Phelan that wanted you dead. Now that Duah's in charge it will be different. Everyone's heard what Phelan said by now." Edan wondered if she meant the two of them, or just him.

"Join the Daesani?"

"Join your family, Edan."

Edan looked over at Tara, half visible beyond the flickering flames. "I'm already with my family." He stretched out a hand to touch her belly, and this time the warmth in his voice was truly genuine.

Cinnia looked confused for a moment, then her eyes widened. "How … how is that possible? Edan, what have you done?! This is against all Tradition!" She clutched at the charms still hanging around her neck, ready to use them to ward off this evil.

Edan made to stand, to hotly defend them both, but Cinnia had already let her hand fall again. To his amazement she began to laugh. "Oh, what am I saying! What use is Tradition now? Have I not broken it a dozen times over already, and likely to break it a dozen more?" She gestured back at the distant lights of the Daesani fires. "I've thrown in my lot with the wolves, Edan, and they know nothing of our Traditions. Who's to say that your choice is any worse?"

"But … you could still visit with us, at least. Brina would love to see you, I'm sure." Cinnia cast her eyes across the squatting People. "Not all of you, of course …"

Edan knew that the three kins, denied their battle, had already decided to try and follow the women and children who had gone east. Boll, the Auroch chief, had grudgingly offered him a place alongside them, implying that they would already be burdened by one human, so two would be little worse, but Edan knew that he could no more live amongst The People than Tara could live amongst the Daesani.

"Don't worry. The People will be gone by dawn."

"But you won't go with them?"

Edan shook his head in reply. Cinnia opened her mouth to say something, then stopped. Nervously she stepped forward, coming close enough to the fire to be clearly seen. Edan could see that she was staring at him — no, staring at something on his chest.

"That charm ... the Hunter's charm. It is Maccus' isn't it?"

Edan lifted the charm up on its leather thong, holding the worn bone arrowhead up to the firelight. "Yes, it is."

"You found his body?" Cinnia's hand flew to her mouth. "How? When?"

"After the flood. Many days after. The Fomor threw it up on the shore."

Cinnia turned away from the fire again, so that he could not see her face. He reminded himself that she had known Maccus for more years than he had lived.

"Where will you go then?"

Edan hadn't talked to Tara about it, but the answer seemed clear. "To the Winter Place. And then I suppose that we will see what lies beyond The Great Wood after all."

26. Phelan

A face was staring down at Phelan from the wall, grinning at him through the gloom. He wondered how it had gotten there. One of its eyes was a white smear, the other a burning red point. It made him uncomfortable, and he tried to think where he had seen it before. Had it been in a dream? Everything had become so confused.

Suddenly angry, Phelan leapt up from his deerskin bed and rounded on the face. "Get out! Get out!" he shouted, but the face didn't move. Now that he was closer to it, he could see that it was daubed onto the wall with mud and excrement and blood. Was that his blood?

Outside, through the thickness of the wall, he could hear the sounds of people in motion, the hard slap of dressed skins being stacked on one another and the clack of wooden poles. His people were packing up and leaving, fleeing the Fomor, while he was trapped in the darkness.

"How did you let this happen?" the face asked.

"You know how it happened!" Phelan's head was hurting, pain throbbed from the spot where Duah had struck him with the spear butt. Duah! This was his fault.

"You should kill him," said the face.

Yes. Phelan thought that he could easily smash his way through the wattle and mud of the hut wall with the sharp stone that he kept hidden under his bedding. But then what? Any Daesani he met would recognise him — would report him to Duah, who would confine him here again, 'for his safety'. What good would that do? Who was going to save the Daesani now, if not him?

"But you aren't saving them, are you?"

"Get out of my head!" Phelan shouted at the wall. He clawed at the caked mud with his fingernails, leaving a long scratch that made the face leer crookedly. It cackled, mocking him. He pressed his hands to his ears, stumbling around the inside of the hut, but the sound refused to lessen.

"Fate has deserted you."

No. That couldn't be right. He'd done everything he'd been asked, to win Fate's favour. Fate had put him within reach of the Troll woman, then snatched him away. Cruel; she was so cruel! If Fate wasn't on his side, then he would make his own Fate. But the voice in his head was telling him that Fate didn't want him to win.

"Silence Shaman! I have had enough of your prattle."

"Oh," the voice sounded amused, "is that who you think I am?"

Phelan stopped his erratic progress around the chamber and stood stock-still in the centre of it. If it was not the old dead Shaman who was speaking, then who was it?

"You should see who's at the door," the face said.

Phelan froze, and then turned, suddenly aware that there was someone nearby. The prison Duah had made for him was his own private sanctum, but the hide curtain had been replaced with a sturdy door of tight woven hurdles. Now that the face was quiet, he could hear someone nervously breathing on the other side of the door.

Phelan pressed his face to the door, feeling the cold wood against his cheek. Through the narrow gaps between the hurdles he could just make out a figure in the gloom of the outer hut. One figure. Since Phelan had been imprisoned, it had been Duah's habit to always have two men in place to guard against his escape, but they did not usually come close to the door, and never alone. Duah, naturally, had made his home elsewhere in Tanrid.

"Who's there?"

A hesitant voice filtered through the wood, "Uch, sir, it's Uch."

Uch? Phelan remembered a scrawny man with a shock of black hair. One of the newcomers who had come to them from Edan's tribe. He had a vague memory of the man being at his back when he had gone out to confront the servants of the enemy. Did that make him an ally? He wasn't sure.

"Uch. I know you. What are you doing here alone?"

"I volunteered to guard you." Phelan thought he could hear shame in the man's voice. "I wanted Duah to think that I could be trusted."

"But you can't be trusted?"

"I can! By you!" Behind him the face cackled, but Phelan waved for it to be silent.

"And the other guard?"

"He wanted to help his family pack. I told him I'd cover for him."

Ambitious, desperate for status; that was Uch he remembered now. The first of Edan's tribe to turn Daesani. A mate just as grasping as himself. Was this a sincere attempt to help, or a trick to give Duah the excuse to kill him? Would Uch be desperate enough for favour that he would betray him? He waited a moment for the face to advise him, but there was nothing. 'Oh, now you stay silent' he muttered to himself.

"I'm sorry," the voice quavered from the other side of the door. "I didn't catch that."

Phelan cursed himself for speaking out-loud. If he didn't get out of this place soon, he'd go mad. To trust or not to trust? Unsure, he stalled a moment more.

"Never mind. You are kin to Edan. Tell me, is he here also?"

Uch's voice was hesitant. Distrusting, or simply embarrassed? "No. He left with the Troll woman, not long after ... after the truce. They would not stay with us."

Phelan realised that he had no choice but to trust the man. Even if it was a trick, it would get him out of this cage.

"Just let me out."

Now he heard fear. "Let you out? No! I can't do that. I just wanted to tell you that I was sorry for what had happened. To tell you that not all of the tribe, the people who used to be the tribe, were like Edan."

Phelan gritted his teeth and clutched at the door until his fingertips went white. It hurt, but it kept the sound of anger from his voice.

"I appreciate the thought, but I would appreciate my freedom more."

This comment was met with nothing but the sound of anxious breathing. The man did not have the bravery to let him out, not alone. He would have to change his tack.

"Then I need you to take a message." He didn't give Uch the chance to refuse. "You will go to Newlyn and tell him that I must leave Tanrid before it is abandoned. Tell him that it must be at night. He will know what to do."

* * *

After Uch left, the face on the wall did not speak to Phelan directly again, instead it whispered in his dreams. He found that he slept frequently, but never for very long, and took to pacing out the time between rests, back and forth across the tiny space. He tried to make sense of the things he thought that he had dreamt, but none of them were clear. There had been rushing water, biting cold, the terror of the flood and the taste of blood. One evening he awoke certain that creatures woven out of buckthorn and bindweed had been raking through the corners of his room. None of these things told him more than he already knew, but he felt increasingly desperate to be let out, before it was too late. He felt certain that Edan had not lied. The doom of the Summer Lands would come with the full moon, and the days were slipping by.

"Fate is no longer your ally," the face whispered.

"So, you said before."

Phelan dreamt that he was standing on the lip of a vertiginous cliff, poised above a sheer drop into a pounding sea. The waters below were stained red with blood, crashing and washing against the rocks. Flocks of gulls flung themselves at something rolling in the waves, then beat crimson into the air. The voice spoke directly into his ear, as if the speaker stood just behind his shoulder, but he did not care to turn and see it.

"Then you should find another. One that will serve you better."

"And where will I find this ally?" Phelan flung his words into the teeth of the wind, letting it blow them back to his unseen companion. "Everyone has turned against me. Even my own pack! Duah will go back to Eburakos and take my place at the Great Wolf's side." Dream logic imagined Duah wearing both his headdress and his face, the Great Wolf unaware that a substitution had been made.

"Do as we desire, and we will spare your people."

"We?" Now Phelan wanted to see the face that spoke, but he could not move. "Who are you?"

"Do you really need to ask?"

In front of him a spire of rock was toppling into the sea, splintered by battering waves, massive chunks of it crashing into the water. Overhead, a black sun cast rays of darkness across a glowing sky. Phelan opened his mouth to demand answers of the Fomor, but suddenly he was falling too, tumbling through the air to land with a shock on the heaped-up skins of his bed.

Phelan stared up at the thatch above his head. It was almost pitch black in the closeness of his cell. Only the faint glow of moonlight through the gaps at the top of the wall gave the chamber shape and dimension.

He grasped at the fleeting tails of the dream that had awoken him, but they were gone as soon as he reached for them. Instead, he realised that he could hear voices in the main part of the hut, the long room where his pack had once made their home.

He scrambled to his feet and went to the door, crouching in case anyone was looking through the gaps from the other side. The waxing moon was high, shining through the smoke holes in the roof. By its light he could just make out two figures — night-time guards.

"I can manage alone, if you want to sleep." Uch's voice, nervous.

"It is no problem." Phelan tried to place the second voice. It might have been one of the marsh fishers who had joined them in the spring. "I enjoy these clear nights — the silence. There has been little quiet of late."

"Of course, of course." Uch's anxiety seemed plain to Phelan, but the other man appeared to miss it.

Why were they here? The second man was clearly no conspirator, therefore no friend of Phelan's, but then why had Uch returned? He had not come back after that last visit. Was this part of some plan, or was he simply Duah's man like all the rest? Had he even spoken to Newlyn as he'd asked?

Phelan considered the door. It was just a frame of woven branches, fixed to the upright logs that bore the roof's weight and braced with poles of wood. If he flung himself hard against it, maybe it might break. He could not prevail unarmed against two men, not quietly enough to avoid rousing the camp, but would Uch stand aside as he had stood aside at the river, or help him?

On the other side of the door, Uch started to try and make the marsh man leave again. Whatever he wanted to happen, he wanted it soon.

Suddenly there came the sound of running feet, the unmistakable slap of calloused soles on the hard earth of the long hut's floor. Through the slats of the door he saw swift shadows charging headlong from the entrance. The fisher just had time to cry out before one of the figures collided with him and the cry was cut short.

There came the soft sound of a body being laid to ground, and then the poles were knocked aside, and the door opened. In the half-light beyond his cell he saw Newlyn and Cuall, with Uch standing behind them wringing his hands. Newlyn was bulky, carrying a heavy leather bag across his back, while Cuall had wrapped himself in a deerskin cloak.

Phelan clasped hands with Newlyn, forearm pressed to forearm. Newlyn was dependable, faithful. He would have rather it had been Kaman than Cuall, who could no longer run. Even Uchdryd, who had more reason than most to hate Edan and Tara, would have been preferable; but he must take what he was given.

"I'm glad to see you both. I thought I would never be free of that place."

"Not free yet." Newlyn kept his voice low, just a burr in the darkness. "We must get you away before others come." He went to the door, glancing out into the darkness.

Phelan needed no further hints, and he made for the exit. Newlyn and Cuall fell in before and behind, but Uch held his ground. "You too." Uch looked reluctant, but he grabbed him by the arm and hauled him out between the huts and onto the high ground behind. The last time Phelan had seen these slopes they had been piled with supplies gathered by the Daesani for their long trek. Now they were moonlight bare, with furze and heather the only cover.

"Here, I brought you this." Newlyn held out his hand, proffering the knife of sharp obsidian that had been wrenched from his hand after the fight with Duah.

"Thank you. And my crown?"

Newlyn shook his head. "Duah has it."

Of course, Phelan thought. Duah had won the challenge, the mark of the wolf was now his to wear. Well, let him wear it. He would save the Daesani without it.

He turned on Uch instead. "Tell me where they have gone — Edan and the Troll."

"Why do you need to know that?"

The blood anger flared at the refusal, filling Phelan with rage. For a moment he felt as if the face was pressing up inside him, as if it was his own face, as if he was looking out of its bloodshot eyes, or it was looking out of his. He grabbed

236

hold of Uch's clothing and hauled them tight around his throat until he was on tiptoes. Frantically Uch clawed at Phelan's arm, but he clenched his fist, the muscles stood out like cords.

"Phelan! He helped you escape!" The others protested but he paid them no heed.

"You spoke with them, you told me! Now tell me where!"

Uch choked out the words. "No! He's my kin, I won't help you hurt him!"

In response, Phelan threw Uch to the ground. The blood lust filled him now, and he slammed his heel into Uch's side, hearing something crunch wetly under the impact.

Again, the cry of protest, again he ignored it. If the others were going to try and stop him, they would already have acted.

He dropped to the ground next to Uch, putting pressure on his injured side with his knee, and leant close, pressing the obsidian blade against his cheek. "Tell me what I want to know, or should my blade turn its attention to your mate when it is done with you? Or to your child perhaps?"

"To the north!" Uch choked out the words. "To our winter home. That's where they said they were going."

Phelan eased the pressure from his knee but kept a hint of contact to remind him of the consequences of silence.

"Where is it?"

"Round the curve of The Great Wood, near the shore of the river Udso."

Phelan snarled in annoyance. "That word means no more than water in our tongue. This land is drowning in rivers. I need a landmark!"

"The mere! Where you met us. The river you crossed when you chased us, that was the Udso. Follow it south from the mere to where it meets the forest, and that is the place. I swear it!"

"You wouldn't lie to me?"

"No! No!"

Satisfied, Phelan put away his blade, and ran his hands quickly through Uch's clothing, delving into the leather pouches tied at his belt. He found dried moss for tinder, a scallop shell with a sharp edge, a handful of antler points and then, best of all, a pouch of hazelnuts. All these he took, tucking them into his own clothing.

"Newlyn, Cuall, now is the time. Will you hunt with me, one last time?"

Cuall looked away, and Newlyn hung his head, unwilling to reply. Phelan felt the rage rise again but held it back; these were his pack mates.

"Neither of you?"

It was Newlyn that spoke. "There was no need for this violence. He was in your pack — our pack. Your lust for blood has driven you mad. This land is already done, the waters rise faster every day, the wind brings snow even in the summer. You have already saved the Daesani. Forget this obsession and come away with us to the west. There will be hunting enough in the new land."

"Forget?" Phelan held himself taut, ready for more violence. "No, there is every need. I have been promised. With one death I will buy life for the rest of us."

"Promised by who?"

Phelan ignored the question. Even these two, who had once been as close to family as he would allow himself, had betrayed him. So be it. He would go alone.

"You have food there, an axe, that deerskin cloak, give them to me." He directed the last at Cuall, who offered no argument, divesting himself of the cloak and holding out to him. The moonlight reflected faintly from the bare skin of his arms, betraying a sheen of sweat.

Phelan wrapped the cloak quickly around his shoulders, then looped the leather satchel that Newlyn handed him over the top. He could afford to carry no more. The boy and the Troll had at least eight days head start on him. He would have to travel at his fastest to catch them. He could only hope that he knew the ground better than they did.

"You will catch them."

He jerked around, wondering which of the other three had read his thoughts, but it was not they who had spoken. The face was with him still. The Fomor, ever watching.

There was nothing more to be said. He allowed himself one nod, a farewell to Tanrid and his people, and he was gone.

27. Edan

The sky was clear, cloudless, and as blue as a starling's egg, the day that the world ended.

Edan and Tara had allowed themselves fourteen days to reach the Winter Place, out of the score that remained before the Old One's deadline. They wanted to get as far away from the Daesani as they could. They had learnt that the wolf-men were making for a place called Eburakos, a camp at the edge of the lands of Gok where a mighty river flowed out of the forest, the same river that made its way to the lake of Tanrid from the west, and they wanted to be nowhere near it.

Edan had thought that fourteen days was a generous estimate. The Winter Place could not be that far away, but he had been wrong. The landscape they had to cross was at the very centre of the Summer Lands, as far from either coast as it was possible to be, and yet even here the encroaching waters made themselves felt. For the first four or five days beyond Tanrid they had slogged their way through a mere of countless channels and hummocks, until at last they had reached a swathe of higher ground that trailed from the forest edge down to the marsh below.

Neither of them knew anything of this land beyond a name, Esa, supplied by one of the boar-kin before they had set out. If any people, human or troll, had ever made their home on these slopes, they were long gone now, with no trace left behind except an occasional heap of flat stones that might as easily have been the work of spirits as men.

Streams sub-divided the land with monotonous regularity, cutting through the soft earth on their way to the marsh. Each was a struggle to ford, and the open fields between them were claggy with mud and squelching with water. When they came across patches of woodland, they offered a welcome relief from the constant damp. They stayed a night in the first one, a whole day in the second.

More than once Edan considered abandoning the slog and entering The Great Wood. It was so close now; they could be under the boughs of the trees in less than two days if they wanted. What did it matter whether they entered the Wood now, or trekked a score of days to do so at the Winter

Place? All of the forest was equally unknown to them. It was the logical choice.

And yet he couldn't bring himself to suggest it. Maybe it was simply the desire to stay near the lands he knew as long as possible, or maybe it was the last little hold that Tradition had over him. The thought of entering The Great Wood terrified him; there was a fear he hadn't conquered yet. If the Elder had been there — if the Elder had been alive — then he would have insisted on the familiar ways, the time-worn paths. Surely, they owed at least that much to the ancestors.

Thinking of the Elder reminded Edan of the First Man's tale, which he had told to the Daesani so many months ago. In the long winter nights, he would tell the other tales that followed from it: The First Son's Tale, The Sea Hunter's Tale, The Wanderer's Tale. The last was the one that laid down the timings of the spring and autumn journeys, the boundaries of the hunting grounds and the dangers of straying from these rules.

Edan did not have the Wanderer's charm, but he remembered the tale well enough. He had told it to himself as they headed north from the second patch of woodland, taking comfort in the familiar cadences and the memory of the Elder's voice.

The Wanderer was the grandchild of First Man and First Woman. Like them, he followed the path from the Winter Place to the coast and back each year, taking from each the food that could be found in that season, but he chafed at the routine.

One spring, instead of following the rest of the tribe to the coast, the Wanderer set off on his own. While his family went north, he went east, into a land where the people had the heads of aurochs instead of men. The Wanderer tried to make peace with these people, offering them a gift of nuts from the forest, but the bull men drove him away and he was forced to flee along the banks of an immense river. In the river the Wanderer found a people who had the lower bodies of fish instead of legs, and who lived in the water. Again, the Wanderer offered them a gift, the flesh of a deer that he had hunted, but the fish men only ate water weeds and fled from the gift of meat.

Next, the Wanderer journeyed alone across a great plain where there was no food and only the wind kept him company. For five score days he wandered, until he came across a tribe of people who were woven out of grass. Once again the Wanderer tried to offer them a gift, though by this time he had no food and no water, only flint that he had picked up from the plain, but the Grass People were terrified of the fire he struck from the stone, and they lifted up their feet and blew away with the wind.

At this, the Wanderer finally gave up his journey and turned back for home, but it was now winter, and the snow came down thickly, freezing him to the bone. Though he eventually found his way to the coast, there was no sign of his people, and the Wanderer thought that he might die alone, out in the wild. Then he remembered that his people would follow the rules that his Grandfather had laid down, as they did every year. He knew exactly where they would be on that day, and so he was able to find them. After that he wandered no more.

Edan couldn't help but laugh at the irony of it, making Tara, who was walking ahead, turn back to look at him. He had met auroch men, and grass people, and travelled all of the lands that the Wanderer had, but with better results. The tale had been no more than a tool to scare them into staying to the little corner of the world that they knew, and what use was that now?

"Something funny?"

"Just a story I remembered."

Tara smiled at him indulgently and he had a sudden rush of delight. 'That's my mate!' He must have smiled foolishly himself because she raised an eyebrow, then shook her head and walked on.

That was thirteen days before the end of the world.

They had received a little food from The People, shared from their common supplies, but rations had been low and so they had to forage as they travelled. The land of Esa wasn't as empty of game as the grasslands had been. Many times they saw deer grazing in the distance, but they had neither the time nor the energy to hunt them. They gathered what small food they could on the move: rabbits caught on the run by an arrow; duck eggs from a few late summer nests; field mushrooms and dandelion roots. Mostly they lived on fish. Edan had finally put his fishing spear back to the use that his father had intended for it; no more weapons for him. The small streams were full of fat trout and he speared as many as he could reach.

The fish took them five days on, around a massive curve of The Great Wood which protruded into the Summer Lands from the west. Here the forest loomed from the top of a steep escarpment of mud coloured stone, capped with a narrow stroke of white chalk. Although this detour was unexpected and put them at risk of failing to reach their destination in time, Edan was perversely glad, because the cliff took away the threat of having to enter the woods early. At the Winter Place, at least, he knew that the forest could be entered, if they could reach it before the Fomor.

The old tired fear of drowning raised its head at the thought of the Fomor, but it was worn out and no longer had the power to terrorise. Instead he worried about Tara, about his unborn child, about the practicalities of the future. When would the water come? How would it come? How fast? Or … was there some chance that The People who had gone to confront the Fomor might prevail, and prevent it? Truth was, he didn't really believe that. He had fought along with Tara to give The People their chance, but he'd seen the Fomor too.

Seeking reassurance, he asked Tara if she had any more visions to guide them, but she could offer him nothing. They had taken shelter at the mouth of a cave at the foot of the pale cliffs — just a little thing no more than a few paces deep — at what had finally seemed to be the limit of the country of Esa. At the going down of the sun they had seen that the land opened up to the west of them, a sparkling plain of marshlands and hills that shimmered beneath the low sun. The sight lifted Edan's spirits. He knew that he must be close to home, and it gave him the courage to talk to Tara about his concerns.

"I can't tell you more Edan, I'm sorry. The vision is over now, at long last!"

They had gathered twigs and brush from the slope, blown down from the woodlands above their heads, and built a fire just outside the mouth of the cave, where the smoke could be carried away by the northern winds. The dry wood caught fire easily, blazing up quickly and then falling back. Tara poked at it idly as she spoke, stirring the embers with a blackened stick.

"It is a strange thing. I've dreamt that same dream since I was a child, without even knowing it. Now that the time of its coming is at hand, it is no longer needed. I close my eyes and I do not see the three suns, even though I know that the Black Sun is coming so very soon."

"I suppose it's silly of me to doubt."

"No! It is natural for you to doubt." Tara gestured with her stick, indicating the invisible landscape beyond the fire. "This is all the world we know, except for the stories that Morikatus told. How can we believe that it might vanish in a single stroke?"

"The Elder never believed it."

"I would not have believed it if I had not seen it."

Edan put his doubts aside. "Then I'll believe it too. After all, everything your visions predicted has happened."

The smile on Tara's face faded a little. "Yes, they have."

But the next morning Tara woke him with an anxious shake and told him that she had experienced a vision after all. He blinked awake to find her leaning over him. "Phelan has escaped."

Edan sat up, rubbing sleep from his eyes with the back of his hand. "What do you mean? How do you know?"

"I saw it. He is coming after us."

"I thought the visions were done?"

"Not this one."

Her words brought him awake quickly. Phelan. Of course, it would be Phelan. Closing his eyes for a moment he imagined Phelan racing across the landscape behind them, chasing them as he had chased them so many times before. Would he have hunters? Dogs? Fomor? His mind painted in each of the possibilities in turn, until he was visualising a whole horde of men, dogs, and monsters charging after them.

Could he catch up with them? Maybe. They had travelled slowly, shepherding their strength, and pausing always to gather what they could. It was plausible that one man, travelling fast, could overtake them before they reached the Winter Place. Could he find them if he did? Edan glanced in chagrin at the ashes of their fire, they could hardly have built a more obvious beacon.

He wrapped his arms around Tara. "It doesn't matter. He doesn't matter. We will get away."

Tara pushed him gently back. "Oh Edan. You know he will find us, before the end. He was there at the beginning; he will be there at the finish. But don't worry. We've beaten him before, and we will again."

After that they hurried. They stopped hunting and sought better cover in the long grass and scattered trees of the valley. In the shelter of the scrub the late summer days were hotter, buzzing with flies and lousy with spiders and ticks. Progress was more difficult, but Edan hoped that they were making themselves impossible to find. 'Unless he has dogs … or Fomor,' he thought morosely. He spent half his time looking over his shoulder for Phelan and half trying to spot some trail or landmark that he recognised, but everything was turned about or from the wrong direction.

Three days passed, and three days more. Edan notched each on a scrap of wood that he had tucked into his pack. The skies were empty now, clear of birds, just as the woods were empty of deer and foxes and people. Clouds came and went, and the days swung from cold to hot with no apparent pattern.

On the seventh day they came across a sluggish fat stream winding its way through the rushes. An old wooden post, weed coated and beetle-bored, stuck at an angle out of the mud, with the tip of another visible just above the surface of the water. Edan recognised an old abandoned fish trap. He was certain that it was one he had helped set when he was just a boy. They were in the Winter Lands at last.

Edan stopped and looked around. Everything looked different without its winter coating of snow and ice, but the big features, the hillsides, the shape of the land, were the same. Somewhere well ahead the river flowed out of the woodland, which meant that the tribe's winter lodge was there too. Somewhere to their right then, out beyond the cover of the aspen and the birch, was the lake where he had first met Tara.

"You know where we are?" Tara asked.

"I do. Close, but not close enough."

"Not close enough?"

Edan fished the tally stick out of his pack, and showed her the marks he had cut, counting them off with his fingers. "One moon, Cuinn said. It has been nearly that long already, give or take a day. The moon was half full when we reached the Stone Forest and it's nearly the same now."

He sighed. "I don't think we can get to the Place in time. Maybe we might just reach it, but neither of us knows how the flood will come. It might be a slow creeping that we can easily avoid, or a crashing wave, or everything might fall into the sea in an eye blink. We can't take the risk."

"I know how much you wanted to get there."

Edan thought of the leering image of Bal waiting alone in the long hut's darkness. "Or maybe not."

Tara let that pass without comment. "Where then?"

Edan pointed left, up towards the distant peaks of The Great Wood. The forest edge, with its line of cliffs, was hidden beyond the horizon, but he could see the white clouds that gathered above the distant trees.

After that it was a two-day dash, out of the lowlands, up the slopes, looking for a place where the cliff could be easily scaled and where the forest looked inviting. On the first day squalls of rain chased them up the rising land, sweeping in from the distant sea on the back of a freezing wind, but on the second the sky was as clear as a freshwater stream, without a breath of wind or a scrap of cloud. To Edan it felt like the whole world was holding its breath — waiting.

And that was the day that the world ended.

They had pitched camp amongst broken mounds of soft crumbling rock, each capped with a mat of dry knotted grass. Exposed layers of ochre stone, as soft and friable as packed sand, emerged here and there, heaping up until they became cliffs; crowned first with bands of red and white stone and then with the grasping roots of trees.

"Edan, get up!"

Tara's urgent voice woke him in the half-light. The sun was just clearing the horizon, and he was cold, inside and out. "What is it?"

"It is coming. They are coming. We need to get out of here."

He levered himself up, swigged water from the leather bag, and got to his feet. The rising sun shone red on the cliff face at the top of the slope, and pale white on Tara's frightened face. Eyes wide, she made the sign for haste: 'hurry!'

Edan took her word for it. He scrambled up to the top of the slope, looking for a suitable spot to enter the forest. Here and there was a dangling root, or a fallen boulder, that might have given them a way, but they seemed too precarious to be safe. Experimentally, he tried a few handholds, but the rock crumbled at his touch.

Think! Think! In winter, the cliffs were all but hidden by snow, which drifted up against them like a tide, but it all looked different now. There was nothing to the left, but to the right, at the limit of his vision, a bare slope of rock seemed to break the slope. From Edan's angle it looked something like the head of a sleeping man, mouth open, nose squashed against the soil. All at once he knew it, a great outcropping of grey rock that they had sometimes hunted near. Morna had always called it Gok's head and joked that Bal hadn't thrown it very far when he cut it off. Gok's head would be their route into the Wood.

He set off back down the slope back towards the camp, calling Tara's name and waving a hand to get her attention. He could see her, looking up at him. To his surprise she flung her arm out, pointing towards the northern sky, and he heard her voice echoing up the slope, desperate and urgent.

"Look Edan! Look!"

28. Tara

A cliff edge like a knife in darkness; a sea that glowed with fire; an island of ice upon the green mirror of the water. Stooping on the night wind in a falcon's body, Tara saw The People and the Fomor clash at the edge of the world — a phantom battle of shadows and displaced stars. There was Anagar, bear-strong, wolf-wise, wrestling on the edge of the precipice. There was Kaman of the Crow, deftest at spear thrusting. There was the monstrous war master of the Fomor race, a giant of shark's teeth and drowned bones, whose every sweeping blow tumbled a dozen of The People into the sea. Only the Fomor's chieftain — Bal — was missing.

Inevitably, Anagar came to face the Fomor champion. The warrior stabbed with his spear, sending black blood spraying, but the Fomor raised its claws and the whole cliff face convulsed, sending man and Fomor alike into the black ocean. Disembodied, vision led, Tara knew that this battle happened the very night that she dreamt it.

She awoke to find the pre-dawn darkness stained green and purple by sheets of light in the sky. 'The spears of the Fomor,' she thought with a shiver. The rising sun washed the lights away, but the memory of the battle she had dreamt was as clear as the new day. There was no more time.

Throwing off her sleeping furs she woke Edan and sent him off in the half-light to seek a way up through the cliffs. Had it been twenty days now as the Old Ones had predicted? Edan hadn't been sure of his count.

The rising sun revealed a landscape as thin as a dried-out carcass, with rotting stone bones poking through the fragile skin of grass. The whole Summer Lands suddenly seemed dead and buried to her, as if the Fomor's work was already done. Everything that mattered was already gone, save Edan and herself. And Phelan. Always Phelan. How close was he? She did not believe for a moment that he would not come; the mystery was what would happen when he did. What would he do? Would Edan fight him? Could she?

The previous night they had unpacked their assorted belongings and made a desultory attempt to put them in a final order. Now they were scattered around their camp in apparent disarray. It was tempting just to abandon them — to grab up the few nearest things and run to join Edan, or simply to let them lie and wait there for whatever was to come, but Tara had a family to consider, both born and unborn.

She forced herself to reach for the closest thing at hand, a collection of fish bones that Edan had plucked from the remains of past meals. They were tiny, fiddly things, with no use that she could think of, but Edan had assured her that they would be useful and might be hard to find in the forest. The pile of flint nodules at the bottom of her pack had far more obvious value; they had gathered them from the stream beds of Esa, where they had been easy to find.

The fish bones went into the pack and other objects followed: herb springs tied up with grass, an antler hammer that had been a gift from Ama, the fine string of red beads that Edan had given her. She kept a nervous eye on the horizon as she worked, though she wasn't sure what she was looking for. Phelan? A pack of Daesani hounds? The Fomor themselves?

The sun rose higher and bled the chill out of the air and Tara's limbs, but to her surprise it grew no brighter. Instead, the day grew darker and then the chill came back, cutting through the heat of exertion. She glanced up at the sky, expecting to see gathering clouds, but the sky was empty.

Tara rose, shading her eyes with one hand. Something was wrong with the sun. It had grown dark, and through nearly closed eyes she thought that she could see a shadow cutting across the sun's face where no shadow should be.

She felt a chill pass through her that was nothing to do with the falling temperature. The Fomor had made their mark on the moon, now they were doing the same to the sun! She had expected it, but that meant nothing, and she stood nervelessly and watched it happen. Only Edan's yell snapped her out of it.

She saw him coming down the hillside, waving at her, and pointed at the sky. Had he not seen it already? "Edan! Look!" she shouted, he looked up.

As if responding to her wild shout, the ground beneath her feet shook violently, and she fell to her knees. The fragile rocks cracked and threw out tiny avalanches of gravel all around her. She saw rocks the size of fists careen down the cliff faces and off towards the marsh below. The trembling seemed to go on forever. The whole world was a struck drum-skin that would not stop sounding. By the time Edan had slid his way down the shuddering slope to her side, it had grown as dark as night.

"The Black Sun!"

Tara dared to look up; the sun had vanished. In its place a ring of ghost fire shimmered and turned, the blue flames outlining a gaping hole where the sun should have been. Below them the ground finally settled, but she hardly noticed. The Black Sun, it was real! It was one thing to see it in a vision, quite another to witness it in person.

"It is like the river all over again! They are coming! The Warriors failed!"

"Did they?" Edan took her by the arm, urging her up. "You knew the wave would come, you always said so. The Grass People escaped; The People escaped; even the Daesani escaped. Now we have to do the same."

"You don't know that they escaped!"

"We don't know that they did not. Come on love, get up."

Tara blinked at him in surprise. Love? He'd never used that word before! The shock retreated for a moment. "Love?" She signed the word in the most heartfelt way possible, two hands clasped across her chest.

Edan rolled his eyes, grinning in spite of himself. "Yes, yes, of course. I love you. But please ... get up!"

Together they grabbed their half-filled packs and rolled up skins, cramming in the most important things that Tara hadn't yet packed. Unburnt firewood and unstripped rushes lay everywhere, scattered by the earthquake. Above them the sun flared back into the sky; the bright blue day returned. Tara wasn't fooled. She remembered the river, there had been silence there too, between the earth-shake and the flood. They had to get into the forest now.

"Where are we going?"

Edan pointed west. "That way, along the cliffs. It is a little hike, but we will be there before noon."

Noon! It was only mid-morning. "Is there nowhere closer?"

"The cliffs weren't safe before the ground shook; they will be worse now."

Tara snatched her pack from the ground, tying the bark strap of the sleeping skin across her chest. There was no sign of a wave. There was nothing at all out of the ordinary to be seen on the marshlands, but she could feel in her bones that something was terribly wrong. The land was crying out in a voice that she couldn't hear. Even the spirits were gone.

They hurried west in what the tribe would have called a hunter's gait, strides long and chests open, covering land at a steady pace. The temptation to run was almost overwhelming, but if they sprinted now, they would exhaust themselves well before they reached their goal. They had to pace themselves, picking their way around the rockslides and tumbled stones. In some places sections of the cliff had collapsed entirely, leaving trees hanging suspended in mid-air by no more than roots and tangled branches. They gave some of these slips a tentative try, but they were far too loose to climb.

Clouds began to gather, condensing out of the sky in long parallel rows that spanned from horizon to horizon. The sun dimmed again, this time because it was covered by clouds, and the ground quivered as if with fear.

Edan pointed ahead. "There, Tara, that mass of rock, do you see it? We used to call it Gok's head. That's our route up, if anything is."

A mass of exposed grey rock cut through the steep brown cliffs at the end of his pointing finger. Tara thought that it looked climbable enough, but it was still far ahead, and she could be wrong.

Without warning, a wind came howling down out of the north, bowing the trees on the plain and shattering the silence. It was like the roar of a beast, impossibly loud. The kind of sound that said 'run! run now!' Tara thought that it sounded like the chieftain of all the lero, gnashing its teeth and lashing the grass with fierce swipes of air. They barely had time to stagger before rain began to lash at them. Curtains of it swept at them — grey masses of drumming water; raindrops the size of bees, the size of dragonflies, soaking them instantly.

"Come on!"

They staggered forward again, side-on to the wind. After the first explosive burst the rain ebbed, but the last sliver of blue sky was swallowed by roiling clouds, and the wind only gained in strength. Tara tried to keep her eyes on their goal, the grey rocks indefinite behind the veils of rain, but they kept straying to the northern horizon. Was that movement? Was that a wave? Was that a mass of Fomor surging through the rain? Every tossing treetop looked like an uncoiling limb, and every squall of rain a charging monster.

Even so, she heard the flood before she saw it, not even knowing at first what she was hearing. An intense rushing sound drowned out the wind, like an enormous herd of aurochs stampeding towards them. Involuntarily they stopped, hands clasped.

Tara saw the reeds stirring. They went up and down, like weeds on the surface of the sea when a wave passes. She was confused. The ripples were too large to be the work of wind or rain. A little way off, at the base of the hill, a stream threaded its way along the edge of the reeds. As she stared at it, she realised that the water level in the stream was rising, slowly but surely escaping its banks and gurgling up the shallow slope.

"Edan, the water."

"I know." But he wasn't looking at the stream, instead his eyes were fixed on the horizon. Tara tried to see what he was seeing. There was nothing there but another rain shower, sweeping closer.

Only, it was not rain that she was seeing, it was a wave that stretched from horizon to horizon, a wall of water that must already have swallowed half the Summer Lands.

"Edan."

"So big. I didn't think it would be so big!"

Tara gripped Edan's hand and ran. The grey bluffs were now close, just at the other end of a narrow ridge of bare rock that cut across the rain sodden slope. Tara could see that there were trees scattered in a line down the bluffs. Rainwater ran freely between them and flooded out across the grass, and as they raced closer, she saw that the bluffs were actually a stack of flat rocks like steps, heaped around a single jutting outcrop. The fear was sharp in her throat. The wave was so high; it might still catch them halfway up.

Behind them the water rose with uncanny speed, churning its way up every channel and then surging outwards. A mass of it raced past them to the west, along the line of the river, and crashed against the edge of the forest. Mounds of foam-capped water rebounded across the slopes to either side of the river, washing away the hills in a tide of mud. The Summer Lands were becoming an ocean.

Tara had her eyes on the rocks in front, and her mind on the water behind, so she didn't see Phelan until he was already upon them.

A javelin came first, a sharpened dart of fire-blackened wood that whistled out of the rain straight at her. Some instinct warned her, and she twisted at the last moment so that the point missed her, but the shaft slapped her in the chest, and she fell on her back in the mud. The deerskin lashed to her back cushioned the fall, but it also dragged her sideways into the flood water.

Freezing black water surged over her. It was in her eyes, in her mouth. She gasped for air, found more water. There was mud in her throat. Somehow, she gagged her way back to the surface, but the soaking bed roll dragged her back. She folded her arms around her belly while the water drove her downhill. Finally, she managed to dig her heels into the mud and come to a stop. Head above water she looked for Edan. He was two dozen feet away at the foot of the rocks, but Phelan was already on him! Edan had his spear in his hands, but he was fighting defensively, trying to fend Phelan off with the haft.

But Phelan had an axe. He swung it one handed over and again, aiming for Edan's head and arms. Edan caught the blows on his spear. The sound of the splintering impacts rang out through the rain, but each impact drove him back into deeper water.

"Don't do this! It's over!" Edan pled. He was gasping with the effort of holding Phelan back, spitting the words out between breaths.

"No more words!" Phelan's voice crackled with madness. "I live, you die. Her blood for my people!"

With a roar, Tara flung off her pack and ran at Phelan, hoping to catch him in a grab like she had the lero. She got her feet on the ridge and raced along it, but she wasn't fast enough. One more overhand blow snapped Edan's spear, sending shards spinning into the water, and Phelan kicked Edan backwards into the flood. By the time Tara reached him, Phelan had already recovered his balance, and he turned her charge aside with a deft twist of his hip that tossed her into the water for a second time.

"At last!" Phelan raised his hands in exultation, shouting at the sky. "You doubted me, and I prove you wrong! You didn't think I would catch her, but I did. Call off your flood! Honour your bargain!"

Tara had no idea who he was talking to. It certainly wasn't her, but she took the chance to scramble to her knees.

"Stay down beast." This time Phelan struck her with the axe, clubbing her across the back with the blunt side, and she collapsed in agony.

"Witness me!" Phelan roared his words into the lashing rain. He flung his axe away into the water and advanced on her, drawing the knife of black glass from his belt.

Tara crawled away, but he came after her. He grabbed a handful of her hair and used it to haul her back. She scrabbled under the water, trying to pull free, but her hand closed on something hard and sharp instead.

Phelan yanked, and she went with him, exploding out of the water to strike him in the face with her clenched fist. In her hand was the bone point of Edan's spear, and the blow drove it into Phelan's eye.

Phelan reeled back, wailing in agony, the spearpoint jutting incongruously from his left eye socket. His hands flew to his head; blood poured obscenely between his fingers. As he staggered away, he went over the edge of the raised path and toppled into the surging water.

"Edan! Edan!" Tara coughed water but kept shouting. She couldn't see anyone in the water.

"Here!"

Edan was clinging to the rock face a little to her left, where the flood battered the cliff face. He got a solid footing on the slope and flung out a hand for her. "Where's Phelan?"

"Gone!"

"Then hurry!"

She was trying, but the current was almost too much. Her lungs heaved, her back ached, and she was sick at the violence she had inflicted, but she placed one laborious step after another until their hands clasped. Then it was just a matter of hauling herself onto the exposed rock with Edan's help and starting upwards.

The rock face towered above them, all ledges and sharp rises. Rainwater cascaded down the grey stone, adding its fury to the flood. It was a treacherous climb. Tara crossed the first ledge and started up the incline beyond, then froze. Perched above her, Edan turned and reached out again, but she looked down instead, fearful of a half-remembered vision of that very moment.

Below her the water swelled, and then exploded outwards. Bal rose from the waves, his left eye red with blood and his right white with madness. He wore Phelan's body, but the heart was Fomor.

With an inhuman twist, the creature propelled itself out of the water and grabbed Tara's ankle in one clawed hand. She was jerked from the rock but did not fall because Edan caught her by the wrist at the same instant, wedging himself against the stone to hold her there. Now all three of them dangled in a chain, suspended above the raging waters by no more than grasping hands.

Tara tried to find a foothold on the rock, fighting with all her might against the grip that was dragging her downwards, but the creature that held her was hideously strong. Instead of losing its grip it began to climb her, hauling itself up her body hand over hand.

Furiously Tara kicked back at it, trusting her weight to Edan's grasp. She flailed her heels against its head and shoulders again and again, rebounding from the cliff with each blow.

"No more!" She shouted. "Leave us alone!"

The creature looked up at her, transfixing her with its one blind eye, and reached up with clawed fingers, but she put all her strength into one last convulsive kick and struck it right in the middle of its upturned face. This time the blow was true. The creature jerked back, lost its grip ... and fell.

Frantic, expecting the next attack at any moment, the two of them got to sure footing and climbed. Broken roots and dislodged pebbles washed past them; the world was washing out from both above and below. Tara was sure that Bal would emerge again, but nothing came. Even when they dragged themselves, soaked and exhausted, into the edge of the wood, to crouch together amongst the tangled tree trunks; even when they fixed their eyes on the waves, watching them roll in and crash out, crashing away across what had once been land; even when the sky grew dark and the new sea grew still; even then no thing, living, dead, or anything else, emerged from the sea to follow them.

29. Ailsa

In the half-light before dawn, when everyone else was still sleeping, Ailsa slipped quietly out from beneath her furs and tiptoed towards the door. 'Quiet as a fox, quiet as a mouse,' she whispered to herself, mouthing the words as she pressed her weight against the wicker door.

Outside, the moon was still drifting down behind the trees, and the sky was not yet light. Ailsa felt a thrill of excitement when she saw the full moon. She knew what that meant. When the sun rose, she would be six years old, and it would be time to go to the sea!

Normally Ailsa's family stayed well away from the sea. They lived in the woods near the stream, or at the hill camp, where the trees were thinner, and Father could catch the little deer. Ailsa knew that she had family somewhere in the south, way beyond the hills, but they didn't go there. Instead, once a year, they went to visit the sea. To Ailsa the sea was a special mystery, one that she couldn't remember very well even when she tried hard. This year would be different. This year she wasn't the only child, she was the eldest, and she would remember everything.

She was too excited to go back to sleep, so she took the water pail down to the edge of the stream and submerged it in the current, kneeling on the bank so that she didn't fall in. The fast-flowing water foamed over the pail and snatched it out of her hands, and she had to scramble down the bank and grab it before it washed away entirely. Then she had to put both arms around it and push it up the bank to get it out of the water, by which time she was soaking wet and covered with mud.

Indecently pleased with herself, she set about hauling the pail back to the house. She could only move it a short way before she had to put it down again, waddling along with it between her legs, but she was strong, just like her mother. By the time she made it back to the hut, the sun had risen over the oak trees and the door stood open. Her mother waited in the doorway, the swaddled shape of Ailsa's little brother snug in the crook of one arm.

"Look at yourself."

Ailsa looked at herself. Rapidly drying mud was smeared all over her tunic, and it caked her pale legs. She picked off a few flakes and grinned.

"Silly mouse!" Her mother plucked her up off the ground with her free hand, and held her perched on her right side, opposite the baby.

There was movement in the doorway and her father appeared, yawning and rubbing his dark hair with one hand.

"Daddy, I got the water!"

"So, you did." He looked at her mud-stained clothing, but she knew that he wouldn't be angry, not that day.

Ailsa washed her face in the water and fidgeted as her mother dragged a bone comb through her hair. She was saved by the cry of the baby. As soon as her mother turned to see to him, Ailsa swiped a strip of dried meat from the rack by the door and wolfed it down. She had red hair like her mother, and pale skin like her mother, but she was as quick as her father.

When the packs and food were ready, they set out for the sea, following a deer trail through the densely packed trees. Her father carried his bow, and her mother had the baby strapped across her back. Ailsa had her own share of the load, but it was very light, and she skipped ahead along the trail. It was still winter, shading into spring, and the snowdrops and jakkios were dusted with frost, so she ran through them, delighting in the crunching leaves.

Later, her parents took her by the hands, one each, and swung her along between them. In this way they passed the time until mid-afternoon, when they sat down on a bare rock facing the sun and ate. The baby had milk at the breast, of course, but the rest of them ate fish which her father had caught, and her mother had smoked. He was the best fisherman, and the fish was delicious, but Ailsa hardly paid attention, because she was sure that she could smell the sea already.

When the food was done, she ran ahead, sure that the sea would come into view at any moment, but the trail wound on interminably through the sighing forest and she got slower and slower. Eventually her legs gave out on her, and her father had to heave her up and carry her on his shoulders.

In this way they finally reached the coast. The land all around was low, with the waves washing right up into the edge of the forest, but her parents had chosen a high spot, a cliff overlooking the sea, where they finally let Ailsa down.

She crept to the grassy edge and lay down on her belly to look out over the flat sparkling sea. Late afternoon sunlight glittered off the water, turning the scattered islands into inky shadows that could have held anything.

Greedily she drank in the view, determined to remember every detail this time. When the baby was old enough to understand she would tell him every detail of this place.

Ailsa felt her parents come to join her, standing protectively on either side.

"That was my land, there," her father said, pointing out to sea.

"Did you live there too, mummy?"

"No. I lived way over there." She pointed the other way with her free hand, at yet more open water.

"Under water?!"

"No!" Her mother laughed, and the baby woke and gurgled in response. "It wasn't under water then."

Ailsa tried to understand that, but it didn't make any sense. "Did I live there with you?"

"No."

"So, who did live there?"

Her father answered this time. "Many people lived there. Good people and bad people. But they all had to leave, just like we did."

Ailsa considered that carefully and then asked, "So ... who lives there now?"

"No one," said her father, "only dead people."

She peered at the sea again, watching the sun slide lower and lower towards the water. "Are the dead people good or bad?"

"Both!" They all laughed at that, though Ailsa wasn't sure why.

"Come on, little mouse." Her mother held out a hand and pulled her up. "It will be dark soon. We'll camp in the trees and then in the morning we'll go down to the shore and get some cockles."

"Cockles!"

Her parents took her hands again, one each, and they headed back into the shadows of the forest together.

THE SUMMER LANDS

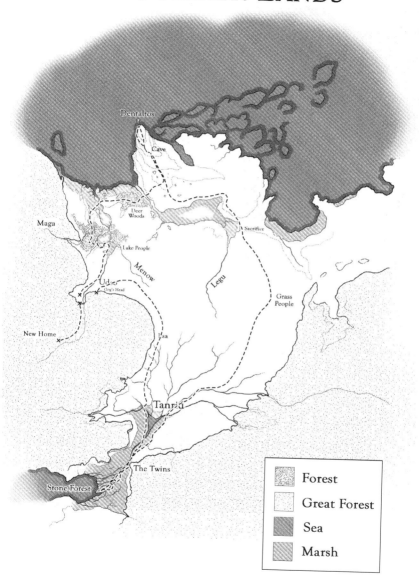

Dentaltos

Cave

Deer
Woods

Maga

Lake People

Sacrifice

Menow

Legu

Ud..

Ong's Head

Grass
People

New Home

Isa

Tanria

The Twins

Stone Forest

Forest

Great Forest

Sea

Marsh

Afterword

The real Summer Lands

In 1931 the trawler Colinda, fishing near the Ower Bank off the Norfolk coast, hauled up a lump of peat containing a barbed antler point that had once adorned a mesolithic fishing spear — the same spearpoint that Edan lost in the Legu river.

The find was the first insight into the lives of the ancient people who once lived in Doggerland — the place that I have called the Summer Lands.

During the last ice age (more properly the *Last Glacial Maximum*), what is now the North Sea was dry land, connecting Britain to France in a broad swathe from the English Channel on up. At its largest extent, up to around eighteen thousand years ago (18,000 BP — *before present*), it stretched as far north as Shetland. Back then, this Doggerland (the name was coined in the 1990s by Professor Bryony Coles, in honour of the Dogger Bank, which was in turn named for the Dutch *dogger* cod-fishing boats of the 17th century) was a cold expanse of tundra, inhabited by mammoths and neanderthals whose bones are still being plucked from the seafloor today.

Ten thousand years later, at the time this novel is set, Doggerland had become a realm of low marshes and gravel banks, constantly threatened by the encroaching sea, running from the Channel Islands to roughly the level of the Humber. In the south, the Thames and the Rhine joined together to flow through the Dover straits in what has been called the "Channel River". In the north, a rich coastal landscape of bays, inlets, marshes, and rivers, created what may have been one of the richest hunting grounds in mesolithic (that's the middle stone age) Europe.

It's possible that Doggerland might have been slowly covered by rising sea levels over hundreds or thousands of years, but there is another theory. About 8200 BP, there were a series of massive undersea landslides at a place called Storegga, just off the course of Norway. The landslides created a mega-tsunami in the North Sea, which rushed southwards and consumed the low-lying Doggerland, washing away its gravel and marsh terrain forever (permanently?).

Over the twenty years following Professor Cole's naming of Doggerland, dedicated scientists, working with the Sea Palaeolandscapes Project (what is now the ERC Europe's Lost Frontiers project), mapped great swathes of this lost landscape. By 2007 they had amassed enough information about it to feature in a special episode of Channel 4's Time Team called "Britain's Drowned World".

Which is where I came in, and The Drowning Land began.

The Time Team special filled my mind with ideas. I was struck with a singular image of a small group fleeing the oncoming waves. I imagined a fantastic fantasy world — a prehistoric Atlantis — consumed by this catastrophe. I thought of Tír na nÓg, the land beneath the waves; Avalon; Hy Brasil; and the Lowland Hundred (Cantre'r Gwaelod) that is supposed to lie under the waves of Cardigan Bay, and which probably inspired Susan Cooper's Lost Land. Tir Na Nóg made me think in turn of the Fomorians, the mythological first race of Ireland, misshapen giants who came from under the sea to fight the first human settlers. The Fomorians were portrayed in comic epic *Sláine* as monstrous fish creatures who demanded human sacrifice and human tears for their one-eyed King Balor, who also stood in for the devil in 1985's *Dragon Warriors*, a paperback-size roleplaying game that had a massive influence on me when I was growing up. I also thought about Robert Holdstock's chilling *The Fetch*, another fable of deep time. From such varied roots, a novel can grow.

It took a while. Other projects distracted me, and it wasn't until the Time Team special was repeated in 2011 that my vague ideas started to come together. As soon as I started to sketch out the plot for the novel, I knew that, even though I was writing a fantasy, I wanted it to be as scientifically accurate a fantasy as I could make it.

What followed was, for an armchair-bound writer such as myself, an epic journey of research. I visited neolithic and mesolithic sites in Jersey, which was itself once a hill in Doggerland, and studied the hundreds of artefacts gathered in the States of Jersey museum. Chantal Conneller, now at the University of Newcastle, was kind enough to show me her dig site at Les Varines, and to share some of her papers with me, while James Dilley (of Ancientcraft.co.uk) ran a flint-knapping evening and showed me how to make cordage from grass and glue from birch sap, as well as giving me technical advice on the novel. James also made a reconstruction of the Bad Dürrenberg wolf headdress, which he wore when I met him, and which you may recognise on Phelan's head. Dr David Chamberlain of the Royal Botanic Gardens in Edinburgh advised me on plant life. All the factual errors in the novel are, naturally, mine and not theirs.

The rest of this Afterword is a summary of some of that research; an exploration of the science behind the novel.

The people of the Summer Lands

Edan's tribe typifies the sort of hunter-gatherer group that made Doggerland their home: small, closely related, and mobile. Similar groups on the European mainland left shell caches, temporary camps, and coastal settlements at the same date, so it's easy to imagine that Edan's tribe would have done the same. They do differ from many recorded groups in one significant way, which is that they move inland in winter, and to the coast in summer. The archaeological record suggests that the opposite was more common, because the shore, with its supplies of fish and — most importantly — shellfish, provided a reliable source of food in the winter. My tribe, however, driven inland by the relentlessly rising sea, seeks the shelter of the wood in winter.

The mesolithic was a time of transition. The climate was growing warmer and wetter. The megafauna of the ice age had vanished. These changes sparked new technologies: bows, microliths (fine flint tools), fishing spears, the domestication of dogs. Eventually, these changes came together in the *Neolithic Revolution*, which brought farming, domesticated animals, tomb building, cities, and religion.

The people of the Summer Lands are in the midst of this transition. The Grass People make unleavened bread from wild grains — they are on their way to developing agriculture. The Daesani have tamed dogs, have welded many small tribes together into something like a society, and built villages. When they move west into the British Isles they would likely become one of the mysterious monument building peoples that filled the landscape with burial mounds and tumuli. The unnamed tribe inflicting the *threefold death* on the boy at the edge of the lake in Chapter 16 are the ancestors of the same tradition that put Lindow Man into a Cheshire peat bog at the end of the Iron Age, six thousand years later.

Although these various groups have quite different cultures, they have pretty much the same phenotype — short, dark-skinned, dark-haired, and blue-eyed. This is the body type of Cheddar Man, a prototypical Britain from around 8,000 BP, which was recently revealed by DNA analysis. If you want to know what Maccus or Kaman might have looked like, turn to Alfons and Adrie Kennis' reconstruction of Cheddar Man.

But, of course, there is another people in the Summer Lands, Tara's people, the Trolls, where do they come from?

It has been suggested that Doggerland might have been one of the last footholds of Neanderthals in Europe, perhaps even later than 28,000 BP, the date of the last attested finds from Gibraltar. Some of the earliest finds recovered from Doggerland were remnants of this Neanderthal population, mammoth teeth, bone fishhooks, and stone tools. Similar finds have been emerging in much larger quantities over the last decade from the Netherland beach of Zandmotor, a piece of reclaimed land made out of 21 million cubic meters of soil dredged from the bottom of the North Sea, a unique window into the archaeology that remains hidden beneath the waves.

The People are not Neanderthals, however, but their descendants. Over the past decade, genetic evidence for interbreeding between archaic and modern humans — specifically between modern humans, Neanderthals, and the Denisovans (who lived across Asia) — has increased, with some studies suggesting that as much as 20% of Neanderthals DNA may have survived in modern humans. It seems reasonable to assume that over the period after the Neanderthals became extinct, different groups may have retained a greater or smaller proportion of Neanderthal traits.

While there is no scientific evidence that a physiologically distinct *half-neanderthal* might have existed as late as 8,000 BP, let alone in Doggerland, the folklore of North-Western Europe abounds with Trolls and Ogres and Faerie races — creatures that are *almost* human, but not quite; just a little larger, a little stronger, a little *other*. The Jötnar of Norse mythology and the Fomorians of Ireland are similar creatures. These legends might have originated from a distant folk memory of the Neanderthals and their descendants, hence my Summer Lands Trolls, who are humans with a strong heritage of Neanderthal traits.

Amongst the Neanderthal traits that I chose to represent in Tara's People are: a broad nose, a large and stocky build, a wider mouth with bulky molars, a strong healing capacity, a shoulder joint less well adapted to spear throwing, and body structure better for sprinting than endurance running.

It has been suggested that Neanderthals could not make nasal sounds, and to pronounce a variety of vowels. Although this is far from settled science, it pleased me to imagine the People as using signs to supplement their speech. As can be seen in the book, however, much of this is cultural rather than genetic — Tara *can* pronounce the Tribe's speech perfectly well once she is used to it.

Another Neanderthal trait that I gave to Tara was pale skin and red hair. The BCN2 gene, which in modern humans is associated with light skin and hair, is 60% of Neanderthal origin. Similarly, Neanderthal DNA shows a variant of the MC1R gene — which controls hair colour — associated with red hair. Not all Neanderthals will have had pale skin and red hair, but it seems possible that these traits may have entered the modern human population from the Neanderthals that they interbred with. As the final chapter shows, Ailsa — Edan and Tara's daughter — has inherited her mother's colouring and her father's build. In time, perhaps, her own descendants might be the red-haired Celts of Western Europe.

Topography

ERC Europe's Lost Frontiers has identified several significant features on the seafloor, some of which have been given names, and some of which appear in the Summer Lands.

The largest of them is Outer Silver Pit Lake, a huge depression just to the south of the Dogger Bank, which would have been a lake in Edan's time, fed by rivers flowing in from the south and out to the north. It is this lake that Edan and Tara skirt as they head south towards the Grass

People. The Fomor men live on its eastern shore, and the Legu (my name) runs from it to the sea.

South of the Silver Pit was another lake, Tanrid (my name again) where the Thames and the Rhine met. Edan and Tara, travelling south from the Grass People, come to the north bank of the Rhine and then follow it to Tanrid. Here, the two rivers joined to become one, the Channel River (or *Fleuve Manche*), which flowed out through the Straits of Dover, then turned west. Its bed is what we now call the English Channel, and some of the hills rising from its flood plains are now the Channel Islands.

The Channel River flowed through the narrowest point of Doggerland, where the huge cliffs of Dover and Calais rose 15 to 45 meters high on either side. It is this region, a vast plain of gravel beds scoured out by the floodwaters of post-glacial lakes as long as 180,000 BP ago, that I call The Twins. Beyond this, the Stone Forest, where mudflats expose the preserved remains of trees from an earlier age of Doggerland. A very similar drowned forest can be found on the beach at Redcar, North Yorkshire, along with the ubiquitous mammoth teeth and mesolithic flints. This preserved forest was recorded in the 19th Century, and recently re-exposed by the storm known as The Beast from the East, in 2018. There's no evidence that such a forest existed in the mudflats south of the Dover Straits, but it is certainly possible that there was.

Even the cliffs that Tara and Edan struggle their way up at the very end of the novel are a real place, the dramatic coloured cliffs of Hunstanton, on the Norfolk coast. These vividly striped formations were laid down towards the end of the Early Cretaceous (108-99 million years ago). The cliffs now are perhaps 20m high but would have been higher in Tara's and Edan's time.

There is one notable feature of the Summer Lands which doesn't appear on any of the Lost Frontiers Project's maps, because it is entirely of my own invention — Dentaltos. Dentaltos lies at the location of the real Dogger bank. The Dogger bank is a moraine, a huge ridge of gravel, rocks, and other material that was once carried there by a glacier. It would never have had steep cliffs or rocky shores, and it certainly wouldn't have had a sea-stack like the Tooth of the North. Features like that certainly do exist elsewhere, of course; Dentaltos was based on the Old Man of Hoy, on Orkney, which I visited as a teenager.

Language

No record remains of the language spoken by the mesolithic people of north-western Europe. Since the 19th Century, extensive efforts have been made to reconstruct some of the ancient root languages from which modern European tongues descend — Proto-Indo-European, and Proto-Celtic — but these still only take us back to Iron Age, when the Indo-European family of languages spread east from its roots in Anatolia. Before that date, the people of north-western Europe would have spoken *Old European languages* (also known as Paleo-European languages), of which almost no trace remains.

As those people spread out across Doggerland, and the lands surrounding it, Old European was replaced with new languages from the east. These, in turn, became Proto-Celtic, then Celtic, then Goidelic (Gaelic) and Brittonic (the language of ancient England). Now, the only traces that remain of the original Old European are a few river names and a handful of unusual words in Gaelic, Welsh, Irish, Breton, Cornish, and Manx (the last two of which are themselves now dead languages).

In the absence of Old European, I drew on the Celtic languages for my names. Tara is named after the Hill of Tara in Ireland, the legendary seat of the High King, and probably derives from a Proto-Indo-European word for 'star'; Phelan is also an Irish name, and means 'wolf'. Cual and Uchdryd are Welsh names, while Edan (little fire) and Brina (defender) are Irish again. Eburakon comes from the Brittonic "yew tree place".

For the words that appear in Tara's language lesson in Chapter Seven, I tried my hand at reconstructing words from the surviving Brittonic languages, and a Proto-Celtic word list courtesy of the University of Wales. For example, Tara's thank-you — "Meru Tu" — derives from the Cornish "Meru Ras", the Breton "Merasta", and the Proto-Celtic "tū" (you). The hand-signs come from modern British Sign Language because, in the end, you can only invent so much.

Conclusion

There are many more titbits of scientific information that went into my creation of the Summer Lands, but hopefully what I've presented here gives you a view of the science behind the story. If it has whetted your appetite, you could do worse than visit the ERC Europe's Lost Frontiers project website and take a look at their map of Doggerland for yourself, browse the videos on Ancientcraft, or dive into one of the scholarly books on Doggerland published over the last decade.

Hopefully what you find there will inspire you as it did me.

About the Author

David M. Donachie would like to be a reclusive polymath tending his collection of bones in a rattling house overlooking the ocean, but is actually an IT professional, writer, and artist residing in a chilly garret full of reptiles, cats, and books.

David's first book of short fiction, The Night Alphabet, is available on Amazon. As are the many anthologies and gaming books to which he has contributed.

If you'd like to know more about David's work, he strongly encourages you to visit his website, follow him on Facebook, or check him out on Goodreads.

Website	https://www.teuton.org/~stranger/
Facebook	@DavidMDonachieAuthor
Amazon	dmdonachie
Mailing List	https://bit.ly/ddonachiemailinglist
Good Reads	www.goodreads.com/dmdonachie

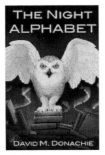

Also by this Author

The Night Alphabet is a collection of 26 short stories dragged from the edges of sleep: marrying nightmares to detective fiction, ghosts to science, and the weird to the nonsensical.

Printed in Great Britain
by Amazon